"I loathe you, Mo..."

"Nothing is real to you except Malvie, a pile of stones. It is an insult to my husband's memory to name him here, but he did more for Malvie than you ever, with your idle dreams and boasting, could do in a hundred years, you brutal, lying, murdering, ravishing criminal! Do not touch me, now or ever, I will not, I will not—"

"Ah, but you will," he said, still smiling, and seized her.

"A whopper of a story . . . comes close to rivaling *JANE EYRE* and *WUTHERING HEIGHTS*, maybe even *REBECCA*."

—CHATTANOOGA TIMES

Fawcett Crest Books
by Pamela Hill:

THE DEVIL OF ASKE

THE MALVIE INHERITANCE

Pamela Hill

The Malvie Inheritance

A FAWCETT CREST BOOK

Fawcett Publications, Inc., Greenwich, Connecticut

THE MALVIE INHERITANCE

THIS BOOK CONTAINS THE COMPLETE TEXT OF THE
ORIGINAL HARDCOVER EDITION.

A Fawcett Crest Book reprinted by arrangement with St. Martin's
Press

Library of Congress Catalog Card Number: 73–77057

Printed in the United States of America

First printing: March 1975

1 2 3 4 5 6 7 8 9 10

The Malvie Inheritance

PART ONE

I

On a still, sunny afternoon in late May, Annabel Doon, the young heiress of Malvie, sat in her aunt Retford's flower-garden at the nearby dower house, the Mains, in the shelter of a great and ancient yew-arbour. The rest of the garden itself was not what it would later become, few folk yet having adopted the southern habit of troubling to grow flowers for the look of them. Mrs. Retford, a provident lady, still maintained a long bed of kitchen-herbs behind a discreetly dug path of gilly-flowers and, at the end, a small yellow Scots rose bush in early bloom. The resulting admixture of onion, chive, fennel, clove-pink and rose came to Annabel as she sat, slippered feet together and slim, bone-stayed back correctly upright, in the arbour, stitching at her embroidery-frame. Her nose wrinkled in appreciation of the spiced, beckoning odour of the sun-warmed garden; but much as she would have liked to go and bury her face in the gilly-flowers, savouring at close quarters their heady scent, she did not. It would have been unladylike, and one must always, even when apparently unobserved, behave like a lady.

A tangle of coloured silks lay nearby on the arbour-seat and Annabel reached down, selecting a blue thread and inserting it in her needle. She was engaged on a tester, which when completed was to be stretched, lined and hung above one of the beds at Malvie, when the great house should be opened again for them all to live in. Aunt Retford had promised that, if little more, and would no doubt fold away the completed tester with matching chair-seats, footstool, fireguard-panel and other such objects Annabel had already completed. The girl's mind, briefly rebellious, wondered how much longer Malvie would have to remain closed. Papa had been dead now for almost three years.

The tears pricked, interfering with any clear view of the design of leaves, flowers and pomegranates aunt Retford had chosen, whose centres Annabel was at present filling in with

8

Jacoby-stitch. Papa had loved her less than her cousin Morven, because she was a girl and they had little about which to converse; but he had been kind, and had allowed Annabel to run wild and, as long as there was any money, to ride a pony. One of the first things aunt Retford had done, after turning Morven away from the door of Mains, later, was to sell the ponies; Annabel flushed now with indignation, remembering. There was nothing at all she herself had been able to do about it, neither tears nor, in those days, temper being of any avail. Young girls, aunt Retford had said, must learn their manners and their stitchery, not romp about the countryside like hoydens; and so Annabel, still red-eyed for Papa, had been whipped, then strapped into a back-board to prevent her developing a stoop, and put to master samplers, which she hated; then, by the time hate had been further flogged out of her, to be replaced by apathy, the footstools and the like. They were, by now, a welcome enough way of passing the days, which, as aunt Retford kept small company, were lonely.

The sun shone on irreverently, prevented from freckling Annabel's roseleaf skin by the clipped, solid presence of the yew-arbour. This was so old it must have been there before the dower-house was built, perhaps even before some parts of Malvie. By contrast, in its dark stern frame, Annabel herself seemed ephemeral and young; a very young girl of fourteen, attired in a carefully-ironed white muslin gown with pale blue ribbons, exactly the shade of the small satin slippers she wore, whose heels were flat. It was necessary, aunt Retford said, always to be dressed ready to receive any company by noon, whether or not the company ever came. The Mains was eleven miles from the nearest post-road and it was unlikely any company would, except Uncle Hubert who at times rode over; and he had come less often of late.

Annabel stared down at her dress, reflecting that next time it was washed, a new laundry-maid would have to be found. These were hard to come by, and aunt Retford had said she might, this time, try the Grattan orphanage forty miles off for a waif trained to domestic service. Those were not always available, and one had to wait; meantime, Mrs. Betts, the cook, would no doubt do Annabel's gowns. One must not, of course, even if the new arrival were one's own age, consort with maidservants. There were a great many things one must not do.

As if to deny all this, and remind Annabel that she was not a puppet without life of its own or choice of movement,

9

a soft, escaping ringlet of brown-gold hair slid out of its confining riband, cascading down over her shoulder so that she had to put aside her work and tuck it back. Its warm, resilient quality made her think of silk, and of her own long lashes which, she knew, could touch her cheeks when lowered. A doll, she looked like. But a doll had blue eyes. "Mine are hazel," thought Annabel unaccountably. She raised them, letting the stitchery remain in her lap, and again surveyed the warm, untenanted garden. Hazel eyes, with gold flecks among the green, and a small neat mouth like an unopened rose, that seldom laughed nowadays. She was pretty; she knew it, had always done, though no one had told her. Even Morven, who'd teased a lot when they were together like brother and sister in old days, hadn't ever told her she wasn't pretty, only stupid because she was a girl, and—and because of Malvie.

Annabel closed her eyes; the brief instant's withdrawal hid a sudden expression of deep, intuitive awareness and pain, doing away with any suggestion, despite the flowerlike prettiness of the face, of insipid folly. That she knew what she could not yet name was true; certain things were unsafe to dwell on. It was better, as aunt Retford would certainly say, to return to one's obedience and the day planned for one, and stitch uneventfully on. Obedient, pretty Annabel; hardly a ghost of the rebellious child there had once been . . . She had obtained permission, today, to sit in the garden for an hour and a half, until tea; and to come in at once before then if it should show signs of clouding over, lest she get her new satin slippers wet.

She had once, long ago at Malvie, run barefoot about that hill of grass lying now beyond the trim hedge, to where Morven was waiting then; and together they'd sat down on the woodland moss and looked at the white wild garlic, just in flower. It seemed long ago. Morven . . . she'd hardly seen him this year, or perhaps last. What was he doing now? Taking the boat out into the bay, holding the irons for old Aaron Judd, the blacksmith, with whom he lived now at the smithy-cottage, having unclassed himself, as aunt Retford said, by so doing? But what else could poor Morven have done, with Malvie closed and no roof over his head, after aunt Retford said she would have none of him at the Mains? Morven was too wild to live with them, Annabel had been told; it was too much responsibility for a lone widow-woman. But there was more, far more, to it than that.

She herself was not permitted to go and visit Morven, any more than he was allowed to come to the Mains. The blacksmith's cottage was no place for a young lady, aunt Retford said predictably; in addition, certain matters took place there one should not know about.

Certain matters . . . "It will be the smuggling, a part of it," Annabel thought, without undue concern. Everyone, Papa when he was alive, and Sir Hubert Melrose, her own maternal uncle, who was a Justice of the Peace over at Maddon, and the parish-minister, and aunt Retford herself, all bought brandy and, in the case of the gentlemen, pipe-tobacco in such ways because it was cheaper, and saved tax. "Their wives get French lace," Annabel reflected. If Morven was smuggling sometimes, it was understandable, she thought. He had nothing else to do, and no money.

A low whistle, which might have been a blackbird's, came at that moment from beyond the hedge, across the remembered rise of blowing grass. Since it was empty of the ponies Papa had used to keep grazing there, the grass was by now too long; aunt Retford talked of putting geese on it. Beyond, the far ground disappeared over the hill, studded along its top with the gean, the wild cherry tree, which in autumn would yield small bitter fruit, useless for pickling. It was from this region that the whistle came. Morven would be up there, inexplicably waiting for her, his thin face expressionless, his eyes dancing.

How could she go? How could he even expect it, so long it was since she'd had word with him, so that it was almost as if a stranger called her to come? Once, a year ago, perhaps, when she was still a child, it might have served; but now, she was a young lady.

Annabel changed colour, and dug her needle into the cloth with such force that the point stabbed her finger. Persons like Morven thought everything stayed the same. They didn't know how people like herself had to alter.

She sucked the blood from her pricked finger. On no account must she venture beyond the garden: Aunt Retford had been explicit on that point. On no account. The yew-arbour, for an hour and a half, till tea-time only. It was almost that now.

The blackbird's call sounded again. Morven wasn't used to being kept waiting. In the days when they had been together at Malvie, she'd always obeyed him when he whistled, on the instant. Morven was the elder, Papa had told her, and one day she was to be his wife.

There was, she knew already, a thin place at the back of of the arbour where one could wriggle through. At first when she had come here, a wild and undisciplined child from Malvie, she had done exactly that, emerging with crumpled clothes and her hair full of spiders and beetles into a briefly recaptured world of grassy freedom. Aunt Retford had seen it and sent Betts to catch her and he'd brought her back at once, and the whipping she'd had still made Annabel's cheeks hot, remembering. It wasn't, when all was said, worth risking that again; especially now she was fourteen.

The whistle . . . Morven knew about how she was treated here; it wasn't fair. It was as though he deliberately tried to get her into trouble, to laugh at her punishment, a kind he himself had never experienced. Morven, as a boy, had never been whipped, hardly even rebuked. Papa wouldn't let his tutor use the birch on him. It was all because of Uncle Richard, Morven's father, the true laird, who'd died abroad shortly after the 'Forty-five. "Morven's the son of his sire, the true heir of Malvie," Papa had used to say sombrely, whenever the subject came up; hearing of some new, wild thing Morven had done, he would laugh, and toast him in contraband claret. "If the coin had fallen to the George and not the rose, in 'Forty-five it would have been I who rode off north, and not your uncle." But Uncle Richard, the elder twin, having won the toss, had gone; and had had his estates forfeited. In the end, after lawsuits and much expense, which ruined the family, Papa had been permitted to inherit Malvie because he was the brother who had stayed at home and hadn't joined the Prince. But Morven's father, who had, was an exile, never again to be allowed to come home. He never even saw Morven, who'd been born after Culloden at Malvie.

Morven. "Unless he marries yourself, my lass, he can never come into his own," Papa used to say. And he himself had had it all arranged before he died that this should be the way of things, only aunt Retford and Uncle Hubert Melrose, adding up the debts afterwards, had said the marriage wasn't the answer and Morven must go. And they'd closed Malvie up, after Papa's funeral, and driven Morven out as a vagabond with no home, and taken herself and brought her up as a little doll, a correct young lady, sewing samplers, sewing chair-seats and footstools, bribing her with promises that one day Malvie should be opened again.

"Perhaps on your marriage," aunt Retford would say with her tight, narrow smile. But the marriage, it was clear, mustn't be to Morven now, but to some rich man who would clear the debts and wouldn't mind the lack of any real dowry. Most of the money Papa still received had gone, in twice-

12

yearly consignments, to Uncle Richard in Paris while he lived, and afterwards to educate Morven. Even poor Mama's dowry had been used for the purpose. Mama was too meek to demur. In any case she'd once been betrothed to Uncle Richard herself, when he was heir of Malvie, and had only been married to Papa some years afterwards, when Morven was already a motherless small boy living with his uncle. It was to find a mother for Morven that Papa had in fact married, in the end; and who better than the young woman who should have been Richard's wife? Morven's own wild Highland mother was by then long dead; she hadn't survived his birth at Malvie. It was Annabel's own mother, gentle, inconsiderable Grace Melrose, who had brought them both up as her own till she died of phthisis when Annabel was five.

"I can just remember Mama," Annabel thought. Odd to think that she, with her smooth fair hair and gracious, placid smile, should have loved Uncle Richard always despite his betrayal, and wept at his exile and refused to marry anyone for a long time, only she had been prevailed upon, at last, to marry Papa. Young women were not consulted about their wishes; one might as well be a parcel of French lace. After Mama died Uncle Hubert Melrose had offered to take and bring up Annabel with his own son Peter at Maddon, but Papa wouldn't agree; then again on Papa's death Uncle Hubert had been expected to offer, but this time had not. "No doubt he was afraid you'd beguile Peter or even little Paul, and you with no dowry to speak of," Morven had said unkindly, when he heard. That had been during the last days when she herself could still see and talk to Morven; the last time he had the chance to be cruel.

He had often been cruel. Sometimes she was sure he hated her.

She stayed resolutely in her place, not risking the spidery exit from the arbour. It made it easier not to answer Morven's summons now if she remembered certain aspects of their youth together. Annabel was not a jealous creature; in her heart she had almost worshipped the cousin Papa loved so much more than he ever loved herself. This had been the case since long before the time when Morven, six years older, rode a large pony and she a small; since he'd taught her to play cricket, then mocked unkindly at the sight of her short, childish legs endeavouring to make the runs in spite of hampering petticoats, so that she stopped and cried. Later there had been the time, worst of all, when he'd dared her to climb out of the high turret-window of Malvie, easing her way along to the narrow ledge below the roof, where the ghost of Susannah Doon, her own great grandmother, was said for some reason to walk. This however happened in daylight, and there was no sign of the ghost who walked presumably under the moon; but halfway along she, Annabel, had stuck, and grew frightened and, mistakenly, looked down. The ground below had seemed far off, green and swaying like the endless sea beyond; hens pecked about nearby like flies, and Morven's upturned face among them was pale, narrow, and expectant, a new moon in reverse. She'd known then what she should have known at the beginning; that he wanted her to fall. He wanted it, because Malvie was hers and could never be his. He wanted to kill her, for revenge, or whatever it was. He wanted it . . .

"Cry-baby! Cry-baby Annabel!" His mocking call had floated up from below, like a gull's from sea-rock; but the mockery reassured her, for it was customary to Morven, and she knew he meant to make her angry enough to forget her fear. But the height of the ledge, the merging of green land and greener water, the breakers in the distance white like the hens at their feet, made her sick with terror; she couldn't move either back or forth; her fingers gripped the ledge helplessly. Clearly now, after all this time, she could still recall the tiny, star-shaped flecks and patches of lichen, golden in colour, which inhabited the room and walls, and their rough dry feel against her clinging, useless fingers. Below her, Morven had begun to call again.

"Jump, and I'll catch you. I will, I promise. I'll catch you so's you don't fall." But one could never believe him; the voice had changed, was loving now and trying to help her, to save her perhaps, but she couldn't take the leap . . .

Luckily Sam Aitken the groom had come along, and had seen what was happening. He'd climbed up and rescued Annabel, and got her down. Later, she was told, he'd aimed a cuff at Morven, which in those days was like slapping the face of the king in council. But Aitkens had worked in Malvie stables for three generations and Sam could risk Papa's anger, which never in any case showed itself on that occasion; after all, Sam had saved Papa's only daughter. Then, shortly after that, as it seemed, Papa had died.

And so she would not go to Morven now, just because he was whistling, and kilt up her skirts and run through the long grass uphill, and risk aunt Retford's whipping though she was now too old for it, and sit by Morven again among the springing mosses and the white pricking of garlic flowers that gave out so beguiling a scent in the summer woods that it wasn't like their relative, the tamed cookery-herb, at all. She wouldn't go . . . and what did he want with her? He hadn't come near, or sent a birthday-remembrance or any other word for a long time. It was as though, now Malvie was gone, she herself meant nothing to him.

More than anything in the world, though, she would like to go. If he whistled again . . .

Her head stayed cocked like a bright-eyed thrush's, listening. But there was silence now from the hill. It was almost as though he'd known what she was thinking, and given her time to go over it all and change her mind, then stopped just in time to torment her. Morven was like that.

Morven Doon, lying up in the spinney, had himself shed the mood which had led him to try and summon his young cousin today. He'd known she would not come, any more than a little wax doll would propel itself, on jerky, uncertain limbs, across the field. His feeling for Annabel remained as it aways had; a mixture of affection, resentment and a certain deep abiding envy and hatred, the latter on behalf of Malvie. He had always felt this, even in the days when Uncle Philip complacently assumed he could right the wrong by marrying Morven to his cousin, later. Uncle Philip had died too soon.

Morven himself was light-eyed and slim, a youth still, with a thatch of silky-brown hair not always confined with a ribbon; he had a fey, pallid, moonlit beauty. He stared now at Malvie's tall chimneys, seen beyond the geans in their silvery summer leaf; farther off was the sea. That latter was in all of Morven's awareness, waking and asleep; the pull of the tides, the deep-running currents back and forth to Man, had been in his ears since birth; ay, his first conscious knowledge must have been of the sea, sounding below the great Flodden tower of Malvie, where his mother had borne him! She'd chosen, he knew, to make her lying-in there in the brief time she'd been with them, as though the raw cold stones resembled more nearly her fastness in the Highland north than the tame house below would ever do, with its panelled walls and carpets already a trifle threadbare. So she'd borne him, Morven, up there, and then died; as though in resentment that his pending birth had prevented her from following his fugitive father, Richard Doon, into the heather after Culloden, and later to France.

15

Morven Doon had never seen his father, but he knew him, or felt sure he did. Uncle Philip had nourished his orphaned nephew on legends of the glorious elder twin he himself had all his youth copied and admired. Good, inadequate Uncle Philip, turning in the end to the slight solace of an evening's wine; everything else had been a little unreal; his own emulation of Richard, even to marrying the latter's erstwhile betrothed in the end, from a sense of duty no doubt, had produced only a daughter, then solitude. Morven could remember his aunt Grace well enough before she faded, in gentle apology, out of life when Annabel would be about five: the mother had never seemed to live, breathe and feel like other women. They said, and it was whispered long after her marriage to Philip Doon, that her heart was buried with his brother who had died in France; that she had never recovered from the earlier news of Richard's impulsive wedding, in the north, in the flush of triumph which had begun the 'Forty-five, to a Highland woman.

Love and heartache . . . he himself had never felt it, perhaps never would. He stared between the trees now and thought, not for the first time, that no woman would ever mean to him what Malvie did, his house of Malvie. His house, despite what the government of the day had done in forfeiting all the possessions of his exiled father. His house, not Uncle Philip's to whom it had been, after lawsuits, allotted. His house, not young Annabel's who had happened to be born of that prudent, later marriage of his uncle's and the woman who should have been his own mother. He'd have been fashioned of a different stuff, no doubt, had his dam been Grace Melrose and not Helen Colquhoun; gentler, more acquiescent, more like Annabel.

And, now, they wouldn't let him marry Annabel. They wouldn't even let him see her; and they'd trained her, like a little horse, with whip and bridle, not to come when he called, not to turn her head to his whistle.

Well . . . they'd all see.

He turned again to Malvie, surveying it with the lids half-closed over his strange, light, catlike eyes, which could be the colour of cold water or else could shine with inward achievement. He'd achieved nothing of late, since losing Malvie. The house had furnished the stuff of his dreams since ever he could remember; each evening, in the old days, riding home alone or with Uncle Philip, he'd been used to draw rein and look across at the golden lichen covering the stones, so that roof, pediment and tower seemed made of gold, an elfin blessing. Gold! Morven's thin face grew bitter. There was little left of the real commodity; after Philip's death, the lawyers had come and burrowed like beetles, then there had been aunt Retford's small indomitable figure standing on Mains threshold, forbidding him the house; and Malvie was closed up.

"You must find your own way in the world, nephew Morven; you're a man now." He remembered her tight, complacent smile, and Sir Hubert Melrose, dead Grace's brother, fidgeting behind her. Sir Hubert had, no doubt, been ashamed of the treatment of Richard Doon's son by Richard and Philip's own sister; he'd tried to give Morven a sovereign as he left, and the boy had flung it back at him on the path. He could still hear the ringing of the gold, and see the swift, predatory movement with which aunt Retford had bent at once and scooped it up.

"I can find my own, never fear; to hell with you all." And he'd turned and gone, not knowing yet where to, and in the end he'd gone down to the shore as usual and the near caves, and brooded there till Bart's boat came, and gone out in it. Bart was the blacksmith's son and after—it was fishing that day, no more—they'd beached the craft and gone up together to old Aaron's cottage for supper, to cook the catch; and somehow he'd stayed on with Aaron. That had been three years ago and everyone said—'everyone' being the genteel country, remembered from the time when Philip's tolerant affection enveloped Morven and he met them daily as equals —everyone said he had gone to waste, was wasting his life, should be in the army or studying the law. To hell with that too, Morven thought; he could make more on the rum-lay over from Man than ever he'd make in a scrivener's stuffy office in Edinburgh, or following the drum. And he had his freedom; and he could, day and night, be near Malvie.

He watched the house constantly, seeing it now as something in a dream; it hardly seemed possible he had spent his boyhood there. He had a way of entry, not easy and not by the door; it hadn't been needed nor had he entered the house again since aunt Retford and Sir Hubert had turned the great key of Malvie, three years ago now. He didn't need to go in. But as day followed day and time passed, he would evolve one scheme after another for growing rich, purchasing the house back or else marrying Annabel; he didn't care which, provided Malvie ended in his own possession. Annabel herself was another matter; he was used to her, she'd never touched his heart. To rob a mail-coach, and get away undetected with the loot . . . to hide away a small fortune made from rum and gin . . . to pick pockets; some made a fortune at that in the London play-houses. But to go to London would mean leaving Malvie alone in daylight and dark, Malvie remote and lonely already behind its gold. He must stay here; Bart's lay seemed the only answer.

Aunt Retford meant Annabel to make a rich marriage, he knew; she was bringing the girl up for that purpose, turning her into a correct, pretty, spiritless thing. Uncle Hubert had stopped Peter Melrose from mooning after her last year; he said he didn't countenance marriage of cousins, but it was more than that. There wasn't anyone else hereabouts. Once or twice Morven had heard talk, drifting down into the blacksmith's cottage of an evening, that the debts on Malvie could still not be cleared by any means and the house must be sold. Malvie sold! Sold to strangers!

But no strangers had come. The roads were bad from the south, and no one in the north had any money. Malvie, the inheritance of Doons for centuries, since King David's time that had the wanton queen, was safe still. Morven would lie, as now, watching the house, and thinking of how ever since King Davie, who liked his English comforts, Doons had fought in Scotland for the true king; for Montrose; for Claverhouse at Killiecrankie; for King James at Sheriffmuir; for Bonnie Prince Charlie. His own father Richard had been the last of the name of Doon to draw a sword for the royal house. And the result of all that had been that he, the heir, was left now landless . . . and poor.

What was to be done? What could he do, not yet being rich, to save Malvie for himself and his sons? For he must breed sons. If the prim, timid, correct wax doll Annabel had lately become since aunt Retford whipped the life out of her had run out today, and up the hill to him, should he have raped her to settle the matter? He'd have done it—he had thought of that answer sometimes—if there had been any help in law, by so doing, for Malvie. But he and Annabel were still minors and the debts must be cleared. He'd be left, in the event, with Annabel and not the house: shackled to a girl who had no interest for him. Anyway, she hadn't come today.

His thoughts drifted from present to future and he rolled over on his back, staring up at the silvery gean trees. To-morrow, Aaron had said, they were going out, the pair of them, without the fire-signal, when the tide should be right after midnight. The moon would be in the dark quarter and with the wind right they could make all speed to Man, and back again by next evening. There would be bales off a French ship to bring home. Morven grinned, showing teeth white as a fox's. Respectable Abel Judd, Aaron's elder son who owned the Fleece as a careful taxpayer, would come later with his dray; a certain number of excise-approved barrels were always on it. There would be stronger stuff than ale hidden among the straw in the double bottom; not only the dray, but Aaron's cellar at the smithy also, had that. So had the Fleece. Abel however was too careful to come out with them in in the boat himself; Morven and Bart would see to the stowing, and the hiding afterwards of other packages, and their delivery elsewhere. The list of high-ranking customers was a fairly long one; all the names on it were those with whom Uncle Philip and he used to visit, and drink wine brought no doubt from somewhere or other, tossed over the throat in one another's stately halls. But not now. He, Morven, in a woollen cap and leathers, would come after dark, oh, ay, and hand in a package through a closed shutter, while they snuffed the candles. And afterwards, they'd leave the money by arrangement.

Money. It was what he himself needed, much, much more than he already had—and he had made a little in such ways—to save Malvie. His will was like a coiled serpent inside him, ready to spring at need; he had spent little or nothing on himself all these years; he still wore his old clothes, or Uncle Philip's. He hadn't had a woman or cast a guinea at play, or drunk ale in Abel's Fleece that he must pay for. Mean as the devil, they'd begun saying he was, young Morven. Sometimes he wondered if the red blood of the Doons in him, and of his wild Highland dam, might be running thin and sour; but there was always the sight of Malvie, to set it pounding again. One day, when the plan was perfected, he'd be the laird there, and play chess in the evenings by his own fire in the great hall, with his boots eased off, like Uncle Philip; and when he dined it would be in powder and ruffles, with a servant at his elbow plying wine, and the candlelight shining on the long polished table among the meats. Doon of Malvie, he'd be then. There was a woman at the opposite end of the table, but he couldn't see her face.

He still lay about on the grass of the spinney, relaxing his lithe thin body in its patched shirt that had once been Philip Doon's. He had given up expecting Annabel, or thinking of her; his thoughts drifted now to women in general. Of these he was ignorant; except for the fading memory of his uncle's resigned wife, and the legends of his own mother; aunt Retford he hardly classed as a woman at all, and Sir Hubert Melrose's wife had been always ailing before she died last year: no one latterly saw her. Aaron was a widower and had been for years. Women were, accordingly, a closed book; but Morven felt that, if he opened this, he could read it without difficulty. He had not yet, however, had a woman or attempted one, and Bart laughed at him for it: Bart, sexual as a tomcat, spent his own free time, his money and all his landward thoughts on legs and bosoms, generally those of the lasses in the Fleece kitchen, who were handy; or young casual workers on the farms. There were bastards everywhere already with Bart's hook nose and sloe-dark eyes, though he was only twenty. He, Morven, wasn't like that; a certain fastidiousness took him when confronted with easy wenches, or perhaps he was in any case cold, his only real love being Malvie. For Malvie, he'd marry . . . but before then, no doubt he should find out about women, as his father had perhaps done before taking the untamed, green-clad Highland creature he'd met at the famous Holyrood ball in 'Forty-five. Richard Doon had married her next day in her green silk dress. There were those who said all the misfortune had stemmed from that; there was never any luck in green. Morven pulled a stalk of green grass now and thoughtfully nibbled the pale, juicy end nearest the root. Luck! He'd no faith in that; one made one's own. With a trifle of common sense and caution, there was no need to be caught doing what didn't suit other folk. Society had made an outcast of him for no fault of his own; he would take his own way with his life. The will in him was, he knew, his mother's; she had followed easy Richard south, then north, then come home to Malvie to have her son and passed the waiting time striding the rooms and corridors like a caged tigress, before taking at last to her tower. From it there was the sight of the road along which tidings never came, except of disaster. She'd left the wish that her son should be called not for his father, in the end, but for her own land, Morven of the blue hills which she would never see again. He had her eyes, pale as water: and her thin wiry frame. The silky thatch of brown hair was his father's.

He himself had no wish yet to see Morven of the north. His heart was here, in his father's country, which they said had such charm that no man could willingly leave it. Every stone and every cranny was known to Morven Doon, the least crack and mark on the long flight of stone steps running down from Malvie's steep back to the sea. He knew that well, and also the caves deep under; there was a place where the seals came in from the open seas to lay their young, that no man could reach for long because the tide ran inwards to the concealed shelf of rock within minutes again, except for one single day in the year. Morven had been, that day, for the allotted hour: he'd go again. He was free to come and go as he would, no man owning him.

Doon of Malvie! There was no man must tell him what he should do. He would do his will. He'd get back the house . . . somehow, anyhow. Silly Annabel, the wax doll in a sunbonnet —he'd seen her last year, following aunt Retford about with a flat basket, while the old woman snipped off rose-heads with scissors—Annabel should have bred his heirs. If she should breed them now instead to some rich man aunt Retford found, and they peopled Malvie, like Bart's bastards peopled the farms . . .

A nucleus of an idea, ruthless and cruel, sprang to Morven's mind at that moment. He was not yet certain of the details of it. But it had come; and as he thought best after activity he rose, jerked his coat across his shoulders from where he had slung it meantime over a branch, and strode down again to the road which led towards Aaron's. Peter Melrose's horse would be shod by now and if so, before they set off tomorrow night, he'd ride it over to Maddon. Peter was one of the few people who still acted in a friendly manner since the closing of Malvie, and Morven's choosing of the blacksmith and his son for company. It would be pleasant to see Peter again and talk as they had been used to do while Philip Doon still lived.

The sun had gone by the time Morven descended from the hill. There was, by now, no sign of Annabel in the Mains garden. No doubt she was in the withdrawing-room, drinking their pale and punctual tea. Morven was assailed, again, by a curious, vindictive fancy that sometimes beset him, thinking of their separate lives and what they had become; a fancy to take and ravish Annabel, to feel her silly pink mouth fall open on the shape of an O under his hard kiss; stifling with that the cry she would presently make as he hurt her, deflowered her, made her bleed inside her lifted petticoats, so carefully laundered by aunt Retford's successive maids. One day, it should happen. One day . . . he'd work on it in his mind, fit it to suit his own eventual purpose for Malvie; no reason for it otherwise.

Later, much later, he was to have leisure to reflect that if

Annabel had in fact come up the hill to him that day, and he'd done as he said, not ridden over to town on Peter's horse to see Livia Millarch by chance that first time, their lives, the lives of all three of them—Annabel, Livia, himself —might perhaps have been different. But, again, perhaps not. Morven was unable to ride Peter Melrose's gelding until after the return from Man; the beast had an inflamed foot, which did not settle to shoeing for two or three days. In the end Morven saddled him and, having changed his own clothes, rode off. It was by then late on Saturday, and he knew he would not return till after the Sabbath; trouble waited for those who made journeys on that day, except to and from church. No doubt Peter would give him a meal.

Morven shrugged; he would, he thought, lie up in a hay rick meantime. It was already growing dark as he rode; the clip-clop of the great beast's iron hooves struck sparks from the road, lying pale and narrow in the moonlight. He had by now left the rough places behind, and had come to the way the mail-coach passed; he himself felt, again, like a gentleman, seated up here on Peter's fine bay. He spurred it on, seeing, as mile followed mile, the fire Aaron had made come out from below the flying, obedient hooves; old frail-seeming Aaron at his forge, wresting durability and strength from bright-red iron, then stopping it to signal to the incoming ships . . . Morven smiled. They'd got the cargo back safe enough, and stowed, and some delivered; he hadn't been idle these two days. Now, in Uncle Philip's cast-off coat of black velvet with frogging, and his hat, he himself might be Doon of Malvie, riding the roads. The laird himself casting a long shadow athwart the unending greystone dykes, passing them swiftly as night changed to dawn. Morven came on the town's spires pricking up into the sunrise before he remembered; damn, he'd have to attend church service, it was too late to hide. Already, parties of men and women were emerging in their best clothes, carrying packs of food to eat between the morning and afternoon sermons. He dismounted, begged a bowl of milk for himself, and a drink for the bay, from a dairymaid at a nearby farm, and presently rode on. The morning was by now clear and cool; Uncle Philip's velvet coat-sleeve had lost its glamour with the night, and looked rubbed and shabby.

He had drawn up the bay horse at last by the church gate, and was about to dismount, hoping perhaps to meet the Melrose carriage as it came in with the rest; but had not yet done so, and a procession along the street gave him pause. It was a pitiful one; he realised it must come from Emmett's orphanage. The young girls who composed it were, some of them, mere children; they wore cloaks of hodden with plain hoods, and were scraggy and thin, as though the summer's day itself would not warm their bones. Morven had heard of Emmett's; the inmates were spoken of with pity, for they were waifs who were taken in and trained, these days, in laundry and domestic service, from the payment of which, later, the authorities were recompensed for their keep. It was like a lifetime's slavery; the governor, in his beaver hat, and his cold-eyed wife in her pelisse, walked ahead of the sad little procession as if ashamed to own it; behind again was a subordinate dragon, keeping the girls in order.

Morven sat his horse and watched, his own arrogance for the time forgotten; nevertheless, at the back of his mind, was the certainty that these poor young women would think him some grand, important personage, perhaps a relation of Sir Hubert Melrose. On the whole, they gave no sign of any such assumption; keeping their bleared eyes meekly on the path as they went into church, scuffing their patched footgear on the cobbles. Only one young woman was different. She raised her eyes, which were direct, grey and stormy beneath straight-set black brows. Her hair also was black as a crow's wing beneath her hood. She might have been about sixteen. Her gaze—it was arresting, yet cool and impersonal—met Morven's and held it. He would remember her face, with its broad cheekbones and full soft mouth; she showed none of the ill-health of the other underfed young women. There was a difference about her, which at first he could not pin down or name; she was different from any girl he had ever seen anywhere. That hair, smooth and shining and black! When it was let down it would reach, he dared say, below her knees; he'd like to touch hair like that, to play with it. There were other things he would like to do.

The dragon's elbow thrust; they had been staring at one another too openly. "Livia!" a voice called. "Keep in the line and mind your ways."

Mind her ways, eh? Livia, the wife of Augustus. The line moved on. The twist of her young body under the shoddy cloak as she rejoined the rest had showed Morven another thing to remember; she was pregnant. A wanton? There could be small opportunity there . . .

Afterwards, when he'd met Peter and his father coming in with the carriage to church, he asked them of it. There was a part of Emmett's foundation which was a separate correction-house, they told him, for those who had strayed in their first assignments outside to domestic service, when they were recalled and disciplined for such time as it should take to cure the fault. Morven grinned; there was only one cure for that kind, as far as he knew. He said so to Peter Melrose; that golden-haired young archangel looked grave.

"Their lot is not an enviable one," he said thoughtfully. "Who are we to say that we in like case would do better? It reminds me of the stone cast at the adultress; who was fit to throw it? You'll come back after church, Morven? There's cold mutton and bread and cheese for supper, as the servants stay on for the second sermon."

He hadn't asked for news of Annabel; but his father, glooming in the rear seat of the carriage, wouldn't encourage that, Morven thought: the old man had other plans for Peter. The lad was in any case too good for this world, Morven decided; he and Annabel together would have made a pair of saints, begetting cherubs. It had been as well to separate them.

II

Four or five months after these happenings, the young woman with grey eyes, whose name was Livia Millarch but who, for good reasons, called herself Mary Reid at present, jolted and swayed in the post-coach along the uneven highway into town.

The coach was hardly full; they were near the end of the journey and the driver, looking forward to a draught of ale at the Fleece, let his horses have their heads for the last mile. Livia looked dully out at the road, with everything beyond nipped black and bare by frost; she was going to her first situation, and the prospect seemed as bleak as the landscape. This Mrs. Retford lived miles from anywhere, and it would be necessary, for the final stage of her journey, to walk. It was unlikely anyone had troubled to come and meet her. She clutched the modest hamper which contained her few belongings, and drew her grey cloak round her against the cold. The coach drew to a halt at an inn; she could see its lights and open door across a square cobbled yard, but did not intend to go in.

She alighted with the other passengers and, having enquired the direction of the departing driver, set forth with her long, easy stride. Before long she heard running footsteps and, turning, saw the young mother with her child who had occupied the opposite seat in the coach; she beckoned Livia.

"You goin' to Malvie? Like a place in the cart?"

The farm cart was welcome, though open to the cold and frost; she huddled in the back, watching the young woman's husband, an agricultural worker, settle his wife in and hoist the little boy, who was delighted with all of it, up by him near the great, patient shire-horse. Livia watched them, a certain bitterness in her expression softening and almost fading as she did so; but it returned when the young woman turned and asked her where she was bound.

"The Mains, to Mrs. Retford." Her voice was deeper than most women's, and did not hold the slurred a's and lazy consonants of the region. It was difficult to know where she might have come from. The farmworker's wife clucked her tongue.

"In service there? They never stay. She's a terror, mean as they're made; she'll see you work the skin off your hands." Her eyes goggled pleasurably, ready for further exchanges as regarded Mrs. Retford. But the young woman in the grey cloak said little more, only adding shortly that she didn't mind work; so the other was disappointed, and turned back to watching her little boy with his father, to see he didn't fall off the cart; one never knew with restless children. The horse jogged on and they soon left town behind, taking the path that led by a steep fall westwards to the shore and a sight of Man.

The sudden revelation of the glittering view made Livia draw breath. She had never before seen the sea. The sun sparkled on it as though it were molten silver; forgotten were the bare, black fields and her own cold heart. What lay beyond the width of the horizons she did not know; did anyone know what lay beyond for them? But she took comfort from the sight of the sea. If this Mrs. Retford was a terror, she could always take a minute off now and then and go and look out at it. In any case, it couldn't be worse than what she'd come from.

Her mind ran back over the only life she could remember, and this, in turn, as always, ended in blankness, the dark, a

25

time she knew she ought to remember but could not; a time which had made her as she was and would always be, no matter what befell. In her blood coursed a strangeness she could not understand, a quality which had kept her, always from the beginning, separate and different from Alice and Milly and the rest; separate from Mary Reid. For all those, one day would be like the next, the next like the last; with no blank left in the memory, no warm sudden racing invitation in the veins that made gladness out of nothing, even the light of the sun on the sea.

She should have no gladness left in her; they'd tried to beat it out. She was a bad girl; they all said so. Matron and Mrs. Park at Emmett's had said so, time after time since Livia first was sent there as a stubborn black-haired little creature of seven years old, brought in by old farmer Ransome's kin. Old Ransome himself wouldn't have parted with her. But of late his mind had begun to wander and his limbs had grown too stiff for him to get about the farm, and those who came resented her because she wasn't Ransome's own. Why should he trouble with a gipsy's get? It wasn't as though she was his. And Livia partook heartily of the good farm fare, the porridge and cream and curded cheeses, and the small-ale and home-baked bread and stored russet apples. It was time, accordingly, old Ransome's kin said, that she went; to Emmett's, where there was provision made for such folk.

There hadn't been farm fare at Emmett's, or anything like it.

Livia's mind shied away from recent memory, jerking back like a wilful foal to what must have happened before she could remember. While she had still lived with old Ransome in his house, while they would sit together by his fire of an evening, he would tell her of the early things. There had been a woman with loose black hair, he said, lying in the straw of the byre one winter's night seven or eight years gone; he'd heard moaning, and had gone out with a lantern in the end to see if it was one of the beasts. Bitter cold it was, so that rime silvered the roofs of the house and shed, and made the cattle stamp in their stalls. The woman was in labour, too far gone for Ransome to carry her back again into his house; the child was born there in the straw. Afterwards he'd gone to fetch a blanket and hot posset for the poor mother to sup, but by the time he got back with the bowl, being even then a bit slow, she was dying; he could tell by the fallen-in quality of her face, and the great sunken eyes surveying him impersonally in the light of the lantern. "She'd

26

have been pretty once," he would say reflectively. She must have come a long way.

He had bent over her and asked her name, when he saw she was going. "Livia," she told him, adding proudly. "It's a queen's name."

"You'd want the bairn called after ye?"

"Ay."

Her eyes had closed then and he could find out nothing further. Later, after she was dead and they'd buried her, farmer Ransome busied himself with trying to find out one or two things more. The times were troublous, and she'd been a gipsy woman, and not much could ever be found out for certain, in any case, about those folk. The fact that she'd left her tribe gave him a lead; and the stir then over Jacobite fugitives in the north country. Some were still hiding in the heather, others making all sail to France if they could find a ship, still others, all of that same year, trapped and shot or hanged or drowned without trial. There was a tale, and farmer Ransome was to hand it on to the child Livia for what it was worth, about a fugitive from the north parts who had been a great lord's son, and who had gone out against his father's wishes for the Prince when he came over in the previous summer. Later, after Culloden, the lord's son took up with a gipsy woman, who hid him and left her own kin to follow him. He was a fine, handsome fellow, they said, with a head of long curling hair. The redcoats found him at last and took him from her, and tied him up by his long hair to a horse's tail, and dragged him by that towards the next town. When they got there he was dead, and the woman who had followed, wailing, made off then alone, to have her child. It was impossible, in the confusion of the times, to be more certain of anything than that. The man's name, the officer in command of the detachment told farmer Ransome later, had been Millarch. It needn't have been his real name.

The old farmer had christened the baby and brought her up himself, weaning her from ewe's milk as though she were an orphan lamb. She thrived well enough, and diverted him in the evenings, when the day's work was done. There was, in those days, an old woman who came up from the village to clean for Ransome, and she helped with Livia; but she died in the third spring. After that things went from bad to worse, and old Ransome grew increasingly addled and rheumatic, so that his married daughter moved in. The child Livia had meantime been neglected, and by the time they persuaded Ransome to let her go to Emmett's orphanage—it was only for a while, they told him, till things got straight—her hair was matted so thickly they had to cut it, for no comb would go through, and they picked her scalp and body free of lice.

If the old man had had his wits about him, Livia knew, he wouldn't have parted with her. He died that same year, and the parish buried him.

Emmett's foundation, where Livia spent the next nine years of her life, had been brought into being by two brothers of that name not hitherto renowned for their piety; they had been burgesses of the town in the time of James the Sixth. By then, it was no longer possible to shrive one's soul by leaving mass-silver, and as an alternative the brothers left a certain sum for the education and maintenance of twelve young women who were, the titles stated, to be indigent and without other means of support. They were to be taught, and thoroughly instructed in, those arts which go to make up a good housewife or domestic servant; they were to be brought up in the fear of the Lord; and on departure to a paid assignment or to marriage were to be given—and this was one of the few tenets still adhered to by present-day authority—twelve pence as dowry, to be paid, on their departure, out of the fund.

By now, certain modifications had crept into Emmett's. The instruction in housewifery mostly covered public laundry, which the orphan children took in and did with great benefit to the fund which absorbed the payments. A provident clause in the contract ensured that, when work was found for them —and with the shortage of domestics everywhere this was not likely to cause inconvenience—the first three years' payment should be sent direct to Emmett's, who would deduct one-third against the back costs of the orphan's food and board from the age of seven. In this manner a nice balance was ensured for the municipal authority, who had some time since absorbed Emmett's original foundation and had moreover, providently for these times, added the initial town correction-house to the earlier endowment financed by the brothers' trust. With suitable physical barriers erected, there was no reason for the inmates of the two buildings ever to meet. Processions to church were an exception; but as they were not permitted to speak on that occasion, no harm was done to the orphans' morals. On such a day, Morven Doon had already glimpsed Livia.

Livia remembered the correction-house walls, of yellow brick, rising beyond the high windows of the communal dormitory in which she had slept, with eleven others, since the farm-folk delivered her to Emmett's. On asking what that building was she had been told not to ask questions; and after a few days had no leisure or energy to ask more.

The orphans were kept hard at work, and fed badly. Clappers came round at five in the morning, wielded with a certain enjoyment—it was her only one—by Ada Park, the second-in-command of Mrs. Priddy, the governor's wife and orphanage matron. Ada had herself been an orphan and could remember nothing before Emmett's. She had long had individuality and the milk of human kindness flogged and probably laundered out of her; it had proved impossible to find her a situation despite her hard-working capacity; she stank. The stink, which Ada could not help or remove, pervaded the dormitory, the privy, and any other place where Ada was known to have been. After a time one grew used to it. She was a thin bitter carping creature who disliked the orphans and could never be free of them: even her bed was in the common row. They assumed Ada as a necessary evil; they were long since beyond hate.

The dormitory was not private, any more than most other parts of Emmett's except the privy and the governor's office. It was not permitted to talk there, and even whispering between one bed and the next was overheard by Ada, zealously reported by her, and the culprit flogged. No doubt this helped to account for the singular state of innocence in which Livia herself grew up, despite her child's memory of farm animals and nature. By the age of twelve she had still no idea what men were for, except to thunder prayers and read the Bible. Governor Priddy, the only man in sight except at church— due to what lapse in the lifetime of the long-dead Emmett brothers no one knew, there was no provision made for anything but young women—Governor Priddy was there at all by virtue of his wife, who was own sister to the Provost of the burgh. He was a tall, lean, cold-eyed, mean-faced creature, who on Sundays added terror to his appearance by putting on a black beaver and stock. At church he would sit among the elders; at meals at Emmett's, in so far as the twice daily issue of thin cooling gruel could be called by this courtesy, he excelled himself: from the table-head, where his own served viands differed enough to bring hungry sniffing to the twelve poor little creatures placed below him, he would emit a lengthy grace. Early in the morning, and before retiring at night, there were more prayers, and a Bible-reading; the minor prophets were favoured as they gave Governor Priddy an opportunity to render the adverse thunderings of Jeremiah about a situation the orphans could but doubtfully understand. They were visited also by the town-minister, his wife, the kirk session who were hereditary governors of Emmett's, and now and again by prospective employers. A close relationship was maintained between these good ladies and the authorities of Emmett's, who could always be relied upon to relieve the shortage or, at worst, to put them for a consideration on the waiting list. They would also assist in the not infrequent escapes or lapses of the employed from found situations: at worst, they would take back these unfortunates for a variable period of correction. It was a service not freely available in other towns, and the authorities prided themselves on the maintenance of so fine a tradition of public service in the burgh.

The spectacle of Governor Priddy, lofty, black-clad, and infallible, confused itself with the probable image of God in Livia's earliest thoughts on the subject; she was, in accordance with the rules of the foundation, thoroughly instructed in Holy Writ and in the fear of the Lord. The latter emotion was taken for granted more than would, perhaps, have been the case had the children not been so tired out physically. Instruction in laundry-practice exceeded even instruction in the prophecies of Jeremiah, Nahum, and Habakkuk. From the time the little girls were nine years old they would participate in the full rota of housework at Emmett's; the encouragement of a fine national tradition of independence was an expressed clause in the contract for acceptance. The rota involved sweeping-duties, cooking and washing up the crockery bowls; scrubbing the long wooden tables, their very knots worn flat with such toil over the years, with lye; sanding the cleaned floors, and—a break from monotony—drawing chalk patterns afterwards, according to one's fancy, on the still damp redstone tiles of the governor's newly-washed corridor. Livia liked this exercise, except that the stones were cold and in winter, one's hands and feet grew chilblained at the task. There was no protection from cold or respite from heat; the girls wore hodden grey, in summer as in winter. In former days they had spun and woven it into gowns themselves; now it was supplied by a weaver in town at low cost, to allow more time to be spent in the laundry. The ,purchase of hodden did not happen often; one gown would be handed down from the last owner, well patched, to the girl coming up. When a girl grew too big for the largest size available it was time for her to move out of Emmett's.

The twelve pence had been intended as dowry, but this was seldom needed as such; Emmett's allowed few opportunities for meeting bridegrooms, and citizens' wives were constantly in need of maids. A small, meek, underfed orphan, who could launder and had no great opinion of herself, was worth keeping from an employer's point of view; girls from outside were flighty nowadays. Besides, the compulsion to repay a lifetime's board out of wages, which were low enough at three pounds a year, would discourage the most ardent suitor on an ordinary wage: whether a girl married or not, she still had to go on working to repay the debt till this was clear, and could bring little to a husband and family. Otherwise, there was the correction-house. Certain enterprising young women had in fact married, then fled elsewhere, or reared so many children in so short a time that it became impractical to pursue them for full gain. But these were the lucky exceptions, not in any case spoken of by anyone left behind.

The public wash came in each working day; it was the task of the smallest girls to carry it down to the laundry. In those days there was not yet a boiler at Emmett's, and all the water had to be carried up from the river by hand, or else the girls took the wash down to the banks in summer and trod it repeatedly in the shallow water. Certain fine linen, however, needed indoor treatment. One orphan—in Livia's time it was a rickety child named Alice Greer, whose bow legs toddled manfully back and forth between the irons and the lye-pot—would stoke the fire, while one or two others trod the linen-tub. This last job was the favourite, as it somehow gave rise to a dance, skirts hitched high out of the water, bare legs flying; it was the only approach to levity the orphans had. By the day's end, however, the joy had mostly been taken out of them; everything must be finished, the wash hung out or ironed, the fire cleaned for next day and its surface rubbed with sand, all buckets emptied and put back where they came from. Mrs. Priddy, who never showed herself while there were tasks to be done, would make an inspection, at the day's close, to ensure propriety and thoroughness; Ada Park was not allowed near the clean linen. If anything was found to be undone, or badly done, matron's gimlet eye would spot it; then the miscreant would go without supper. Supper wasn't much, being no more than thin gruel and a manchet as usual, except on Sundays when there was broth; but on Sunday there was of course no laundry.

Livia was a good worker; something in her rejoiced in the fact of tasks to be done, thankless and grim though these

31

often were. Besides, she had a fund of health accounted for by the early rearing on Ransome's farm; ewe's milk and curd had set her good teeth and straight bones, not like poor Alice who'd never known anything but Emmett's from a baby. Because Livia grew tall and strong, she was given the heaviest tasks to do; generally, when there was extra laundry-work, it was she who was set to it often in solitude.

She minded this less than might have been expected. Her own company was enough for her, and in ways always would be. It was, in fact, less dull than that of Alice, Milly, Ada and the rest; the defeated grey look that made them seem already like little old women had entered their souls, and talk was sparse and mostly forbidden. Livia thrived on silence. She knew also, though she had no mirror, that she wasn't like the rest, either in soul or body. Supple and strong as a young tree-sapling, she knew her body was; despite Governor Priddy's exhortations, she seldom troubled about her soul, and she had breasts already; they'd formed over a year ago. There were other matters one put up with, but which had never been explained; they were on the matron's forbidden list. Sometimes, when huddling down at night beneath the single greyish blanket on her bed, Livia would be aware of her own smooth, sliding limbs; and in the river sometimes, if she got down first to wash the day's lot before the others came, she could see her own reflection in calm water. It was already as Morven would see it, and remember; a face broad and strong in the cheekbones, the mouth full and generous, the eyes shadowy in reflection beneath the tight laundry cap.

Livia was treading the tub by herself as Alice had snuffles, the day the governor passed by, whether by accident or not she never knew, or wondered later. She had her skirts bundled high and was kicking and dancing in the wash, while her bare toes dripped beads of dissolved lye as they left the water; she knew no tunes except the paraphrases they chanted on Sundays in church, and in some manner she'd altered one of those, so that it fitted the dance-rhythm; jigging and dancing, as her ancestors had done from the Hungarian plains to the north shore of Scotland, over a century and a half ago now, despite the law and its rigours. The rigour overcame Livia as, seeing God's pale intent face at the door, she stopped fearfully, and bobbed a curtsy in the tub; it got her skirts wet. Lord knew what he must have seen, she thought, as she kicked her height moments ago. He didn't seem displeased, however, he closed the door and latched it. His lips, she noted, as he came towards her, seemed purplish today in his pale set face; like the plums in thin dough they had sometimes in summer. What did he want with her? Livia began to tremble; there was almost nothing one could think of doing which wasn't punished, somehow or other, soon or late.

"Come here," he told her. He didn't trouble, that time, with her name.

Livia stepped out of the tub, and stood trembling on the stone floor, barefooted, the wet dripping from her legs and skirts. What would he do now? But it wasn't—queerly— punishment. The governor, instead, was doing an unexpected thing. He had put forth a hand and was, almost reflectively, stroking her breasts under the grey bodice. Livia watched in fascination. She wasn't to know—how could she or anyone have known, such matters being almost like piercing the veil of the tabernacle—that Governor Priddy's wife, the Provost's sister, had denied him marital rights now for a matter of five years? The sneck on the laundry-door would hold.

Governor Priddy got at Livia four times more after that; after the first, she was no longer surprised, hardly even frightened. It gave her, in a way, a sense of power. One time was in the broom cupboard, another in the privy, and twice it happened when he was supposedly wrestling with her immortal soul, in his office. That last was a place where everyone, sooner or later, came on Fridays for punishment. Livia herself had been chalking the flagstones outside when he'd wrestled with Mary Reid, who had gone away now from Emmett's and was at work somewhere in the town. Mary had had a villainous squint and a stubborn Scots disposition; no doubt that was why Priddy's nasal whine had risen, on that occasion, particularly high over the Book of Isaiah. Or was it Ezekiel? The sounds Priddy was making now, with little groans coming out from between his teeth as though he were in pain, as he got at Livia wedged up hard against his desk, were like those he'd been making then. Livia closed her eyes and let him get on with it. If it was what he wanted, she'd be better off no doubt, as long as he was pleased with her. Already, twice now since it all started, matron had sent her down to town by herself on an errand to the baker's, a thing that had never happened before; and had given her a penny for herself to buy gingerbread.

Livia thought of the gingerbread; of its hot, spicy smell; of the friendly spotty face of Tam Imrie, the baker's boy, across the counter as she bought it. The recollection occupied her until Priddy had finished and had taken his hands off. Then he said, as always,

"Are you a good girl, Livia? Do you say your prayers?"

"Yes, sir."

"You say them each night, kneeling by your bed in your shift?"

"Oh, yes, sir." It paid to tell lies. It wasn't so bad now as it had been at first; after that first time, she hadn't been able to stop bleeding, and the wash wasn't finished, and she'd stilled the trembling of her limbs by the only way she knew, by getting back into the tub and finishing the job, so that the blood went away with the washing-water. She hadn't dared say anything to anybody. Who could she tell? Matron would say she was a wicked liar, and have her whipped. Ada Park would only tell matron. If it got back to the governor himself, he—well, he—what would happen then? There was nobody who could tell Governor Priddy what he must do and what he mustn't. (In this Livia was wrong.) There was nobody, nobody at all, now farmer Ransome was long dead, who'd take her side, or to whom she could run. No, she must just say nothing, and go on as usual. As long as it pleased old Priddy, that was all right . . .

"I am glad that you say your prayers, Livia. You may go now. And remember—"

"Yes, sir?" His tongue passed, uncertainly, over the purple lips. He looked ill, she thought. It must be bad for anyone to get as caught up in praying, and the like, and—and what he'd just done. One thing seemed much like the other, after all. Livia kept her face straight till she should get outside the door; but it was comical, she knew. Nobody here would ever let her say so, but it would make a cat laugh.

"Keep silence, Livia. You understand me?"

"Oh, yes, sir."

She bobbed her curtsy, and went.

The first day she felt sick over the gruel at breakfast she didn't pay much attention; sometimes, with seeing it every day, that was what you felt like with gruel. But it happened almost every morning after that. Then, about a month after, she fainted in the laundry with the hot iron in her hand, and burnt herself, which didn't matter, and somebody's washed linen petticoat, which did. Matron was sent for.

The remembrance of matron afterwards added to the queerness of the whole thing, from the beginning. Lately, matron had been almost a friend, with her gingerbread money;

but now—well, she'd come and slapped Livia's face. That might have been to revive her, but then matron went on slapping, and Livia started screaming, and in the end they were both on the floor with matron kneeling, and Livia lying on her back, screaming with the pain of being constantly slapped, but it wasn't clear why matron was screaming in return. Presently she started to emit words.

"Harlot! Brazen Jezebel! Whore! Whore!"

It was poor Tam Imrie they blamed for it.

Tam and she, all the enquiries being over, were made to stand side by side, not looking at one another, on the repentance-stools in church on Sunday morning. Livia was sorry for Tam, whose fault it hadn't been; she could only give half an ear to the hellfire preached over them both by the minister. Say what you liked, you couldn't go to hell for what you hadn't done. But everybody in the place thought he had, and as for Livia herself, there was nothing bad enough. The elders, among them Governor Priddy in his best blacks, sat there looking as if they and he had nothing to do with it; *she* could tell a different tale, of him with his breeches open. It didn't seem possible now. The elder, the prophet of God, the Provost's brother-in-law, the governor of Emmett's, all the rest of it; Priddy couldn't be interested, let alone responsible. She was glad she hadn't mentioned him; nobody would believe her.

Afterwards, the Emmett's authorities had Livia whipped; it was in any case the recognized punishment for a wanton. Governor Priddy sat with a gleam in his cold eyes, watching, in full view of her exposed flesh and what was happening to it. Afterwards she was to be sent to the correction-house for some months. It wasn't usual to go there straight from Emmett's, but in her case they hadn't had any choice; and in any event, they couldn't have kept her on at the orphanage once she was known to be pregnant. So Livia found out what was behind the yellow walls. If one waited long enough, there was an answer to all one's questions. She was taken in as an inmate of the adult house some days before her sixteenth birthday. At least old Ransome had left her the date of that, and her name. She was left in contemplation of these possessions, and of a flayed back and thickening belly, seated on the edge of just such a pallet bed as she had left behind in the orphanage, with a hodden blanket fashioned, no doubt, by the same weaver under the self-same contract.

There was not so much difference as might have been expected between the correction-house and orphanage. The difference was in Livia herself; not because of her pregnancy, not because of anything that had happened to her physically, but because she was filled with rage.

The emotion was so foreign that she did not at first recognise it, or herself in harbouring it. For a poor, downtrodden, shamefully pregnant young woman, a mass of quivering and publicly chastised flesh, it was unexpected; Livia might have assumed never to raise her head again or open her mouth. Her punishment had taken place in full view of the provost and session, the governor, matron and the two women officers who would be in charge of her, this coming year, behind the murky, yellow-grey walls of the correction-house. On first sight of the interior, however, Livia's rage increased; it might have come from her father's proud blood, never the devious gipsy half of her; such folk endure everything in silence. A smell of defeat pervaded the flagged passages; the familiar smell of old hodden, poverty, harsh soap and lye and repression and cruelty. The latter was by statute; all female inmates were to be flogged twice a month, to maintain them in an awareness of their fallen state, and to encourage repentance. The proviso dated from the seventeenth century and was seldom now adhered to by the two women officers Livia had already seen, and who were known respectively as Gammer Whitehead and Gammer Bell. They were in fact too idle for the exertion, and would lie like troopers instead, if the Provost were to ask a question regarding it, which he seldom did.

Livia had already seen the Provost, in his great wig and chain. She had also seen the Governor, and he'd seen her, stripped part naked over a bench in front of them all and beaten with rods till she bled. Smug, Priddy had stayed through all of that; the expression she'd caught on his face had been one of pure pleasure. It wasn't she who had a devil, Livia knew now; it was Priddy and his like. The knowledge of what he'd done to her came more fully as the weeks passed; in the correction-house, the inmates could at least talk.

They talked most in the dormitory, free of any Ada Park; the two old women had separate quarters. In this way and others, life was if anything more private than it had been in the orphanage proper. As Livia's child grew in her, so did her soul.

Some of the inmates she already knew. It was not a large town, and two at least of the girls had been formerly in the orphanage, having been returned from situations, one for petty theft and one for soliciting. The petty thief was Mary Reid, whom Livia remembered from Emmett's. She was the same sharp-faced, bitter-tongued little wench with one skeery eye, and had not grown an inch; it was hard to credit that she had a young man outside, and that he was Tam Imrie.

"I knew he hadn't done anything with you," she told Livia. "I knew who had." They had all known, evidently, what the governor was like; he'd got at three of the girls Mary knew of. "One day he'll get what's coming; but they wouldn't believe *us*. Did you take a black draught, dear?"

Livia said she hadn't, and Mary shook her head. "It's too late now; should've taken one, it'd have loosed it," she said. "Thing is, their ladyships won't take you once they've seen you looking like that; it might be their husbands next time," and she scanned Livia's waistline. "Better stick to pinching, like me." She grinned, showing degenerate stumps of teeth. "It's the money," she explained, "what the hell do they expect you to do? Three pounds a year, and half to go back. Tam and me'd get married when he's free of his bond, that's this coming quarter, and he'll be a master baker." She closed her lips on what might have been more, and looked at Livia reflectively with her weird eye gleaming. "It's better here without that laundry," she added. The depraved and abandoned inhabitants of the yellow house were not permitted to go down to the river; their task instead was plain sewing, which occupied the daylight hours with propriety.

Besides this there were visits, made more frequently than to Emmett's proper, by those charitable ladies of the town who took an interest in such things and were, moreover, like everyone else, on the lookout for domestics. It was unlikely that they themselves would accept the correction-house inmates into their own homes, though they prayed over them; but an acquaintance in the country might be glad of a maid, and might even advance the fare and other perquisites to the finder of such a treasure, even if it meant waiting for a while. Brief factual versions of the successful applicants' careers were sent before them, so that the prospective employer could take her own precautions. Mary had experience of this. She was, she confessed at last, in fear of the well-doing ladies and the way in which they might separate her from the prospect of bliss with Tam.

"Don't you say a word to anyone," she hissed one night from under her grey blanket. "Tam gets his articles next month, see? He's found a place, oh, miles and miles from here; somewhere east. It's got a brick oven, and a house for us to live in. It isn't much, but it'll do me. But s'pose in the meantime they tie me up with some old bitch who won't let me go, and Tam goes off with some other? A man can't wait for ever, but it'd kill me, I think." She'd feigned sick, she said, last time they came with a place for her; she'd scratched and rubbed her face with harsh lye and let them think it was the pox. "That sent her off fast enough, but the folk here got the apothecary to me next day, and he soon saw it wasn't. They warmed my back, I can tell you; but it was Lily got that job." Mary gave her eerie grin. "Only thing is, that tale won't do twice, if they come for me again; no way of catching the real thing in here, I'd say. I wondered if you'd help, knowing Tam?"

Livia had half listened, then and at other times; the tale by now was like something she'd heard long ago, but which would never happen. If any of them got out of here, it would only be to some drearier place; to some old woman who skinned the meat off the bones before serving, or beat one constantly; not but what they all did that. She stared at the high barred window, beyond which rain could be seen dropping down between here and Emmett's. There was nothing else, only Emmett's and the rain. On Sundays they all assembled, and formed a procession for church, wet or dry; she remembered the young fellow she'd seen one such day, mounted at the gate on a bay horse. He'd had light eyes like a cat's; they'd stared at her, and she'd stared back. There were folk like that outside. She herself would do anything, anything, to get out of here; it didn't matter whether it was to Tam Imrie or another. If Governor Priddy himself came with an offer to set her up as his doxy, she wasn't sure, by now, that she'd refuse him.

She glanced down at her swollen body. It hadn't—they'd tried twice or thrice in the first weeks after she came, without telling her why—proved possible to relieve her state with purges. It'd gone too far, Gammer Bell said, agreeing with Mary unknowing; glaring meantime at Livia as though it were her fault. They'd made her sick, however, and as though her inside were all running out of her in a constant mess of black draught; but that was all, and this remembrance Priddy had left her with grew bulkier as day followed day. It began to seem as if there never had been a time when she wasn't pregnant. They'd stopped purging her now.

She would lie beneath her blanket night after night and

38

half listen to Mary, and it was with no sensation of anything snapping open at last in her own mind that she said one time dully, as if it couldn't matter much either way,

"If Tam can fix it so's we both get away, let him; I'll do it if I can, if he can wait till after." Her belly by now raised the covers as she lay. Mary turned on her side, smiled, and said, consideringly,

"Thanks, love. When's it come?"

Livia said she didn't know. "Lord, you innocent," said Mary. "Looks as if it wouldn't be long to me; say any day now. I'll get word to Tam when he comes in with the loaves. Funny they never notice who's delivering daily; used to bake their own, then we'd be done. But the sacks of meal are big enough, in the dray."

Livia did not answer; she was already asleep. A silence had settled down on the yellow house, to be roused some hours later by the sound of Emmett's clapper. Livia's labour began that same day at six-thirty, where she'd gone after breakfast to wash up the bowls. It was, at the beginning, like washday and flooding again; she dropped everything and yelled for Gammer.

They said to her afterwards that it had been an easy birth. All Livia could remember was the pain; agonising, recurrent pain such as she'd never felt, nor hoped to feel again. In this state they removed her, somehow, to a narrow grey cell, and a truckle bed, and she lay there all day grunting and crying out dolefully; most of the time, Gammer Bell stayed with her. The odour of spirits came, because they were always to be found where Gammer might be; one time, someone put the flask to Livia's mouth, and it burned all the way down. Then pain again; then a lasting screaming agony. After that someone put a hand over her mouth and said she must bide quiet, the session was visiting; and Livia opened her mouth and damned the session, and bit whoever it might be on the hand. If it was Gammer, she didn't hold any grudge; later, when it was all over, she brought Livia a posset. Gammer Bell had a face like a great slab of ancient curd, immobile, expressionless and mostly evil; she dived presently to the blanket below which Livia lay and, beside her, by now, a small scarlet creature which had cried at first, and which looked like Governor Priddy. Gammer then said, in her flat everyday tone, "Well, it was the good Lord's mercy, without a doubt," and lifted away what by this time was a dead skinned rabbit, like those seen hanging in the poulterer's shop. Livia, who had thought she could feel no more, felt

39

her heart turn over. The baby was dead; they'd killed it. That suited everyone here well enough, no doubt, but it hadn't done any harm, the poor baby. Gammer had done something to it with the grey blanket, after it had cried; it had been alive enough then. It had been awkward, no doubt, on a day when the session was visiting, for a baby to be born in here who had a face like Governor Priddy. She'd seen that much clearly for herself, as Gammer bore it away.

Not quite two months after that, word came of a place for Mary. It was with an old woman in the remote country, who couldn't seem to keep her maids. Her name was Mrs. Retford, Mains of Malvie. There wouldn't be any chance to pilfer there, Mary was warned by the authorities; Mrs. Retford was informed of Mary's weakness, and there would be no chance to get rid of stolen goods in any case, so far from town and with no coach-road. So it was arranged.

Sorrow however awaited the authorities; the devil claimed his own. Tam Imrie the baker's apprentice had, as is known, already shown signs of levity, for which he had been duly punished by the session and by his master. Tam however would complete his indentures, which had prevented his marrying, within the week. On the day this happened, he delivered the order of loaves and meal for the last time to the correction-house, going round as usual by way of the open kitchen-passage in his dray. The dray moved off afterwards; and that was the last anyone ever saw of the youngest inmate, Livia Millarch, who as it happened had been taking her turn at cook-service that day and was not, as afterwards became clear, fully supervised in this process; it was not in fact possible to keep an eye all the time. But Livia had been proved a wanton before she was sixteen and her bad end was a surprise to no one. She and Tam had made off; even Tam's master did not know where, although he said the boy had decamped, ungratefully, with all his gear the day the apprenticeship was formally concluded. He himself had no further hold over Tam and nothing could be done.

For Livia, lying snug in the dray behind meal-sacks, something could and was; she hid that night in a place Tam showed her, and he brought her food. Next day, Mary was to board the coach for Mrs. Retford's. "You'll keep your hood pulled forrit?" said Tam anxiously. The only time when things could go wrong, for all of them, was in the market-place before the coach drove off. Tam couldn't be there himself, for obvious reasons; it was a matter for Mary and Livia alone, and perhaps Ada Park if she should come to see off the passenger.

Ada came; but no doubt Tam had said a word to the coach-driver, for the latter spent some moments in dalliance with that poor civet. By the time he stepped aboard, one grey hooded figure had been exchanged for another; Ada was too busy waving to the driver to spare time to look for the departing countenance of Mary Reid at the window. This was as well; by then, round four or more corners, Tam and Mary were embracing one another with swift, triumphant happiness before they vanished in their life together. "I gave Livia four of my twelve pence for herself," said Mary when she could. "She'll need them with that Mrs. Retford. She's got the papers too."

By then, the coach had gone.

The farmworker's cart set Livia down about a mile from Mains where the lane turned up again towards the moors. Carrying her hamper, she walked slowly on, holding her skirts aside from the high central ribbon of green grass which, even in this winter season, cluttered the narrow road.

At last she crested the rise from which the gables of the dower house could be seen, with Malvie itself a brooding ghost beyond. In that first moment as for all of her life, it was the smaller, more intimate house Livia would love best; a warm, welcoming little house, with pitched roof and walls honey-yellow with age on their plaster, covering the old stones. A glimpse of the wintry garden, bare now except for the dark yew-arbour, met Livia as she passed by. It all added to the wonder of the sight; she had not yet seen a garden. She made her way almost fearfully up to the rear door, and knocked on it. To live here, to help cherish this pretty house, would be all she asked, no matter how bad the mistress might be. If only she herself could continue in safety as Mary Reid! Surely with the papers and the letter, and the distance away it all was she could *be* Mary Reid; nobody from Emmett's would ever come here. Every waking moment, every effort of muscle and will, should be spent in turning her into Mary; a new Mary, who worked hard and didn't look at men. Livia the wanton was dead and fled, gone long ago into a different country with Tam Imrie. Let her be forgotten; a new servant had come to the Mains, who would work as no maid had ever worked before. Even this Mrs. Retford shouldn't have any complaints if she did exactly as was wanted, every least thing . . .

The door had opened and a middle-aged woman stood there, in cap and apron; a cook, perhaps, or housekeeper. She looked Livia up and down where she stood waiting in her hodden. "You're Mary Reid, I daresay."

Livia bobbed. "Yes, ma'am." It was done now; too late to change, she was Mary. The woman, whom she followed into a stone passageway, didn't look as bad as matron, Priddy or even Gammer had done; but one hadn't yet set eyes on Mrs. Retford.

"I'm Mrs. Betts. Best leave your hamper," said the other woman, knocking on a closed inner door. As Livia went to answer the summons she heard Mrs. Betts' footsteps shuffling away.

She closed the door behind her, and found herself confronting Mrs. Retford.

That lady sat alone in her room, at her desk, summing up accounts, a goose-quill held firmly in one small fine hand. The light was, designedly, behind her—Agnes Retford had not let full light fall on her face of late years—and her features were difficult to see. The voice when it spoke was cultured, with an overtone lacking in the late charitable ladies of Emmett's. Without being told, Livia knew she was in the presence of county. She hadn't met county before; they didn't interest themselves in the busier aspects of charity, only sometimes giving money to it. But this Mrs. Retford wouldn't be giving money to anything, that was certain. Her eyes were too close together. They were flat, blue, somehow repellent eyes, with no more depth in them than a pair of buttons. Mrs. Retford in her day had been a blonde, and her faded locks were still somewhat coquettishly arranged beneath her widow's cap of cream-washed lawn. She had long ago left off full mourning for her spouse, who had been dead forty years, not much lamented.

Livia waited, hands held respectfully clasped beneath her mantle; her new employer looked her up and down.

"Mary Reid?"

"Yes, ma'am." And she curtsied. That was the second time they'd asked her; soon, perhaps, she'd get used to it and stop jumping inside herself when they called her Mary. Mrs. Retford nodded, as if satisfied in one way. Then she said, as if she were an adder sliding out from behind a brake.

"Mrs. Priddy of Emmett's Foundation wrote to me about you. She says you pilfer." The tone held no accusation, only a calm weariness. Livia flushed scarlet; she'd forgotten about that part of it "It was the money, ma'am," she said lamely.

There seemed nothing else to say.

"If you are caught stealing here, you will be whipped and dismissed within the hour. You understand that clearly?"

"Yes, ma'am." One didn't dare mention the forty days by law. In this country, everyone knew, they had to let you work that out before you left; except that, granted, sometimes you wouldn't want to. She wouldn't in any case want to fall foul of this terrible little lady. She opened her mouth to say it would be all right, there wouldn't be any danger of her stealing here, there was no need; or some such thing. But Mrs. Retford seemed to have forgotten about it. She asked Livia to hold out her hands for inspection, to see if they were clean.

Something flared then in Livia. It had been dusty in the coach, and there'd been the mucky farm-cart afterwards and she'd walked since then, carrying her basket. She kept silence, however, and extended her broad, capable hands, soiled with the journey. Mrs. Retford's mouth tightened a little.

"That will not do for serving food, Mary; you will see that they are cleaner than that when Mrs. Betts hands you the dishes. I understand, however, that you are a capable laundress; that will clean them." She smiled at her own mild pleasantry, but Livia did not respond. Old bitch, she was thinking; one's as bad as the next. Still, it's a pretty house. I'll keep it clean as well as my hands. She wondered where one went to fetch water; perhaps there was a well.

A glint had showed already in Mrs. Retford's refractive eyes; the new maid's silence was like a wall. She must be broken, that was evident. "There will be plenty of work for you to do, Mary; I expect a high standard. You will be responsible generally for the lighter housework, dusting, sweeping the stairs daily and polishing once a week; cleaning the glass panes inside and out, and caring for the curtains and the linen, also serving at table. There are other tasks Mrs. Betts will show you. She will also show you your room."

There hadn't been mention of time off, Livia thought; but the news of a room was cheering. She had never in all her life had a private sleeping-place; as a rule, no servant expected it. She stammered a word of pleasure, anxious to please this difficult, unpredictable lady; Mrs. Retford raised her flat eyes.

"The reference from Mrs. Priddy also says that you need supervision, Mary, or else you are lazy; that will be provided here. She adds, however, that you have no flighty inclinations, which is as well; they would not be tolerated."

"No, ma'am." It was her luck, of course, that most things wrong with Mary had been right with her; she certainly wasn't lazy. As to flighty ways—well, such as they'd ever been they were done with. After a day or two this little, old county bitch would no doubt find there was less need than she'd thought to keep a strict eye. Till then, she herself would just have to put up with whatever came. And there was her room; at nights, there'd always be that. Dismissed from the presence, she followed Mrs. Betts' toiling skirts upstairs at last with thankfulness.

The room was small, hot, and directly under the roof; it contained a mattress and a row of pegs, and a ewer. But it was hers; she'd never before had anything of her own. She listened to Mrs. Betts' gabble with half an ear, longing to be alone in it.

"Don't mind being up here on your own, I hope? I live with Betts over the stable. Thirty years, we been man and wife; I come from beyond Solway. Betts is the coachman here . . . not that they run a coach now. There's the little carriage, when they use it, for her and Miss Annabel. Grows a good vegetable, Betts does. If he didn't, he'd hear from me." Mrs. Betts smiled mournfully. "Quiet, everything is here; they never see company. Sir Hubert Melrose comes sometimes, but it was sad about losing his son."

Livia listened, perforce, to the tale of Peter Melrose's death; he had been killed in a riding-accident last autumn. She was only half aware of the names conjured, the Melroses, Miss Annabel; all of her mind was attuned to the necessity of making them want her here, making it impossible to do without her even if they found out she wasn't Mary Reid. First thing, she'd scrub that passage, with its grimy stones. Where was the sand? She asked Mrs. Betts about it.

"You can call me Betty, everyone does," said that lady sadly. "And if you want a bite to eat, when you've got your gear hung up, it's in the kitchen. I'll be glad of a hand; there's Miss Annabel's things, and all the bed-linen. Come down when you're ready."

Having eaten well, on a bit of a cold meat pasty and an apple and a cup of fresh milk, reminding her of the old days at Ransome's, Livia set to on the pile of soiled linen. Who was Miss Annabel?

She first set eyes on that young lady next morning, when she carried the tray of chocolate upstairs to her room.

The room was in semi-darkness—it was still fairly early,

although Livia had already lit fires and carried up cans of hot water to Mrs. Retford and to her niece, who was not yet awake. She set down the chocolate-pot and fetched the can, which had been left outside the door, and put it over by Annabel's flower-patterned ewer; then she drew the window-curtains. The day outside filtered through the branches of a large old pear-tree, at present bare of fruit; it still left the room in a green twilight.

Livia went across then and drew the bed-curtains, which were of printed India muslin, not new. The underwater light may have accounted for the breath she drew then; she stood holding the chocolate-things and looking down on Annabel Doon, asleep like some princess of old fable. Livia thought that in all her life she had never seen anyone so beautiful.

Annabel awoke, lifting the long gold-brown lashes which had lain quietly all night on her smooth cheeks; she wore a frilled night-cap of white linen, tied with a tape beneath her chin, and the long hair cascaded under it to her shoulders. She sat up, yawning a little, and accepted the chocolate. Presently she noticed Livia, and smiled. "You must be the new maid. What is your name?"

And Livia, bemused, sunk in the contemplation of beauty and delight such as she had never known existed—this girl's eyes, her hair, her flowerlike skin, her exquisite smile, were of fairyland, and her tiny hands seemed almost too fragile to hold the cup from which she drank with, granted, a human enough appetite—answered unthinkingly, "My name is Livia, miss."

Afterwards, she remembered.

III

That something like friendship should have sprung up between the two girls after that would perhaps have been impossible in a less lonely situation. If any servant was considered as a friend, it was after service of long standing, in certain cases only; Mrs. Betts herself had never achieved it.

The young niece of Livia's employer—of any employer, implying a probable ignorance of toil, hardship, hunger and lack of privacy, for such folk lived differently—would not have been a candidate for Livia's heart, back at Emmett's or nearer town. But Annabel was lonely; hungry for Morven, missing even the sparse company of young Peter Melrose, news of whose death had come as the first personal shock of her life; she could hardly recall gentle Mama's demise, and her father had been some weeks dying, which had prepared her.

So she was shorn of young company; and the morning chocolate-visits of the new maid tended to grow longer and longer, stretching by the end from minutes to a full quarter-hour; Livia dared not stay longer away from her duties, although after the first week or two Mrs. Retford ceased to spy on her constantly. There wasn't much, in any case, for Mary Reid to pilfer; any small saleable object, a silver snuff-box of the late Retford's or a cameo brooch of his widow's, had discreetly gone long since, to be turned into money. Money was a passion with Mrs. Retford; the scrimping and saving of it on small things, tedious to relate, her heart's desire. But she never scrimped on Annabel, her chief investment: the girl's appearance was always neat and pretty, and she was given enough fresh gloves and slippers, white hose and beribboned linen, to deny any rumours there might be about the Doon lack of dowry. Once Annabel had offered a pair of white satin shoes to Livia when they were slightly rubbed; the latter shook her head.

"Why? You only have one pair; I've never seen you in any other."

"They do me. Your aunt wouldn't like it." And she folded her lips over the rest. Annabel lay back on the pillows and looked at her, a considering, bright-eyed sparrow.

"Aunt is very pleased with you, although she will never say so, Livia. You work hard, and—and you do things you needn't do; you draw such pretty chalk patterns on the flagstones after you've scrubbed them. I never saw anyone else do that." She smiled, and prepared to chatter on; it was pleasant to do so, for aunt Retford and she talked seldom, and then only regarding correct essentials. Annabel would have been, had she had the opportunity, a company-loving person; the presence of other people in a room stimulated her. This luxury had seldom been afforded; she was still to discover herself. Now, the new maid challenged her with silence, covering no doubt a great deal she herself didn't know; where had Livia come from? For aunt Retford, to whom it had not occurred that there would be any need, had not disclosed to her niece that the new maid was from a correction-house and, accordingly, cheap. Perhaps she should have done so; but the likelihood of talk, let alone some intimacy, between the two young women had not manifested itself to her: the imagination of the correct of heart is limited.

Livia, now, showed no signs of pleasure at news of Mrs. Retford's own. She hung her head and pleated her apron's stuff with her fingers. "Please, Miss Annabel, will you remember to call me Mary?" It wasn't the first time; one day, the silly little thing would let it out.

"But you told me your name was Livia," said Annabel, opening her eyes wide.

"It's my other name. They never use it, miss." Livia, who could quickly lie her way out of any unforeseen emergency, had found this recurrent one a growing embarrassment. She flushed scarlet, and lowered her grey eyes before the clear, amused hazel ones. "My name's Mary Reid," she said firmly, and turned away. "If you're done with the tray, I'll take it." She did so and went towards the door. Annabel called after, laughing.

"I shall call you Livia Mary. That'll do, won't it?" A dimple showed in her right cheek which was rarely seen, situated near the upper lip which seldom laughed. "Livia suits you better, though, I think. It is an unusual name; where did it come from?" For Annabel, educated on no account to be a blue-stocking, had never heard the wife of Augustus, barely indeed of that emperor. Livia, still standing at the door with the tray, and with her own clear memory of what old Ransome had told her in childhood, opened her lips on a breath; she had been about to say, proudly, as her mother had done, "It's a queen's name," but remembered in time who and where she was now. Miss Annabel, no doubt, thought her queer in the head already, sometimes one name, sometimes the next. Best say no more, or the old woman'd get hold of it and ask questions, perhaps even write back to Emmett's. No, that was fanciful: madam'd grudge the expense and anyway she herself so far was giving satisfaction. Mrs. Betts had told her so, at the same time clucking her English Border tongue about how that poor dear, Miss Annabel, was completely under the thumb of madam; no life of her own or friends at all. There had only been Master Morven, if one could call *him* a friend. And he'd been sent to the rightabout the moment the old master was dead.

Livia, who had heard Morven Doon mentioned once or twice by then, asked a question. "You steer clear of the likes of him, Mary, if he comes skulking round," was all she received. Her supposedly untutored ears were then regaled briefly with a list of the dangers an honest girl might be in from lingering even one unguarded moment in the company of such as Morven Doon. "Were you even seen to pass the time of day, it'd be the end of your good name in these parts; and once that's gone it don't come back, no matter what." And Mrs. Betts, whom it was difficult to picture having any cause to know, had turned back to her vegetable-chopping and to a discreet silence.

Livia herself had had more to do than trouble further about Morven Doon. Her duties, which were constant by day, took her about the place but not beyond; she hadn't seen him, or met anyone who had. Her sole company since she'd come had been the Betts couple, Mrs. Retford—if she could be called company, Livia thought wryly—and Miss Annabel. It wasn't enough servants for a house even this size. She remembered now that Miss Annabel and she had been disagreeing about something a moment ago and, recalling what it was, said firmly that it would be better, wouldn't it, if Miss just remembered to call her Mary by itself? But the pretty face frowned.

"I don't see—" Annabel was beginning, and Livia changed course abruptly. At such moments, she'd often had reason to know at Emmett's, it paid to divert the attention of whoever was being awkward. Now, she racked her brains, and hit on something. "I did hear say there were folks coming soon to look over the big house, to buy it," she said. "Where did I hear that? Can't say I remember." Betts, she supposed; there was no one else who'd have any news. She stooped to pick up the hot-water can, fetched upstairs earlier that morning. "Shall I pour out into the ewer now, Miss Annabel?"

But there was no reply. If Livia had hoped to distract the other girl's attention she had more than succeeded; the heiress to Malvie sat quite still, face white against the pillows. "Buy the house?" she said. "Buy Malvie? Oh, no, it can't be—it can't be, Livia!"

So I'm Livia again in any case, thought the other grimly. It seemed there was no help for it; best say nothing more. Miss Annabel didn't speak up often enough in presence of her aunt to be likely to mention any servant's name. Perhaps, now, she'd say more to the old woman about Malvie sale, and Mrs. Retford would ask where she'd heard it. Perhaps—

48

oh, what use in thinking up more ifs and perhapses? She had her own work to do, and provided she got on with that, and kept mum, nobody could say much. She bobbed a curtsey to Miss Annabel, still staring ahead from her bed, and herself departed with the used chocolate-tray.

The news about Malvie had indeed come from Betts, who'd got it from Abel Judd the son of old Aaron the blacksmith, at his Fleece. Betts was permitted to escape there for some hours on a Friday. Two dark-clad gentlemen, he'd heard, lawyers by the look of them, had come riding in lately from Edinburgh, and Molly the maid had taken up their gear and a posset before they slept that night, and had overheard something before she knocked on the door. Next day the two gentlemen went up to visit Sir Hubert Melrose at Maddon, and he rode back down with them at night to partake of wine, and the three talked together till all hours. Twenty years older, Sir Hubert looked, and grey of face and hair since the death of his son; it was the first time, almost, he'd ridden out since Master Peter was killed. There'd only be little Master Paul left now to inherit Maddon. Sad, that; and sad too about Malvie. The times were coming when these great houses would all be in crumbled ruin, with no money to keep them up, unless they sold in the south to some rich buyer. Time Malvie was sold, perhaps in time to get back to the grand place it had once been; not but what there was hardly ever a Doon with enough silver to put back a roof-tile if it fell off, or mend a window. They were a feckless race, the Doons.

The Doons! Miss Annabel, now, kept prisoner by that aunt of hers; and young Master Morven, knocking about the shore and Bart Judd's boat all day, and whatever they did at night . . .

But everyone at the Fleece, and in the countryside, knew very well what Bart and Morven did with their boat at night. It was politic not to mention it, any more than one had once mentioned the devil.

A restlessness had taken Livia after that conversation with Annabel Doon.

After the day's work was over—the fire-lighting, the carrying upstairs of heated water, the scrubbing and sanding and chalk-patterns, the polishing and sweeping and dusting and cleaning of small many-paned windows up and down the house; the brushing of curtains and rubbing up of handles and latches, as well as the great tirling-pin so seldom used on the Mains front door—the washing and ironing and pleating of caps and cuffs and under-petticoats, the starching and rinsing, the threading in again of ribbons and darning of the ladies' hose—after all this, and more, it would be near evening, when Livia's work, with the speed she made at it, was done. Sometimes, lately, she'd walk out for a breath of air, beyond the house, beyond the hedge. Once or twice she'd cover the half-mile down the lane, and stand for a while looking out over the sea. There was Man always on the horizon, a dark blotch out of the almost constant mist about its base. Once there'd been a long ship in the channel with furled sails, still in the evening. She'd asked Betts and he said it was a revenue-cutter; they sent them to cruise up and down on occasion, and keep watch. Watch on what, Livia didn't ask; she was sharp, and she knew. Once, again, in the near distance, across the curve of the small bay, she'd seen the dark hump of the smithy-buildings, and an open door and an old thin man bending over his forge. She'd known he was old by the slowness of his movements; he was tall and thin as gibbet-meat, a mere hanging together of old bones. But he could work; she watched him for a while, leaning in darkness and silence by herself against a wall. Often after that she'd come out and watch the slow, dedicated, busy old man; he'd forge and hammer objects nearby the fire, which he kept bright orange against the night. Anyone who worked as hard as that deserved to get rich, she decided.

Then, one night, Aaron Judd had stopped working at his forge. It was a night when there was no moon; a wind had risen. Dark as the devil, the old thin figure had straightened up from the forge, with the fire bright in it; and had come to the door and looked out over the bay. Livia had wondered if he sensed her watching presence, and resented it; she almost moved away, but something warned her to keep silent, keep still. Presently Aaron went back again to the forge; and slowly, deliberately had passed and repassed his hand and arm in front of the glow, so that flickered light and shade alternated with one another on the rock-surfaces and out to sea. The sea was quite dark, and one could see no ships.

She hadn't asked Betts, next day, what Aaron had been doing. Any fool would have known; and it was in any case none of her affair, so she kept silent.

Annabel's uncle, Sir Hubert Melrose himself, rode to Mains a few weeks later. The girl was brought to him where he sat with her aunt in the small withdrawing-room. She knew what he would say, and how he would say it. Uncle Hubert was entirely predictable; he had never in his life said anything to surprise Annabel, and Livia Mary had told her, in any case, what was going on, concerning Malvie. For it was about Malvie, her own inheritance, that he'd come today; the house which had been her home and Morven's, and which, she knew, neither her uncle nor her aunt regarded as anything but a tiresome necessity, to be sold if possible. Everything had, for some reason, to be turned into money.

"It is fortunate," Sir Hubert was saying, "that a suitable offer has been received. With the place in such bad repair—" he helped himself to aunt Retford's wine absently, as though he were still at Maddon—"and in so remote a part of the country, with the roads scarcely passable in winter, we have been indeed fortunate in receiving an offer with the quoted price."

"It was not niggardly," put in aunt Retford eagerly. She had watched the absent-minded hand of Sir Hubert, half in resentment, half in hope; if he felt so much at home here, being a widower, then perhaps she—

Annabel did not ask about the price. She sat with her feet together, upright in her chair as she had been taught, not touching the back. She listened to Sir Hubert's calm tones and her aunt's matter-of-fact ones, settling all their fates as though it mattered what size of offer had been received. For anyone, anyone at all, to buy Malvie, Malvie which had been Papa's house and which should have been hers and Morven's! She dared not ask if anyone had informed Morven yet. Perhaps no one would trouble to. Could she herself find a way? It was difficult these days to be free of supervision for long enough to get word to him, though perhaps if she told Livia Mary—yet she'd rather do it herself, it was her matter . . .

Planning for herself made Annabel bold and, presently conquering her awe of the small proud-capped figure of Mrs. Retford, seated there in her best blacks, and the portentous presence of Uncle Hubert in his, she made herself speak. "Must—must the house indeed be sold?" she stammered, and then felt foolish. Uncle Hubert was smiling indulgently; aunt Retford flushed a little beneath her unaccustomed paint. She'd daubed herself, Annabel knew, today, because she still hoped to marry Uncle Hubert; long ago, in all their youth together, she'd once loved him when he kept company with her brothers. A queer thing, the changing of such love till it had, by now, almost a comic quality. Sir Hubert, though always courteous to the household at Mains and prepared to

51

act fully in his capacity as Annabel's trustee, had given Agnes Retford no opening for dalliance since his own wife's death. If he married again, it would be for heirs. He did not return Mrs. Retford's eyebrow-raising over Annabel's speech, but replied to his niece with grave punctiliousness. "It must indeed, my dear Annabel," he replied, looking down his nose as he did when on the magistrates' bench; the gesture concealed his feelings usefully. "As you know, all the outlying land, the farms also, have gone their way. It was at first hoped to maintain Malvie until you yourself might make a suitable marriage—"

The tester, Annabel thought; the embroidered firestools. It had all been a waste of time, as Malvie was to go. The knowledge of how she had been deceived and used, her childhood spent, came to her as she sat there, eyelids demurely lowered, listening to Uncle Hubert prosing on. Aunt Retford got up presently, without calling for the servant, and herself closed the shutters and lit up the sconces on the walls; it was by now evening. Sir Hubert spread out his hands so that his gold ring, given him by his late wife, flashed in the new-lit candle-flames. "How are we to take you to town, my dear, and give you a season, eh, and introductions to eligible young men? Nothing of the kind can be done unless there's some money, and a dowry. Your father's debts . . ."

"And Richard," added Mrs. Retford, who as a good Whig had not approved of her eldest brother's Stuart affinities. "The allowance to Richard Doon, and for his son, drained away much of what was left; it is right that Annabel should be informed of these things."

"Morven hasn't got any money now," said Annabel.

Mrs. Retford frowned a little; the talk was getting out of hand. She cast a glance for help to Sir Hubert—how handsome, with the powder on his grey hair, he still looked by candlelight! He had had the looks of the family, she'd always said, though poor Grace was spoken of as being pretty. But Grace had had no spirit, nothing to redeem her loss of youth when it went, suddenly as everyone said, after Richard Doon rode away.

She returned to her notion of duty towards Grace's young daughter; Sir Hubert hadn't come to her aid about Morven Doon. "A man has other prospects if he is penniless," she said coldly. "In this country, he can article himself without loss of face; many noblemen's sons are indentured to some attorney, or have joined a regiment. Your good uncle here offered to do both, or either, for your cousin Morven at the time your poor father died; he rejected all offers of help, and not courteously. We need spend no more time in considering him, I think." And, this time, she personally leaned over and, smiling, replenished Sir Hubert's glass. She herself drank little.

"Well, well," said the magistrate peaceably, "there's the matter of this Englishman, whose name is Devenham. I know nothing of him except that he's rich; the lawyers are seeing to it. They want to settle in by the spring; it's fortunate, very, as it avoids delay and uncertainty. There are young sisters, I believe; some company for Annabel." He already spoke of Annabel as if she were no longer there.

Mrs. Retford did not fail to aid him in her turn. "You may leave us, my dear, I think; there is another matter to discuss," she murmured, and the young girl rose and curtsied, and went out. Nothing had been achieved except to tell Annabel, formally, of the coming sale of Malvie; they could have done no less. After she had gone the widow turned to her visitor.

"She looks well, you think? I've carried out my task?" She smiled with closed lips. "It wasn't initially easy; she was as wild, when she came, as—as a young filly." Mrs. Retford conjured up a vision of horses, which she had always disliked, and gave a little well-bred *moue*. Sir Hubert was murmuring obediently that Annabel seemed increasingly beautiful, and a credit to her upbringing. He would permit himself few stronger feelings on the matter; talk of Annabel's growing beauty reminded him, unbearably, of Peter's brief infatuation, and Peter was dead.

He dropped his eyelids; and presently, in the waiting silence, raised the ringed hand to sketch a little toast with his filled glass. It was uncertain for whom the wine glowed red in the light of the candles; for themselves, Peter, Annabel, Malvie, or Morven waiting outside in the dark about the other matter.

It was, as it happened, a customary thing with almost anyone to have such matters, little or great, somewhere in their lives' hidden places. That night, in addition to bringing the certain news about Malvie, Sir Hubert had had a reason for riding over. He himself was an abstemious man; and as a Justice of the Peace and magistrate, had to preserve his countenance on public occasions, somewhat better than many of his neighbours did; but he, the local doctor, the town-lawyer, and the minister in his manse, with others, all liked their brandy. Nor did they see any reason, any more than other folk did, to pay the excessive tax demanded by London. Mains of Malvie, hard by the sea, was a better place for Sir Hubert to receive his consignment tonight than Maddon would have been, for the latter involved a long ride inland for those who had already brought the stuff across from Man, where a Frenchman had delivered it. A short two nights back, Aaron the blacksmith's hand had again passed and repassed before his fire, his tall thin figure visible well out to sea. And so Sir Hubert would be satisfied.

The polite talk went on between the man and woman, neither of whom had any real contact with one another. The little matter could not openly be mentioned. The talk, instead, centered round young Mr. Devenham, concerning whom Mrs. Retford was naturally very curious. Despite the magistrate's having denied any knowledge of the new English purchaser, she was able, by discreet probing to find out much that she wanted to know; Mr. Devenham, besides being rich—his father had been, one understood, in the East India Company —was something of an invalid, and single. His widowed mother and two sisters would reside with him.

"A long way north from London," Mrs. Retford murmured; why were these people coming so far? The metropolis, where even as Agnes Doon she had never been taken, represented to her untold, unsavoured joys; the sight of a world where the beauteous Miss Gunnings, without either fame or fortune, had won the respective hands of a duke and an earl, and immense sums of money changed hands each night as cards. Mrs. Retford sighed briefly. While her brother Philip, ten years her junior, still lived, there had been occasional diversion in this way; they played for low stakes. But of late years, alone here with Annabel . . . If even an invalid Englishman came, it would bring other company, provided he were rich. And, provided he were rich, there was Annabel also. The pattern of things worked itself out with surprising speed inside Mrs. Retford's head, while she listened and conversed with Sir Hubert, and the night outside grew dark. Annabel, marriageable with the portion culled from the sale of Malvie . . . a neat trick to sell the man Malvie, then wed it to its erstwhile owner dowered with his price! Agnes Retford almost laughed; then thought better of it, in front of poor Hubert. One could never tell how a man would view such matters; and with his own elder son so recently dead, who might have been permitted to wed Annabel after all if

54

the price came in time for Malvie . . . but now it was too late. Poor Peter, the coffin-dust on his bright hair already in the vault at Maddon! It was a bay horse, which they said young Morven had ridden over to him from the smith's. Ill luck accompanied Morven. It wasn't that there was anything amiss with Aaron's shoeing, but the fact that Morven came with it had brought a curse. Agnes Retford's face darkened. She'd been right, more than right, to cast that damned boy from her door, not permit him to enter here. It would have been like housing the devil, and she'd had enough trouble in her life.

"The sconces," murmured Sir Hubert. A knock had come beyond the shutter.

Mrs. Retford moved quickly, going to where the hat-shaped douser leaned against the wall on its long stem. One after another she extinguished the candles in the room. With the ensuing darkness and silence a flicker showed itself beyond the opened shutter, no more; starlight, perhaps; no moon had yet risen. The shutter closed again, and instantly, without a word spoken, Sir Hubert found his tinder and relit the sconces for his hostess, the revived flames briefly etching peaked shadows on his well-fed face, making it a wizard's. A bundle lay now on the sill. Sir Hubert went and lifted it carefully, passing it to the lady; opened, it revealed a number of bottles, some of which he pocketed and the rest, speedily, were caused to vanish into a corner-cupboard. Hostess and guest then sat down and finished their wine, as though nothing had happened, and discussed the news of the day from Maddon and France, rather than London; that remained a foreign city. The matter of the doused candles, the brief interruption at the window, might never have occurred. It was late when Sir Hubert left, and the stars lit his journey past the dark, untenanted water below the road. On the opposite rock, Aaron's forge had gone out.

Long before then, something else had happened; a small figure in a hooded cloak had accosted the departing smuggler, earning a curse from him. He pulled the figure into the nearby shadows and jerked back its hood. It was Annabel. Morven swore again, looked quickly round at the silent dark; little fool that she was, he'd thought it was the gauger! "There's danger, d'you hear?" he hissed. "There'd be trouble even for those two if it was known," and he nodded to the window. "You must know nothing, nothing, d'you hear? Say to no one you've seen me tonight. How did you know?"

"Livia Mary the maid told me there was something afoot. Anyway I guessed. Uncle Hubert doesn't often stay as late. Morven, I had to see you."

He was still angry, disengaging her hands which clutched at his seaman's coat. "Don't speak my name, you fool! Not here—"

"Morven, they've sold Malvie."

"What?" He stood quite still; the starlight, vaguely outlining his face, showed it thin as a boy's. She began to cry, helpless against what she knew troubled him.

"Do you suppose I'd have stopped you for less, knowing what it'd mean if—if they caught you? Morven—" she could not seem to stop, despite his prohibition, saying over his name, it was too dear to her—"Morven, they've sold the house to an Englishman." She told him the man's name. "I don't know any more, except that they sent for me tonight, to tell me. That means the thing's done; they never tell me anything as a—"

"Quickly; someone may come any minute. Did you sign anything? When does this man come?"

"No. Uncle Hubert signed, I think. The lawyers have been. I—I couldn't stop it, Morven. Say you're not angry." She pleaded with him, a drifted rose-petal in the dark; he shook her off.

"Angry! Malvie sold, and I not angry? What can be done, what can be done?"

"Can we do anything, together?"

"We? We're minors." He came back to a realisation of their danger here, and of the risk she'd run to come and tell him. He patted her, absently as though she had been an obedient puppy. "I'll do what can be done," he boasted, "never fear. If anything can be altered, it's I who must alter it. Go you back inside." He seized her shoulders and gave them a quick, absent squeeze; he was no longer thinking of her, as she knew. He watched her slip away presently in the darkness and re-enter the house; then recalled a thing she had said to him, and which in his anger he hadn't fully taken in.

Livia Mary, the maid. Where had he heard the name Livia before? He remembered now . . . Anyway, damn that; it was Malvie that mattered; only Malvie. He must make plans, if not to prevent the sale—too late for that—then to make it impossible for the Englishman to inherit; Doons had always owned Malvie, and always should.

He stayed there brooding for moments in the dark, oblivious now of the danger. Then he went, and within minutes the place where they had both stood was empty, as though not a soul had been there tonight, or any other.

Afterwards, Agnes Retford took some time to mount to her bed. She walked, bearing a guttered candle in its oak holder, through the silent house, telling herself it was prudent to inspect this after the nearness of smugglers, the identity of one of whom she would not, even to herself, admit. She had shut her brother Richard's son out of her heart from his birth, and out of her scheme of things from the moment poor Philip, his protector, was removed. Morven Doon no longer existed as a fact in her reckoning.

This house, Mains of Malvie, which had been allotted to Agnes for her life, on marriage, was her constant pride; it made up, perhaps, for a union so loveless that nowhere in the whole house, least of all in her curtained bedchamber, did any trace or remembrance of her short-lived husband, Neil Retford, remain. She wouldn't have married Neil, everyone knew, had there been the least chance of Hubert Melrose in old days. But she'd been more than twenty and one didn't want to die an old maid.

Bolts and bars being satisfactory, she went back to the corner-cupboard where the newly acquired brandy lay, and took a bottle upstairs with her. On the way, she continued to cast a sharp eye for dust, neglect, or careless polishing, visible in the raised candle's light. But every surface shone, and Agnes went up to bed pleased enough with the new maid, Mary Reid, who worked and seemed, despite her history, trustworthy. It might be a case, still, of a new broom; Mary hadn't been here four months yet. Mrs. Retford's mouth tightened, in time to reveal an unbecoming, raddled likeness of herself in a passing mirror. No matter; youth passed, also, and pretty Nancy Doon, that she'd once been, was no more; but there were other satisfactions. Work was one; she herself had never permitted the Doon idleness in her blood to prevail. Tomorrow, she had already decided, she must send the girl Mary Reid to open up Malvie, and at least remove the upper film of dust from such articles of furniture as were left there. At Philip's death they had, of course, sold what would sell, but the purchaser had agreed to take what remained and it would be politic, Mrs. Retford now decided, to look as though someone had cared for them a little these past years. She'd inform Mary Reid of that tomorrow. She got into bed presently and, before extinguishing her candle, poured herself a tot of the contraband brandy in a small glass. As she sipped the burning, satisfactory stuff she smiled, and still smiled afterwards in sleep. For a plan to come to fruition which had seemed, for many a year, as if it might end in dust was pleasant . . . it hung still, of course, on many factors, but she could vouch for Annabel's obedience, in the event. It depended of course on the young Englishman and whether or not he was susceptible to the girl's undoubted beauty. Yes! She'd been fully justified, to herself and her conscience, in getting rid of Morven Doon and the absurd pretensions nourished in him by her brother Philip, poor Philip who had no idea of money . . .

Morven Doon had edged his way into Malvie by a postern door whose boards were shrunk loose, so that his slim fingers could slip the bolt by squeezing between the ill-fitting splats of wood. Once inside, he mounted the back stairs and found himself in the attics which ran the full length of the house. They were filled with débris many generations old, most of it not worth having been brought down to the clearance-sale at Philip's death. Filtered sunlight picked out one object after another as Morven passed by, emphasising in melancholy fashion their age, neglect, and dust. Nobody but himself had troubled about this part of Malvie for years; since he was a boy old enough to climb, he had known every inch of the attics and all they contained. Annabel, he recalled, had been too timid to come up here; deliberately, he'd frightened her with tales of ghosts.

He went now to the place where his father's violoncello lay swathed in a cloth. Richard Doon as a child had been taught well and, with his brother and sister, had entertained the country to performances at Malvie, anticipating the famous Mozart children who would later visit London. They hadn't —Morven smiled—reached the heights of the young Mozarts; Uncle Philip had told him the agony it'd been when he stuck, accompanying Richard on the harpsichord, because their elder sister Nancy had muffed the pages and couldn't get back to the place. Aunt Retford then had been a dainty young creature in powder and lace, the little boys in powder also and blue satin coats. Uncle Philip had told him of it all.

Nobody had instructed Morven in music; he knew he had a natural ear. He drew away the cloth from his father's great, neglected instrument and found its strings gnawed lately by rats, since last time he'd come; they hung loose. The sight angered Morven and he plucked vainly at the sole remaining string, making a booming, eerie sound in the long garret.

He flung the cloth over the 'cello again and turned away, a sense of failure and of death and dust, the end of all possessions and all hope, overcoming him. Yet how old was he? Twenty. When his father was his age he'd been full of the joy of living, making ready to toss a coin with his twin for the honour of going out for the Prince. And little more than a year later, it was all over and Richard Doon a fugitive, Morven himself about to be born at Malvie of a stranger from the north, and the girl who would have been his own mother, and Richard's wife, left broken-hearted at Maddon. But hearts could mend.

He went to the place where, leaning against a gable-wall, was the unfinished portrait of uncle Philip and his new bride, who had been that same Grace Melrose. Grace by then had mended her heart, at least to outward view; the gentle, high-bred face looking out from the canvas roused no emotion in Morven any more than, he could guess, it had ever done in his own father during their betrothal. Uncle Philip no doubt had loved Grace better. He bent over her assiduously on the portrait now, attired in riding-gear which he in fact seldom wore, and a tie-wig; a small lap-dog nestled on Grace's yellow satin lap beneath the oak tree which still grew on the main front before Malvie. Of all of them, the man, the woman and the dog were gone, only the tree remained now, almost unchanged above its carpet of grass. Morven turned away from the canvas, unconsoled, and wandered aimlessly about the attics for some time. He was uncertain why he had come.

The rising tide of bitterness in his blood would not be stilled as he went: almost, it clamoured like a voice. Why was there no single portrait of his own father here, either as boy or man? He had no idea what Richard Doon had looked like, except from Philip's descriptions. His father had been tall, his uncle had told him, and had had brown hair. As for his mother, the Highland girl in the green ball-dress, there was nothing of her here, neither portrait nor card-case, fan or embroidery-box. What did he know of his mother except that she had been wild and sad, and had regretted coming to Malvie? But he'd been born of love. He had that to console him, he, the outcast who lived now from choice with Judd the blacksmith and his son, and kept rough company. No Doon but had once worn silk . . .

A woman's shoe, the broken heel showing traces of the red paint with which they aped France, at one time, lay about as he passed; Morven kicked it viciously aside, watching the cloud of dust it raised settle. Some woman's long dead, Susannah Doon's perhaps with whose ghost he'd frightened Annabel. He himself was no ghost; he was alive, the power of life pulsing in him, stronger now for coming here; given time, he could have saved Malvie. Time! There was not enough of that to do anything but watch, resent, and plan. In a day or two, a week or two, depending on the slowness of the lawyers, or the roads, the English purchaser would be here, and in residence.

The plans raised themselves again in his mind, vague and malevolent. They had already begun to take shape like these seemingly unsubstantial drifts of dust that raised themselves in wreaths as Morven went by, and settled again on cloth and wood and canvas. Dust. The stuff of the dead, but damnably difficult to get rid of . . .

Dust he'd be if necessary; a ghost, unsubstantial though always present. If a man was invisible he could accomplish a marvellous deal. He'd use the night as day, and by day hide himself. Somehow, in the end, he'd win.

He turned presently and went downstairs by the main staircase. It swept from the third floor to the hall, in a wide curve copied from a French château of the Renaissance; but it had been carved in England, and brought home to Malvie in sections by Morven's great-grandfather, who had diced with King Charles. Its balusters were thick with dust at the top but by the lower floor, he noted, someone had lately polished them. He saw the figure of the housemaid presently, dusting with a cloth tied round her head. She'd have been sent over by aunt Retford, he knew, to make all ready for the arrival of the purchaser. The fact of her presence, and that she had been enabled to enter by the main door when he had not, angered Morven further.

"Who sent you here?"

As he called down to her, hearing the multiple echoes of his voice through rafters and passages, the instant's thought came: if I were Doon of Malvie, this is the way I would stand here, calling to my servants.

The girl gasped, and looked up. He had already noted, with that part of his mind which was not constantly engaged with himself, that she had a graceful, generous figure; the long limbs moved easily in the process of wielding duster and broom, making it pleasing to watch her. He had seen the deep breasts moving gently under her bodice; now he saw her face. He knew her at once. She was the young girl he had

60

noted in advanced pregnancy last year, walking to church in the correction-house column at Grattan.

Her eyes flashed in instant recognition and panic; no, she hadn't forgotten him either! Morven descended the stairs slowly, looking her over. She would do, he was thinking; she would do very well. The hair, black as a raven, he remembered, was concealed today by the housemaid's cloth. Before he'd done he would make her take it down, let him play with its thick tresses, bury his face in their length. He'd never yet touched a woman's hair.

But not here.

Now, standing as he was still a step or two above her, he watched her regain quick possession of herself; she bobbed a curtsy. Morven recalled that she could not know for certain who he was, though she might have guessed. He heard her answer his question.

"Mrs. Retford sent me—sir." The title came unwillingly; he was, after all, in his oldest clothes, dusty from the attic, but last time they'd met—did she remember?—he'd been riding Peter Melrose's bay horse, and had his hat and cloak on. She must know him, at any rate, for a gentleman. Morven looked at the stair-curve at his feet, dismissing the memory of the next time Peter had ridden that horse, and it had thrown him at a fence and killed him instantly. The luck of the Doons . . . But they couldn't blame *him*. "What is your name?" he asked the maidservant. It had, he remembered, very well, been Livia.

But she herself recalled nothing but the remembrance of this man's light, shining eyes seated there last year on the bay. He had, she was sure, noticed her state at that time; those eyes would miss nothing. The colour rushed like fire into her face.

"Mary Reid—sir." He must, she was certain now, be young Master Doon. Nobody else could maintain such assurance, standing there as if he owned the house, the great shadowy house. Herself, she didn't like it. She'd been hurrying through the work to get down, as soon as might be, to the sanity, the known warmth and cheerful welcome, of the Mains. This great house was full of ghosts. And he, standing up there like one of them—

That he had discovered her, and knew at least some of her secret, was too terrible a thing to think of all at once. Mrs. Retford would send her packing, back to Emmett's, and then—

Morven Doon was smiling now, with closed lips. He looked

like a tall young devil. Suddenly Livia knew she was in his power, to do with as he would. The light eyes shone.

"You're lying, Livia."

"Oh, sir—" Suddenly she began to scrabble with her hands, red with constant scrubbing, against her apron. It was no use denying anything. "I'm not doing any harm, sir," she pled. "Please—"

"If my aunt has a maid named Mary, whose name is really Livia; and who, last year or so—What became of the child you carried, my wench?"

"It died." She was sullen now; it was only a matter of hours, and it'd all end. She should have known it couldn't last; nothing did. Why couldn't she hate him more? She wasn't perhaps, a good hater; she hadn't hated even Priddy, who'd undone her; or Gammer, who'd killed off her baby. He was still talking, that terrible young god on the stairs. What did he want of her now? It didn't matter, it didn't matter.

"What is your other name, Livia?"

"Millarch," she said dully. Morven rocked on his heels a little, savouring the firm wood of the staircase. He was enjoying his power over Livia. He would, he had decided from the beginning make her do whatever he wished; it was all part of the plan. To know a woman . . . and those breasts, when he could handle them, would ease his dissatisfaction with himself, with life. Already he felt less dissatisfied.

He took a step nearer. "When did my aunt say you were to return today, Livia?" he asked her. Her new colour fled. "Please, call me Mary, sir. The reference says Mary Reid. I—I swear I'm not doing anyone harm, sir. If you'd keep silence, I—I work hard here, sir. It's a good place; I—ha'nt had a place before. If you send me back—oh, sir, you don't know what it can be like, back there; you couldn't know."

Her voice had dropped, not raised itself like most women's into a wail. He had begun to admire her; he found her, already, a challenge; most servant-girls would have become a weeping mass of jelly by now, but she—Morven came down the two remaining steps and took her chin firmly between his fingers, lifting her face.

"You have a pointed chin," he said, "and the eyes of a witch. You are a bad wench, Livia, I think. When did you say my aunt told you to return? I asked you, and you should have answered me. Answer your master."

She had closed her eyes. "Sir, four o'clock, but—"

He kissed her briefly, handling her in a way that left no misunderstanding. Afterwards, he was pleased with himself;

she couldn't know, from that, he thought, that it was the first time he'd even kissed a woman. He kept up the swaggering pose he had allotted himself. "Four o'clock leaves little enough time to lay you down on a bed," he said. "I shall be in the north spinney this evening at half-past seven. You will come to me there."

"Sir—oh, no, sir! Please, sir, no!"

"If you do not come—" he varied the words with kisses, nips, more fondling—"if you do not, I shall tell my aunt you are not Mary Reid, but Livia Millarch; that you have had a child by someone; that you are not the good, reliable young woman the reference says; that you have wanton ways. Have you not, Livia?"

"No, sir, please, you see—"

"Then she will whip you, and send you back whence you came. And without a reference you will never find another situation. Is that not so?"

"Maybe." Livia was defiant; the pryings of his mouth and hands had aroused unwilling fires in her. Her red mouth set obstinately, tingling already where he had kissed it. She heard him laugh.

"Are we not sun and fire, wind and water?" he asked her. "You will see."

He watched her whisk away then with her broom and duster, saying she'd work to do; he was not deceived, she would come to him. He let himself out at the front door shortly and walked down the moss-grown steps, Doon of Malvie in his own mind, more so than an hour since. It wouldn't be the last time he crossed the threshold, or his sons. Livia should help him at the commencement of the plan. Afterwards, it would all become clearer.

She did come that evening, but not till he had almost ceased to expect her and was taut with anger. The sun had gone down and she wore her grey cloak and hood. Her face was still sullen and he could see, in the half-dark, that she'd been crying; when he drew her to him her cheek was still warm with late tears. "Why?" he asked her, mocking. "You're used to it, are you not?"

She did not reply. She let him handle and unlace her passively, as though she had been a doll. He was aware of a mounting excitement in himself; this was his first woman . . .

Morven was not clumsy. Afterwards he remembered that he had at some time shaken her hair free of its riband, let it tumble down and run his fingers among it, just as he had promised himself a year ago he'd do. By then, there could have been no need for his hands elsewhere; they were lying together on the grass.

"There was this man before," he kept saying, bewildered, still half angry, at her passivity. "Was there only one, Livia? Was there?"

That it should matter was, he should have known already, strange. She herself knew. "I came, didn't I?" she said. "What more d'you want?"

"Don't you like me—Livia?" He had taken her swiftly by then; was it the first, the second time? He remembered asking, afterwards, again, if she liked him. Why should it matter? She'd do as he said. He was more than himself, now, more than any man had ever been; emperor, conqueror.

"Livia . . ."

She was lying quite still, the darkened grass beneath her averted cheek. He could see the black crescents of her lashes, as though she slept. She wasn't really asleep, she couldn't be; he shook her. "Livia, Livia!"

Suddenly she turned to him and he could see the slate-dark pools of her newly-opened eyes. Slowly, she slid up her arms and drew his head down, and kissed him on the mouth.

"It's different when you do it," she told him. He wanted to shout with laughter, exultation. She went on talking. "I'd meant it should never happen again," he heard her say. "I'd meant to turn into a good hard worker for her, and the rest. But now . . . well, it's different." She could explain nothing further to herself or him. He was her man, she knew. She would obey him.

He kissed her again, and laughed. The moon rose for them presently above the trees. They hadn't felt the creeping cold of night, either of them, where they were lying together; now he felt her begin to shiver. "I'll have to go," she told him, "before they lock up." He watched, presently, while she entered by the garden-gate and into the house by the door which led through the kitchen. Morven waited for a while to make certain no untoward light shone out, meaning Livia was discovered; then he made his own way slowly back to Aaron's. They couldn't taunt him any longer, after tonight, with not having had a woman; no, by God; He felt himself, striding at last through the moonlight, different also, more massive in some way. He was a man; Doon of Malvie. The plan wouldn't fail.

IV

Events tended to make Livia clumsy, and within the next few days, tired as she was with the assignations with Morven in the spinney each night, she dropped and broke a large salt-glaze butter crock. She stared incredulously at the fragments, lying irrevocably on the stone floor with their white lining revealed; she'd been washing the great crock while it was empty. There was no help for it with a loss that size; she'd have to tell Mrs. Retford. It was the first thing she'd ever broken, but that wouldn't make for any less fuss. She went, grimly, to her employer's room at twelve.

Miss Annabel was present, seated with her stitchery in the window-seat. A horrifying sight had met her eyes, much, much worse than the butter crock. In fact, the latter probably wouldn't even matter now, she thought. On Mrs. Retford's table, lying nearby her hand, was a letter in Matron Priddy's handwriting. Livia knew it well; it was unmistakable, with florid curls and twists, like an old whore's wig. It was as though matron put the omission and dullness of her life into her handwriting, to compensate. Anyway there it was; she'd written for some reason, perhaps to say they'd found the real Mary living with Tam under some rural thatch, and taken her. Into the silence, with her innards still turning over, Livia heard herself blurt out the story about the crock. Mrs. Retford's pale eyes raised themselves, expressionless.

"It is completely broken, you say? That was extremely careless, Mary. How did this occur?"

"I dropped it, ma'am." The answer was obvious, if one thought of it; what she herself was thinking was that, some-how, even though the letter had been read the worst hadn't happened yet; Mrs. Retford still called her Mary, not Livia. A mercy Miss Annabel never spoke up in her aunt's presence. Livia prayed, in as far as she ever indulged in that over-stressed exercise for Emmett's. If God listened to this one, she might forgive Him a good deal.

65

The cold, flat eyes assessed her. "Indeed? No doubt you would have been more careful of your own property. You will of course pay for the crock; it will be necessary to purchase another." Livia said nothing. "Your wages are paid at the quarter, and it is not that yet," said Mrs. Retford. "What are we to do for a new crock meantime, Mary?"

Livia shook her head. "I don't know, ma'am." It seemed the only way. Miss Annabel went on stitching, not raising her smooth head. They'd laugh together, perhaps, about this over tomorrow's chocolate; or perhaps not, Mrs. Retford was looking ugly now, in the way matron used to do.

She smiled. "You have twelve pence given you by Emmett's, I believe, on leaving. That will do very well; we will say nothing of the remainder of the price."

Livia flushed. She'd kept the four of the pence Mary gave her, carefully hidden away in her mattress. Lately she'd thought, if a pedlar came round, that perhaps she'd buy a new ribbon for Morven to unlace. What if she said so? The sense she already had, of hidden power, of the ability to bring about chaos in this neat, orderly, lifeless room, grew in her like a great spreading of glorious dark wings. She'd only to say one-quarter of what was in her head for it to happen. Instead she answered meekly, "I only have four of them left, ma'am."

"Then you are extravagant as well as careless, if you have spent all of eight pence since coming here. What can you have found to spend them on? No matter. While I have it in mind, Mary, there is a letter here from Mrs. Priddy at Emmett's. I had written—mistakenly, as it seems—a report to say that I was pleased with you, that you appeared to be settling down here and working hard. She has replied—"

"Thank you, ma'am." One had to get it in. Mrs. Retford gave her one glance, and continued reading coldly. "She has replied to the effect that she is glad of it, and to ask if you have any information about a missing young woman, Liza Millarch."

The silence pounded. Livia dared not raise her eyes or even slide them towards Miss Annabel, stitching away there on her window-seat. Any girl, any ordinary foolish little thoughtless creature, would look up and say "But surely the name's Livia, aunt? This is the Livia here." Then the end would come. But she didn't. Nothing happened, and Miss Annabel stitched on and on, the brown-gold lashes scarcely stirring on her roseleaf cheeks. Darling Miss Annabel. Darling matron—even that—with her curlicues that had led to the unforseen deception. It was possible, Livia's limited knowledge told her, for Livia to look like Liza in a slanted hand. Anything was possible. She drew a breath and said that no, she hadn't heard anything about anyone missing.

"You knew this Liza well?"

Now it had come; one either had to lie like a trooper, or else give the whole thing away; and she wouldn't do that, not now. "I didn't know her well, ma'am," she said carefully. "None of us liked Liza much. She was wanton, you see, and if she'd have taken to better ways—"

Mrs. Retford raised a finger. "That will do, Mary." Her frown was stern and Livia realized, too late, that with Miss Annabel present certain things shouldn't have been mentioned. Mrs. Retford half turned now to her niece and, over her shoulder, as if she'd been another servant, ordered her from the room. The girl picked up her sewing and went. Livia was left confronting her employer. Two red spots, which this time were not paint, showed on Mrs. Retford's cheekbones.

"I had intended offering you a choice between the price of the crock, and a sound whipping, Mary," she said. "Now you will be whipped in any case."

"Yes, ma'am." There was no need to say any more. All mistresses beat their maids sooner or later; she was lucky it hadn't happened sooner, and that this old girl wouldn't surely have as much strength in her arms as matron, or Gammer or the rest. She thought of Morven, her lover; and made a bargain with her own soul. If it was a choice between not having to be whipped, and never having set eyes on Mr. Morven Doon, she'd choose, any time, to be chastised with scorpions. Odd how Holy Writ kept recurring. Mrs. Retford meantime had risen, and had gone to her rod-cupboard.

"Prepare yourself," she said coldly.

Afterwards, she remembered to ask for the fourpence. Livia fled, scarlet-faced, upstairs to get it; Lord, the old woman had more strength in her than you'd think! But the singing dark bird wasn't killed; she could feel it soaring, still, in her own breast, and afterwards, when she'd handed over the money and gone down, with a burning backside, to get on with her work, she felt a pair of arms sliding about her suddenly and hot tears against her cheek; Miss Annabel. She shouldn't be here; her aunt might come and find her.

"I had to come," Annabel whispered. "Oh, Mary—" she'd discarded Livia, the other noticed, and would no doubt take care not to use it again—"did it hurt? She hurts me sometimes. I couldn't say one word; and I haven't any money, so there was nothing I could do, except—except the letter." The dimple showed briefly. "She asked me what that word was and I—I knew all of a sudden, and what must have happened, and I told her Liza, because the handwriting was bad and her sight's short—Mary, what's a wanton?"

The child she was, Livia thought. She put the clinging arms gently aside and said, stoically, "It wasn't bad; I've known worse. Don't get yourself in trouble, miss, for me. And as for wantons, the less you know of them the better; I wasn't one, in any case. Some day I'll tell you what happened." But Miss Annabel, she saw, was looking thoughtful; her butterfly-mind had sped on.

"I've been sad for a day or two; the strange people are coming this week into Malvie. Malvie was my home, you know—Mary." She smiled, as if learning an unfamiliar language. "It's worse for my cousin Morven than it is for me. You haven't ever seen Morven. I love him very much. He loves Malvie better than anything, I think." Her voice trailed into a sad little echo as she moved away. "So forgive me if I wasn't very attentive, at first, about the name. When one is worried over something, everything else seems unimportant; but it isn't, of course, I suppose, to other people."

Livia was staring down at the waiting wash. So that child loved Morven Doon, did she, a child who didn't know what a woman was? Poor child.

The party from England had at last left their travelling-coach to enter the Fleece, where they would stay while their gear was put in place at Malvie. Abel Judd, well aware that money came with the equipage, sent out his ostlers in haste to the horses' heads, and himself came out to light the travellers into the taproom, where a good fire blazed against the night's cold.

He held up a lantern. It showed first his own expression-less, rather heavy face behind the panes, contrasting yellow light with sharply flung shadows. The everyday, stocky figure of Abel Judd had never been notable, with its dark eyes un-readable beneath a fringe of balding hair. The latter affliction had long ceased to trouble Abel, though he had been sensi-tive about it as a young man. Cerrtain things about Abel were also different from other young men; as he himself was aware by now, a mishap in his boyhood had left him incapable of siring children, though not of enjoying a woman, if he would. His father and younger brother Bart had, he knew, regarded him accordingly with derision, almost as a eunuch, though he wasn't that. Abel had endured that situation quietly through youth; then, when the time came, married an acquiescent young bride; now dead. He knew about women, therefore, and he knew about humankind; the sense of difference he still had permitted him a kindly, almost saintly assessment of folk and their faults. Nothing surprised Abel Judd, and he resented little as a rule. Tonight compassion was strong in him, seeing the poor young invalid in the new coach, and the way a footman lifted him out. *That* was a worse affliction than any he, Abel, had to suffer. Still a young man, and no doubt rich; the party were well set out in velvets and furs; but what would riches avail that poor cripple? Abel followed the new arrivals into the inn. The lantern he carried lit up the grotesque appearance of the party. It flared, next, on an elderly stout woman's unlikely golden hair, and elaborate turban; she was much painted, and her eyes were kindly and tired. Abel gave her his arm; once by the fireside, in a gesture like that of a richly-plumed mother hen, she drew her two daughters to her. They were, as Abel could see, nothing to make the blood race, neither comely nor plain. One might have been about nineteen years old, the other fourteen or fifteen. The younger miss gave Abel a contemptuous glance out of opaque, almond-shaped dark eyes beneath her hat: he bowed and withdrew.

"My son will go straight upstairs, to his bedchamber," said Kitty Bowes.

She watched through the door while the footman, who catered for all his needs and had been with them for long, helped Godfrey Devenham upstairs. When the feeble, valiant frame had removed itself Kitty turned back to the fire, and ordered spiced ale for them all. When it came she made everyone drink, the servants also, and toasted Malvie. "To our new home!" And might it be happier than the last, she thought; that wouldn't be hard; perhaps, in this remote part, they could start again like other people . . .

Clairette drank, Cecily drank. As they were doing so a visitor was announced, and bowed in by the landlord; Sir Hubert Melrose, who had intended to be in time to meet the coach, but now would join them in spiced ale . . . Kitty had him served, and watched him with eyes well used to assessing the world, and its opinion of her family. This seemed a kind gentleman, a thought middle-aged perhaps; he was staring at Cecily a good deal, between compliments. It was time Cecily found a husband; there hadn't been any suitable proposals in London for her, as things were. Kitty sighed inwardly. Cecily, at nineteen, was almost exactly as she herself had been at seventeen, a plump golden-haired lamb led to the slaughter, in her own case the care of an uncle and aunt in India when her parents died. It had been a matter of finding as rich a husband as possible, as there wasn't much money; this was easier in India. Kitty remembered the shudder she'd felt at first sight of the stern, cold official of the East India Company, his aspect early observed beneath a fringed sunshade carried by a native servant on the way to a reception to which she'd been taken in her first low-cut evening-gown. It had been horrifying when he proposed for her, and his proposal was of course accepted, because, as Aunt said, he was a senior official and had great prospects, and her niece could at last be rich. Young women were in short supply in hot countries; at home, he'd have married someone else.

"What is your name?" he had asked her coldly, on the wedding-night. As if you wanted, in the usual way, to marry a girl without finding out her accustomed name . . . hers, in those days, had been Amanda, Amanda Catherine. She'd known, for somebody back in England had once told her, that Amanda meant she-who-must-be-loved; it seemed absurd and pitiful, in the circumstances; this man didn't, never would love her. So she'd said, on a sob, "Kitty, sir," and Kitty she'd been, to herself and everyone, ever since. She'd fulfilled her destiny, miserably, as the wife of the nabob, who wanted heirs; she gave him one each year, but the heat didn't agree with her and they were all born dead, except, at the last, Godfrey . . .

Godfrey. Why had it to fall out so, that he was as he must always be, in spite of his father's fine incisive mind which had made him what he, in his own time, had been? Godfrey could never have stayed on in India. He hadn't, with the cruelty of society what it was, even been able to stay in London. She'd tried it, in spite of everything, for five years, for the sake of the girls. Cecily and Clairette must find proper husbands, not like *their* father. For that second marriage of her own to Josiah Bowes had come too late, and mistakenly.

Kitty moved her full white shoulders in the burgundy velvet travelling-gown. Love, for that's what it had been for her, could be a cruel thing . . . cruel, and she a widow at last, rich beyond dreams, but with figure, teeth and complexion gone, and along had come an Irish money-seeking scoundrel;

70

oh, she knew Jos now for what he was always. She hadn't married him soon enough, though he'd known very well what he was doing in getting her with his child, that time she'd been off guard one night on the sofa; she'd had to marry him, there was no other way of arranging matters, and then they'd gone across to France and pretended things had all happened four or five months sooner, but nobody was deceived . . .

Josiah hadn't made her happy, any more than the nabob had ever done. Not a maidservant in the place had been safe, and he'd spent all of her jointure he could lay his hands on; Godfrey's money, thankfully, was safe by his father's will. Five years after Cecily's birth, to her own surprise and Jos's, there had come Clairette.

Society had never accepted them in London. In a thousand snobbish cruel ways she'd been made to feel, even while they accepted her cheques for charities, that she was beyond the pale, that they all were, even the poor girls, even poor Godfrey in his chair, with his books and collections of plants that he loved, which grew about him indoors, like a green sunshade. They weren't ever asked to anything; invitations to the right places, to balls, would never come for the girls or for her. Even after Josiah died, providentially, of an infection of the bowels in the house in Bloomsbury, where they were staying at the time, nobody called, or ever would call, and she'd been left at the funeral with hired mourners only, and the hearse with nodding plumes . . . poor Josiah.

It was the lawyer who'd suggested that they ought to clear out. He didn't put it like that; but Kitty knew. A suitable property in the north . . . an old family, fallen on hard times . . . county society . . .

Well, she'd thought of Godfrey as well as the girls. It was Godfrey's money. If he couldn't ever meet a girl he fancied, and some of the young London misses would have done anything to be rich, well, he'd be happy enough with his plants and his shells, and any other thing he could find growing wild, or lying about on the ground. She'd never known anyone who lived so much inside himself, using the things in his mind and saying nothing at all, for shyness. His stepfather had used to twit him about it, and then she for once had turned on Jos and told him to hold his tongue.

Godfrey would be in bed now upstairs. She'd go in, herself, before they all lay down, to make sure he slept and wasn't in pain. Meanwhile there was this pleasant gentleman, Sir Hubert Melrose, paying quite marked attention to Cecily.

71

She'd been brought up strict and proper, Cecily had, not permitted to see too much of what went on with Jos in the house, being kept mostly away at a young ladies' exclusive school. She'd make a good wife to someone. Clairette was different, Clairette had her Irish father in her and could turn nasty, if she'd a mind; one never knew what was going on inside her head, though she was the cleverer of the two. But men didn't want a clever girl, only a good wife and mother.

"Will you have another round of spiced ale, my dears?" said Kitty. She already included Sir Hubert Melrose as her dear; Cecily's cheeks were quite flushed with his attentions, she hadn't had much opportunity of meeting the right kind of man before. If it could come to anything, it'd be most suitable . . .

The smithy cottage had once been a part of the Malvie estate; it had been purchased by Aaron out of his savings at a time when the trustees were also selling the outlying farms. He had lived in it all his life and his father before him. They had always been blacksmiths, and they had always worked for Doons.

He straightened from his anvil now, a thin, frail-seeming old man with the outward air of an Old Testament prophet. His younger son Bart, who seldom did a hand's turn at the forge, was with him. Bart had the old man's height and leanness, but none of his stern air; he was an idle, lascivious creature, with an eye for the women. His sleepy dark gaze focussed now on the green space beyond the smithy door, presented through a transparent screen of wavering heat from the forge. Across the grass, moving hesitantly, came a young woman; the maid from the Mains, carrying some repair-job in a basket. Bart Judd's eyes widened in appreciation. A fine bosom, a good tight belly and thigh! He murmured of the matter to his father, who did not turn.

"Away to it, then," muttered Aaron, surlily; that was always the way it was with Bart, off at a minute's fancy and back the next. He'd never settle. For this reason Aaron loved Bart best; better than his kindly, God-fearing, well-doing elder son Abel, who'd lost his young wife four summers back. But neither sorrow nor joy made Abel a part of Aaron, as Bart who cared nothing would always be. There was only one creature who lay as near Aaron's heart as his own younger son, and that was Morven Doon. A fierce, silent protective-ness emanated from Aaron to young Morven, scion of the old stock and deprived of his birthright. Aaron had, without saying anything, ridden off himself in former days to the 'Forty-five; but had come quietly home after Derby. He'd seen the way things were going by then; and a man had his living to earn. But young Morven could always find bite and sup with him, and a roof over his head though it wasn't much.

A short laugh from Bart caused the latter's father to look, at last, beyond the door, laying down the harness-nails he was forging. Morven himself had come out meantime from the cottage, which lay beyond, to meet the girl; they were standing regarding one another and smiling. The sun grilled down.

"No room for me," said Bart, apropos of the last statement. "He's got her."

"Do you say so?" said Aaron, who knew already. He had been uncertain of the identity of the woman, but knew Morven had found one, and was now himself a man. The matter pleased Aaron. He turned an experienced eye to look over Morven's wench. "Ay," he said presently nodding. She was, he thought, comely; exactly what he himself would have chosen. "They're in the spinney, nights," said Bart knowledgeably.

"Maybe so. Quiet, now; the young wench is comin' in." And with that Livia's shadow darkened the forge-door, and Aaron pretended to be busied over his fire. The bellows lay nearby; he used them, and the heat blew from cherry-red to vermilion.

"Would you roast us, father?" yelled Bart, over the noise of the bellows. "Here's a lady." He winked, unable to help it, at Livia, who blushed becomingly. Aaron laid down the bellows and turned majestically, waiting; Morven skulked still beyond the door till Livia should have done her errand.

"Mrs. Retford says will you please repair her hammer?" said Livia to Aaron, and took the broken object from her basket. He accepted it with the air of a Marshal of France receiving his baton from the Queen; he still said nothing, and turned away again to the forge; presently he said over his thin shoulder, "It'll be a minute, if you wait outbye." When he turned again, the forge was empty of anyone but himself; Bart had also gone, but only down to the shore to caulk his boat. He couldn't, the father reflected, thole being second fiddle. The lass hadn't even seen the pair of them, in here. She'd already gone off with young Morven.

They were lying together on the straw which still lined a

73

disused byre of Aaron's. It had happened so quickly that there had not been time for more, today, than a survey of her by him with half-shut eyes gleaming through their slits, and a turning of her knees to water. It was always the way with her at sight of Morven, now; what was to become of her?

But the present was sweet. "What'll he think of me?" she muttered into his shoulder. "What'll that old man think?"

Morven laughed. "He'll think what I tell him, and no more," he told her, "and he remembers what'd have happened were he thirty years younger, and he—Ah, damn him and everyone, Livia, Livia!"

Afterwards they sat up. Still holding one another close, they could look out from the byre-door straight across the curve of the bay to Malvie, where the road wound up to the gate past the lower shore. The gate itself, once an elegant double affair in light wrought-iron, had been fashioned by Aaron's grandfather who had been a craftsman. It hung now on a broken hinge, mended with rope like an old cow-gate, to make it stay shut. The sight angered Morven; he could feel the anger creeping up through the late satisfaction of his body, so that he almost forgot to look at Livia. He turned and looked, and presently thrust her down again.

She lay passively in disarray; she had forgotten about the blacksmith, and the caressing eyes of Bart as she'd passed by. She had forgotten everything but Morven himself; and, she knew, she always would. If he whistled, any time, she'd come. There had been hardly a night this summer she'd spent altogether in her bed; lying out with him till all hours in the spinney under the moon, under the wild cherry trees whose tiny green fruit were like peppercorns.

He rolled off her now, again fulfilled, and yawned and stretched himself. "That was good," he said, and continued to fondle her breasts above the pulled-down shift. "It's always good with us, Livia Mary." He laughed; she had told him long ago how she came by the name.

"Maybe it won't always be so," she said, and moved away. Her happiness was like a great caged bird within her, tremulous and still fearful. Morven was, she knew, a natural adept, with every cunning version of the art of love laid bare; who had bequeathed it she didn't know, but she did know what could happen, and might soon. If he'd got her, again already with child—

"What is it?" he asked, for she was shivering. Fear was not, in his estimate of Livia, a natural thing; she was as it should be, unafraid as an animal. Morven nuzzled her re-

74

vealed shoulders; they were magnificent. "They ought to be in a low-cut dress, such as fine ladies wear," he said. "One day I'll buy you one, and candles to sit under; then you'll look like a queen."

A queen! "What's that to do with me?" she said angrily, and thrust him from her; why did he make a fool of her when he'd had what he wanted? "I'll be in the family way by then, most like, and your aunt'll have shown me her door. Fine talk of queens that day." She began to cry.

He laughed, and pulled her again to him. "Never fret, I'll be careful," he said. "I'm always careful, aren't I?" But sometimes, he knew, he forgot; it was generally impossible by the end not to renew himself in her totally, savour the wonderful release and well-being that came when he was with her, as now. He took her again, briefly and fiercely, and then looked up; there was a rumbling on the distant road, heavy enough for a coach to be coming. But it was not the time of day for the post-coach.

"What is it?" asked Livia drowsily; he had solaced her. Morven did not answer; quickly buttoning his own clothes he stood up, so that he could see the coach as it passed by. It did so, travelling at too high a speed for the road, and swaying a little. It was borne by four horses, all grey and evenly matched, and there was a coachman and footman. Morven could not see the inmates before it came past, thundering on towards the gate of Malvie.

He gave an oath, and ran out and across the sward. He did not even hear Livia cry after him; he had already forgotten her. The coach had stopped now at the tied iron gates and because there was no lodge or keeper, the footman got down, untied the rope and climbed up again on the box; the gate was left swinging. The coach itself travelled on, growing smaller till it was the size of a beetle; presently the curve of land hid its arrival before the door of the great house. Morven began to run. Then he stopped, wiping his hot forehead with his sleeve. No need to appear in haste, dishevelment and shirt-sleeves to greet the new purchaser of Malvie, the hated, moneyed Englishman! He himself must go and wash, and put on his coat, and get his hair smooth again. Then he'd go up, properly mounted on Aaron's brown cob, and see.

He dived back towards the smithy once more, and in a quarter-hour was on the road. Livia, left behind, had not moved for a while from her place in the byre straw. He would always be off, whenever there was some matter that interested him more, for the time, than herself; she'd need to get used to it. A small, wise smile curved her mouth as she brushed herself down, then laced up her bodice and smoothed her own dishevelled hair. As long as the old bitch didn't notice straw on her back when she got home . . . She hesitated at the forge-door, shy of going in so soon to ask about the hammer. But Aaron, soul of tact, had left it lying ready on the outside bench. Livia lifted and tried it, set it in her waiting basket and set off. On the way back to Mains she met another carriage on the road. It was slower than the last had been; a dray, drawn by a patient horse. The man seated at the reins wore a broad hat and countryman's smock. His dark eyes were already fixed on Livia.

She knew the man, and did not stop for him, making her own way back up the lane to Mains in the languor that follows prolonged making of love. The dust was thick on the hedgerows and the green herbs, Good King Henry and ragged-robin and the rest, were whitish grey. There hadn't been rain for weeks, and the carriage wheels—She turned, unthinkingly, again to survey the dray.

That was Abel Judd, she knew. He'd be over in his circircumspect way to pick up a few free bales for the Fleece, which Morven had said Abel had bought, in the end, with his own saved money. A careful good man, Abel. "How'd he make the money?" she'd said suspiciously to Morven at the time. He'd laughed; he was always laughing now. "Saved it on wine and on women," he'd told her. "Others spend theirs, but Abel—well, he had a wife once, but she died; now he never spends a drop of his money, even on ale. Forget him," and he'd seized her hand then and pulled her after him up the spinney rise.

She could forget Abel again quite easily now; but he was still watching her. He had, in his slow way, seen her already and taken note of her from the first; repeated sights of her gave him, he found, repeated pleasure. The garnered, shining beauty of the moments when he had gazed at her, or thought about her, had a quality Abel himself had never met before; it hadn't been like what he could remember of courting poor Emmy, whom he'd known anyway since their childhood. This young girl, with her raven's wing hair, the bright carnation colour showing in her cheeks with the heat of the day, her fine eyes and trim, comely figure, had by now stayed in Abel's memory a long time; he was beginning to think he wouldn't be able to forget young Morven's wench. With a peasant's perception, he was apprised of that situation, and resented nothing; they were young, they loved one another, it was a pretty thing. He passed a slow tongue over his lips as the pony jogged off, and continued to remember Livia, after he'd turned the corner to Mains. He'd be surprised, thinking it over, if that Mrs. Retford knew what went on. He'd not tell her, never fear; no need to get the little maid in trouble before it came. And come it would, soon or late, knowing young Morven.

Morven arrived to find the coach at a standstill outside the door of Malvie and, beyond, his aunt's little calèche; she must have driven over already by the path round the field. No doubt she had brought Annabel with her.

Morven scowled, earning a similar welcome from the English coachman, who in the absence of superiors was standing at his ease with a toothpick; the footman was nowhere to be seen. The first fellow openly considered the advisability of asking Morven's business, but thought better of it in face of that young gentleman's haughty light-eyed stare. Doon strode up the steps and in at the great door, finding himself in what should have been his father's hall of Malvie.

A long oak table remained of such things as he remembered. About this, grouped on straight-backed chairs, a polite assembly was already seated; he caught sight of his aunt and Annabel, and old Lady Berry who could never bear not to know anything that was going on in the county. The rest, strange to Morven, had come out of the coach; and first among these was the new master. The young footman, whose disappearance Morven had already noted, stood now behind an invalid-chair of a light kind which could be carried in. In it a stout, pale young man sat; his prominent eyes slewed round to view Morven on entry, in the manner of one who finds it a matter of some pain, perhaps, or trouble, to turn the head. He smiled.

No one else gave Morven Doon any welcome; Mrs. Bowes looked fussed and bewildered, her two daughters surveyed the ground; old Lady Berry, whose forebears had been noted Whigs, glared beneath her grey wig as if an interloper, such as all Morven's kind had been to her since the Revolution of 1688. Mrs. Retford frowned beneath her second-best bonnet; she had attired her young niece carefully today, not in the very best but in green, with a narrow blonde trim at bonnet-edge and throat. The girl sat by her, in her shadow; but Morven felt Annabel's intense awareness of himself, though she dared show nothing.

"This," said aunt Retford's small cold voice into the silence, "is my nephew, Morven Doon."

Her mean, flat-eyed face surveyed his attire a brief instant, and in that instant found it wanting; he'd taken, after all, some care in changing his clothes back at Aaron's, but was made now to feel that he was too carelessly dressed to meet the incomers from London. Unwonted colour stained Morven's cheeks; they themselves were no great sight!

But he bowed to the company; and when it came to Godfrey Devenham's turn was filled with pity and triumph. The pity, never uppermost in Morven, was no more than any strong, normal being would feel for so weak and pitiful a sight. The goggle-eyes, like a frog's, Morven thought, were set in flesh so soft and useless it seemed without foundation, like a shape in dough. The dwindling of muscular power which, since a very early age had prevented young Devenham from walking, made his ankles slender and narrow as a lady's beneath stout calves, grown so for lack of exercise. His body was flabby, his narrow-fingered hand like a fish's. Morven felt his thoughts grow cruel. His own triumph, the prospect of realisation of a hope which had still been shadowy, rushed upon him so that his eyes shone, and he smiled openly at the company; months, years, it might have been, before what was in his own mind came to fruition! But now—

For he had already seen the way Godfrey looked at Annabel.

Mrs. Bowes was exclaiming, as if her son had neither ears nor understanding, as she often did, how he had happened to contract his ailment. The story had so frequently been told by her to hearers that she almost believed it herself, whether or not they did so; in fact, no physician had ever diagnosed the illness' cause. "It was at Weymouth as a child; a chill from the sea-bathing, so newly home as we were from India at that time; they shouldn't have forced him, but his dear father wanted him to be brought up without fear of the sea." She smiled mournfully, as if admitting Bowes to have been the later lapse he was; and went on to explain how for her only son, the hope of her heart (this was true enough) the purchase of a quiet place near the country or the sea had been advised, as perhaps likely to effect improvement. "He will have his books," she went on, and would have catalogued these; but Lady Berry broke in.

"Can he sit a horse?" said the old lady. She herself had ridden over today, at near eighty, a distance of some twelve miles up the coast-road from Invale; and had small sympathy for anyone young or old who could not, for whatever cause, ride to hounds. Godfrey raised his eyes sadly and let his mother answer, as she swiftly did.

"No; but he is a scholar of no mean attainment, reads Latin and some Hebrew, all such things, except that his migraine often troubles him . . ."

Annabel smiled at poor Godfrey; how dreadful, she thought, to have an incessantly chattering foolish mother always with one! Poor young man; he was still, although nearing thirty, not yet old; if he could be permitted to forget himself for an hour, it should be possible to remove the unhappiness from his frog's eyes and interest him in things he could enjoy and do; gardening, perhaps, or drawing in crayons; she herself had been taught to do that, there was still a box somewhere in the Mains cupboard that she never now used, and would lend him. If only Morven hadn't come in, she could pay more attention; but as it was—

". . . if only he would make a suitable match; but he showed no interest in any of the young women we met in London . . ."

Morven Doon, watching outside the circle, was suddenly aware, by a sixth sense he had, of the thoughts going on behind each face at this moment; of aunt Retford's momentarily revealed blink of satisfaction, as if a shutter had quickly opened and closed again behind her eyes' bleak flatness; of the hopeful, beady gaze of the old woman, well aware of all this, and the same time calculating that if she had anything to do with it, her own niece, not Agnes's little green-clad nincompoop, should get all that money; they must be asked soon, this family, to dine and sleep at Invale, with perhaps a card-party, to meet the county. It was known Sir Hubert Melrose had already . . . and so on to the girls, whose thoughts were their own, and to Godfrey, aware now of nothing but the fairylike vision Annabel presented, so that the thoughts racing unwontedly in his scholar's mind made his feeble hands sweat. Her eyes, he had noted already, were flecked green-gold; he'd never seen anyone so beautiful; could his useless body, placed here like a lump in its chair, be overcome by the urgings of his mind which urged him to love her, love her? Could he ever interest her with talk, if he were less shy, if they were alone, and he—Could he, perhaps, if it turned out that they both liked and laughed at the same things, somehow make her like him also, forget his appearance? It wasn't easy, he knew; but he wanted that more than anything in the whole of his life . . .

"If only such a thing might happen," Mrs. Bowes was saying with fond disregard. Aunt Retford looked down her nose to hide her satisfaction; Morven sneered; and Annabel, seeing, blushed confusedly.

Godfrey Devenham seldom spoke to anyone except briefly and with kindness; he never, at this rate, so much as mentioned his father, the nabob, who had died when the boy himself was eleven. Godfrey preferred not to remember him; the character traits which had caused the elder Devenham, at fifty-four, to be able to retire with a vast fortune acquired by way of the East India Company, in which, like most, he had started life as an articled clerk, did not make for happiness in his family circle. Godfrey, the only one alive out of the progression of still-born children poor Kitty had produced, was left in no doubt that he, like his vulgar and inadequate mother, was a failure. Unable to protect her—a wish to protect and solace Kitty was the earliest feeling Godfrey could remember, but there was nothing in this way he might do— he had begun, almost as soon as he could walk, to lose his newly-gained balance in public. The nabob, taking this as a whim, ruled that each time it happened a servant should flog the child till he got up; in this he had royalty as a precedent. Under this treatment Godfrey, by the time he was eight years old, was still unbalanced, and also incontinent; though he differed from Queen Anne's son in that parental harshness did not, in the end, kill him.

He nearly did die, though, of childish diseases, which left him deaf in one ear, affected in eyesight—the staring eyes needed glasses when they read, as Godfrey loved to do despite cruel recurrent headaches. There was also a glandular anomaly which made him fat; he could not, by now, take exercise to correct it. He was by this time mostly hidden away by the servants and his mother, who feared that the contemptuous rage the sight of him induced in his father might lead the latter to do Godfrey an injury or perhaps take his life. But it was the nabob who died, succumbing shortly in course of an operation for the stone.

Nobody mourned him other than openly. When the funeral was over—Godfrey could remember being led downstairs carefully by his mother, all in black, the diaphanous veils she wore enhancing what remained of her blonde, plump beauty —and the harsh face in the coffin was covered, a new life began for the boy. From being an object of scorn and derision—servants copy their master, and he had often found himself a whipping-boy and scapegoat—Godfrey was now the heir, come into his own; the nabob's will had been provident of his immense riches, and it was all, save for Kitty's jointure, left to his son. By the time Kitty had made a fool of herself with Bowes, and had gone abroad with him and had first Cecily, and then Clairette, the boy Godfrey had long ago made his own inner life.

He had always had something of this, even in the days when he was concealed high up beneath his father's roof to avoid the swift, terrible cut of that gold-topped cane, brought down in anger. He had been used to crawl away, sobbing, if that happened, and presently find solace in the pages of a book; and books still solaced Godfrey. They became, as time passed, more real than the world outside; and this was merciful. After his father's death, for a year and more before the Bowes elopement, he continued to suffer physically, though for a different cause; a physician had advised his mother to put the boy in an iron frame to strengthen his legs. Accordingly, they never did bear Godfrey's weight for the rest of his life; he would always remember the cage. It encompassed his ribs and limbs, preventing him from walking, breathing or moving freely; it even, while he was standing in it all day, prevented him from holding a book. As a compensation he had asked them, timidly, to place his cage nearby the window, far enough back for him not to be seen, but near enough to see the street. In this way he would watch life as it went by. It was always, as far back as he could remember, manifest to Godfrey that he could never be a part of ordinary life, never join the laughing, thoughtless, richly dressed young people he saw passing in carriages, or walking below in the street. Small things, instead, had become diverting and important; he could recall the colours in a fly's wings as it stayed preening its antennae on the casement-sill behind which he had been put, while the summer sun grilled him inside his irons. Later, after Godfrey was free of them, he was to extend his interest in anything natural; he knew insects, shells, plants, birds and stones. His mother, returned by now briefly from abroad with Josiah Bowes revealed for what he was, laughed, for she could still laugh, and called him her queer boy, and did her best and worst for him. In the intervals of varying treatments and spa-visits, some good, some bad, she displayed one glimmer of sense; she found Godfrey an excellent tutor, who cultivated his mind.

This young man—he had already taken holy orders, to which he was to return much later, when Godfrey had ceased to need him, and was at present a parson in a Wiltshire living; they still corresponded—was not only a scholar but, like Godfrey himself, a naturalist and scientist; besides the Latin and Hebrew Mrs. Bowes extolled, they would discuss together the proceedings of the Royal Society, and follow with interest the affairs pertaining for instance to Hudson's Bay, as well as the daily papers. Well or ill, Godfrey was encouraged to let no single moment of the day go by idly; even when he appeared to be doing nothing, he would be turning over something in his mind. As Mrs. Bowes told everyone, he knew the whole of Shakespeare intimately. It was not by any means all he knew; but his health continued wretched.

He had been sent on a course of sea-bathing at thirteen, shortly after emerging from the cage. This, the origin of Mrs. Bowes' Weymouth story, was only one contributory factor of many. The repeated dousing of Godfrey's shivering, fat, unprepared body in the icy sea-water—the weather on the south coast was peculiarly spartan that year—brought on a congestion of the lungs, delaying his puberty. On recovery, Godfrey caught mumps, the one childhood disease from which he had not yet suffered. Its results were dire and remained with him. Later, with his sexual development still delayed, he showed signs of a phthisis; was despaired of, recovered, caught enteric fever due to the London bad water, was whisked off to Paris afterwards, then back again for the season at home, unnecessarily. Mrs. Bowes, continually hopeful that, with the passing of time and the tactful death of Bowes, her lapse would be forgotten by polite society, suffered one rebuff after another with equanimity; then, as such folks do, she suddenly crumbled. "For God's sake let us leave," she wailed, and Godfrey could see her face, once plumply pretty, now a sad, defeated network of spidery lines the years had etched below the paint. He never forgot this view of his mother; over the years, while he'd been dreaming his life away with Shakespeare and shells, she'd been suffering, and he'd done very little.

"Whatever you choose," he told her gently, and, because he was now the master, made a show of listening and weighing decisions regarding the place, the site, the new property, its prospects and price. But he knew it did not greatly matter to him where he was, provided his library and rare plants could go with him, and he could be left alone, for the most part, in his own private world, as society had no charms for him that he knew of; he'd tried it, briefly, and shuddered at it more that it did at the sight of him, which was something. He'd learned long ago to shut a private door, to allow nothing from outside to enter and disturb him.

Then he saw Annabel. And, ever since, events inside the private door had been only the folly of an idle hour, and science and knowledge only a way of passing time, until . . . until she came to him again. For the first time in his life, with all the passion of a nature starved and smothered in its physical needs from birth, Godfrey loved.

V

Next time Livia came to Morven her eyes were red as though she had been crying. When he tried to make love she turned away.

"It's happened," she told him sullenly. "I warned you it'd happen, if—" Her voice trembled into silence; what was the use? Even now, on seeing his pale intent face again, she felt the flame rise; it'd go on, doubtless, till Mrs. Retford showed her the door. The forty days by law wouldn't count here. As it was, a wonder the old bitch hadn't complained of her already, with her creeping out night after night to the spinney, and half asleep mornings. No doubt Mrs. Retford was too taken up with Miss Annabel's concerns at the moment, going on with that poor young man up at the big house. Well, young Miss could have a man like that if it was what she wanted; as for *her*—

What was to happen to her, when Morven tired, as he surely would now? Within Livia herself there had always been the wonder that she, a waif, a servant lass without grand manners or book-learning, could keep Morven Doon longer than a day. Say what they liked, he was a gentleman born and had many things in his mind ordinary folk hadn't; the best company wasn't too good for him. He couldn't live out his life in this way, out most nights in the boat with Bart Judd, asleep by day in Bart's father's cottage, and somewhere in between in a barn or spinney with herself, while the revenue-cutters cruised up and down the near water and, any day now, an order would come for the Excise to ride out her and round up a few culprits for the look of the thing, as they often did; everyone knew the tax was wrong and nobody but what went round it somehow . . . but there'd be trouble for Morven soon if they had to find a scapegoat. He'd have to go into hiding or else it'd be the colonies for him; and she—

The thought of being abandoned, for whatever cause, made her give way to rare tears, and Morven consoled her in the way he always used. Afterwards he said. "Why don't you trust me, Livia Mary?" and smiled while he nibbled her ear-lobe; she felt the altering curve of his mouth against her neck. She laughed bitterly. "Trust any man?" she said. "Here am I, the same way's I was before, and this time it'll be the road for me and the baby born under a hedge, for go back I will not." Her eyes flashed; they shouldn't kill Morven's baby. It shouldn't be, either brought up the way she'd been, in Emmett's on gruel, flogging, laundry and the Bible. Together they'd make a life somehow, if— "There's only one gait for a woman, Morven," she said sadly. "Either she's a lady or she isn't; and if she isn't, there's not one of your grand madams will give her houseroom when she's in trouble, scrub and polish and launder as she may."

She drew her shawl back over her shoulders with the age-old acceptance of fate of the outcast, the gipsy woman. It had grown cold. He stroked her and rubbed her limbs to warm her. Her hair had fallen loose by now and hung down her back, like a great shining dark blanket under the shawl.

"You have the tresses of Zenobia," he told her.

"Who's Zenobia?"

"A queen. Trust me, I said, Livia; I'm not any man." He laughed; the notion that he could be in any way ordinary was, today, absurd; were not all things moving his way, as though he'd cast a spell on everyone? Annabel forever up at the house, or down on the shore with poor Devenham in his carriage, shell-collecting; he'd watched them once unseen from the back window of Aaron's; pretty, it had been.

"Give me a little while," he said, "lace yourself tight. A week or two, maybe even a month, two perhaps; then I'll make you a queen on Man. We'll go there together."

"You're mad. You'd leave the sight of Malvie?"

"Even that," he said, and ran his fingers through her hair. "Malvie will wait for me—now."

"She stared at him; what could he mean? When he spoke

84

so, as if he knew everything that was in the world and beyond it, a shiver overcame her, she didn't know why. She turned her head to look at small things, which she knew; the myriad springing golden lances of the late moss their two bodies had crushed; the waiting trees. All the time he was whispering in her ear, seducing her; she wasn't herself, she hadn't her wits, when Morven was with her; she'd believe anything, then after . . . "Trust me, only trust me, Livia. We'll go off together, in the boat . . . have your gear ready . . . there's a little place I know of at the Ayre of Man, where you can lie snug in time, and have your child. It'll be as if we were married over there, Livia; nobody cares where anyone came from."

He sat up, narrow cheeks flushed and eyes brilliant with his own conviction. She watched him, knowing, as she'd known from the beginning, that she would always follow this man; there'd never be another for her. She rose presently to go back and for instants, standing together in the wood, they were like a king and queen of faery, tall light-eyed Oberon and Titania with loose hair blowing; the wind sang in the geans for them, then presently tore on. Livia twisted up her hair and went down to the house.

The advent of Mrs. Bowes and her two daughters, and her invalid son, gave rise at first to a natural stir of interest in the county, fomented energetically by old Lady Berry, so that a number of calls were exchanged. In course of these, however, someone took up the pen to write to a friend living in London, to ask further particulars about the Bowes family; these having been duly ascertained, there was a certain cooling off on the part of the more excessively virtuous matrons, who withdrew to watch events. It might have been the worse for poor Kitty had not a providential circumstance intervened to save her from total ostracism here also and include her, however vicariously, among the county families. Sir Hubert Melrose proposed shortly for Cecily, and the betrothal was gazetted in the new year.

This hurdle achieved—the wedding would not take place for some months, to allow for the preparation of the bride-clothes, which must of course come from London—Kitty and her daughters, rather than her son, set themselves to transform Malvie. This had, in everyone's memory, always been a shabby house, for fines and, before that, gaming-stakes had ensured that no Doon would have money to spend on its interior any more than its roof. The latter had by now been slated in great part; later, with the rooms fired and dry, rich varied hangings, many of them brought by the nabob from India, were unrolled, to cover the walls; there were carpets woven and tufted of silk, prayer-rugs and embroidered shawls; one of these transformed the drawing-room, casting its rainbow fringes over the great gilt harp which had once belonged to Susannah Doon, and had been found in a neglected state in the attic. With its gilding newly freshened and its pegs re-strung, it was a pretty sight to watch young Clairette, who fancied herself briefly as a performer, play it in the evenings, though the child's fingers were too short and her arms and stance not graceful, and she had no talent.

Kitty Bowes would watch, sum up her younger daughter's known limitations, and sigh for the day when Annabel Doon, as Godfrey's wife, should sit by her own great-grandmother's harp and, perhaps, play; and even if she did not, what a pleasure it would be to watch the pretty thing seated there! For Kitty's sentimental heart was now, like the revived furniture of Malvie, in a state of nourished, shining splendour where hitherto only dust and neglect had lain. She had seen at once that her poor boy was smitten; and being Kitty would do everything in her power, and some things which should have been beyond it, to grant him his heart's desire. It would, after all, be a rich marriage for Miss Annabel, and she would regain her old home. More did not, for it could not, manifest itself to Kitty; why, the child met nobody, never had met anybody, down there with her aunt!

And Mrs. Retford was agreeable. From the beginning, it had been evident that that small, punctilious lady—of whom Kitty had found herself, from the first, afraid, for she could see that she was often in danger of putting a foot wrong, and you never knew with these blue-blooded folk—was not only agreeable but entirely determined on the marriage; and as that made two of them with the same determination, and it was what poor Godfrey wanted also, the matter would seem to be, almost, except for propriety, resolved. Propriety of course demanded that there should be a period of acquaintance, and it was desirable that the two young people should come to know one another in any case; but Mrs. Bowes, without words spoken, had entered into an alliance with Mrs. Retford, and each separate minor campaign was planned to capture first one point of vantage, then the next. Already, Kitty knew, the man-hungry daughters of the county no longer hoped, if they ever had, to capture the interest of Godfrey with a view to marriage. No more need be said at present; let things take their course, and she was always glad to welcome Annabel to tea or to their informal supper, and to play at bezique with the girls by the fire after Godfrey had been carried upstairs, tired with his exhilarating afternoon on the shore . . .

There had, of course, been the initial matter of the pony. Clairette had unwittingly helped here; on first arrival, Kitty had ordered a splendid little Welsh pony for her youngest, easy, they'd promised, for a young lady to ride. But Clairette was scared of animals, and had such rigid hands she would have spoiled the poor beast's mouth, and Kitty had vexatiously considered selling it again; she'd so wanted Clairette to cut a good figure among the Berrys and the rest, if the invitations came. But, as so often, Providence had intervened, and had turned the entire transaction to great advantage. It had been Godfrey who had spoken up; Annabel, he said, loved ponies and hers had been sold. It should be kept for Annabel to ride, if she wished.

He'd flushed up, poor boy, as he said it; it wasn't often, Kitty knew well, that he made any positive statement of the kind. Even at that, he'd qualified the matter to happen only if Annabel should wish it; but Kitty and Mrs. Retford had soon settled that. The girl did wish it, of course; she'd passed her little white hand lovingly over the pony's mouth and muzzle, and soothed him, for he'd grown wild meantime out in the field, with nobody to saddle and manage him, and he'd bolted grass. Annabel had got him to come to her, and trust her, and presently Kitty had made it clear she must ride him, and have him meantime in a present, and that the present was Godfrey's. The poor child had crimsoned with embarrassment then, and had glanced at her aunt, as if fearful of a rebuke, the way she often did. But Mrs. Retford had only said affably that it was very good of Mr. Devenham and his mother. She hadn't left Kitty out; and then there was the matter of the habit.

"She hasn't got out," said Clairette, in her blurting way. "She might as well use mine, Mama; I shall never wear it again, I assure you," and the child had turned away, as if that matter was finished with. Miss Annabel hadn't wanted to accept the habit, which was a very pretty one, made of dark Melton cloth with a tall hat, bearing a plume at its narrow brim. It had become her vastly, everyone said, when they made her try it on; it would hardly need any fitting. Annabel wore it, for her aunt saw that she wore it, next time she went out with Godfrey to the shore; after that, the girl on her pony, and the stout invalid form in the light carriage, would go down together, and hunt for shells and weeds all afternoon, coming home sun-filled and happy. That Godfrey was happy induced the necessity, in Kitty, of stating that Annabel was so also; in fact, she had never considered the girl as a separate person. Godfrey wanted Annabel; she must, accordingly, be acquired, as the pony and the harp had been; as Malvie had been, for Godfrey. Kitty by now had persuaded herself of this.

Annabel was not without perceptions of her own; and she felt herself thrust too openly into Godfrey's company.

It was not, she told herself, that she disliked poor Godfrey; on the contrary, sometimes when they were alone together, on the shore among the rock pools, and he was telling her interesting things he'd found out about the habits of shellfish and the slow, bright, wavering anemones which would, at a touch, whisk back again to formless jelly—sometimes, then, she could forget herself and him, and learn and listen; it was all new to her, this love of the different kinds of life, this knowledge that there were other kinds at all; in the existence with aunt Retford, one had tended to think of oneself, of correct behaviour, as solely important, and now, hearing of a time when there hadn't been any air to breathe or life upon the earth, only strange gases, till life came and they still didn't know how . . . God, the Bible and aunt Retford would say, had breathed upon the waters. It was impossible, according to Godfrey, that that was the way it had happened; it had taken millions upon millions of years, not six days. And the water-snails, which often as a child she'd shuddered from, for she'd always had a dislike for slimy creatures, had once been kings, ruling the world like uncounted giants from the sea.

"You know a great deal," she had said to him once. "How did you start to find out about it, Godfrey?" And he had looked at her with great kindness, and had said, in his shy quiet voice, that it had happened gradually, he hadn't been much in the way of meeting people, and so he grew interested in things instead. "They're always there," he said, "if other matters go wrong," and then he'd gone on looking at her with an expression, now, in his eyes that made her feel uncomfortable, and ungenerous for feeling uncomfortable, when he'd been so kind and thoughtful about the pony, and had told her about shells and snails. Once after that she'd begged Clairette to come out with them, but the younger girl had shrugged and had said, with an unpleasant expression in her eyes which didn't belong to a child,

"That would spoil things. Besides, I don't like being near the pony," and she had gone off on her own concerns, refusing to come. Annabel tried to forget it, and told herself she'd sooner have the pony, whose name was Beau, as a companion than Clairette, who was both rough and sly, and said unaccountable things which made everyone feel awkward. The girl wasn't happy, no doubt; she felt no one liked her, which was probably true, and Cecily was busy preparing for her wedding and had no time for her younger sister. They were both, Annabel and Clairette, to be bridal attendants, for Cecily when she should marry Uncle Hubert in a few weeks' time, and their gowns were to be buttercup yellow and edged with sable fur. They had cost a great deal; Annabel had never had a gown in her life that would cost half as much; and they had been made by the mantua-maker to the late Dowager Princess, in London; the measurements had been sent by post.

Aunt Retford somehow heard of Annabel's attempt to persuade Clairette to accompany her and Godfrey, and scolded her. One never knew nowadays what was the correct thing to do. Once, she'd been told that on no account was she ever to be left alone in the company of a man; although, no doubt, poor Godfrey didn't count in that way. But a rejoinder in such fashion did not please aunt Retford either; she rapped Annabel's fingers smartly with her closed fan, which she carried for an evening-visit up to Malvie. Their life now consisted of daily visits, sometimes twice daily; they were hardly ever at home. "Do not answer me with opinions, miss, but do as you are bid!" she snapped, and Annabel folded her bruised fingers behind her back, bit her lip to keep the tears in their place, and said nothing. She knew, for they had at some time spoken of it openly together, that her aunt expected her to marry for money. The prospect and fact of marriage seemed in any case unknown and vague; she could never, as it happened, remember knowing any married couple well. Mama had died early and had left Papa a widower, and Uncle Hubert likewise; and aunt Retford's husband was back in the shadows and never spoken of, and Mrs. Bowes's husband had not come north; one understood he was dead, and had not been satisfactory. What was a satisfactory husband? Once, daring, she had even asked her aunt.

"It is a young lady's duty to settle herself in life, as advantageously as this may be done, and her best course is to follow the advice of her parents or guardian in such a matter," replied that lady evasively.

This was no help. Marriage, to Godfrey—and Annabel now knew well enough this was being considered for her—would be more than appearing daily, correctly dressed, for a canter down to the shore by his side on the fine little Welsh pony. It would be much more, even, than making her own home again at Malvie instead of at the Mains, having rich clothes to wear, two carriages, leisure to receive and visit whom she chose; to do what she liked, instead of sitting all day at aunt Retford's prescribed embroidery-tasks. It meant—she knew this—children; how they came Annabel was not quite certain, but the thought of Godfrey's flabby invalid body, his fish-fin hands, his mouth, touching her was unpleasant. It didn't tally with her everyday opinion of Godfrey as a delightful and instructive friend, once his shyness had been overcome. He wasn't shy with her now, except—except when he looked at her in that way which caused her discomfort. There was nobody she knew well enough to ask about all of this, except perhaps Livia Mary; and the latter was a servant, and one didn't discuss such things. In any case, Livia Mary herself was unmarried. There was nobody suitable to ask.

At times, particularly when she was alone, Annabel's thoughts flew to Morven. It seemed so long since they'd been together; that last, brief time in the dark outside Mains, when he'd been angry, had been almost a year ago. Then there had been the other time he had appeared, still angry and scowling at first, but pleased later on, at Malvie the day Godfrey and the others had arrived. She'd hoped that, perhaps, Morven would be able to visit frequently at Malvie now that Mrs. Bowes, who seemed kind, and Godfrey were living there; but there had only been that one visit she'd ever heard of. Morven hadn't time, she knew, for sick people.

There had however been a subsequent visit of Morven's, of which Annabel was not informed.

Godfrey himself had accepted few social engagements since coming to take up residence at Malvie. There had been one rout-party given by his mother, about the time of the Melrose betrothal, which he had only briefly attended, having one of his frequent migraines. His shyness, in addition, prevented him from improving on many acquaintances, already made; he was, accordingly, often left alone when his mother and sisters were elsewhere.

This happened the day Morven came. Godfrey had not

forgotten Morven Doon, or the story of lost inheritance. He had himself been aware, beyond the enchantment of Annabel's presence seated nearby him that first day, of the advent of that other, and of the watchful, resentful quality of a pair of blazing pale-green eyes. Godfrey's own sensitiveness made him aware that young Morven must in fact resent him fiercely; as he himself grew better acquainted with Malvie, where he intended to start a garden, he could understand this situation very well. To have lost such a paradise through no fault of one's own, when one's ancestors had walked here for centuries, must be bitter. Godfrey thought about it, and conquered his own shyness sufficiently to send an invitation to Morven to come and dine, one day when his own mother and sisters were absent; this would, he thought, be easier for them both.

He spent the time after the invitation had been sent in doubt, half expectation, and some agony of spirit. Perhaps, he thought, Morven loved Annabel and wanted her for his wife. The cousins had known one another from childhood; to have grown up side by side with such an angel would make it impossible not to love her; had not he himself done so in the first moment his eyes lighted on her bright hair, slender body and sweet heart-shaped face? But to ask Morven about that would be impossible; to converse at all with strangers, leaving aside Annable nowadays, was a task which took all Godfrey's fortitude. He could never forget how ugly they must think him; and Morven Doon was straight as a young tree. If Annabel should look at Morven, and then look at *him*! His mind glanced away; he couldn't endure even the thought that she might never love him. He awaited Morven's reply, and ordered dinner.

But Morven would not dine. Later the same day, having sent no word, he strode in, with a shot hare in his hand, the blood dripping from its nose over the floorboards. He wore his oldest clothes, as if in derision; his whole manner was aggressive and wild, like an animal whose freedom is threatened.

"I'll not eat with you, Englishman," he said.

Godfrey was silent with astonishment; he was unaccustomed to open discourtesy. Presently he said, gently, "Why?" as if it were a scientific problem. Morven laughed, and showed his white wolfish teeth.

"Why? Because of my mother's Highland blood, I suppose; we do not sit down to meat with those who have robbed us of our heritage."

"I took nothing from you," said Godfrey fairly; the house

91

had, he knew, been bought of the trustees and Annabel. Dimly, he began to see in himself a protector for Annabel; this fellow wouldn't have been kind to her in the way she needed. She was gentle, more akin to the things of the south. To be English wasn't in any case a term of reproach there. Godfrey waited, but no answer came; instead, Morven Doon turned the talk his own way.

"Here's my dinner," he said, and slapped the dead hare. He saw Godfrey stare down at the gouted blood and grinned. "In the south, they tell me, you hang men or send them to Australia, or to the hulks, for stealing a hare. Save yourself the toil, sir; I didn't shoot it on Malvie ground; I took it on the high road, where it was loping."

Godfrey said nothing more about the hare, which was almost certainly his own; what did that matter? "I am sorry that we cannot be friends," he said peaceably. "I—having no Highland blood, perhaps—have no rancour towards those who have never wished to harm me, and even very little now to those who have. It—it would give me great pleasure if you'd come often to Malvie. It need not be—lost to you."

His face suffused, for he knew he had phrased all of it badly and had, no doubt, wounded this half-Highland Scot more deeply than ever. Why were the two races so different? In England, it would have been pleasant to offer Morven the run of the house, let him shoot over the grounds at any time, act indeed as if the place were still his own. But a bitter snap of hatred was all that showed in Doon's pale eyes as a result. He laid a hand lightly on the table.

"This was my father's, Richard Doon's," he said. "He bought it with his own silver, in a Cumbrian great house where the owner had broke himself, and he and my uncle found it there together. Upstairs, there is a portrait of my uncle, who stayed at home—"

"I have heard of it; we will bring it downstairs, and hang it above the fireplace. Why will you never come to see it there?" Godfrey's tone was pleading; for Annabel's kin to be friends was all he wanted; it would surely grieve her if things fell out otherwise.

"There is no portrait of my father, who rode out for the true King with his sword. If there was such, you would not dare hang it, Sassenach." Morven spat out the word as if it were customary to use it here, so far south; which it was not. "No one remembers my father now except myself, who never knew him," he said. "He should have been Doon of Malvie;

so should his son. He died in a Paris attic before he was forty, of eating putrid food bought cheap in the market; there was never enough money for any of them, the exiles; there is none now for me. How can you come here Englishman, and buy what cannot be bought? You will never bear the name of Doon or have Doon blood running in your veins, or in those of your sons."

He laughed in Godfrey's face; by now, it was white.

"No, I'll not dine," said Morven, "or come through the door here again until I come as Doon of Malvie." And he turned and went out.

Godfrey, left alone, felt sick for some time, as he sometimes did with mortification or shock; later he failed to eat any dinner. What had he said to Morven Doon to make the other hate him so? What had the last saying of all meant? Doon of Malvie . . . But that didn't matter, was absurd. The thing that troubled Godfrey was that he'd failed with Morven Doon, a personal failure, when he'd tried so hard—perhaps too hard—to succeed. How clumsy he was!

It was not possible for Godfrey and Morven to meet again; the affray with the customs-officer happened shortly afterwards. There had for some time been disquiet in informed circles, following a governmental enquiry from London as to the drop in tax for liquor over the area, the previous year. A consignment of boats, manned by such of the militia as could be spared, armed and supported by shore excisemen, patrolled the channel. It was due only to the almost universal support, in the area, for the brandy-runners and salt smugglers that none were yet taken. Contraband was hidden, in such unlikely places as loose window-sills and under roof-thatch and in holes dug in the moorland turf; beneath Malvie itself, there was a cave where the water rose high twice daily, and never a searching exciseman penetrated further, into the upper chamber beyond the lower. Morven Doon went there, however, knowing the tides from a boy, and Bart with him. Bart and Morven stowed the bales away where they knew where to find them, and took the boat out again when the tide was right and the night fallen; and they laughed as they sailed close between the two sets of cutter-lights and made out to open sea, and the Ayre of Man where a French vessel waited. The two of them could do all that was to be done, as a rule, between them; Aaron had charge of the shore-signals, and Abel the bestowal of goods and, also, collection of payment at a later date; he divided this afterwards fairly.

Meantime they took on board the stuff from the Frenchman, spent two nights on Man and sailed for home; by then, there was a gale blowing.

Morven remembered afterwards that he had let the boat slightly off course, buffeted by wind; a wall of rock reared ahead, and by the time he had veered the hull round he had misplaced Aaron's signal. It took a quarter-hour to right their course, and by then the smithy fire glowed clear orange above the rock, with no one about. Aaron would, if all had not been well, have shut the door to or let the fire out. As it was, Bart shouted against the wind and Morven let the small boat run hard in to shore . . . they heard the gravel grate before they became aware of dark, grappling figures in the water and, ahead, a lit flare from a lantern. Someone fired; and Bart, who was never slow to answer, pulled out his pistol.

Morven could never tell for certain what happened then. There were two more shots; both went wide, and he heard the swish of a cutlass and felt Bart's weight slump over against him, vomiting warmth; presently he lay quite still in the bottom of the boat. The men were everywhere nearby; Morven decided to abandon the boat and bales, and Bart, who was clearly dead. He shoved the vessel back with a sudden force that unbalanced the few men clinging to the prow; writhed back, dived over into the dark water and away, swimming for a while under the surface; great areas of submerged rock met him, and he knew them all like the lifelines on his hand. Within moments, guided by his knowledge of the shore, he was striking out for Malvie cave, where the tide rose high in the outer chamber.

Shouts died behind him as he swam on, in the end treading water to look back briefly; their lantern-light would not penetrate so far. He could see, dimly, a cluster of dark shapes like crows; the boat, the customs-men and Bart's body. He'd been sorry to abandon Bart, but knew the latter would have had no sentiment about doing so to himself, if dead; what was a corpse worth? The boat he grudged more, and the bales . . . the bales would damn him. They contained brandy, gin, tobacco and lace. He grinned in the darkness. Difficult to overlook that, even in the dark . . . he'd have to disappear for a while.

He scowled, realising for the first time that he had lost his freedom of movement by day. He'd go in the end, no doubt, to Man, and take Livia. They'd leave together as soon as he could find a boat, and meantime . . . meantime he must hole up in the cave, and find out what had happened to old Aaron, and wait to hear the court-verdict on himself. Uncle Hubert Melrose would do nothing, except save his own face; he wasn't even Morven's kin, but Annabel's.

Annabel. She'd be snug in her bed now at the Mains, perhaps having heard the shots. Perhaps all of them, all the women, were sitting up agog in their beds. Well, he'd see them again.

The cave was full and cool. Morven stepped up, dripping, on dry land at last at the inner end of the cave-mouth, then using his hands to grip knowledgeably, climbed up the further rock-wall. At the north-east corner, not seen from the open mouth by day, was a small aperture sealed tightly by a stone from within. Morven pushed the stone away, and it revealed a wider, ascending tunnel, leading off into further dark. He felt his wet tinder which still lay in his breeches-pocket, cursed, ascended, and vanished inside the cleft. Once inside he found the stone and replaced it as it had been. No one, entering the cave by now, would look for him.

The dark inner passage was long and rough, sloping always upwards; several times he almost stumbled. As time passed, however, he became aware of a lightening at the far end, almost like a shaft of daylight coming down; the moon had risen. He hastened towards the shaft and, as before, set feet and hands with familiar ease in the clefts and fissures as he climbed; it was about thirty feet in height, and if he took trouble to remember this fact and did not look down, he forgot Annabel, long ago forced by him into almost such case not far above. For this passage, as he well knew, led up to Malvie; to the oldest part of all, built centuries before the Caroline front and great outer rooms. This led to the old, central tower, built in the year of Flodden, perhaps on the foundations of an older house still, a house where men had no doubt lain in wait to strike for the Bruce or, before that, against the Dane. What the original purpose of the passage had been God knew, Morven thought, for the days of excessive dues were recent enough. No doubt it had been used for arms-carrying.

He hoisted himself to the top at last, and sat for a moment with legs swinging over the dark void. He was now inside Malvie itself; a trap-door lay above. Morven thrust, and presently the hinge, not used lately, gave protestingly and he came up and out, replacing the door behind him. The room he stood in was empty, no more than a cellar now; to one side curved ancient stone stairs against the tower-wall.

He climbed these, seeing the light of the moon strike, at each narrow window, his sodden sleeve. He had had time to remember that he was chilled, now the exertion of the climb had worn off. He had no food except—he laughed a little, remembering, and fingered a comforting hardness in his pocket, the one which didn't hold the tinder. The brandy-bottle had stayed with him all through the swim; it was good French stuff. He sat down there and then and undid the cork, and swilled deeply. How many days could one live on brandy, and no more? But it had warmed Morven; he felt better already.

The tower led out by a series of half-stairs and corridors to the long attics, running the length of the newer house. Morven moved stealthily, to avoid wakening the Englishman's servants who slept up here. When he had reached the attic proper he made his way to the place he had been in on that day when for the second time he saw Livia, dusting down-stairs. His uncle and aunt's portrait was no longer there. Evidently Mrs. Bowes had been in the attics. Morven yawned, found a place where he could wrap his cold body in a dry old curtain, left among the dust for whatever purpose no one knew, except oblivion. He stripped off his clothes and spread them out to dry; and, naked except for the wrapping, lay down behind where the great sloping canvas had once stood, to sleep. They wouldn't look for him here; not in the re-spectable stronghold, the Englishman's house of Malvie.

"But it's mine," Morven thought before he slept, "it's mine." No purchase-money and no deed could take it from him. He slept, and in his ears drummed the blood of his ancestors. Doon of Malvie, Doon of Malvie, and the spiders scurrying near him in the layers of the wall . . .

VI

He woke: it was broad daylight, and he had no idea of the time. He reached out a hand to his still damp clothes where they lay; then rose, shed his wrapping, stretched, and walked naked to the window. At the back of his mind was faint amusement at the prospect of a maidservant, or one of Mrs. Bowes's daughters, perhaps, coming up here and discovering him thus, screaming and falling in a faint; it would at least give him the advantage of surprise and a few minutes' get-away

Still smiling with his own amusement, he watched the lawn below; they were beginning to level the rough ground and to plant shrubs. Morven's smile vanished, and a cruel light showed in the oblique eyes; any change made to Malvie must come from himself. He watched, resentfully, while gardeners worked on the space far below, studying their faces and knowing they were new men, strangers no doubt from the south. After a while the cold struck his skin and he wandered about the attics looking for dry clothing; there should be, somewhere, an old chest containing things of uncle Philip's. He found it, and rummaged through the contents, selecting in the end a worn satin coat, with a slot for a sword-belt; the braid at cuffs and edge was tarnished and frayed, and there were buttons missing. He found other garments, put them on and returned for his own shoes, which were still damp and stiff from the sea-water. Sometime, when he could get to a town with some of the money hidden by himself and Bart over the months, he'd buy new clothes. It hadn't been poverty—he grimaced, for the thing was relative—but lack of leisure which had left him shabby. Now he might dress like a lord, if he would, and could escape the eye of the revenue-officer.

He strolled in the old-fashioned clothes he had found to the stairhead, and looking down saw a maidservant go past with a coal-scoop ready filled; it must still be early morning. Perhaps, if he could contrive to get to the Mains and way-lay Livia, she'd get him food and they could arrange where to meet later. He knew, early each day, she had tasks which took her out to the wood-stack or the coals, or to fetch water from the house pump. He'd go down now, skirting the main lane so nobody might see him. Arrogantly he left his drying clothes where they were. He could hide out well enough at Malvie until the hue and cry had died down.

Livia changed colour when she saw him; they had met at the place where she came daily to draw water. "Morven Doon, you're mad," she said. "Do you know they were at the Mains looking for you, the same night it happened? 'You're his aunt,' they told Mrs. Retford. She gave the officer a flea in his ear, I can tell you."

She seized him by the sleeve, and drew him out of sight. "Whose old gear are you in now?" she said, laughing and crying. "Ah, Morven, Morven——"

But he had seized her and was assuaging his hunger by kisses, and more. Presently he held her away, leaving her gasping. "Will you come tonight, to the usual place?" he said. "I'll be waiting."

"It isn't safe—not now, Morven!"

"Safe or not, I'll be there! we can talk after." Swiftly, in a low voice, he ascertained news about old Aaron Judd; he'd been set free, Livia told him, after the signalling-time should be over; they'd held him till then, the revenue-men, then when they found the boat inshore they let him go free. "He said he knew nothing," Livia added. "The heart was broken in him, but he said he knew nothing. He said he didn't know how Bart could ha' died."

"You knew about Bart?" he asked her, and she nodded.

"Betts told me; he saw them carry him up. Lord, that was a bad night's work! Whatever will Aaron do now, without that boy? Bart was a fine smith, they say, when he'd take time off to do it. Why can't men mind their right business?"

Morven pinched her hip, and said he'd mind his when she brought it to him tonight. "Get me a bite to eat, love," he begged. "I've lived on brandy since yesterday."

She looked round, went away quickly, and presently returned with a loaf and meat pasty, which she thrust into his hand. "Better not wait about to eat it," she said. "The old woman's up. If she thinks I've eaten all of this for my breakfast, she'll take it off my wages." She looked at him lingeringly with her grey eyes. "Morven——"

"Yes, my love?" He was biting with sharp teeth into the pasty; it tasted good. "Bring a drink of milk tonight when you come, if you can," he told her. She nodded, tears in her eyes.

"If I can," she said. "Oh, Morven, take care! If I come and don't find you, how will I know where you are. How can I reach you, if——" She bit her lip on it; word would mean his arrest, and being marched away by the militia and perhaps hanged, and her belly was getting to show beneath the apron no matter how she covered up, and one day soon——

He kissed her. "I'll be at our place, never fear," he said. He would not tell even Livia of his hiding-place in Malvie. That was private, for himself only, a thing to be assessed in his own soul. Besides, somehow at sight of the tame shrubs planted by that Englishman he'd had a notion, imperfect yet,

98

as to how he could get back Malvie. Annabel, and the pear tree at her window, and Livia to take word, and then the wedding, and—

But Livia, he knew, would take some persuading about that. Tonight should be for her only. He waited, in due course, among the wild cherry trees, and she came, and brought the milk, and he drank it. Then he lay down with her and they made love as they had never made love before; the very earth and trees seemed to tremble with it, and Livia, transported, forgot everything, forgot the coming child and that Morven was a wanted man, and what might become of her if they took him. She only knew that she was in his arms, and in his arms was all she need ever know of heaven; after they were both dead, if there was nothing more for her, she thought, they'd had that.

The tears were wet on her cheeks and he kissed them. "What is it, love?" he whispered. Then he talked to her again of Man, where they would live, he said; only a little while, and then he'd come, when there was a boat again, and take her away, and they'd live in a cottage on the rough north shore, as he'd said, and she could have her baby.

"There's a thing I want you to do for me before that, my darling," he said, fondling her breasts which were swollen a little; "I won't tell you now; tomorrow, perhaps, tomorrow."

Livia sighed and trembled with ecstasy under his hands. She didn't ask more about the other thing she would have to do for him. There would always be some thing or another to do, for Morven, and she'd do it. She'd do anything. Tomorrow he'd perhaps tell her what it was.

She left him when the dew had already risen, and he vanished again along the path towards Malvie.

Annabel turned her reddened eyelids into the pillow and sobbed quietly, as she'd done each night this week. The past few days had been the worst in her whole life; worse even than when Papa had died.

First, and worst, had been the matter of Morven, hearing the shots and knowing some danger had befallen him, and that there was nothing she could do. She hadn't, of course, seen Bart's body carried back to the smithy cottage, but she'd glimpsed Aaron Judd, a changed, aged, trembling old man, helped in by Betts again today for a meal and a drink of spiced ale before he went back to his lonely dwelling now the funeral was over. Bart's funeral . . . it might have been Morven's. Nobody knew where Morven was.

An excise-officer had come to ask all of them questions; he had been a fussed little man with a cutlass and a face like an angry plum. He'd questioned them all, herself and aunt Retford and Livia Mary and the Betts couple and Aaron. Aaron, who was the only one who could possibly know anything, had known nothing, nothing. He'd kept silence even among them all in the kitchen, Betts had said. "He'll not do a day's shoeing again," Betts had added. "They'll need to get their horses shod from now on beyond Maddon." But Aaron, nevertheless, had refused to go and stay with his son Abel, over at the Fleece; it had been the sea he'd always lived for, the sea and young Bart. If he had his way, he'd die by the sea where Bart had died.

Annabel had heard it all, and listened to hardly any of it. Where was Morven? The awareness of his danger beat against her mind like high springtide waves; nothing else was real. All that might have partly accounted for her cruelty, only yesterday, to Godfrey.

For Godfrey had, at last, asked her to marry him. It had happened on the shore road where they had gone as so often together to collect and catalogue shells and weeds. Usually she listened and was interested, but yesterday—

She hadn't wanted to go, in the first place; she'd wanted to wait at home for news of Morven. But aunt Retford had made her put on her habit, and go up to Malvie as usual dressed ready to ride. So she'd obeyed, and listlessly led the pony, and only half attended to what Godfrey was saying; and then, realising that his sad pop-eyes had something at the back of them which was not any longer about weeds and shells, she had said, gently as always,

"I beg your pardon, Godfrey; I was not attending. There has been some trouble, as you know."

"That was why I asked you to marry me today," said Godfrey, flushing beneath his straw hat. He always wore such a wide Italian hat, summer or winter, if there was sun; it shaded his weak eyes. Poor Godfrey. It looked eccentric; but, of course, he couldn't look otherwise. The realisation of what he'd been saying was borne in on Annabel suddenly, making her blush deepest rose. "Oh, no," she said, and then, although she had of course known this was coming, that aunt Retford had meant it to happen from the beginning, "Oh no, no, no, no! I—I cannot, I cannot!"

She had fallen silent then, miserably tongue-tied; she hated hurting anyone. Godfrey's expression had not altered except that, she thought, he looked on her now with great kindness, sadness, understanding; all three; it all made her cry, and she'd gone on crying afterwards at home, when aunt Retford had scolded her to a degree she wouldn't have believed possible, even for that resolute lady.

"Refused him? Refused so rich an offer; and to live at the great house?"

And then, as if Annabel were not already bowed down with mortification and shame—she liked poor Godfrey, she really did, and found his talk very interesting, only . . . and then, her aunt went on to rail at her, saying the sum that had come out of her own pocket for rearing Annabel suitably could only be repaid by a rich marriage, and Malvie . . .

A spark of spirit had shown then in Annabel, and she replied with great daring, "Please, aunt, repay yourself for my upbringing with some of the purchase-money from the house. It's mine, you said, and—and I shan't need it for dowry, or a season." The thought of going far away, remote from any news or sight of Morven at all, was hateful to her; but Mrs. Retford's diminutive form rose in a towering rage and Annabel thought she was about to box her ears, as though she were a child again. Her resistance collapsed and she gave way to tears. "I cannot marry Godfrey, please, aunt, not that, I could not, I could not!"

Mrs. Retford, being a woman of great determination, forbore to press her niece on the matter at present; but she made it clear to Annabel later that she and Mrs. Bowes, who as was known greatly hoped for the marriage for her son, had discussed the proposal Godfrey should make and assured one another that, in a little while, with the natural timidity of a young girl perhaps discounted with accustoming, it would be repeated, and in the end accepted. "After all, my dear Annabel, he is a very eligible bachelor," murmured Mrs. Retford. "Few come to these parts, in any case, and I do not know that I am in health to take you to the capital for a season, to find another husband. I have done a great deal for my brother's child, but gratitude, my dear, is expected, a little, in the event." Mrs. Retford sighed; then her face hardened. "If Godfrey should speak again, my love, as no doubt he will, then pray reconsider, and give him a more courteous answer. I should be loth to be spoken of as a harsh guardian, but I must consider your own best interests as well as mine." And she smiled; Annabel was reminded of a mask over a dead face, hiding all but the eyes.

The memory of how she must have hurt Godfrey stayed on with her, and added to her misery; but the prospect of accepting him as a husband made her tremble. One couldn't dislike or do other than pity poor Godfrey, but the thought of his touching one! She flushed deeply, alone in the dark. The trouble that had come over her mind lately had found no assuaging; she still hadn't found anyone with whom to discuss it, or to ask. Annabel knew her upbringing had been so carefully supervised that there were matters she had never been permitted to see or know; there had been a maidservant at Maddon once, she knew, who they said had been in the hay with the stableman, and had had a baby. She hadn't been allowed to hear any more. What had they done together in the hay, the maid and stableman? What was marriage, and how were babies made? Her own mind, like her body, was virgin; she was beginning to find it a little ridiculous, as though she ought, even as an unmarried girl, to know more than she did.

Something caused her thoughts to switch to the maid, Livia or Mary. She hadn't been as friendly of late, even rather sullen, coming in with the chocolate; yesterday she hadn't said a word, and Annabel noticed her eyes were swollen, as though she'd been crying. Perhaps she'd been in love with poor Bart Judd, whose funeral was so lately over.

For Annabel was blind as regarded Morven, as regarded even the fact that Livia might have met Morven at all. Like many women, the fact that she loved a man sealed him off in her mind from the access of any other love, as though he were in some way marked as hers, inviolate.

Morven. Morven. Where was he now, her cousin who should by now have been her bridegroom, if Papa had only lived? Had Morven a bed to sleep in? Had he enough food, enough money?

The wind had risen. Later there came the rain, swelling to storm and hurling itself, at last, against the roof and walls. The patter of the great drops against the glass of her casement was like gravel, thrown up from below . . . strange that raindrops seemed to be falling upwards . . .

It *was* gravel. It wasn't rain.

Annabel threw back the bed-covers. She flung back her hair and ran to the window barefoot, as she was, in her shift. She flung open the casement with fingers that trembled, fingers that were clumsy and let in the hurricane, tearing at her linen and hair; the cold rain soaked and chilled her body through the shift. But she wasn't chilled in her heart; a great warm rush of blood came, making it pound, making her live again. Morven was waiting below the pear tree, whose branches reached up like arms to embrace the sky and storm. Seeing her, he prepared to climb it: and she watched him come.

It was hoped that the weather, which had proved itself stormy of late, would have considered the matter of Sir Hubert's wedding to Miss Cecily Bowes, but it did not; on the day, as for the past week, high wind drove the rain in sheets about the walls of Malvie, flattening the new trees Godfrey had had planted against their stakes, and breaking off the branch of a great old elm; this fact was suppressed, as it had injured no one and it was thought the bride might fancy that such a happening meant ill-luck on her wedding day. Otherwise she was happy. The guests began to arrive at about four o'clock, and the ceremony was to take place in the evening. It had been decided to hold it in the larger with-drawing-room instead of going down to church, because of the invalid state of the bride's brother, who would give her away. Afterwards there would be supper and dancing in the great hall, and on the morrow the bridal couple would depart for Maddon.

The bridegroom arrived with the minister and friends, and everything went as expected, with the bride's party decorously making its way at last between the standing rows of guests, along the first-floor corridor, which had been already lit with many sconces and hung this morning with flowers, and into the drawing-room. The short journey across the silken carpet Godfrey's papa had bought afforded many a clear view of the bride, with her golden hair and pink cheeks, the latter enhanced by the warmth from the candles and the crowd. Wagers were laid that in a year, there would be a son born with the same golden hair, to resemble poor Peter Melrose; it was well known that Sir Hubert had chosen a fair-haired lady for this very reason. Little Paul, the remaining Melrose son, accompanied the bride-party to bow it through doors; he was just eleven, and his suit was of pale yellow satin, to echo that of the attendants.

It was these, or one of them, who attracted far more attention and wagers than the bride. Annabel Doon had never been seen in greater beauty. She seemed to eclipse both Miss Cecily and her sister, Miss Clairette, who also carried the train; both girls were in the buttercup-yellow creations of the Dowager's modiste, which hung gracefully, rustled richly, and enhanced the complexions of the two young ladies with their trimming of soft dark fur. But it was not a matter of attire which beautified Miss Annabel; she seemed to glow from within. Whispers were passed, and nudges made, about the hardship to poor Godfrey Devenham it must be, seeing her approach, but not yet as his own bride. However time would remedy that. Mrs. Retford, who was of course among the throng, and Mrs. Bowes had let it be discreetly circulated that the betrothal-announcement had been delayed a little, on account of Godfrey's health. Everyone wished them very happy, or would do shortly. Then they turned to witness the ceremony, which took place among more flowers, at the head of the drawing-room.

Annabel did not hear the exchanged vows between Sir Hubert and his bride. Her mind was in retrospect; in a vague, stimulated happiness that was purely physical. She knew now, none better, what married people did . . .

And she was married. She was married to Morven. He'd said so, adding in the low voice they had both used, so that aunt Retford through the wall shouldn't hear, that in Scotland a handfast-ceremony was law, and all one said was "I take thee . . ." and "I take thee."

"I take thee, Cecily, to be my wedded wife."

I take thee, Morven, to be my husband . . .

Where was he now? Where did he hide, by day, after dawn had come to reveal him catlike climbing down the tree beyond her window, as he'd climbed up? And tomorrow, for it wouldn't be tonight, he would come again.

Delight recaptured Annabel. It had hurt, of course, at first; Morven had had to put his mouth over hers, to prevent her foolish outcry, then, once it was over, there was such bliss as no one had ever known; she still couldn't describe it in words. And it would happen often. It would happen again tomorrow night, when he came up. She was his wife, and—and when he could make arrangements, he'd take her away with him, once she was of age. It would have to be somewhere abroad. They could live on the Malvie money.

Uncle Hubert and Cecily were married now, till death did them part. It was queer and unlikely to think of their being as happy, in the same way, as Morven and herself had been, would be again. Would be again! It was possible to smile at poor Godfrey, now, as she turned after the bride, and they made ready to go out of the room and then back again among the guests for polite smalltalk and cake and wine. She wouldn't hear or taste any of it, although it was pleasant to receive so many compliments on her appearance; radiant, one old gentleman said she looked. The radiance was all, she knew, for Morven. She wished he could see her in her grand yellow dress, with her hair in side-curls in the new fashion.

He did see her. She happened afterwards to look up above the long trestle tables, packed with delicacies on silver and crystal, and the rows of seated guests. A fiddler had struck up and the sad, nostalgic sound—why was fiddle-music always sad even when he played a merry tune?—vied with the howling of the wind outside; every now and again the massed candles would gutter, like an obedient flock of yellow-skirted ladies curtsying.

They'd placed her, of course, beside Godfrey. She'd felt a slight, shameful irritation rise as they led her to her place; certainly she was a bridal-attendant, certainly everyone who had been in the bride-party sat together, Uncle Hubert, the bride, Clairette, Godfrey, herself and little Paul. But she was so placed that it looked, to all these seated rows of curious guests it must surely look, as if she and Godfrey were—well, almost betrothed; and it was no help that he couldn't take his eyes off her. She tried to be civil, however; talked to him gently, because she knew he must have a headache, with the heat and crowd and bright lights. "You like the flowers?" she said once. "Clairette chose them, and told us what to do, and we all helped to make the swags." Blooms had been picked from the new garden here, and from Uncle Hubert's place at Maddon, and sent over. It hadn't been difficult to make a show with the splendid, well-nourished blossoms with their waxy leaves. But, she thought, she must earn some praise for Clairette. The girl was sulking, as she often did, because nobody had praised *her* grown or said *she* looked radiant, because she didn't; she had, Annabel guessed, no reason. Annabel smiled to herself.

The fiddler passed by, his strings wailing; and it was then she looked up and saw Morven.

She couldn't have said what made her do it. She hadn't even, for that particular moment, been thinking of him; only how hot it was growing in the hall, and how they'd most of them eaten too much, so that it would be not everyone's pleasure if the trestles were shortly cleared away, as they would be, for them all to dance. She herself didn't want to dance with anyone; it would, in a way, be pleasanter to stay here where she was, seated quietly by Godfrey. But that would no doubt lead to more talk.

She looked up towards the roof, where the old hammered beams were almost invisible in the mounting haze of heat from the candles. The wind sounded again beyond; and through the sound of the wind and the fiddle-music, up there in the hazy darkness, where there was the old minstrel-loft, she raised her eyes and saw, for an instant only, Morven's face; pale like the new moon, staring down on them all, and then it vanished. He'd seen that she saw him. A great rush of emotion, relief or terror, flooded Annabel, and she saw the servants come in to the hall and begin to clear. It was the right moment to go; she knew what to do.

"Excuse me, I beg," she said to Godfrey, as though he were a stranger; and leaving the hall among the stir of scraping benches and couples pulling one another out to the centre of the floor ready for the first dance after the bride and groom, she fled. Someone called after her, asking for a dance from the bride-attendant; some man who'd drunk too much wine. Annabel picked up her yellow skirts, and ran out alone into the darkness; through the waiting silent nether house, to find the kitchen-stairs; she passed the bridal-chamber, its bed waiting ready all decked with flowers. She ran on; in the far distance the fiddles had started up; they would be dancing.

The stairs were dark, unlit in this forgotten part of the house. But she knew her way; stumbling, groping over the landings and the places they'd once known together, she and Morven, below the ghostly attic where he wouldn't let her go. What was he doing here? Was Malvie attic the place where he was hidden? She should always have known, of course, that he'd hide somewhere in Malvie.

An arm shot out of the darkness at her, nearby the gallery; by that time the fiddles sounded again loudly below. He'd placed a hand over her mouth; no need, she wouldn't have screamed. She wrested free and looked up at what she could see of his face in the half-dark; the eyes shone strangely. For the moment, as had often happened in her life, she was frightened of Morven; frightened of what he might mean, what he wanted, what he wanted now . . . it wasn't the same, in any way, as it had been between them gently in her own quiet room, down at the Mains. He was like a different person; a sudden, demanding, bitter stranger. She sobbed, as he handled and disarranged her; this wasn't, with its swift, contemptuous bundling up of skirts, Morven, her husband, her lover.

But he took her; there, in the full sound of the fiddles, almost within sight of the dancing lines of guests, of the sad gaze of Godfrey. Far below, they went on dancing; and when he'd done with Annabel, he thrust her away, laughing. She could see his teeth. She was gasping, sobbing, dishevelled, shamed; why had he taken her brutally like that? Hadn't he known she had had to come because they were man and wife, Morven and Annabel, not—not a maid and stableman in the hay? But it was over. She adjusted the London-made clothes carefully. Perhaps her skirts had got grubby on the stairs; cobwebs, dust. Why think of that? She gazed up at Morven, wordlessly. He took her by the shoulders again, gripping hard.

"Now go down and sit by him, while the others divert themselves. Don't stand up to dance. If anyone asks you, decline. You're to sit by him till the end, you hear me?"

"Morven—" That raping of her, that rough cruel usage as though she were a servant, a chattel, and now—

He smiled, seeing her fright and shame. "Is it too hard to obey me?" he asked her. He put a finger under her chin, raised it up and kissed her. Even the kiss was impersonal, as if one of the guests downstairs had given it; as if two strangers kissed. She began to shiver. "Go down," said Morven again, "into the warmth."

He patted her, a small kindly derisive gesture of farewell. "Don't look for me again here," he said. "You understand me? If I'm taken, we won't ever meet again."

"Ah, Morven—" She was trying to form words which would make it clear to him that she'd never, never tell; that nothing she might say or do would give away the fact that she'd seen him tonight, that they'd—

"Then go down. Sit by him. Isn't that what I'm asking you to do?" He smiled, winningly in the way he could do always. "Do this for me, and tomorrow night, if I can, I'll come to you at Mains."

"You promise?" She was like a child; the prospect of his coming to her, of its again being as it should always be between them, not—not like tonight, was enough for her meantime; afterwards, it didn't seem clear what would happen.

"Kiss me, Morven. Please kiss me again, and then I'll go." And he kissed her; it was a pleasant, friendly enough kiss, now he'd got her to agree to what he wanted. He waited in the shadows while she regained the hall; then watched the obedient, yellow-clad little figure thread its way to where Godfrey Devenham still sat, and take its place by his side.

Morven smiled to himself; the sweetness of revenge had been his in full measure tonight, taking his will of Godfrey's girl in, almost, full view of that poor incapable creature, of them all, all the sycophants who'd come to gape and dine now money, and gilding, and flowers, and the prospect of social gain, had come to Malvie. But he'd found his way already under the petticoats of the chief player, the feminine lead. He could, in time, find his way to bed, board and hall again at Malvie. It wouldn't, judging from that sorry hulk downstairs be long, perhaps no more than a year or two; in the meantime, Man, and, always, Livia, his own dear woman. He'd never desert Livia or her child. That hand-fasting to Annabel had meant nothing without witnesses, but the little goose wouldn't know that.

He left the throbbing of the fiddles shortly and went to his own place, and slept more soundly than the bridal-couple till morning.

Livia had to cross a part of the vegetable-plot at Mains to carry the house-ashes to the heap; some days this couldn't be done till the afternoon. As she picked her way across between the rows of young growing kale and late beans she glanced, almost shyly, over to the yew-arbour; Miss Annabel was in there, had been there now for an hour, ever since she left her aunt's room. It's happened once or twice that way, lately. The figure in the arbour did not respond or smile and she had, Livia saw, her flushed cheek averted, so that she must be staring at the close dark wall of yew. God knew what that'd tell her. There was nothing to do but get on with one's work, and—and think of Morven.

She emptied the ashes and saw, as if with half her eye, the smoke-like drift eddying and settling in fine dust, some of it on her skirts; she shook them fastidiously. Life was queer, if you thought of it; queerer the harder you thought, and neither she nor Miss Annabel was a lightskirt, if one had to think of skirts at all . . . yet both of them, most like by now, in the same way, and to the same man, and yet *she* hadn't the strength to tell him what was the truth, that he should leave the poor little devil alone, she'd enough to put up with; her aunt, and that pop-eyed poor creature at Malvie who wasn't a man at all, wanting to marry her. That was, of course, what all the trouble was about; Livia had heard Miss Annabel before now, sobbing and crying out in her aunt's study, not willing any more to go to the shore with Mr. Godfrey, go up to Malvie and the like. There'd been more trouble, lately, because the old woman said she'd made a show of herself last month at that wedding-feast, sitting beside poor young Godfrey Devenham all night, and why, if she didn't intend to accept his offer and make fools of them all . . . and so on.

Livia picked up her pail grimly. Mrs. Retford had spoiled one thing, she thought; Miss Annabel wouldn't be sitting a pony for a while, after the way she'd whipped her again today. She'd heard it herself, and the sounds that came; wicked it was; some folk could bear more than others.

She made her way back out of the garden quietly, not making any further greeting to Miss Annabel. In a way, each knew there was something the matter with the other; they weren't, even in the ordinary way, at ease; it wasn't as if she herself had even known too much, until one morning, a while ago now, she'd found a coat button of Morven's in Miss Annabel's room. That had decided it, but she'd had her own notions, before then, of what was going on. That first morning, it must have been, she'd seen fit to take away the sheets, although it wasn't the day for laundry.

She wasn't asked to think, that was it; servants didn't, except to themselves; even Morven, when she'd said nothing and handed him the button, with an offer to sew it on, hadn't told her much. "I said to you I had a plan," he reminded her. He'd let her repair the button, in the manner he had as though he were a king, and she an attendant putting the jewels back in his crown; then he'd turned away to the window; yes, he'd been with her in her own room by then, having come up, straight up, from Miss Annabel, whom he'd left sleeping that time, he said. She herself had been aghast at sight of Morven; supposing the old woman saw him, mooning through the early morning passages and up the stairs?

"I needed you," he'd told her on arrival, and fallen on her although it was by then dawn. But later, staring beyond the window at the sunrise, as though he'd forgotten her again and was once more with that other,

"She shall bear me a son. He will be born at Malvie. Later, he will inherit."

"Oh, you're mad, you're mad," she had cried, flinging him back his mended coat. With her own belly grown so big someone was bound to notice it soon, couldn't they be off, to Man or wherever he'd said he was taking her?

But Miss Annabel still would not conceive.

It was over a year since Annabel had sat with her embroidery in the yew-arbour. That thought drifted through her mind now, among others, staring at the tiny, close dark needles of the yew. The yew had been here for two hundred years. It had outlasted that prim, unaware little creature who'd once sat here, who had been clear of bewilderment in body and mind, not as now, a burning battlefield of assaulted flesh and, within, a medley of mixed sensations, some of which still came strongly.

She no longer knew herself. Even the recollection of some of the things that had happened, that she herself had caused to happen, made her blush now hotly, here in the privacy of the dark arbour, remembering. Last time her aunt had whipped her—it had happened fairly often lately—it had been in the evening; she'd lain in bed afterwards sobbing, and Morven had come; climbing up the tree, vaulting with one leg over the sill into the room, into her bed, without a word, as so often . . . and she'd given herself to him like a maenad. She wouldn't have thought any woman, any gently bred correct young woman, could behave so, and he'd laughed. It hadn't seemed to surprise him, he hadn't disliked it, he'd . . . he'd taken advantage of it, instead, as though—as though she were an unprincipled woman, a harlot; harlots were spoken of in the Bible. And now her harlot's flesh, longing again, burned for Morven in the way her seat had lately burned under aunt Retford's birch. Why did one never know one's body until some dire thing befell it? What else was there still to know?

Annabel's tongue, tentative, rose-pink and pointed, came out like a little cat's, and wet her lips; her mind glowed with the recollection of Morven. It wasn't clear to her how she'd lived before. Tonight, if he could come again . . .

They didn't often talk together. It was too dangerous, because of aunt Retford so near. Annabel eased her bruised body on the wooden bench and ceased to wonder when Morven would take her away or where they would go. The movement of her limbs had released new, unfamiliar sensations in all of her flesh; the prickling tenderness of her nipples against the tight bodice, the way they'd grown just lately; the responsive quality, as though she lacked a skin, of all her body; so that even the rubbing of a leaf against her face gave her pleasure and strange, intimate pain. She was a different person; and, accordingly, angry at the invasion of such privacy by aunt Retford and her birch. If she would marry Godfrey, aunt Retford kept saying; if she would agree to marry Godfrey Devenham, it should stop.

She'd almost forgotten Godfrey. He wasn't a person any more. She could remember him at the end of a long, long tunnel, something of the shape and darkness of an elongated yew-arbour; she was sorry for Godfrey, that was all. But Morven, Morven was real . . .

She moved again, and eased her hurts a little. The sun shone now and bees buzzed. She was able to spare a thought for Cecily at Maddon, and how they said, Mrs. Betts had told her, that she had already started a baby. Perhaps *she* . . . but what did she know about it? Afterwards, when they were abroad, there would be more time to think.

She'd seen Livia Mary going across with the ashes to the heap, and saw her come back again with her bucket empty. She smiled this time, but Livia pretended not to see her. She'd been queerer than ever lately, not so much sullen as showing a gruff kindness, perhaps to make up for aunt Retford. If only there could soon be an end to that! Morven didn't perhaps know she was being whipped so often.

A quarter-hour later, Livia came to her down the path; she was carrying Annabel's cloak and bonnet.

"Your aunt says we're to go today to the almshouse, to take quince jelly." She spoke tonelessly, her eyes on the ground.

Annabel felt sudden weariness and pain overcome her. She couldn't walk so far today; aunt Retford should know . . . then she realised that, of course, it was part of the punishment; aunt Retford was saying, without words, that as she wouldn't go to Godfrey on the pony she could trudge on foot, four miles it was to old Ellen, with the jelly.

Ellen was an old servant, who had somehow stayed with Mrs. Retford since the days of the latter's marriage till she retired; she was one of the few now living who remembered Neil, briefly the master. It might have been hoped that a sum of money would be available to Ellen for her old age after having served so faithfully; perhaps this was the reason for sending a pot of quince jelly once a year. The almshouses —they had been founded at about the time of Emmett's— were inhabited by five or six old women; they were beyond the village on the road that ran over the moor.

Annabel put on her cloak and bonnet listlessly; there was no way of evading the journey. Perhaps, if Livia had been more friendly, she'd have asked her if she could sit down for a while, somewhere in the heather, and let the maid walk on by herself with the quince-pot. It was on Livia's arm now in a flat basket covered by a cloth. It had been made last autumn.

"Shall I carry the quince, Miss Annabel?"

She started; had the other known, somehow, what she was thinking, that she couldn't bear the trouble and weight even of that today? A trifle of haughtiness showed itself in Annabel; she made herself survey Livia Mary, not giving way to her own confusion. One didn't grow confused before a servant. She said, coldly, after a moment. "If you will carry it carefully," and, walking before Livia to the garden-gate, set out, followed by the maid. Neither looked forward to the long walk in one another's company; the sun shone hotly down.

Annabel achieved her wish without the necessity of saying a single word to Livia; halfway along the moor paths, she began to droop. The heather, with its dark twining stems and little hard bells of unopened flowers, seemed invitingly near; she could see a blue butterfly in it, very small, early, the colour of harebells.

Livia watched, the sullen gleam that had been in her grey eyes changing, swiftly, to pity. If she had hands on Morven now, the devil. "It's all of two miles yet to the almshouses, Miss Annabel," she said gently. "Would you care to rest, and I'll go on? We needn't say anything."

So Annabel sank down thankfully among the heather, and watched the maid stride off. What a strange girl Livia Mary was! But not unkind.

Livia reached the almshouse, presented Ellen with her year's quince, having found her seated among a row of equally patient, cloaked and capped old women waiting for death; and shortly shook the dust and the smell of institutions off herself again and turned back towards the moor. Her own old age wouldn't be spent in a place like that, she swore; better die in a ditch than eat charity. And that, my girl, she told herself grimly, is where you'll maybe find yourself soon enough, if anything happens to Morven before we can get away. With Miss Annabel perhaps breeding they'd be able to go sooner from what he'd said . . . but must she sacrifice Miss Annabel? What was to befall *her*?

As if to remind her of danger, the gauger, the customs-officer who'd come to Mains that time Bart was killed, clattered past. He rode a weary horse and his cutlass clanked as he rode; there weren't enough gaugers to go round, Betts had already told her. The officer passed her the time of day, and she answered civilly; nothing more was said between them about Morven. Morven was only one more missing man, wanted for handling contraband and being among trouble. Depending on the judge it could mean Botany Bay for Morven, or else hanging. How did he think he'd ever win free, to be lord of Malvie? For she knew now that was his dream.

"She shall bear me a son. He will be born at Malvie, and inherit."

It could have been the angel Gabriel himself talking, Livia thought irreverently. He'd find, maybe, after all that he was mortal flesh, the same Morven Doon. When would he send word to her again to come to the place by the trees, or even, as he'd done lately sometimes, visit her on the way back from Annabel's room? A queer coil, it was . . . and she herself queerer still to countenance it. But if Morven Doon came to her now, she knew, she'd receive him gladly, unable to resist any more than at other times. She'd never be able to resist Morven.

A dray moved patiently towards her in the near distance; it was Abel Judd, looking exactly as he'd done that other day, making this same journey. He drew up beside her and offered her a place in the cart. "I'm for the cottage," he said. "Care to come?" Livia saw his dark, shy glance assess her and felt, as one sometimes did with people, that Abel knew or, at least, suspected her state; lucky old mother Retford hadn't. She shook her head over the proffered lift; Miss Annabel was still back up there by herself on the moor; they'd better walk back together, in case there were questions. "How's your father managing for himself?" she asked Abel.

He shook his head. "He shouldn't be there alone," he told her, adding, as she knew already, that he'd asked old Aaron many times to come to him at the Fleece, to make his home. "But he maybe won't feel it's a home, without any woman," he blurted out, his eyes resting on Livia. She heard him with amusement; Lord, was this another of them? He needn't look at *her*. She made it manifest to him, in the wordless courtesy which can be used, at such times, by all women; there are ways of leaving it clear when a man can hope, and when he can't. Abel showed neither pique nor dismay at her manner.

"You can always come to me, you know," he said gently, as though they had said more than they had. "Remember that if aught goes wrong, Livia; any time, you can always come to me."

She watched the dray draw off with its humped barrels, like monstrous prehistoric shapes, rocking in the back of the cart, and Abel's hat showing in front, pulled down over his eyes and to cover the bald patch on his scalp. He'd called her Livia, she noticed; everyone did except Mrs. Retford. It was as if they knew, from the start, that she couldn't be Mary.

The two young women returned to the Mains dower house without mishap or further adventures; Annabel was rested after her sojourn in the heather and no one had passed her by on the moor road. Aunt Retford cross-questioned her about the appearance, welfare and thanks of old Ellen; she answered routinely, only half aware of deceit, glad Livia had already briefed her with replies. Going upstairs afterwards to take off her outdoor clothes she was conscious of a growing intimacy with, almost dependence on, Livia. It should be the other way round, and the maid should depend on the mistress. But it didn't matter; she was too tired. Would Morven come tonight?

VII

It was some nights later. Morven was lying with his cousin. The light from a risen, waning moon streamed across the bed; having shown the branches of the tree outside almost as bright as day, they then outlined, with more precision, Morven's breeches, cast arrogantly over a chair. He caught sight of these and thought how, erroneously, he'd grown familiar enough, with repetition, to think himself safe in coming here, when in fact it was as dangerous as it had ever been. If that old woman through the wall heard sounds, she'd come in at once; and within the hour the clamour would reach the ears of authority, whether he'd got away meantime with or without his breeches. He smiled. By the dark of the moon, there'd be less danger; but by then, in any case, if all went as it should, he'd be well across to the Ayre of Man with Livia, leaving his plan for Malvie to fulfill itself in natural course. This might, he thought, be his last night here; he'd have to tell Annabel what she must now do, before he left, in case he didn't see her again for some time. The prospect aroused some unwillingness in Morven; he could see she'd take it badly, however he put it to her.

114

She stirred and sighed, and he let his mind dwell briefly on her, sometimes fingering the bright hair which lay scattered over the pillow. A part of him, he knew, could still feel pity, and the thought of Annabel penned up, perhaps for years, with that grotesque at Malvie roused it in him now. He himself wouldn't abandon her, of course, or the son she should bear him. In fact—his satisfaction deepened—as a result of what he himself had, knowingly, taught her it might be necessary for him to come across and solace Annabel, once or twice a year from Man. Otherwise, if she were compelled to take lovers, the inheritance might again be in doubt . . . one had to make due provision, foresee everything of that kind. Poor little Annabel, like a little bitch in season. Women . . .

He caressed her knowingly, using certain ways he'd learned from Bart by word of mouth, then proved later for himself. They didn't fail him. Annabel had altered, he knew, from the innocent, unaware little virgin she'd been when he first came here to her, the night of the storm some weeks ago now. He'd been aware, none better, of what he was doing to her, as time went on; destroying, after the beginning, almost like a second stubborn maidenhead, the quality she'd kept of a certain natural delicacy, of innate withdrawal. He hadn't had time for that; and in the determined pursuit of the business he'd made, even Bart couldn't have bettered him, he felt certain. By now, the pantings and sighs, the receptive upward thrustings of Miss Annabel proved it. He smiled. Her tail would burn, doubtless, while he was away on Man. The part of Morven that had been savagely resentful of Philip's daughter, of the heiress, the prim little person who, last year, wouldn't come to his casual whistle, rejoiced at this achievement. A handful for Devenham, perhaps.

Was she pregnant yet? She should be, Morven decided; and watched, in the state which he had now reached of being able to assess Annabel's responses; and his own. It was as though he watched a mime-play, each action of the wordless players significant; impatient as he'd been, early on, he knew, with the green child's womb that refused, time and again, to accept his seed, by now he was considerate. It had been worth it to watch and control the slow, sure ripening of Annabel's inclinations, her awareness, the hot Doon blood coursing in her alongside the pale maternal Melrose. Not, he thought now, that she would ever be Livia; with Livia one didn't ever have to go gently, for fear of hurting her; Livia, who filled a man's hands with all promise, ripe fruit and golden corn!

He must accomplish this present task here in good time to take Livia away to have her baby. They'd both go at the earliest feasible moment after Annabel should be proved with child.

He returned to Annabel. He was almost sure, by now, that she must have quickened to him; discreet questioning of Livia about the state of the linen had given him the answer he wanted; how she'd sulked at that! She hadn't wanted to tell him anything, hadn't wanted to know. But there were, in any case, other signs. He slid his hands up now under Annabel's shift, and found her breasts, swollen a little and soft, no longer so much like small hard apples. Bart had said—how often he still had recourse to Bart!—that you could tell, almost at once, that way, when a woman was pregnant. At his touch, he heard Annabel moan pleasurably; he hushed her, always remembering aunt Retford nearby through the wall. Livia said she was taking a drug to make her sleep, she hadn't been well. Let the old harridan sleep forever. He didn't concern himself with her health.

He served Annabel in course, feeling, again, as the seed left him to enter her, an almost sacramental quality attaching to the moment and the act. It was as if he himself remembered the centuries during which his ancestors had, in such a way, perpetuated the blood of their ancient house. Doon seed, garnered and sown again to ensure Malvie for Doons for a generation to come . . .

It was done; he turned again from her, thinking once more of the different way he himself had spent the past four nights. He hadn't been able to come to Annabel, urgent as it had now become to be certain of having impregnated her before he left. He'd been away, some few miles down the rocky coast, seeing about hiring a boat from the Luith fishermen to go across to Man. Aaron, who still had his own boat, had been afraid of the revenue-cutters and said he'd had word they would be sent, next week again, to cruise up and down and eye the near channel. More trouble wouldn't pay. Then there was the money Morven himself had made over the past few months, and Bart's. After that was all stowed, perhaps after three or four days, or a week, he could come for Livia.

Livia! The thought of her again strengthened Morven, rendered him complete; even here, in bed with this narrowly fashioned, immature child with her thin resistant sticks of limbs. Too quick, it had all had to be.

She responded then. Suddenly, she began kissing him; full

deep satisfying kisses, a grown woman's, trusting, loving and unafraid. Presently, she herself had already often learned, her body would turn mysteriously to flame; she lay expectant. Presently it came upon her, the sweet inward turbulence, the demanding storm, as always when he'd served her, her husband, her husband . . .

Afterwards, she lay again quiet, obedient and still. It was then Morven saw fit to instruct her further, placing his mouth close against her ear and whispering, so aunt Retford still wouldn't hear through the wall.

"No. Oh, no, *no!*" The sound she would have made was almost a scream. He stifled it.

"Quiet. Lie quiet, will you, Annabel?"

He glanced round at the door, and listened for some moments; it was all right, the old woman's drugs must be strong. But it mustn't happen again. He turned to the crying girl and subtly, carefully tried to make clear to her that he himself must go away for a time, the law was still after him and it was better to be, meantime, elsewhere. She would be safer and happier by far at Malvie than the Mains; nobody there would whip or supervise her; Godfrey would be her husband in name only, and would protect her till he himself came. "And I will do so," he said. His voice had a prophetic ring in his own ears. What other outcome could there be than that in some way, sometime, when the affair with the gaugers and poor Bart should be long forgotten, he should return triumphant to Malvie?

"But you promised. You promised we'd go away together. And how can I marry him when, when—" She was sobbing, a child again; a defrauded, deceived, ravished child. "He can't do this, can he?" Morven whispered. "I'll come, and we'll do this together often." But she would listen to nothing; she was his own wife, his handfast-wife, she reminded him piteously; how could she marry Godfrey?

"You'll still be my wife. It's only to ensure Malvie for us. You know I love Malvie, don't you, Annabel? You know it's really mine. Would you refuse it to me?" He tried that, and more; but she was not persuaded, and her crying, if it grew louder, would surely wake someone. In the end he stopped her mouth by taking her again quickly, fiercely, part to console and part to subdue her; almost viciously wreaking on her flesh the anger he felt at further unnatural delay. First so much time lost till she conceived by him, and now . . . but she must, should obey him! He would convince her of it in

117

time; this way, he could at least establish mastery over her, leave her lulled and perhaps comforted.

But she still wept, and at first struggled under him; then clung fast to him with her limbs later when he would have risen from her after all, and made him stay; the dawn was at the window, he knew he should be gone long ago. The light had already grown clear enough for him to see her tear-stained little face. "Don't go, Morven, Morven, take me with you, take me now, I'll do as you say, wherever we go, I'll do anything, anything." She saw herself, he knew, as a smuggler's wife, a mender of hose, a patcher of nets; anything but what he wanted. He told her as much, coldly. "You won't consider my wishes," he said. "It is always only your own." He freed himself from her at last, and went and dressed himself. The tears poured down Annabel's face as she watched him; he'd go soon, and after the horrid, horrid things he'd said . . . as if, after him, she'd go to Godfrey or anyone.

Morven turned suddenly and smiled, using all the charm he had. There wasn't any point in frightening her further.

"Give it some thought, chicken," he said, and came and kissed her and tucked the disturbed covers back. "I promise I'll come to you again. We'll talk of it further." He would have, he decided, in any case to come once more; he couldn't leave matters in such a state of uncertainty.

He felt her arms slide round his neck; her cheek was hot with tears. "You promise?" she said, and her voice trembled. "Tomorrow . . . you will truly come?"

He lied to her, knowing tomorrow was unlikely for several reasons. He promised everything, in an effort to accustom her, now she was aware of it, to the suitability of his plan for Malvie. Tomorrow, or as soon as he could, he'd come again, make love with her, talk persuasively this time during the act, not later; in that state, he knew, she'd see anything from his view, agree to anything. But there was so little time left for patience; Livia's child was almost due to be born. If he were to tell Annabel of that, or perhaps get Livia to tell her? Surely the quick resentful pride of the Doons would make Annabel do then as he wished, and go straight to that other . . . if only he could be more certain, meantime, of having got her with his child! If it were a false alarm, it'd be all to do again, somewhat differently; with less ease, no doubt, once she was Godfrey Devenham's official wife at Malvie. Malvie . . . it must not, so nearly regained, be lost now for a child's spoilt whim.

He had left Annabel partly comforted with his kiss, and his

118

promise. It was to be her last comfort for long. Less than a week later, Morven Doon murdered the gauger who had been sent over with others from Grattan.

Godfrey Devenham had been planning his garden at Malvie.

As he made his way down the vistas of newly implanted shrubs and trees, past the lake, and the dug plots where, next year, flowers would grow, and the weeded avenue, he was aware of a sense of inward purpose, of deep and growing pleasure; all this should be a frame for Annabel. Whether she came to fill the frame or not did not perhaps immediately concern Godfrey, or much deter him; he was used to having plans and dreams which failed to reach fruition. He had not, initially, thought of this retreat in the north as anything but a means of escape from wretchedness, and it had brought him love; the love transformed him, making him no longer a creature of a separate dimension, causing him to see her at every turn of the paths, or seated amid summer roses that had not yet bloomed, roses from Persia that the nurserymen had had sent this year from the south. It was as it had been in the days last summer when she was often with him, when he would watch her pick up a shell and bring it to him, and gently follow with his weak forefinger the delicate whorls and spirals she had touched, shading from their peripheral pallor to exquisite inward rose. Holding the perfect shape to their ears, they had used to listen together to the sound, brought home to Malvie walls themselves, of the sea; the imprisoned sea, so that at night, when Godfrey was alone again, he would pick the shell up, and listen to the sea and think again of Annabel. He thought constantly of her, at the same time as he gave his full attention to the grouping of lilacs or the framing of a disposed virgin's-bower. She was his life, and made his heart beat.

He hoped her aunt was kind to her. Lately, she hadn't come so often, and she seemed, he thought, peaked and pale: perhaps she was worried about her cousin, lacking news. The pony moreover had strained a fetlock, and it was understandable that Annabel would not come as frequently to see him here when she couldn't ride; his own company would be dull, he knew. But he wished he could see her soon again, and perhaps discuss the water-garden with her; a notion had come to him lately about diverting and clearing the narrow muddy stream which meandered nearby the gate, to make a small pool there for water-plants, and perhaps some of the bright metallic fish he'd seen in tanks on dealers' booths in London, driving by as he used to do in the coach. Here, one was closer to the things which made the waking hours pass pleasantly; he'd hardly used the coach since he came, only his light garden-chair. Water-soldier, perhaps, and the yellow flags which grew so well in the north, and valerian, reflecting its fire in the pool in summer, when the flags had already made long fruit. Any bright, perfect thing to contribute to Annabel's delight, so that he could watch as she stooped over the pool, and looked down at the circling fish, and saw her own fair face reflected in the surface, like some fairy princess with a magic mirror which could preserve her for a hundred years in unaltered beauty.

But no magic could transform *him*, he knew. It was only in fables that the frog-prince, the monster, the beast, turned to comeliness. If she came—surely she must in the end, when his heart so longed for her!—she'd have to see him, daily, as he was. Was it too much to ask of any young woman? Could she ever, knowing his very mind and heart, let him love her? For that she should ever love him in return was beyond the bounds of possibility, Godfrey thought; one couldn't hope for the impossible. But perhaps she could gradually accustom herself to him; he hoped, at any rate, after their excursions together with the weeds and shells, that she liked him, was interested, knew she no longer made him shy.

How he loved her, he thought; a love so strong as his could give rise to no denial, in the end. He could give her so much she'd always wanted; not only things like the pony, like the pool, fine clothes, a harpsichord, her parents' portrait hung above the grate. He'd give her Malvie itself in gift, if she came. If only she would, before he died of longing or had to retreat, as he was doing now, into a world of the imagination . . . if only she would come!

"She was sick again this morning," said Livia.

They were seated side by side in the spinney, hands touching, she and Morven. It was already night, there was a chill in the air and the very leaves had thinned, and Livia began to shiver. I must go in soon, she thought. They hadn't made love. These days, she was too tired for it; and still angry with him.

"You know why I had to do it, don't you?" he said, reading her silence. He could forget, by now, that he hadn't ever told her directly about himself and Annabel; she knew, had probably always known from the beginning. He hardly needed to explain to Livia, for she would know, knowing him, that it was all for Malvie; but when he mentioned the house she merely moved her shoulders away with a bitter, sideways shrug.

"What's a heap of stones?" she said; no one else would have dared say it to Morven, and he did not answer. She went on. "It'll hurt that pretty, innocent dear," she said, "that's all I know; and *him*. Oh, you laugh at him for a cripple, I know that; anything's weak or off the straight, and it's like the worms to you, made for no more than being trodden on. But he's seen trouble already, Mr. Godfrey; and he's a good kind soul."

"And I'm not?" He tried to fondle her, but she drew away. "No," she said, "you've maybe no soul at all. You're maybe one of the damned, Morven Doon; I know that, but—" Suddenly she hid her face against his shoulder. "I'll be damned along with you, then," she said. "Best take me away soon." She sat up, and laid a hand on her belly. "Each day I go to *her*, I think she's noticed," she said. "She's sharp; it'll happen one day." She could see, in her mind's eye, Mrs. Retford with the birch in her hand, so often lately used on Miss Annabel, and not sparing at that. She herself would be spared much less. They'd be going to Man, maybe, but—

She found that his talk of the whitewashed cottage, and the life they would have together above the Ayre, had never seemed real. It hadn't been safe to make it seem so, maybe. She heard Morven's talk of a boat he'd found now, along the coast somewhere. "Get your gear all ready, lass." He'd said it before; but his eyes sparkled. Livia wished she could rid herself of the heaviness that lay in her; not the child's weight, she was used to that. It was like a fog in the mind, a damp blinding thing creeping up from the sea. She wished they were away, she and Morven, together. Three days from now . . . She made herself think of it, and then think of Miss Annabel.

Morven put out an arm to draw her to him; she evaded it. "What about *her*?" she asked him. He surveyed her, his eyes glinting in the light dark.

"She will marry Devenham, naturally. What more do you want to know?" He was mocking her, his mouth gently smiling; but she knew that he was not pleased. She felt anger rise high in her; did he think he was God, in the Bible, saying this should be and that should be? "You'll leave her, like that?" she said. "You'll sail with me away to Man, and—and just leave her to find out for herself, all of it, and go to him, if he'll take her? She'll—she'll—she'll make an end of herself."

"No Doon has yet done so."

"Ah, damn your Doons."

He laughed, and turned to her whether she would or not; and caressed the place where the child lay, feeling it swell the gathers of her apron. It was sweet to have his hand there; but that still didn't take care of the matter of Miss Annabel, or of how she was to be persuaded into that cripple's bed in time to let everyone think, including no doubt himself, that the child was his; and all for Malvie.

Malvie, Livia thought, casting a glance almost of hate at the tall chimneys rearing beyond the slope of the near hill; Malvie, as much a part of Morven as any woman would ever be! If he had a soul, Malvie was part of it; if he hadn't, then what was left of him after death would merge with Malvie earth, and come up again in the grass and growing trees. Malvie, a house. She wasn't jealous of it; it wasn't jealousy, rather fear she felt: fear lest Morven overreach himself, in this grand plan he had, and bring them all three, Miss Annabel and himself and her, to ruin.

She stared at him now, seated by her confident, well-fed and young and lithe as the devil; the devil would always be served, and she and Aaron, and his remaining son Abel Judd, had kept Morven Doon in bite and sup, though the Lord knew they'd not always conveyed it easily. Why did she love Morven so? His hair, even in the twilight which concealed much, was unkempt and dusty: he hadn't washed or combed it during all of his stay in Malvie, and he needed a shave. A tramp, he seemed like, with Philip Doon's old coat hanging loose on his shoulders, and buttons gone. But he didn't look like a tramp, Morven Doon, and never would; wherever he was, in whatever company. "God help me," thought Livia unaccountably. The love she felt for Morven tugged at her heart, making a silver chain between him and the unborn child. His child, that she'd bear gladly.

She said what was in her mind, as was her custom. "Morven, as you don't want to tell her of it, shall I?" She spoke half timidly, expecting him to be angry with her; but, instead, he turned and smiled, with the swift loving curve of the thin lips and half-closed eyes, and sliding of the fingers over her arms and waist, approving her. The waist she knew had grown thick; she was clumsier than she'd been when he first saw her, but he still liked her. That was well seen, and Livia lived by it; if there ever came a time when he couldn't be with her, could never or would never come to her again . . .

"I knew you'd offer to do it," he told her triumphantly, about Annabel. "She hasn't a mother, poor child; she knows little of such things. It'd be a kindness in you, Livia. Will you tell her for me tomorrow?"

It was somewhat late that last morning when Livia appeared as usual with Annabel's chocolate; she herself was beginning to feel heavy and sluggish in the early hours and it was, accordingly, an increased effort to rise and do all she had to do; but the fires got lit. She had been wondering lately, from Mrs. Betts' silences, whether or not the cook suspected her state; there had never been great confidence between them, they minded one another's business and got on with the work, but it all showed that, one way or the other, her own time at Mains was coming to an end. Two days from now, she'd be across the channel with Morven; he'd spoken again yesterday of the cottage they were to have on Man, a little place with thick whitewashed walls, set high by itself in the jagged rocks above the sea. It'd be queer to look across and see the shore here, instead of the other way round; and get used to the foreign talk of the Frenchmen, and their lawless ways. They'd be like man and wife there, herself and Morven, he'd promised her; she should have a silk dress and lace even on her shifts, and a pair of slippers with high heels, and the Lord knew what else. She doubted if it was all true, but some of it might be, if only they were once safely away.

Annabel's face showed wan today against the pillow and she turned away at the sight of the silver chocolate-pot. "I don't want any," she said, and averted her eyes; there were shadows beneath them and her colour was not what it had been. The sooner this is done with the better, Livia thought, quailing at the task she'd been set; and putting down the tray by the bedside she settled the curtains, to keep her hands steady, and said, not looking at the girl in the bed,

"You know what it means, Miss Annabel, don't you, this not taking the chocolate, and sickness in the mornings, and other things? You haven't had a monthly, have you, lately? You haven't, I know."

Annabel flushed scarlet; one didn't correctly speak of such things. The figure of Livia was somehow like doom, tall, implacable, standing by the curtain in her spotless cap and gathered apron. It was true she herself had wondered—and not dared to ask. Morven and she were married. It was what happened to married people. When it did happen, Morven would arrange something, tell somebody. They hadn't discussed it, on the nights he came; one had to keep silence because of the nearness of aunt Retford, and the nights had passed and dawns had come in loving, loving . . .

"You should not ask," she said primly. The primness infuriated Livia and she stamped her foot.

"Don't you know, you little fool? You're going to have a baby,—*his* baby. And so am I.

And she bunched aside her apron, and showed clearly—for Annabel in this moment saw many things clear—the bulk of Morven's child, lying well forwards inside her. For instants they stayed as they were, the two young women, staring at one another, neither saying anything. Then Annabel said, pale as death now, through dry lips.

"Tell me." And then on the next breath, pitifully, "It isn't true."

She could not have listened; Livia did not expect her to do so. She herself tried to explain, drily and factually, the situation as regarded Morven; the words fell on dead ears. It might have been a little wax doll, sitting rigid in the bed, making pretence to listen. In the end Livia told Annabel all of it; that she wasn't Morven's proper wife, there had been no witnesses to a handfasting; that she must marry Godfrey quickly, if she wanted to save herself and the baby. *"He* won't marry you; *he* won't take you where we're going, me and him together, till my child's born. It isn't that he wants from you; it's Malvie. That's a thing *I* could never give him; he had to have you, a Doon, to get it back. Get it for him, and for his son, now, the only way, marry the Englishman, let him think this child's his. You can do it, if you do it quickly."

She was leaning across the bed now, in her earnestness to be understood; if only the poor child heeded her! "Listen, Miss Annabel, it's the road for you, I doubt not, if your aunt finds out what's been going on at nights in this bed," she said. "How many young ladies—" she used the word with unfamiliar bitterness—"find good husbands once they've had a by-blow to some man? It's happened otherwise, my dear, and if you heed me and I'm your friend, you'll do as we've said, and go and marry Mr. Godfrey, who'd give his eyes to be your slave." And she remembered, in that instant, Godfrey's eyes and wished she hadn't mentioned them; he wasn't, when all was said and done, a pretty bridegroom, though his heart was in the right place and they said he had a scholar's mind. He could, maybe, make Miss Annabel happy in the end; no one else could, not Morven, not now, even if things were different. For it was like turning a knife in a baby's heart to watch the poor little face contort. "Lord, what have I said?" thought Livia. "What has Morven done? Between us, we've betrayed her." It hadn't been so easy, given other things, to think sooner of the full effect on Annabel of their plans with one another.

But Annabel by now had grown withdrawn and cold, and cast her eyelids down as, in future, she would do all her life when matters grew too close to reality and beyond her control. She had reverted, without knowing it, to the state of mind drilled into her from childhood; one didn't discuss certain matters with servants; they should know their place.

"Leave me now, please," she said icily, "and take away the tray, Mary, and close the door."

When Livia had gone she rose, staggered to her ewer and tried to be sick, but nothing came. Then she went and dressed herself.

Annabel could not afterwards remember going to put on her bonnet and cloak. She must have done so, because presently she found herself going, with small quiet steps, across the garden of Mains towards the gate that led out to the lane. She could recall seeing the late marigolds in the beds, and that their petals were beginning to fall and brightly litter the neat flagged path. Betts hadn't swept them yet. Nor was there any sign of aunt Retford. She hadn't been feeling well lately, and slept late. She'd been taking something, Annabel knew, to make her sleep. Perhaps that was why she hadn't ever wakened, when . . .

She herself mustn't think of Morven again. She didn't even look over at the yew-arbour where, a lifetime ago now, a young girl had sat with her embroidery and had listened to a whistle from the hill. She mustn't meet Livia Mary again either, moving about no doubt already on her morning's tasks as if nothing had happened, wearing her apron that covered everything . . . she must never see Livia any more. Perhaps today, perhaps tomorrow, the pair would be gone together; that took them out of her own life, and from now on this must be different. She was another person, finished with Mains, with the obedient, innocent fool she'd been. She would make it now so that, even if she desired to return to that former existence, it couldn't be done; she would alter completely. She knew what she had to do; and still and cold, only her limbs obeying her mind's direction, she emerged on to the high road and presently entered the gate of Malvie.

Godfrey was sitting where she'd known he would be, in the garden. He had a physician lately who said he must eat out of doors whenever possible, and he was having breakfast. A table had been laid with a white cloth and silver and glass, and a coffee-pot steamed there; he smiled with delight at seeing her, and gestured to the servant to go away, and handed her into the place by the coffee-service and asked her to pour. "I hadn't started yet," he said shyly. He was wearing his straw hat, against the coming day's sun. Mrs. Bowes and Clairette must be over, as they often were now, at Maddon. She was glad to find Godfrey alone. It wouldn't have been easy for Annabel, as she had once been, to say what she had come to say. But the new, cold person within her now framed the words with ease.

"I came early because I have something to say, Godfrey," she told him, and poured the coffee steadily. The fragrant brown stream emerged in to delicate fluted cups, fine as eggshells; how much luxury there would be here! "I have decided—" she handed him his coffee—"to accept your offer of marriage, if—if you still want me for your wife."

There, it was said; and his great pallid face flushed pink. He tried to rise, and almost spilled his cup, and she put out a small cool hand to stop him. "Don't try to stand up," she said, "there is—there is one thing." She looked down, stirring the contents of her cup carefully with the silver spoon. She sipped her coffee. It was hot and very, very refreshing and welcome. She remembered now, she hadn't had any breakfast before leaving, and Livia—

"You must marry me today," she said, smiling. "Will you do that? You see, I—I never want to go back to Mains; I wasn't happy there. You could make me happier, I believe, and I—" She flushed, almost matching his own recent colour; for the first time, some of her newly acquired self-possession deserted her. "I will try, I promise, to become everything you would want in a wife. You—you love me, I think." Her voice trembled; it was pleasant, after all, to have someone who wanted her for herself, not as a part of a plan for regaining Malvie. She saw the house, rising in towered newly-cleaned splendour behind; it could become a fitting home for herself and Godfrey, and the child. A determination, rising from more fierceness than she had ever known she possessed, rose in Annabel at that moment; whatever happened, the child should be born and brought up as Godfrey's own, he should believe it and so, from now on, should she. Already the notion that Godfrey's child lay in her womb possessed her; she'd make it so that it was a part of him, that they were part of each other. And everything else; he'd suffered so much, all his life till now, she knew. She'd make it up to him, as far as anyone could. She watched the dawning joy on his face with a kind of withdrawn pleasure; that was as it should always be between them, only pleasant things, things of interest and cultivation of the mind, being allowed to persist there. She saw him come nearer, moving with difficulty as he always did.

"May I—may I kiss you?" he said shyly. He was like a being transported; his joy made his whole body tremble, and when his lips found her cheek they slobbered uncertainly over it. She closed her eyes, and endured this.

Godfrey sought for something to say to cover his clumsiness. He had never in his life felt so tongue-tied with sheer delight; a dream come true, in a moment when, as had almost been the case, he'd abandoned dreaming and given way, as he'd been doing before Annabel came, to misery, to lonely desolation again, like a monster at a fair after the crowd has departed. But now—what could he say to describe the images that already thronged his mind of the things he'd buy for Annabel, do for her? Gowns, bonnets, furs—a carriage of her own, so that she could visit and drive about where she pleased—a little dog, perhaps, like her mother had had in the portrait. Annabel hadn't ever, he knew, had anything of that kind in all her life; he remembered her great pleasure over the pony.

He almost forgot to agree to her latest request, and to say he'd order the carriage and they would go at once together to find the parson, as he still called the minister here, in the nearest town. He asked no questions. On the way he'd perhaps tell her about the water-garden, and take her advice about plants . . . oh, they'd be happy! But he must speak to her again before that; he had, unaccountably and wretchedly, run out of anything at all to say.

He looked at Annabel. She was dressed in her usual bonnet and cloak and, in that, looked more beautiful than anything anyone could imagine, a princess of fairyland; and her little shoes, as always, were of satin and had got damp in the water running always by the gate.

"You've spoiled your shoes," he told her; it was a thing to say. "I'll—I'll buy you new ones."

"Dear Godfrey," said Annabel.

127

It was to be a matter for some days' wonder, when the news leaked out, that Annabel Doon and Godfrey Devenham had married one another in secret, without so much as an advance word of the ceremony to the young man's mother, who was absent at Maddon, or to the girl's aunt. Even in the known state of poor Godfrey's health this seemed a trifle secretive; there might be other reasons; the county waited avidly. Agnes Retford—who was said to be ill, by the way, at Mains—had dangled the girl so openly and shamelessly, permitting her to go down on the beach alone with the young man, frequently all last year, that perhaps haste had become advisable; best to say nothing. The Doon fortunes needed retrieving, without doubt, both in the matter of money—there was plenty of that now, of course—and in the continued lack of news about disgraceful young Morven. It was an unfortunate situation, and the young bride had perhaps acted advisedly in cutting loose from her family in so understated a way: one had better call.

However, calls at Malvie were postponed, tactfully, as a result of the further terrible news of Morven; after which it was no longer advisable even to mention him in genteel conversation.

VIII

Morven had gone by night to the place where, all last year, he and Bart had hidden money together; bags of gold guineas and, in a small leather pack, a sum in *louis d'or* to bargain with the French runners on Man. Now it was a question of getting it back again near shore, and Abel dared not help him with the inn's dray. Morven had been up by himself twice now, carrying what he could and stowing it ready in the place below Aaron's double cellar; from there, when it was ready, he would get it to the boat.

He walked across the moor quickly, head down and wearing a hat; it was bright moonlight, a fact which he had forgotten. One lost count of time and the days, the hours, alone, and the tides running to the moon, though almost second

128

nature to Morven by now, had caused him to alter the time of the boat's leaving tomorrow. For tomorrow, he'd planned it all, he and Livia should leave the mainland for a while; only till things had blown over, Morven told himself. The future was vague, and involved many journeys back and forth across the water, to see Annabel, by then at Malvie, and his son. Livia would tell her about that tomorrow, and then . . . He smiled, pleased, up at the moon.

The money was still there, hidden under a stone in a certain place. In summer the heather had concealed it, and in winter the ground was fissured with frost and the place itself not noticeable. He opened the bag and ran the golden guineas through his fingers, not from miserliness but with a pleasurable sensation of what he would buy with them; a silk gown for Livia, a French lace cap, a christening-robe for the baby to be born on Man. The other, at Malvie, would in due course wear the time-yellowed silk, embroidered with ferns and flounces by some far-off Doon lady, which he himself had worn, and Annabel, and Uncle Philip or his own father, he was uncertain which; and their father, and theirs, back to the time of the Civil Wars. But this child, his child and Annabel's, would bear the name of Devenham; a pity.

He would carry the bags two in each hand; there were others to come, and he replaced the stone. No need to take all the money; he could come back at any time during the year, by night, and replenish his coffers; by then, with the boat, he'd be making more. He made his way down to the cottage, quiet as death now Aaron slept alone within. Aaron, even if awake, would know nothing of what was going on; in a lifetime between the sea and the smithy, he had learned to hold his tongue. Morven slewed round the sill-shaped stone from its base by the cellar, pivoting it with his foot, and stowed away the bags he had brought from the moor, beside the rest already placed inside. As he stood again after replacing the sill before its aperture, the moon flung his own long black shadow on the wall. Morven frowned. A fool's night to choose! If he were not already certain that they'd abandoned the search, being as ever short of government-men, not to mention cutters for constant cruising back and forth, to watch the shore—

A shadow moved. Morven stepped back suddenly, and whipped out the sword he carried, hung by its scabbard to a loop in his belt. The moonlight glinted along the blade.

Nothing befell, and he put back his sword. Then he left the place swiftly. If there *had* been—as he'd imagined for a moment—someone watching nearby, he'd as soon they didn't lay hands on the money, in its hiding-place. At least half his hoard was brought down by now, and the boat wouldn't be in until tomorrow. One day he'd buy a sailing-cutter . . . perhaps, when he and Livia were on Man, he'd take up the calling in a larger way, as certain men did, owning storehouses for smuggled goods in places as law-abiding as Edinburgh and Leith, and their own fleets for sending back and forth to France. He smiled, and walked on. Malvie, his house, was over the rise; round the next corner he'd see it, clear black and silver in the light of the moon, with the trees behind; he, Doon of Malvie, with a house and ships—

They closed in on him then, two before and one after; coming down out of the concealing shadows of the greystone wall, where a gate broke it and they had defined, in watchful silence, maintaining the advantage on a lone man walking below them on the open road. One raised his bludgeon, and struck, but missed; Morven spun round a second too soon, and drew his sword, and swept it in a wide curve, like a janissary's. The gauger screamed, caught in the place between neck and shoulder, and went down clutching his throat; the other two, who were armed, flung themselves on Morven, when they could; still wary of the terrible sword. He used it, like a man possessed, as if he knew this hour, this moment, might be his last of freedom and of sight. When and how he killed the first officer he did not know; the other drew his pistol, and fired straight at the back of Morven's head. It was at this second man, and the first with the wounded shoulder, that he hurled himself in the last instants before darkness overcame, the colour of blood; and in a welter of grunting injury and pain, a grappling of limbs already aware of growing weakness and bled to the bone, he went down with them; in the end, struggling up to sitting positions on the abandoned road, they saw a dead man, their comrade, and one another in their wounds; and that fourth, whom they had come to take, lying face down with his skull's base shattered, and the dark blood staining his neck-linen and dripping slowly down on the road where he lay. They thought that, like Bart Judd, he was dead.

One other came then; out of the dark, having been summoned by whatever means they never knew; the shots had been fired later, as she came running down. She was a young woman with a veil of loose dark hair which fell now over the prone body of Morven Doon like a pall; she knelt down by him, her skirts soaking up the blood and the night's dew, and slid her hands tenderly beneath his head, and raised it; cradling him against her like a child. The pale face in the moonlight was that of a corpse, the features in profile waxen and fine. Livia crooned over it, in a tongue none of them later knew, from what place beyond memory she could not herself remember. This was her love, her king, and he was dead; this was her dead lover.

But Morven was alive. He moved against her breast and flung a hand out with a jerky, uncertain gesture, and tried to speak and to raise his eyes to her. It was, in some way, like the movement of a blind and fluttering thing, a maimed moth, a wingless bird, a mole trapped in daylight. For Morven was blind, though they would not yet know it, nor would he himself till he lay in prison, in a darkness unendingly dark, know it. For now they would take him, and her, in the end, on a cart to the town jail and carry him inside. Then they would say to Livia, as they had said to her mother also when she stood weeping for a man whose blood stained her skirts, and whose child moved already in her womb,

"You can't go with him, lass. Get you along home."

And she stood outside the gate with the wind whipping her blood-stained skirts, and townsfolk beginning to stare at her.

Livia did not know where she went after that at first. The time between leaving Morven and turning, again, out of town was confused in her later memory, a limitless space of bleakness, wind, the dark and the rain. Soaked and foot-sore, she had found herself at last at the Mains road-end again, with, rearing ghostlike beyond out of the dawn, Malvie. It would be about time for her to begin, in the ordinary way, to light fires and carry water at the Mains. She shivered, and looked helplessly from the road to the house, then turned and, for no reason which her mind could ascertain, trudged up the slope towards Malvie gate and went in.

The great house was already awake in the dawn; in the servants' attics a few lights showed. This place, which Morven had loved as he would never love any woman, was stirring into life with as much fickleness as a woman would do, who'd forgotten him. Livia stood there watching the ordained, orderly progress of a day-by-day world forever removed from her, a rich, secure world served by footmen and grooms, housemaids and the upper hierarchy, who still slept. Somewhere, Miss Annabel also would be sleeping, in a bed with satin curtains and her new husband by her. Livia kept her mind on Miss Annabel, her feeling for the other girl nothing but love now, kindliness and a sort of interdependence: they had both of them been necessary to Morven.

Miss Annabel was secure, at any rate. She'd give birth to Morven's son at last on feather-down. He would be reared —Livia's mind did not encompass anything but the son who had been Morven's wish—like a prince. A prince to inherit. Already she thought of the child's father, as irrevocably dead, as having to die. It it didn't happen of his wound in prison, they'd hang Morven.

Standing there, she felt her own child move in her womb. It was a week yet till the birth, or should be, but already he was stirring restively, he'd be, no doubt, in the event, an active wretch, taking all of her strength in the bearing and the nursing of him. What was to become of her meantime? That old woman at the Mains—she was yellow as a guinea these days—wouldn't keep her in the house five minutes, once she knew. There wasn't, for all the personal property Livia had left there—an old pair of shoes and her shawl, and comb, and two shifts which might have been useful—any reason to go back. But where else to go to?

It was then she remembered Abel Judd, and what he'd said to her that time about coming to him at the Fleece, if she ever had to. Then, she thought wryly, it hadn't seemed likely; perhaps by now he'd have changed his mind. Men did; but, maybe, she should risk it. She was a good worker, she knew; she would, in any case, give value for shelter and a bite of food; scrub and sand the floors, wash and polish the ale-mugs, launder Abel's linen. All of it, and more, if only he'd take her in at least till Morven's baby was able to walk. After that, they'd follow the road, the two of them, if they had to.

The remote future had never seemed real to Livia. All of it, future and past, merged in a sum total of experience in her veins; for the first time in long, she thought now of her mother. Once long ago *she'd* taken the road, without her man, and his death-blood on her skirts, and had given birth to her child in the end with less hope than there seemed to be now, with the prospect at least of Abel's roof over her own head. All of it gave Livia fresh heart as she turned and, without even glancing over the Mains hedge, walked straight past the house and back again to the road, and the way she had come.

PART TWO

I

Paul Melrose, aged almost twenty, had ridden over early from Maddon by way of the town. By now, it was afternoon. He drew in at last where the gaunt, empty half-ruin of the smithy cottage stood, untenanted since Aaron Judd had left it some years back and gone, after all, to make his home with his remaining son Abel at the Fleece. Paul stared about him for some moments with the direct, square-set grey gaze which resembled his father's; and presently dismounted and, carefully stowing away in his greatcoat pocket a package he had brought, tied the horse's reins to the doorpost of the old smithy, and wandered into the yard. Nothing met him there but blowing straw, a sense of abandoned desolation, and a view of the sea. Paul stood awhile to look at this last unaccustomed sight, thinking less of himself meantime than of his disgraced, long-absent kinsman Morven Doon.

The sea alone made one remember Morven; Paul, recalling him from his own childhood, always connected his half-forgotten memory with boats. Once Morven had taken Paul out, in the days before his elder brother Peter had been killed and Papa was less watchful of his safety; they'd had a clear run on the inland tide and had surveyed Man, brooding and near, so that its secret places and inland bays, and sharp rocks, were visible. Paul cherished the remembrance of that day, which had been the last time in fact he'd seen Morven; later, he'd heard of the killing of the customs-officer, and that Morven himself lay in prison awaiting trial. The result of that could hardly be in doubt; again, Paul remembered his father, coming into the hall at Maddon afterwards still clad in his riding-cloak, his lined face grave.

"They will hang Morven Doon, I doubt not."

But they hadn't; and whatever folk might say of Sir Hubert's own activities in that matter, and the high-placed palms he'd greased, he'd got Morven sentenced instead to transportation, seven years to Botany Bay. That the sentence had been so short had been due to Morven's blindness resulting from the fight. One couldn't be too hard on a blind man; although Lord Braxfield, the hanging judge, Papa had said, had it been he who conducted the trial in Edinburgh, would have finished Morven off, blind or not. The poor devil of a customs-officer had left a wife and children; one had, Papa said, to think of those.

No one since then had heard anything of Morven in Australia. It was hoped, Paul knew, that he would settle down out there, as many transported men did, and grow rich, instead of coming home. And old Aaron Judd, when at last he died, had left Morven most of his money; a surprisingly large amount, Papa said, but the blacksmith had lived frugally and, besides, had had a hand in most of the contraband running Morven favoured. Honour among thieves, Papa had called it; no doubt old Aaron had looked on Morven as a son, as much almost as Bart Judd who'd been killed. Abel, the well-doing eldest son at the Fleece, had inherited almost nothing; Paul had seen him again only today.

The young man jerked his thoughts away from that recollection, and of the strange character who'd sat in the taproom, like a visitant from another world. His own orderly collection of tame, humdrum, everyday things, the things which made up his daily existence at Maddon, asserted themselves; since Peter had been killed it had become evident what his own life must be. Paul's stepmother, who had been Cecily Bowes, had borne her lord a yearly brood of daughters only; so many to find portions for, said poor Papa, and looked to Paul, as the young man knew well, to set himself to learn the things it would be necessary for him later, as head of the Melrose family, to know. He must begin to take an interest in the title and estates which he would one day inherit; he must not—Paul would see the old magistrate's face darken, remembering golden Peter, killed out hunting, breaking his neck by a fall from his horse at a wall—he must not run risks. Paul stroked his docile mount's obedient neck now; Papa would never permit him to ride anything but a gelding.

He sighed a little; Papa likewise, fearing what might happen to his only remaining son, had only allowed Paul to go last year on the Little Tour, not the Grand; to have to be content with a modified circuit of Holland and Germany, and parts of France, had not, the young man knew well, given him the polish he himself would have liked to acquire. Naturally shy, and acutely conscious of himself, still, as a bumpkin, the thought of today's visit to Malvie was agony

135

to him, although he tried to tell himself it was only to deliver a package to Cousin Annabel, a sovereign cure for headaches his stepmama could vouch for and had had made up specially, only today, by the apothecary at Grattan Juxta. But Cousin Annabel was so finely dressed nowadays, and kept such elegant company, that it was difficult to think of her as the sweet young girl he and Peter had both, in their different ways, loved. If only he himself could have gone to Florence, Rome and Venice as he had desired, and seen the palaces and famous paintings, and the sun on the Grand Canal of an evening, he would perhaps have been able to converse in a suitable fashion with Cousin Annabel as she was now, when she wasn't prostrated by one of her headaches. But as it was, all he could think of to say to her would probably concern Maddon; his stepmama's health, the factor's doings—one couldn't discuss the accounts, in which Paul in fact took an informed interest—or what was happening in the coverts he visited almost daily in company with Papa, the latter walking more slowly now he was getting to be an old man. On the way there, certainly, Sir Hubert would hold forth, in an instructive manner, about what might be taking place on the Bench, or perhaps the doings of the London government, which Papa, in common with all thinking Scotsmen, thought less and less of as year followed year. It didn't follow, Sir Hubert said, that men would keep the law unless the law was made more reasonable; and until Billy Pitt cut the tax on liquor and imported wines, smuggling in the north would continue to be profitable. All of it brought one back again to thoughts of Morven Doon; who, Papa had once said, would be a true son of his father Richard if they thought to hang him. Papa's face had grown bitter then, like it did when he remembered Peter; and Paul thought again how he himself, in order to try to remove that shadow from the old man's eyes, would do his best to copy his brother in every least way. It wasn't easy; he didn't resemble Peter physically, being shorter, darker, and not at all handsome, and with no aptitude for field-sports and such things. His own preferences would have been scholarly, if he could have been left to himself; perhaps he'd have been a preacher or even a dominie.

But to talk to Cousin Annabel was still difficult; her standards were exacting and finicky. He must make do instead with Cousin Godfrey. The thought of Godfrey's kindly, invalid presence at Malvie today cheered Paul; he found it easier to take up the reins again and ride, having overcome his momentary diffidence, towards the great house, with, safely in his pocket still, the sovereign herbal cure for migraines recommended by his stepmama. While it was being made up today Paul had gone in, almost for the first time in his life without the tutor or Papa, to the Fleece taproom, and had encountered the queer personage there while he was ordering himself ale. The man had given him news, which he must not fail to relate to Godfrey and Annabel, about poor blind Morven.

Paul found the family, including Mrs. Bowes and Clairette, drinking tea in the withdrawing-room at Malvie, nearby the great hearth above which, again dominating the place for which it had originally been painted, there hung the portrait of Philip Doon and his fair-haired wife Grace, with her lap-dog and her yellow gown. A low fire of logs burned in the hearth, for it had been a cool day, though with as yet no hint of rain.

The fact of Paul's long ride alone was commented on, and he was made welcome as befitted a young man; he placed his bow correctly, crossed the carpet—its alternate squared and floral patterns, yellow on white, were Chinese, he remembered hearing, and matched the well-hung portrait—bowed again, and kissed Cousin Annabel's hand. It was a white, fragile hand, scented faintly with some essence, orange-flower perhaps, which gave her skin an additionally exquisite, rare quality like the fluted translucent china of the tea-cup she now handed him. Paul accepted the cup, his own fist seeming to him like a ham, holding it uncertainly; obsessed with a fear of dropping such delicate gewgaws—they had come from the East, no doubt, like much of the Malvie gear —he hastily downed a mouthful of hot, scented tea. Manfully, he neither spluttered nor lamented his burned tongue; and looked about him, still shyly. There had been alterations since he'd last visited Malvie; perhaps they would give him a subject for conversation. That plant, now, in the newly-installed long window, with beads of water still lying on its great waxed leaves—the gardener must have watered it, as there hadn't been rain—and bell-like showers of creamy blossom; what was it called?

He turned to Cousin Godfrey, as always now in his invalid-chair. How transparent the poor fellow's flesh seemed! It was an accursed thing, the unknown disease which consumed him, leaving as it were only his mind untouched, so that the fire of intelligence shone like a kindly beacon behind the eyes. No treatment availed for his cure. Paul asked him

137

for the sake of something to talk about, what the plant's name might be; and Godfrey smiled and said it was Solomon's Seal.

"Why that?" said Paul, diverted with the name. His stepmama had a plant named Diligent Eliza, which she grew indoors in pots. Perhaps the names of plants would afford a teatime topic; but still Paul's tongue stumbled. He looked rather wildly at Cousin Annabel, tastefully clad today in lilac stuff, with her hair done in the new fashion of side-curls, bunched out glossily above the ears. She lay on a Turk-ish sofa, as the doctor had said she must do for two or three hours each day, ever since the birth of little Sybilla some years ago had left her delicate. But Annabel only smiled, and raised a finger to induce them to listen to the the faint tinkling notes of the harpsichord struck up by Eliza Berry, who with her husband was over at Malvie as usual; and Paul looked for guidance instead to Sybilla herself, aged six and a half, disposed, like an attendant cherub, by her mother on a small embroidered footstool. Sybilla was, Paul had often thought, a copybook little girl, all golden curls, blue eyes and dimples; not unlike his swarm of small half-sisters at Maddon, but prettier. She wore a tucked and frilled muslin gown, with a pale-blue ribbon high above the waist beneath her plump, rose-petal arms, revealed by the brief puffed sleeves of the gown's fashion. Her slippers were tiny, and made of matching satin. She was eating a cake. Paul wondered why she wasn't with her governess at this hour; no doubt they allowed her to come downstairs a great deal, for Cousin Godfrey adored her. Paul let his eyes rove again from the child to her mother; what an exquisite pair they made! If the effect was perhaps a little too artificial for everyday, as though the first rough wind would disturb it, it didn't greatly matter, Paul decided; there were no rough winds at Malvie now, and all of Cousin Annabel's days, as a rich man's wife, would be sheltered and tranquil. He heard Cousin Godfrey call out to Sybilla about the question Paul had asked con-cerning the plant, and she got up from her stool and ran over, fair curls bobbing. He heard old Mrs. Bowes, from her place across the room, call out, oblivious of the harpsichord, "My colour! My own golden colour; I had that same hair when I was a child." Sybilla was her favourite grandchild; she made the two statements often.

"Tell Paul what I told you yesterday, about why the plant is called Solomon's Seal when there are no seals to be seen," commanded Godfrey. His expression as he watched the little

138

girl was doting; he put out a finger and inserted it in one of her bright curls, as if to draw life from it. Sybilla laughed, and sidled up against him in his chair. "Papa, I half forget," she confessed, and the dimple deepened.

"Then you have a brain like a butterfly, and can remember only sugared almond cakes and the like." He stroked her silken hair. "I will tell you again, sweetheart, because Paul is enquiring; perhaps he will remember if you do not. The seals are underground, on a creeping stem that grows there; each year there is a new scar, as though Solomon had impressed it."

"How could he, when he's dead?" said Sybilla practically. They all laughed; Annabel frowned a little, and said they were being uncivil to Edgar and Elizabeth, who were playing for their diversion, had they not best listen?

"Shall we sing a Scots air?" called Edgar Berry from his place nearby the harpsichord. He and his wife made an incessant business of visiting the great houses in the neighborhood, and were believed hardly ever to dine at home; by way of singing for their supper, no doubt, they had a repertoire of musical pieces, sometimes rather indifferently played. But the Scots air was nostalgic, and prettily enough sung by the pair, while Elizabeth Berry showed off her fine white arms at the keys. It was early in the day for music; but, as Miss Clairette Bowes had been heard to remark in her acid manner, Elizabeth Berry had brought her Italian singing-master north with her on her marriage, and would have been at a loss for any other subject on which to converse.

Paul only half heard the Scots air, for on release from the necessity of polite talk his thoughts had flown back to the encounter in the ale-house that morning. Suppose he were to describe now, in this elegant, fragrant drawing-room, the rough character he had seen in the taproom? An impish urge, despite his shyness, impelled him to do so; Cousin Annabel's salon at Malvie was the occasion of frequent sly hints from his otherwise placid, uncomplaining stepmother. "Had she her hands as full as I have, with five children and yourself and Sir Hubert—" Cecily always like a good wife of the old school, gave her spouse his full formal title— "there'd be less time for musical evenings, and card-playing and painting in water-colours." It was well known, Cecily then added robustly, treating Paul as already fully informed on such matters, that Godfrey and Annabel had occupied separate bedrooms since the birth of Sybilla.

"The dear little angel!" Paul's stepmother had added then,

for nobody, and Cecily Melrose was not an envious woman in any case, could dislike so fair a little creature, who never gave anyone trouble for all she was an only child. "When she's of an age to have a London season, she'll be a beauty as well as rich; then Cousin Annabel will needs bestir herself, and become less precious and taken up with her own health," and with that Cecily had bustled off to supervise the maids at the fruit-preserving, for it had been a good year for damsons at Maddon.

But the strange man today at the Fleece . . .

Paul had strolled in there after leaving his stepmother's receipt with the apothecary, to be made up for Cousin Annabel's headaches. Leaving the dark little shop and its mysterious, spice-filled air, and its shelves where great delft jars, many of them dusty, contained no doubt the sovereign remedies for most things, Paul had first made certain they were watering his horse behind the inn-yard, as he had already instructed; they would find him, he then told them, in the taproom. As he bent his head and entered the Fleece he was, as in the apothecary's shop, assailed by odours; but this time they were of fresh sawdust, soap, beeswax, and the familiar, tonic smell of good ale. It made Paul feel manly, and glad he'd given his top-boots, under the sardonic eye of Papa's valet, an extra polish yesterday; he still would not have had the courage to ask that dignitary to do them for him, but he had wanted them to look well for riding to Malvie. He had then approached Abel Judd behind his counter shyly, and asked for ale on draught; Abel, in almost arch-priestly dignity behind his leather apron, had drawn it himself, and brought it to the young master; everyone remotely connected with the Doon family was known to Abel Judd, and rated extra attention from him, though he himself, with the growing fame of the Fleece since his second marriage, was now a very important personage. The taproom at this hour was not as full as it would become later; a handful of sheep farmers, returning north from Carlisle market, wagged their bonnets angrily together over the mean English prices they had fetched. Otherwise, only one customer sat near Paul by the taps, drinking in silence. Paul glanced at him, and could hardly repress a shudder of distaste; the man stank, and looked like a cadaver.

One thing intrigued Paul; he was sensitive enough to perceive it. Between Abel Judd, stout, balding and prosperous in his pontifical leathers and whitely laundered shirt-sleeves, and this ragged, greasy, malodorous skeleton was a link of some kind; their eyes never met, and it was evident to Paul that, on his entry, they had been discussing some private matter. The ragged man raised his arm now, to quaff more ale, and a rancid, indescribable smell came from his clothes as he moved; they might once have been of blue-grey hodden stuff, perhaps a prison-issue. Now they hardly held together; a stubble of beard on the man's jaw was almost the one sign of life. His eyes surveyed Paul incuriously. Another young gent, he was evidently thinking; a sprig of the county, whom at one time, no doubt, in his younger days, he'd have cozened and fleeced. But the half-dead gaze by now conveyed less interest in the present and future than the past; a not too remote past, redolent of living death, infinite distances, untamed silences.

He interested Paul, deprived of experiences such as the Grand Tour. The young man brought out, with an air he vainly tried to deprive of bravado, a handful of coins from his pocket, and offered to buy the other more ale. Over this, although his manner was grudging and ungrateful, the ragged fellow talked. His own name, he said, was Tom Neilson. He spoke of things Paul had never heard of. He was, he said, back lately from Australia, from Sydney Cove, from Botany Bay.

Paul was strongly tempted to ask at once about Morven; but the habit, ingrained in him by now, of being ashamed to mention a kinsman who had been sent out there prevailed, and he said nothing, only listened as Tom Neilson talked, his tongue less taciturn now with the flow of ale. "I walked north from Tilbury," he said. "Took two weeks; been out there seven year. Not many changes here, 'cept that it's greener than I'd remembered. I forgot how everything here's so green." He wiped his mouth; the lack-lustre eyes slewed round hopefully to Paul, who immediately ordered more ale; seven years, the same sentence as Morven!

Abel shook his head warningly; Tom Neilson had had enough, his expression said. Paul settled down to listen to all Neilson would say; sooner or later, he'd get in a question about Morven. The man spoke of the voyage out. "First they brought us up out o' Woolwich hulks, and that was no Ne'erday dinner. Five stinking months we had of it after that, us chained two and two together in the orlop by night—"

"What's the orlop?"

"The between-hatches; where no man wants to go. Couldn't neither sit nor lie there, or move much, by night for fear o' waking them: couldn't but vomit and do all else over the

141

other man, see?" The dead eyes stared. "Twenty-four on us there were, below decks in one hole like that; ten on 'em died, and never saw Australia."

"What had they done?" Paul had been about to ask. But he did not; even for Morven, who'd killed a man, it was inhuman; nothing was bad enough to have to chain men together in an airless hole below the waterline for five months, living in their own excrement, and the food—"Was the food bad?" he said aloud. Again, the eyes slewed round at him.

"Ay."

"What did they—" But he didn't, he realised, want to hear about it; he, fed twice daily on fresh fish and game from the estates, and new-baked bread and eggs straight from the home farm, and Cecily's small-beer. For sightless Morven, the voyage must have been black indescribable hell; how had he survived it?

Perhaps he had not. What had any of them heard since then of Morven, to prove that he was still alive? Oh, ay; old Aaron's legacy, Papa had told him. But the need to hear direct news of Morven had overcome hesitation and shame, and Paul blurted out, "Did you know Morven Doon?" and the name echoed through the room; he saw the farmers stop their talk for a moment and look round curiously, then resume as though nothing had happened. He blushed with confusion, unaccustomed as he was to making himself conspicuous. But Tom Neilson answered squarely.

"Morven?" he answered. "I should know him; chained together half a year we were, with his plank by mine. I did all things for Morven," he added hopefully.

He might be lying; but in so vast a country, and across endless leagues of sea, the colony was still small enough for most men to know one another. And he'd known Morven was blind. Paul pressed a crown into his hand. "Tell me all you can," he said.

Tom Neilson had lost sight of Morven Doon for a while after landing. Himself, they'd sent him to the Island, he said, for near a year; he didn't say why. When he left Morven, the latter had been set to polishing the Governor's silver. "Neat with his fingers, he'd learned to be already, being blind; and his high and mightiness liked all his gear bright and shinin', and couldn't be sure but that the likes of me would make off with it, but never Morven." A grin showing the remains of black teeth, showed and Tom scratched his pate. "Then when I come back to the port again, there was Morven in charge o' cornstores, and a black fellow along with him. Samson, he called the boy."

"A native?" Paul knew little about the Antipodes; but he'd heard they had savages there, and that Captain Cook had been killed; more than that, he realised, he knew almost nothing. Tom shook his head.

"Na. Them's no good to the likes o' Morven. Eyes to him, this one was. How do I know where he come from? When I left, they was still together. He got me to say—"

The burnt-out gaze turned again to where Abel stood, inscrutably, at the counter. "He got me to say I'd bring word," said Tom Neilson innocently. "Whatever's the way of it, here I am!"

That hadn't been what they would have said together had he not been listening, Paul decided; to his sharpened awareness it seemed as if everything in the room was suspended for a moment in time. No one moved. His presence, he knew, as an incomer, incommoded the two men; but whatever the message was it had been delivered, no doubt, before he came in. He stayed for a while, turning his tankard in his hands and refusing to allow them to shorten his sojourn by silence; after all, he was Morven's kinsman, wasn't he, and a Melrose besides? He'd go, in a moment or two, when it suited him; not when it suited Tom and Abel.

"Will he come home?" he asked Neilson clearly. He'd heard the man say at some time, during their discourse, that some found the voyage so fearful that they would never again risk a return, but stayed on in the far lonely land. Would Morven stay? Would he never come home again? But the released convict looked at Paul Melrose indulgently, as one looks at an importunate small boy.

"Ay," he said in a low voice. "You can tell them that up there at any rate. Morven Doon'll soon be home."

Abel had moved sharply then behind his counter. "Leave that, leave it now," he said, gesturing Tom to be silent; becoming, suddenly, himself, no more than a troubled, sweating, middle-aged man, the bald patch on top of his fringed head shining with moisture; he wiped it absently. He could never bring himself to wear a wig.

Paul turned his head to observe the cause of so sudden a silence in both men. A black-haired young woman had come in and was crossing the sanded floor, leading a little boy by the hand. The child's hair was black also, thick, shining and rough. He was eating an apple. Idly, he threw the core on the floor.

"William Judd, pick that up and go and put it on the midden," said the young woman. "How can I keep the place clean and decent, or Tib either, when you go on so?" And she cuffed the boy absently. William ducked and presently ran out by himself into the sunlight; Paul saw him kick the retrieved core across the yard. "More trouble there," he thought, smiling; he himself would have liked a younger brother. He heard Livia Judd tell her husband she and William were going out for an hour. "To the butcher, and that," she said. "You'll manage, Abel?"

Abel said he would manage. He had turned away and begun to polish the tankards with a clean cloth. Everything here was clean. Paul remembered—he wondered afterwards how, being a small boy at the time, he could have happened to be permitted to hear it—how on Abel's second marriage about seven years ago or so, to the young woman who had just come in, folk had talked. They said she was a bad lot, and the child she was about to bear wasn't Abel's; but Abel had nevertheless married her and given the boy his name. Since then, the Fleece had become renowned for spotless comfort, and was now a famed hostelry, for Livia Judd was a good worker; even her enemies admitted that. And she hadn't so many enemies now; folk forgot, as the years passed and they found other scandals to occupy them, and Livia had a pleasant manner to the women as well as the men.

She went out after the boy, and Paul caught a passing glance from her grey eyes where he still sat doggedly over his ale. She was beautiful, he thought, perhaps like a black-haired goddess of plenty; but sad. She looked as if she ought to be made to laugh more, as if she'd once often laughed. Perhaps—

She had gone, and the room, Paul thought, seemed darker; presently he took his leave, as word had come by them from the grooms. He retrieved his freshened horse and Annabel's package, and rode off thoughtfully, still aware of the change that had come over the taproom at mention of the fact that Morven might be returning soon. It was as though a blight had touched it, almost in quality like that on the death-ship where many men had died. That tale was not, in any case, suitable for tea-time conversation at Malvie, in Cousin Annabel's elegant drawing-room.

After the Scots air was sung and the harpsichord abandoned, Godfrey's mother beckoned Paul to ask for news of her daughter. He went over, having disposed of his fluted egg-

144

shell cup, and sat down by Kitty to hear her searching, not always discreet enquiries, and later wordy messages to be conveyed to Cecily at Maddon. That she had been a loving parent to his stepmama Paul did not doubt and unquestionably still felt an affection for her married daughter; but the pouched, disillusioned eyes, which alone among her features Kitty could not disguise with rouge and haresfoot, rested always on the group made by her son and his wife and child, as some penitent might gaze hopefully on the Madonna. It was, perhaps, nearer the mark to say that Kitty might feel she had somehow acquired a set of priceless Dresden figurines, and could heed nothing else. She nodded absently at Paul's information that his stepmother was well, the newest baby daughter also, and that they had made forty-odd pounds of jam at Maddon this summer, and bottled as many gallons of elderflower wine. "She was always adept at such things, and will make an excellent wife," said Kitty, suddenly as though discussing a stranger. Then, as wives were in question, she launched forth into a panegyric on Godfrey's beautiful Annabel, so well-born and accomplished, such a constant joy to Godfrey and them all; how pretty it was to see them together, so full of affection! Did Paul know the Doons had once sent four knights on crusade? Paul had been aware of it, but listened with indulgence to Kitty's oft-repeated relation of this happy discovery. As her own folk had once (it was never spoken of) kept a draper's shop before dying in order that she be shipped out to the nabob, it was all the more miraculous to Kitty to have acquired, even at third hand, eleventh-century knights for her personal escutcheon. Then she returned to the present; did not Paul think dear Godfrey was looking stronger than he had? "He has taken such delight all this year in planning further improvements to the house and garden, that it will be bound to have done him good. Dearest Annabel is such a helpmeet to him; together they pore over botany-lists, and she seems to understand what the names mean, although I swear I don't."

She helped herself to a third cake, and began to extend her rapture to include small Sybilla. When Paul had come in today at first she had hoped Clairette, though a year or two older, might catch his eye, for he was an eligible young man of the first social order; but poor Clairette was so plain, and made no attempt to please, and the moment had passed, although perhaps later . . . But meantime, Sybilla in a few years would be a rich young lady. What could be prettier than that she should marry her cousin Paul? There would be no danger, then, of fortune-hunting; the Melroses were very well endowed, as she'd taken the trouble to find out, never fear, when Sir Hubert offered for Cecily. It had been providential, at the time ... Kitty tried, now, to inveigle Sybilla over, holding out a piece of cake to her, as if she had been a puppy; but Sybilla, shaking her head till the golden curls bobbed again, dropped a little curtsy and refused it.

"Mama says I must not have any more."

"Oh ... perhaps just this once? Then you shall give it to Paul's pony, my darling, before he leaves. And first you must show him the garden Papa has planted so beautifully."

Paul hastily said that he must ride back. Sybilla held out her hand for the cake. She would like, she thought, to give it to Paul's horse; he was too old, she felt sure, by now for a pony; how silly Grandmama was sometimes! Sybilla adored all animals, even the strange foreign ones whose names she had learned from Papa, and had seen only in drawings. She retrieved the cake carefully from Kitty and held it away from her own muslin dress, in order not to sticky it. "There's a tidy child," said Kitty approvingly. She turned to Paul and began to tell him what a pleasure it was to see a child so well brought up as Sybilla; of course, this last year, they'd had a governess also, an excellent young woman, Miss Glover her name was, from somewhere near York.

It's much too good for him," said Paul, as regarded his gelding and the cake. Sybilla smiled angelically. "Oh, it won't keep till tomorrow. You must not go away until you've let me give it to him. Will you promise, Cousin Paul?"

Poor Paul promised, and was rescued by Godfrey, who had long ago finished his tea; he ate sparingly. He beckoned the young man over to ask knowledgeably about affairs at Maddon; for the first time that day, Paul felt at home, and he thought again what a pitiful thing it was that Cousin Godfrey should be a lifelong invalid, carried—as everyone knew—to the privy and to bed, for he could no longer stand or walk. How could he show such courage as he did from day to day? No one ever saw him pine, or lose heart or interest, or fail to sustain people; look at the way, just now, he'd rescued Paul himself when he was tongue-tied before old Kitty Bowes.

Their talk ceased, and as such things will a silence fell upon the room. Paul was trying to broach the subject of the man at the inn, and had almost been about to tell Godfrey of it; but at that moment Annabel smiled, and clapped her magnolia-petal hands together to have the tea-things removed. "And here is Miss Glover come for you, Sybilla, my dearest," she said in her clear and sweet, of late slightly affected tones; she had heard, as Clairette Bowes unkindly put it, the way the polite English talked, and was trying to imitate them and erase the native lilt from her tongue; only at times, under stress, she forgot.

Sybilla went away obediently, having curtsied to the company, and kissed Godfrey in his chair. His eyes followed her as she went out of the room with the plain, unexceptional, good young woman in a drab round-gown and un-adorned cap who was Jane Glover, the governess. Edgar and Elizabeth Berry shuffled the music they had with them at the further end of the room, and made ready to start again or, perhaps, take their departure. Whichever it was to be, Paul felt it necessary to blurt out the news he'd had from the returned convict earlier; otherwise, he'd never get it said.

"I met a strange man at the Fleece today," he said carefully. "He was from Australia."

He flushed at the discovery that every one of those in the room, including the two Berrys, had stopped talking to listen. It was too late to draw back, and Paul felt his tongue stumble. "He—this man—bore company with Morven on the voyage out. He says—" Paul made himself leave out the parts about the Governor's silver, the negro who acted as eyes, the terrible facts of the outward voyage as he had today heard them. One must, Papa was always saying, remember ladies were fragile beings and there were subjects not suited for their ears. "He says Morven will soon be coming home."

The silence fell again, and it was like that at the Fleece, in some manner; then young Edgar Berry played an impromptu, soft arpeggio on the harpsichord. It broke the hush that had come over them all, in which Annabel lay quite still on her Turkish sofa, as though she were indeed a china figure; her face white beneath its rouge, her gold-flecked eyes dark and blank.

Paul left shortly, aware that his main contribution to the talk of the afternoon had been clumsy, and that he'd perhaps brought on a headache for Cousin Annabel instead of making her better. It was the kind of *gaffe* he would never, he

147

told himself, have made had only Papa permitted him a more extensive social education. One learned by experience, but today's had been mortifying, and he still felt several kinds of fool. Only Cousin Godfrey had taken his hand on departing as though he'd be pleased to see him again, and had pressed him to stay for supper, but of course he had not.

He was about to mount when the plain-clad governess appeared, with Sybilla and her cake. "I hope we do not disturb you, but she would not have it otherwise," the young woman ventured timidly. Her maidenly eyes scarcely raised themselves to survey the well-set-up young man, of a kind she would never, in her circumscribed existence, meet as an equal. Sybilla fed the horse, and after some agreeable small-talk Paul rode off. He later found that the memory of the golden-haired child, laughing unconcernedly up at him and his beast, solaced him, at least in part, for the fool he'd made of himself . . . if he *had* made a fool of himself. Perhaps, after all, he had not, as Morven was after all kin to all of them; why shouldn't one mention his return?

II

Livia Judd awoke from sleep to find the grey light of early morning filtering in between the curtains, revealing the bed where she lay and, on the other pillow, Abel's head, the bald patch concealed by a tasselled nightcap. His mouth was open and he snored slightly. Livia closed her eyes. Abel was good to her, she knew, but she couldn't love him. Last night, for the first time in long—he was undemanding in the frequency of his rights upon her—he'd possessed her body fiercely, avidly, with the kind of brooding protective tenderness he always showed intensified in some way, for some reason. Abel would always have a reason. Perhaps it was to do with the ragged man who'd been in yesterday, and who had talked alone with Abel a long time, in the kitchen after the tavern-part was closed. She'd gone upstairs and left them still talking, and couldn't have told anyone what time the man had left. She hoped he didn't come back; they wanted another kind of customer at the Fleece nowadays.

Livia knew now what had awakened her at this early hour; she'd had a dream, and the dream had reminded her of another life, another young woman whom Abel, for all she was a good wife to him, never knew; a ragged tune ran through the dream, a tune called 'Kenmure' that Morven used to whistle often . . . What had made her dream now, again, of Morven? During all the years she knew he'd be in a living hell, she herself had thrust him down and out of memory, the way they'd done, she dared say, to his body on the hulks where they changed men slowly into animals. There was nothing she could do for him.

Morven, Morven.

And he was blind. She'd never seen him like he must have become; like a child, to be led by the hand, fed, guided, supervised, ordered. No doubt now old Aaron had left him his money, Morven would be better looked after than he had been, in the place to which they'd sent him. She hadn't grudged him the money, even though Abel, she suspected, did, after caring for his old father four years like a baby till Aaron died. Poor Abel; something about him was always unlucky, even the way he'd gone quite bald as a young man. Aaron had left her, Livia, also, a little bit. "To buy yourself a ribbon, lass," he'd told her at the end, when he was dying; he'd been fond of her. She hadn't bought ribbons, though; she'd set the money aside, to be used, some day, for William.

William would be stirring soon; he never lay long abed. He was as full of life as a small half-broken pony, Livia thought, and did nothing she or Abel bade him. Abel was good to William. Now that the Fleece was showing profits— it was herself had helped him there, Abel often told her; the place was clean as a whistle, she and the girl Tib, who'd come to them before Aaron died, kept it scrubbed and wholesome; travellers could come and be assured of a welcome and a good fire and meal, and no fleas in the beds—now that the inn was acquiring fame, and some money, they should think about sending William to school and a university, perhaps, later, to become a preacher or physician. That was what Abel said, and he meant it kindly, but herself she doubted if they'd ever see William in a pulpit. He was too much Doon's son; might he not end as his father nearly had, at a rope's end; she wouldn't wonder at it.

She opened her eyes again, staring upwards at the gathered folds of the central tester; the bed itself was made of oak. Fine things . . . she should consider herself lucky, and in ways did so, she the half-gipsy who'd come, weary, pregnant and out of a situation, that night on foot to the inn. Abel had taken her in, as his servant, for the time; next day, she'd started on the floors. The bulk of the coming child made her groan as she scrubbed and sanded, but she'd gone on with it; only, a short while after that, Abel had asked her to marry him. She'd gaped, knowing she wasn't much of a sight, by then, for any man; and he had begun to reason with her, kindly and quietly. It was for the child's sake as well as her own, he said. From the beginning, he'd seemed prepared to take full responsibility for William. This astonished Livia, remembering Governor Priddy in like case; Abel was, she dared say, some kind of saint. In the end, she'd married him.

It was at the bar-counter, where she heard most things afterwards, that Livia had the news of the amended sentence of Morven. Before then, she'd thought of him as a dead man, or as good as dead. That they would not now hang him, that they'd be sending him, instead, to Botany Bay, was taken by most of those present to mean mercy and that the magistrate, Sir Hubert Melrose, was kin to him; Livia had her doubts about the former. She knew nothing of Australia, but they wouldn't be sending the men out there if it were a pleasant life, or a free one. She'd carried on serving ale, and had said little, and no one said much to her; it wasn't generally known Morven had been the father of her child; as a rule, she supposed, folk thought Abel was. By then, William himself, hair already black as the King of Egypt's, was asleep upstairs in his wooden cradle with the maid, the one they'd had before Tib Willcock, rocking it with her foot; he'd been born in bed without any trouble, even choosing a time when the tavern was closed. After Abel had stated quite quietly that the child was his, nothing more, as far as Livia knew, had been said about that; though Abel had no doubt had to square the kirk folk with silver, to avoid the necessity of having to appear with Livia on public repentance-stools. That'd have been a queer state of affairs, if anyone liked; but it happened, Abel being a warm man and respected in the village. Now, folk respected Livia also.

She hadn't changed much. Those who, if any, were still on the lookout for trouble—there had been one or two forward fellows at the bar, at the beginning, looking down her dress

150

and so on; but Abel had soon altered that—those who still watched her saw only a tall, calm, comely young woman in a drab gown, spotless apron, and clean linen cap covering her black hair. She'd become famous for her laundering and the way she trained her maids, who told each other Mistress Judd was a demon for work, but didn't spare herself. The rest of life could have gone on in such a way, evenly enough, though something, Livia thought, had died in her till that tune of Kenmure in the dream came, to bring it to life. Then, if only briefly, she lived again.

After her first few weeks at the Fleece a fresh item of gossip had come to the taproom; first, someone heard the dead-bell ring; Mrs. Retford at the Mains had been taken. Livia, as may be imagined, felt some relief, for never now would the dead woman come demanding her runaway serving-maid; not that it would have happened, with herself big as a gourd at the time and Mrs. Retford, no doubt, glad to have seen the last of her had she known. She must have been ill for a long time never to notice, for her eyes were as a rule sharp enough; she was not much regretted. Abel, because the dead woman was a Doon and of the old family, ordered that the tavern-door be left shut on the day of the funeral. Old Aaron stubbornly determined, in addition, to go and pay his last respects; Bart would be there, he said. He often spoke of his dead younger son by then as if he were still alive; he had forgotten recent events and treated Abel, who looked after his needs with devoted tenderness, as though he were some paid hireling. Livia's company he enjoyed, he said, and she offered to drive the old man over in the dray that day, taking William with them.

Aaron set off in his best blacks, his teeth for once shoved in his head; the grim necessity of wearing them reduced his speech to a minimum, and on the return journey he carefully took them out. Livia waited for him—women did not attend funerals—at the deserted smith-cottage, bestowing William by her in the straw. He was beginning to crawl and she found, with attending to him, that she had no time for sadness or, very much, for memory of herself and Morven, hurrying towards one another across a space of green summer grass here long, long ago, in another life. Perhaps when she was an old woman she'd be like Aaron, confusing the past with the present; as it was she'd had more, far more, than most women ever knew of; in herself, she was whole. Where was Morven

151

now, in some ship on unimaginable seas? She thought of him as already afloat; had she known he was still lying in prison after so many months, she would have gone to him. But Livia was ignorant of the slowness of the law, and thought of Morven as far away, far further than the distance of a coach-journey. Nor could she write; and Morven being blind, they could send no word to each other. Would he know that, nevertheless, she thought of him constantly? Did he also think of her?

"It'll be the house he thinks of most," she told herself without bitterness, seeing Malvie black against the winter sky, with a single light burning, and a few flakes of snow beginning to come down. It would be a white funeral. She gathered William to her, and hushed him to keep him warm; and pictured Mrs. Retford's hearse, its sable plumes already sodden, driving towards the church, and later the snow lying whitely on the mourners' shoulders, as they saw her buried at last in the family tomb at Malvie.

Aaron rejoined her to say the funeral had been poorly attended by the family; Mrs. Annabel was fallen in her labour, and the physician had been sent for.

"She's early, they say." Livia had been thinking that it was late, the birth. She'd seen Annabel only once, in the carriage driving with her mother-in-law, and Miss Clairette; they hadn't noticed her where she was in the street. Miss Annabel, she'd thought then, from the look of her, was too big; the baby was misplaced, perhaps, and strained the small body till it seemed to draw away all its strength, leaving the limbs like thin sticks; and she'd lost all her pretty colour. Pity had assailed Livia, bringing fully home to her for the first time what Morven had done. His ruthless gift might well kill the recipient, such a birth couldn't be easy, for all the care and comfort Miss Annabel would receive in her silken bed. And the date was awkward.

Now, Aaron was saying he'd heard, Mrs Annabel had slipped and fallen while she was walking in the garden, on the snowy path. That'd help things, Livia thought; a late-born baby supposed to be premature. Folk would gossip still, without a doubt; they always did, and they'd say Miss Annabel and the poor invalid gentleman had done what they shouldn't, perhaps, on the shore last year when they were supposed to be gathering shells, but what did it matter? Morven's child had a father, in any case. They should be thankful for that.

Old Aaron watched her as she gathered the reins; she was a pretty young woman, and he liked those. Shyly, at that moment, he went over in his own mind the provisions of his will. He'd already left a small something to Livia, who was a good wife to his son, and had loved Morven. The latter was more important to the old man than the former; now, as the old do, he remembered clearly that Bart was dead, and that the bulk of his own savings, which were considerable and which Bart would have had, and the boat, and the cottage, he'd willed to Morven. Morven would be back, without a doubt, whatever they all said, and would need money; he, Aaron, had seen him right about that; it was wrong that Richard Doon's son should go without this world's goods when his father had ridden out that time for the true King.

For Aaron, was, at heart, a romantic.

Only one thing went wrong with Morven's plan, as they heard at the Fleece next night, after a terrible labour of Miss Annabel's lasting well into the morning. It was a little lass, they said, with dark-gold hair. The old woman—Kitty Bowes qualified for no other description among the tavern-folk, who knew her at once for what she was, not for what she tried to be, and judged her not unkindly—the old woman had been overjoyed, and had cried out that it was the exact colour her own hair had been when she was a child, and the baby would be pretty. They did say, also, that Mrs. Annabel could never have another child; that was whispered, but in any case the poor gentleman, her husband, was known to be in no state now to father another in any case, so rapidly had he grown weaker over the past winter. He'd sat, as they knew, all through the labour behind a screen at the bed's head, with the tears running down his face with joy at last, when he knew his wife was saved for him. Then immediately, as soon as he'd seen the baby, he'd taken the coach and driven off, weak as he was, through the storm, and that young footman George Oakes with him. George wouldn't give it away where they'd gone, but it was, he said, at the request of Mrs. Annabel; there was some word she wanted carried, about the birth no doubt, and Mr. Godfrey would never refuse a single one of her requests, let alone now. Meantime the baby, little Miss Sybilla, had been put out to nurse, for the poor mother had no milk and was in a bad way for a day or two; but now, praise God, better and almost herself

153

again, though never what she'd been when she was a young girl.

Yes, Livia heard it all; and set herself still more tasks to avoid thinking about that other baby. It would be loved and cherished, that was certain, the small bundle of flesh which was both Morven's and Annabel's; good fathers had been found for both Morven's children. "Oh, my lad, my lad," she thought sometimes, "do you ever think of it all, and do you know it's only a little lass you'll never see, after all your grand planning?" But where he was now it wouldn't make any difference, although she might have known, knowing Morven, he would surely mean to come home at the end of the seven years. But she'd hardly noted their passing, and one day when a new-gilded carriage drew up in the yard, for the grooms to tighten one of the horses' girths that had worked loose, so that the inmates would not be alighting, she'd seen Mrs. Annabel; her hair high-dressed and her pretty face rouged a trifle, under her small French hat; and by her a little fair-haired creature who was Morven Doon's daughter. They hadn't seen her where she stood looking at them from the door, and she'd gone away, and instead seen to the linen.

"Do you care to play cards this evening, Mama Bowes?"

Kitty smiled, pleased at her daughter-in-law's attentions; she was never, she thought, made to feel in the way at Malvie, the dear, beautiful little creature had an eye to her every convenience and comfort, her least wish. Should she play with them? She put her too-bright head on one side for instants, like some gaudy foreign bird, considering. She had herself taken pleasure, after the marriage, in teaching Godfrey's delightful, adaptable bride the intricacies of whist and faro, the latest refinements of vingt-et-un, from which Annabel had, with her strictly cloistered upbringing, of course, been as far removed as a nun. It would be a pleasure now to watch her pretty fingers deal and select the cards, while the two heads, Godfrey's and her own stayed close. How charming, how suitable, to see their devotion to one another! And if she herself had helped, in only the minutest fashion, at the beginning, although it had made Annabel so angry . . . but there, Kitty told herself, it had made her, the grandmother, perhaps responsible for Sybilla's very existence. And the child brightened all their lives now that poor Godfrey—

"I do not wish to play, Mama," said Clairette.

The toneless words recalled Kitty; she downed annoyance at the disturbing of her dream. Her youngest child was often a problem, ungracious, even ungrateful; after all, Godfrey gave her a good home. But unmarried young women were notoriously difficult, and it had proved, with Clairette's plainness, poor dear, so far, impossible to attract an offer for her. Kitty smiled, revealing a flash of porcelain teeth, and gallantly laid her hand on Clairette's arm.

"Why, then, we will take a little turn instead in the garden, as it's stayed fine," she said. "Will you perhaps accompany us, Annabel?"

"No, I shall play chess instead with Godfrey, if he'd like it." Godfrey brightened; Kitty smiled on, and bade Clairette go and fetch the small boxwood table, to avoid tiring her sister-in-law, and the chessmen, before they set out. Clairette obeyed unwillingly; why was Annabel so much like a doll, seated there on her sofa with her skirts outspread, that she couldn't get up and fetch her own game? There was nothing the matter with her. Everyone always deferred to her because she was pretty, and the mistress of the house, supposed to be delicate; but why? It was seven years, or very nearly, since Sybilla's birth. Annabel could ride and walk when she felt like it. Clairette set the chess-things out roughly, so that the bevelled legs of the small table dragged the Persian rug, leaving a fold.

After they had gone Annabel helped Godfrey set out the spiked ivory chessmen. They were so deeply and meticulously carved, and seemed so fragile, that it might have been thought that a careless touch might snap the haft of a pawn's spear, or the elaborate raised device on the turban of a king. But they had survived centuries, and would survive Godfrey and herself. Annabel moved a pawn languidly, smiling at the man she had married. She had become used to be surrounded with exquisite, priceless things. She herself had become one of them.

Her fingers moved the pieces in the game, at intervals of watching Godfrey's clumsy movements assemble the red against her white; he knew what he was doing with them, but no longer had the power of total control over his finger-muscles, and sometimes knocked a piece over. She let him pick it up from where it had fallen sideways on the board, herself silently retrieving, from time to time, the pieces which rolled on to the floor. Godfrey, she knew, preferred to do as much as possible for himself, and that she should not help him. Presently he raised his head and smiled at her.

"Did you want to play tonight, Annabel? Mama arranged it, I believe; or perhaps Clairette did so."

"I always like to play with you," she told him. "I still learn moves from you; you are a better player than I."

She smiled steadily, and moved a pawn; it was a routine move, which would keep her, now the others had gone, from having to give too much thought to the moves, or to keep up appearances before Kitty and Clairette. Godfrey, she knew, felt as she did; always kindly and welcoming to his mother and younger sister, he was able, as she was, to relax when they were no longer present. It was possible, also, for Annabel, playing this age-old, leisurely game, to be able to give way a little to the inner turmoil which had been with her, rigidly suppressed by day, since the news had come of the imminent return of Morven, brought by Paul Melrose the other afternoon. Of course one had always assumed that Morven would stay abroad, at the end of his sentence, as so many transported men did; what had he to come home for? It would have been better if he had stayed out there, and had left them at Malvie to live their chosen lives, which had grown, she hoped, over the years, happy and contented.

"Your move, Annabel."

She started; he had been waiting, she realised, for some time. She must be more careful; she hadn't even seen him make the move, and so many things, like the possible return of Morven, if permitted, could interfere with the bright, inflexible way she'd adhered, over the years, to her own promise to herself, which was that at all times, in every least way she could, she must make Godfrey happy; must let nothing interfere with the promotion of his happiness.

Had she made him so? If Morven should come home . . .

She moved, and watched the puffy, transparent hand reach out with difficulty, and capture her white knight. Godfrey was the kind of subtle, far-sighted player who, moving in from understated beginnings, swept the board in the end time and again; she herself could not have ventured to suggest how he'd taken the knight so soon. She was stupid, she knew. "That was quick," she smiled at him. "You will win tonight as usual; I despair of myself."

"You could win at times if you would think what you were doing. Is it the news of Morven that still troubles you, my dear?"

"I—yes." He thought of Morven, she knew, as the blind man she'd made him go to, that time of the birth, with the news of it as he lay in prison. That they had been cousins

156

and had spent their childhood together, so that she must be fond of Morven, would be enough explanation for Godfrey of that. Now she prepared to go on playing such a part; he mustn't see, must never even suspect, how her heart thudded now beneath its high-waisted bodice, and the colour crept up in her face beneath its rouge. "It hardly seems real," she heard herself say calmly. "Yet, knowing how fond he was of it here, he might have been expected, I daresay, to come back again; though I had hoped he would perhaps settle in Australia. If only he need cause no further trouble!" And her hand, her steady delicate white hand small as a child's, moved over the board and edged its remaining knight near Godfrey's queen, but the latter was hedged about with red soldiers.

Godfrey had stopped smiling, or even thinking of her or of the game. His face was pensive, and she knew that he was giving to the problem of Morven both the pity he accorded any offender—men didn't, as he repeatedly told her, become criminals in most cases unless through poverty, intolerable conditions, or despair—and with the experience he had acquired when, in the early years of their marriage, it had still been possible for him to be carried to quarter-sessions, to act as justice of the peace. He had become much respected and loved for his handling of these matters, more often than not helping the men and their families, she knew, afterwards from his own pocket. But he had not been able to prevent sentences such as Morven's from being carried out, although it was probable that his influence had helped withdrawal of the death-sentence. The fact of his confirmed responsibility displeased Annabel, fiercely resolved to be guardian of her invalid husband's happiness. Morven, if he came home, should have no part or lot with them here, he must not be invited to Malvie. No doubt, as he was blind, he would be content enough with some obscure existence nearby, perhaps in Aaron's cottage, although that was still too near.

She shuddered. It wasn't possible, she found, to picture Morven as blind. Would he feel the gratitude he undoubtedly owed to Godfrey and Sir Hubert, for preserving his life? She herself doubted it; he had never been grateful for anything, even from the days of her own father's affection for him, which had surpassed any Philip Doon might have felt for herself. The disinherited heir of Malvie had taken all that should have been hers except that: childhood, love, honour, virginity, peace of mind, health. Why should she think further of him?

But she could not prevent herself, she knew; and also knew that at night she'd lie awake, thinking of Morven.

Godfrey had won the game of chess. He asked if she wanted a return match, and she nodded; they set out the pieces, and halfway through Mrs. Bowes and her daughter came in view again, leisurely walking up the approach to the long windows, along a stone terrace flanked by urns in which Godfrey grew rare hanging plants. Kitty was talking vivaciously, with Clairette's plain long-nosed face giving no sign of having listened, or enjoyed the chatter. Poor Kitty was another, Annabel was thinking, who maintained appearances; who hadn't lowered the flag even that one time, years ago now, when Annabel herself had been deeply angry with her. Kitty had never dared act so again; as it was, she'd done harm to Godfrey, and he had been ill afterwards and had not completely recovered.

Annabel's cheeks flamed. Even after all this time, it was degrading to think of; an embarrassment to herself, and as for Godfrey . . . but, at least, he hadn't fully understood what had happened. It had given, moreover, some credence to the fact, accepted everywhere now, that he could have fathered Sybilla; and with the birth coming late . . .

She closed her eyes, remembering. It had nearly killed her, that birth. The physician had said, afterwards, that she could never bear another child, and she was glad. The distresses and humiliations of pregnancy, the prolonged agony of labour, the final wrenching of one's body apart, as though one were a mere vessel devoid of will, was something she would never let herself recall or think of. It was—it was like the animals, coarse, painful, grotesque, unmentionable. And before that there had been the other things she would never mention again.

For Morven had been wrong; Godfrey at the time of their marriage was not quite impotent. Godfrey, whose mind was as fine as a surgeon's knife, as a great painting, as a cathedral, and whose body was a pitiful thing, with so little strength in its reins that he could only stimulate, never satisfy . . . Godfrey had tried to become her lover. She had endured all of it; the uncertain, groping touch, the obscene jerking and fumbling, the growing awareness of failure which had ended, always, in the same way, with his head laid like a child's against her breast while he sobbed in bitter humiliation and distress. Annabel had not withdrawn her breast, or herself; she had tried to comfort him.

Then Kitty had taken a hand. Kitty, filled with her usual overt curiosity, knowing, though no one had discussed it with her, that all was not fully well with the marriage; determined, in her foolish and mistakenly loving dependence, that it should be; Kitty, serving them both night after night with wine which tasted bitter.

It had happened, accordingly, soon after that; but not in bed. It had happened in the small shed with glass windows where she and Godfrey, before winter should come on, were constructing an indoor garden on low shelves he could reach from his chair. He's been seated in it by her, and she'd turned and laughed up at him about some small matter, whatever it was; and had seen at once that something troubled him, and the great pearls of sweat beading his forehead; and had gone to him to wipe them away. And then it had happened. It had been embarrassing; she hadn't liked it, but she'd endured it, for as long as it took for the thing to be done. Afterwards Godfrey himself had been ill. That evening she herself had gone straight to Kitty Bowes and told her, with unaccustomed anger burning bright in her cheeks, that she must never, never do such a thing again; it was bad for Godfrey's health and she had no right to do it; what had she put in the wine? And Kitty, trembling and giving way to facile tears, had shown Annabel a little box, in which she kept irridescent green powders left over from Bowes in the days of his excesses; they'd never failed her and Bowes, she said.

Well . . . she'd felt soiled. But it had let the fact of her pregnancy be announced, a little while later, without question from the family. Only Clairette, with her furtive dark glance and her half-smile, had made Annabel feel uncomfortable . . . And, since the birth, of course, with Godfrey's condition and her own, and the migraines which troubled her and for which Cecily's cure, which she'd tried after Paul brought it over and which had proved to be no better than anything else . . . with all that, separate bed-chambers were a necessity. It was understandable; certainly Godfrey understood it, and it was never now discussed between them.

"Shall we have a quick round of vingty after all?" said Kitty indefatigably, coming in by the long window. "The lilacs are in grand leaf, Godfrey darling; we walked in the shade of them, and they've only been planted three years; how well they've grown!"

"It is becoming a pleasure-garden," said Annabel, smilingly dealing out the cards as they all sat down, Clairette evidently

159

having been persuaded to behave more graciously than was her habit. It was an hour yet till the meal; they played till darkness fell, then desisted when the servant brought the candles in, because of Godfrey's eyes. These had grown weak lately, and he only played in daylight. Afterwards Annabel half regretted the absence of the young Berrys, who would have made music for him; but they were elsewhere.

Later, after the two Bowes women had gone up to bed, he had an asthmatic attack. These often assailed him in summer, and the physician put it down to the heat; so Annabel obediently went and opened the windows, allowing the mingled night scents of stock and honeysuckle, grass-flowers and early roses, to flood in; was it her fancy that Godfrey grew worse with the scents? She went out, and shortly brought in what sometimes relieved him, a small, freshly-plucked sprig of peppermint from the herb-garden; the tiny round leaves emitted a charming fragrance, which sometimes refreshed him. He gasped, pressed the sprig against his nostrils willingly, and when he could, thanked her. But his face was still swollen and his eyes ran, and he put a hand to his chest; there was a pain there, he managed to tell her, which wasn't asthma; it came sometimes.

The attack passed and with it the pain, and she closed the window again; as always, in his courageous way, Godfrey began to talk after that of other things, as if nothing out of the way had happened. But his breaths were still laboured, and later Annabel eased his pillows and sat by him till George Oakes, who slept on a pallet in the room nowadays, came. Godfrey was meantime talking of a letter he had received that day; he had meant, he said, to ask her about it.

"You know I'd have made over Malvie—to you—and the remaining farms and—and Mains." He struggled for breath, and she soothed him; what did it matter, she told him again, the marriage-settlements made it unnecessary, a complication, leaving out the question of Sybilla. "We share everything, my darling." She felt her deep affection for this brave man rise; it wasn't like other love had been, not physical, but—but lasting; sometimes, when he was ill like this, she wondered, with a clutch of terror at her heart, what any of them would do without Godfrey. He talked on. An English firm of lawyers, he said, had written to know if he would be prepared to consider a tenancy for Mains; their client wanted a retired life, and was returning from abroad, and would like to take the dower house for a period of five years, at the outset. "What do you think?" Godfrey asked Annabel. "I'd thought of keeping the house lest Clairette marry, but so far—"

"Five years," she echoed. "How did this man know of the house?" The country was remote; he must be someone who knew of it, had been here once, perhaps, or—Fear sprang in her.

"Have they seen this man?" she said sharply. "Do they know him?"

"Presumably, as he is a client." Godfrey smiled through his remaining breathlessness; it gave him, at times, a pleasant sense of masculinity to instruct Annabel. He told her, as was true enough, that the dower house would be better to be lived in and fired, having had only occasional attention since aunt Retford's death. "I'll set them tomorrow to clear the garden," he said. "At present, the Englishman won't get through to his front door. Fosse of course will have to deal with it, and can take instruction from the London firm." Fosse was the Edinburgh lawyer.

So he had already decided on it, she told herself; and tried to quench her own disquiet. There was, after all, no reason why the Mains should not have a tenant, if any desired to come.

III

Some weeks after the foregoing events at Malvie, a hired coach was negotiating the steep, crowded cobbles of Edinburgh High Street. The comings and goings of the law-courts impeded its progress and caused one of the inmates to rap, impatiently, for the driver to bestir himself. That personage shrugged, and gave a routine flick of his long whip above the horses' idle rumps; as if they were used to this treatment, they shrugged likewise, so that the sharp reminder might have been no more than the bite of a passing cleg or gnat; and continued their slow pace.

"This is intolerable!" said Morven Doon to his companion,

who lounged opposite him in the coach-interior, a plain beaver hat pulled down over his eyes. "We are an hour later than we intended already; the attorney will have gone to his tavern."

"Not so," replied the other soothingly, in the accents of a foreigner. "The courts are only now emerging."

"Scaling, they call it here, if nowhere else; add that to your vocabulary, Samson. What a country! Since the Parliament left it, in my great-grandfather's time, the capital is nothing but a lawyers' warren where proofs pile up." He himself, long unable to see even so unworthy an aspect, stared with sightless eyes beyond the window, where, he knew, past the press of black gowns and white wigs the brooch-tower of St. Giles' raised itself, and further up the bulk of the Castle; the light eyes, bright as a falcon's, rested on them unseeing. Morven Doon had lived in darkness since the customs-fight, seven and a half years back; the deep wound to the nerve-centres at the back of his brain had taken his sight, though the eyes themselves were uninjured. The passing of time, in such a condition, had altered Morven in immediate appearance very little; a thick white lock of hair grew at the site of the old injury, but he had covered it today with the wig which he wore beneath his hat. A ruthless quality about the thin mouth, a masklike lack of expression in the face, might have told those with eyes to see that this man had lived long with horror; but most men, seeing him pass by in the coach, would notice only a well-to-do citizen clad in the fashion of, perhaps, ten years back; he had had the suit of clothes made to order in Port Jackson, and they were still of the cut he remembered before leaving home. His coat was of broadcloth, of good imported quality, with modest braiding on the fastenings and turned-back cuffs, and he wore a gay waistcoat of French brocade, which had cost a great deal; his shoes had silver buckles. He had made, as his appearance suggested, a reasonable fortune in Australia; old Aaron's legacy had come at the right time to permit him to buy, at a low rate, a strip of land to clear up-river. With Samson as foreman, and native labour, it had shortly become a productive farm; before leaving, Morven had sold the land and equipment at auction, making a good profit. He smiled; that wasn't the only pair of irons he had in the fire; the man Tom Neilson had been sent to Abel Judd, with instructions to proceed in a certain way over the money still hidden, and the contacts they retained in France.

Morven's companion in the coach was attired similarly to his master, although his waistcoat was plainer. The noticeable thing about him—leaving aside the dusky colour of his skin, for he was a mulatto, a half-black—was his strong frame, compact and massive as a bull's rather than very tall; he had average height. His eyes, surprisingly, were smoke-grey, and surveyed the teeming streets now with a kind of resigned acceptance. Now and again he would pass a pink tongue across his lips, and his teeth, when once or twice he smiled at some saying of Morven's, were ruinously decayed, more like a white man's than a negro's.

His name was in fact Nathaniel Weeks, but Morven, who had rescued him up-river in circumstances which ensured the young man's lifelong gratitude and service, called him Samson because he was so strong. Samson's hands, with the palms showing pink and the nails, against the fingers' dusky tinge, pink also, could perform feats with pig-iron and copper bars, as though the latter had been cheese; his prowess with women was likewise considerable, though less prodigious than Samson himself made out. He had been born in Sydney Cove shortly after the early consignments of prostitutes sentenced to lifelong transportation had landed, and his mother had been an Irish Protestant named Matilda Weeks. She took to her trade with vigour both on the transport-ship and off, and one of her customers was an immense buck negro ashore from galley service, whose ship had called in at the port only briefly to take on water. He was also an ex-pugilist. Tilly found, after the ship had left, that the tickler of the fancy had left behind more with her than his money, and, as she herself told her son later, she tried every damned means to be rid of the little bastard, even knitting-needles, but he was set too high up inside. He emerged, in due course, to the light of day in the bawdy-house, and knocked about there for the first part of his childhood. He was growing, surprisingly, a pretty little boy, coffee-coloured, and shaped like a god, with Tilly's Irish eyes deeply fringed by long black lashes. He learned, quite early on, to steal untraceably; all his days he was to keep a happy knack for this, and for such foresight in general.

When he was six years old Tilly had a bit of luck. A French vessel landed, and with it an elderly travelling aristo-crat who had found it politic to leave court circles at Versailles for some time; *ennuyé* with life on his estates, he decided to see the globe, and brought with him a great deal of money, two valets, and a brocade-hung bed. He was in fact extremely eccentric, and why Tilly's shopsoiled charms should have appealed to him when others were available was one of the mysteries which time never did unravel. She stayed on, in fact, as the Comte's mistress for two years, during which time Samson learnt to converse almost entirely in French. He forgot, as events turned out later, that he had ever known another tongue, and for the rest of his life adopted Gaelic turns of phrase and its accent, which amused Morven later.

Samson left the *émigré* establishment at very short notice. He had been aware, as a much stupider little boy would have been, for some time that the old Comte had a marked fancy for his company, and would send for him, often while Tilly was still present, and take him on his knee and fondle him, and feed him comfits (this may have been the beginning of his history of bad teeth). In course of the improvements in his knowledge of the French language which Samson thus picked up, he learned the words for turban, tunic, silks, feathers, satins; the Comte would like to take him back to France with him, as his little page. "In England it is all the rage, the ladies, ah! They have a little page, a little black boy. He carries the train, so! He stands behind, while the great lady is at the opera. You have never heard of opera? They sing, so." And the Comte gave a short falsetto rendering of Rosina's air, which he had heard the Queen herself sing badly out of tune, once when they staged a performance in the theatre at Versailles. Samson digested this experience, with others. He could not later remember whether or not Tilly had been present to hear the Comte sing, but he was aware of some hauteur at being called a little black boy. He was brown, not black.

Tilly came in when he was at the privy afterwards; it was the only place where they could be alone. "For the dear Lord's sake, pull on your breeches and get out of here," she said. "I'll tell him you've run away."

He stared at her. "Do you know what they're going to do to you, you poor little varmint?" she said. "He's getting a barber to trim the balls off you, the way they do; that way, it's safe to hand you for a page, as they call it, to his lady-friends when you're older. Ah, for the love of God, go!" And she shoved some money into his hand. He hadn't delayed more than instants, after hearing that one; he never knew if it was true, or found out what had happened in the end to his mother. He dived out of the house and away from the port, and lay up by himself in the bush for a while, living on yams; after that he fell in with a native tribe, and the women there were kind to him and fed him. Afterwards he stayed with

164

the tribe for four years, finding out about natives, and learning their language; he dared say he knew more about them than any settler in the Bay. After that—

"You're silent today," said Morven, chaffing him as he sometimes did. "What are you thinking about? This damned coach hasn't moved an inch; let's get out and walk."

They paid off the coachman, and made their way on foot to where the attorney had his office, flush with the arcaded street; Samson unobtrusively guided the blind man by walking behind him, but never took his arm. Doon, he knew—his master had asked to be addressed as Doon—had an uncanny instinct for knowing where he was going, for avoiding objects another sightless person might have knocked into; besides, he would remember this place from a boy, perhaps, before he was sent to Australia. Samson waited, patiently as a lion by a waterhole, to hear more of Morven's youth; he had never forced himself upon the attention of the white man, which was one of his attributes.

Now, they were to sign a paper about a house; this was all Samson knew of it, except that the house would be for them both to live in and was somewhere near the sea. Samson remembered the sea without sentiment; he had had four months of it on the voyage home, and had seldom been without a sight of it all his boyhood. But to Doon, he knew, the sea meant something different. Of course, the thing they were to do about the brandy-running would all come from the sea. Tom Neilson, he knew, who had come home two months before them, had had instructions to see a man called Abel Judd. Samson knew no more than that. No one disobeyed Doon, or tried to evade his orders. He, Samson, would in any case see that they did not.

The attorney Fosse came bustling to meet them. "Mr. Doon? A great pleasure, sir; I had not expected you for a se'nnight yet, though they wrote of your coming from London."

"We made all speed from the south. There was no reason for delay."

Mr. Fosse showed Morven to a chair, and by a kind of occult process involving no spoken orders to anyone, produced a tray of Madeira wine brought in by the scrivener, his wig a trifle awry. Morven could see none of that, but smiled, and sipped his Madeira. The obsequious reception by this crow in Devenham's employ amused him, coming as he did with credentials from the London lawyers, and with the name of Doon. A different kind of usage would have been his seven years back, when he, a convicted half-reprieved criminal, had been lodged nearby in the Tolbooth for a night or two, prior to his removal by Leith Roads to the prison-hulks in the south, and Botany Bay. Best not to remember that . . . except that old Aaron's legacy, news of which had been received by Morven out there in the Governor's house at the port, had ensured his later prosperity, and this libation of wine today. He was, despite any past he might have, by now a respected customer; money made any man respected; after this interview he had one more, with a different lawyer, less well-found than Mr. Fosse. Let not the right hand know what the left doeth, Morven told himself; the purchase of certain derelict warehouses on Leith wharves would shortly come to a very reasonable conclusion. If his hand was against every man's, the hand should be in firm control of the project he'd planned, all those years in the savage country half a world away, which had made him rich. He, a blind man, could buy and sell this lawyer; was in a fair way to buying and selling Devenham himself. The prospect pleased Morven.

He listened to the flurried apologies of Mr. Fosse, explaining why the contract was not yet made out. "Write it out now, then, and let us be gone," said Morven impatiently. The scrivener came scurrying, and was instructed to set aside everything else; the draft of the five-year lease for Mains of Malvie must be made out forthwith. "We'll have it signed and witnessed while Mr. Doon is here with us. More wine, sir?"

"No, I thank you. My kinsman has agreed to the lease?" Morven spoke smoothly; he must remember to invoke Devenham frequently as his kinsman; the latter was, after all, Fosse's known client. He took the quill the attorney finally handed him, and, with Samson leaning forward to steady and sand the page, signed his name, with unwavering fingers. He was pleased with this; he had, in fact, held a pen only once or twice since becoming blind. Fosse watched in some mortification; it had only just become evident that this well-found personage had any disability. His respect grew. No doubt Mains of Malvie, being remote and quiet, would be an ideal retreat for the poor blind gentleman. Fosse came forward in his eagerness.

"Where am I to reach you, sir? Have you a direction in Edinburgh?"

Morven frowned. "No, I have small business here now; I shall go straight down to Mains, I believe."

"But, sir, my client—" Mr. Fosse knew embarrassment. Mr. Devenham had not yet signed, and, although he had signified his willingness for a lease, it would perhaps have been advisable— "The draft will be sent off this very day, sir," bleated Mr. Fosse. But Morven held out his hand, as though he could see the paper.

"I shall be there myself before the mail. Mr. Devenham is my kinsman by marriage, as you are aware. I look forward to seeing my cousin." He smiled. "You may send any urgent message, should there be such, to the Fleece, Grattan Juxta; but I do not anticipate any delay in moving into the Mains."

He rose, and, taking the paper with him, left Mr. Fosse in only a slight degree of perturbation; it was irregular, but what harm could come? As Mr. Doon had truly stated, they were kinsmen; in fact, no doubt, a lease itself was redundant. Mr. Fosse sent, after the departure of Morven Doon and his well-trained coloured servant—how valuable such an acquisition was here in these days!—out to a tavern, to fetch himself some ale, which in fact he drank seldom. But his days in ordinary course tended to be somewhat tedious, and he felt the need of a minor dissipation.

Morven had hired a coach which took the bad roads more swiftly than the equipage they had lately dismissed had contrived Edinburgh High Street. Despite the dangers of a night-drive, he would hear of nothing but that they should go straight on; dark to him was the same as day, and each turn of the wheel brought him nearer Malvie; Malvie, of which he had dreamed for seven interminable years.

Samson accordingly cocked his pair of duelling pistols, of which he was proud, and held them at the ready all the way. With neither master nor man asleep, therefore, each followed his own thoughts, no longer seeing the carriage-lamps pick out stone walls, trees, and sleeping houses and inns on the way.

Morven was thinking of Devenham, his enemy, and the last time they had encountered one another. To say he had seen Godfrey would be inaccurate; at that time, he himself had been newly blind. He had lain on his pallet in the cell, aware of the sentence that had been passed on him, unable even to feel much relief that he was not after all to hang. The world was dark, would never be otherwise for him again;

he would never see Malvie more except in dreams; and seven years was a long time, and Australia half across the world; how many men, after sentence, ever even reached Botany Bay?

He had lain day and night with such thoughts; he had felt young and alone, for the first time acutely feeling the need of Livia, not as a woman but as a breast to lean on, a mother's kind breast; she would have comforted him, he knew. Where was she now? She must have had their child; had she borne it in a ditch, and was she safe? Annabel he thought of less, and never as a person; often, and urgently, he wondered if the boy were safely born, and if he would be reared in all ways as befitted the heir of Malvie. The mother's safety did not trouble Morven, as did Livia's. It was useless, in any case, to repine; it was on the cards he himself would never hold either of his children. He was obsessed with thoughts of his own death; here in the stinking prison, stiff with blood from his bandaged undressed wound, which had festered and brought him a fever; or again on board the ship they would take him to, down in the south, scarcely a seaworthy ship for long voyages, with men chained together between decks like animals. Soon, it would be time.

They had announced a visitor for him then, and Morven felt himself smile wryly as he guessed who it was; almost certainly, Sir Hubert Melrose, filled with last precepts, his cloak muffled high about his face supposedly to keep out the prison-stench, but in reality to avoid being recognised. Sir Hubert had his position to keep in mind; he, Morven, so nearly related as he was, must be an affliction to his kin. He was aware that, for his own sake as well as Morven's, the magistrate had done what he could to have the sentence lightened, and had contrived so much; he must now thank Melrose, he supposed, for his sightless life. How was a man to live on, being blind, in a strange country? How could he learn to do anything at all, when he—

Self-pity might have overcome; but a gentle, known voice came to him, and he realised with a shock that Godfrey Devenham was in the cell. He must have had himself carried down. With hearing that had grown acute and analytical even in the few months of lying here in idle darkness, Morven guessed the young footman was with him, and had set him down in his chair on the soiled straw and ordure of the floor. He lay and waited, aware of some anger. What did Devenham want of him? To gloat?

"Annabel asked me to come, Morven. She—she has been

very ill." The voice trembled, and Morven assessed the situation curiously. To this eunuch, this creature who could never fully have her, Annabel meant everything, was seemingly the dearest object on earth. He remembered that she must by now have been delivered; trying to keep the tremor from his own voice, he asked the child's sex. Godfrey answered patiently.

"A daughter, a beautiful healthy child with fair hair." She had been born late, he added; had been so large they'd feared she and the mother would both die, and they'd had to use instruments. "It was so long a labour," Godfrey said, "poor Annabel, I watched . . ." He himself, at his own request, had been placed behind a screen, to be near her; he had suffered torments every time she strained; there would never, the doctors already said, be another child, and he was glad her fragile body need not endure such agony again; but one couldn't tell it all to Morven.

He was about to speak further of it, though not everything, when the sight of Morven, which had shocked him with the thin pallor of the blind face, and the undamaged eyes staring at nothing, arrested him. Tears were pouring down the sick man's cheeks; they seemed to follow one another without volition, and the bleached hands, lying on the dirty palliasse the prison provided, made no effort to raise themselves and wipe these away.

"No heir for Malvie," Morven wept; then remembered the presence of his enemy.

"Go now, for God's sake. Don't say to her you saw me in such a way as this. Is there news of Livia?"

But Godfrey had not heard of Livia's marriage to Abel; and at lack of any word Morven thought he would die of misery. After the chair had been carried away he turned and sobbed for a long time against the wall, inconsolably.

He had trained himself, even so early as the hell-ship where they chained him beside Tom Neilson between decks, to do without his eyes.

It had to be done, in any case; as well do it cleverly and precisely, and Morven set his wits to pit themselves against the tormenting eternal dark, both at sea—the slapping leagues of endless water, which he heard more clearly than most now, embracing the ship like a helpless fly, so that one more sinking would hardly be of note except that the owner-company would be out of pocket to the extent of twenty-four poor devils' board, and some driftwood—the knowledge of that came either to drive him mad, or else anneal him; the latter happened, and by the end of the voyage he could endure most things; many men had died meantime of the bad food, and of fever. Morven was landed, and visited in time by the Governor, who was curious to see a blind prisoner, and asked him what he could usefully do.

"I need a man I can trust," he said at the end, and to Morven it seemed amusing that he, a convicted murderer, should be spoken to in such a context, as if anyone here could be trusted among the killers, thieves, horse-stealers and other expatriate scum that abounded and lodged, as he himself did initially, in small brick-built houses disposed about the growing port, with the Governor's residence among them like an elephant in a field of lambs; he'd heard Tom describe it so. But in fact not all the transported men were villains, and villainy in any case took on a different aspect here; the quartered army men, the dragoons, caused more trouble than the prisoners ever did, and the Governor waged his own war constantly and sent plaintive letters home, which were not listened to, of the hollow authority he enjoyed as the King's representative. Morven soon, as a civil-spoken clever fellow who could adapt easily, became much employed by the Governor and his deputy, on assignments; at first, he merely polished the silver and the doorknobs, and later was given the precise task of measuring out the Indian corn when scarcity one year threatened a famine, and the natives of the region would come by night and steal it, so that a man to whom dark was the same as day would be of more value here than rubies, and he could for the time be night-watchman . . .

That was how Morven had acquired Samson in the first instance. He tried to listen to the other's breathing now at the opposite side of the coach, to see whether or not he slept; he would not ask him, and the coach swayed on. In a matter of hours they would be, with the dawn in Grattan Juxta, if nothing went amiss.

Samson was not asleep and, as it happened, his thoughts followed the same pattern as his master's; he was thinking back to his own first encounter with Morven Doon.

He had lived with the native tribe for four years since evading the Comte's intentions, and in many ways had become, himself, a bushman, and could trap, spear fish and speak their tongue. The tribe was friendly, and had he desired it would have initiated him, thus making him one of themselves by means of certain mysteries which included knocking out a front tooth and burying it beneath a tree, so that the great spirit Dalamulun would take care of the rest, and of him; but he had resisted this, preferring to remain an outsider among the tribe. He had grown used, however, to their low estimate of their women; these were treated like animals and subject to innumerable taboos which made their lives wretched. He saw little of them except when he slept in the clearing at night, and by day was away hunting for food with the young men and boys.

This grew scarce. The tribe lived mostly on yams in the hard season, and these grew, or had done, thickly nearby the river. Now the white man had come, and cleared away the yam-plants for his farming; increasingly as the convicts were released, or had come near the end of their served time, they were given, or could buy cheaply, a strip of land which, with diligence, could grow corn. But the hungry bush-men would raid the corn as it grew, leaving bare stalks in the morning. A watch was set at each man's land, and as soon as it could be done the harvested corn, amounts of which were very small, was locked in store; the guardian of the latter was Morven Doon.

He had received a supply from up-river one day, and had heard the great open crocks in which it was brought and stored rolled to their places; then he was left alone and the night settled down. He waited in his place, hearing in faint trickles the settling and running of the disturbed grains of corn; his thoughts were not pleasant, and for once did not concern himself and his fate. Word had come that the dragoons had made a raid on the thieving bushmen, and had hanged the men outright in chains, to be left on their gibbets as a warning. Morven had grown inured to cruelty in prison and on the voyage out, rather than since; but he knew these tribesmen had been spoken of as friendly to the whites, and that they were starving. As often, he felt awareness of the infinite unknown land behind the settlement, the limitless silent spaces; often the silence seemed to have a voice. He had heard of men who'd run mad in the outback, merely by reason of this very silence, from which there was no escape; it pressed in on one. He himself could be the prisoner of silence as well as dark.

He shivered; and at once heard a sound which was neither the movement of his body, nor the faint, persistent settling of the corn. It was a scrabbling, whimpering sound; too large for a rat or dog. Perhaps he was shut in with some strange animal here, brought in the crocks with the corn.

He waited; then stealthily, uncertain against what he might have to plan action—some animals here were tame, but not many, for the hunters and, of late years, the white men had taught them caution—rose and moved along the wall. The sound had come from one of the crocks near a corner. There were no windows in the store because of thieves, and the door was fast shut; only Morven in his blindness was at no disadvantage in the dark.

The sound came again, and he reached out; he was certain now that it was a human animal, probably a thief. A cry met him, as his fingers closed on a skinny, almost skeleton outthrust arm, a child's, he thought. Instantly teeth met in his hand; they wrestled, he and the skeleton, together for moments, and then he dragged the latter, sobbing, from its place of refuge in the corn-crock, shaking it briefly to the sound of scattered grains of Indian corn. Neither had spoken, but Morven cursed now aloud at the pain in his bitten hand; he could feel it running with blood. He was about to shout for aid, but as yet did not. He could, he felt, deal reasonably with one skeleton, pot-bellied with eating raw maize.

"Are there others of you?" he said clearly, still holding the child—he was certain now it was only a child—by the scruff. The boy was naked. He whimpered, then struggled briefly and gave up. He'd seen all the men he knew, the men of the tribe, old as well as young, taken and hung in chains for the birds to pick. He'd dived among the corn early on and hidden from the soldiers. Stumbling, for he had almost forgotten how to speak this unseen guardian's tongue, he told Morven of it.

"Do not let them hang me!" He sketched a gesture with his emaciated finger across his throat; the whites of his eyes rolled upwards in the dark to where the strange, still figure of the white man waited. He knew it must be a white man because of the way he spoke. But why did he remain so still? Other whites shouted, strode about, were angry. The boy remembered them from the days of the brothel, the later days of the Comte. He bowed suddenly and said, "*Je vous remercie, monsieur,* you no let soldiers get me. I no hang." Suddenly he slid to his knees and gave way to sobbing. "I no hang? I no hang? Please."

Morven hid the boy till he himself could obtain clothes for him, a ragged shirt and a pair of breeches; he did not for a long time take to shoes. He padded about at Morven's heel thereafter, rapidly putting on flesh with the shared rations, and became the blind man's eyes in a number of ways; he could run errands, after instruction cook and mend; from the beginning keep watch, listen and report accurately; he could also steal, but after the undetected replacement of a watch of the Lieutenant Governor's, and the instruction that he most assuredly would hang after all if such doings were repeated here, the boy settled down to become a useful and later, an indispensable servant to Morven. He grew out of the breeches, and then out of the shirt; he put on weight and inches almost to the extent of his unknown and putative sire, and in particular the privy organ, which Tilly's intervention had preserved entire, was of a size the bushmen themselves, Samson assured his master, had latterly regarded with astonishment; it was evident that he was, even so early, under the special eye of Dalamulun. He soon put the life in the tribal clearing behind him, but did not revert to his earlier origins; by now, he was the perfect white man's servant, and his feeling for Morven was unique, blending a protective understanding of the other's blindness with firm tolerance of the fact that they were slave and master, man and dog. Nobody asked where Morven had found the boy; it was assumed he came from the farms up-river, or else had been picked up from among the swarms of homeless children about the port, the sons and daughters of imported prostitutes. There was no longer any sign, or word, by now of Tilly and the boy never heard of her, or asked about her as far as anyone knew, again. The present was enough and he was happy, and could do more or less as he liked apart from carrying out Morven's orders. When Morven also bought himself the land up-river, it was Samson who acted as foreman there; under cultivation, with the corn cut and sold yearly, and the money which had meantime come from somewhere across seas, his master grew rich. When it became a question of selling the farm, and going back across the sea, there was no doubt that the blind man would take Samson with him now that he was free. And Samson, by now an impressive figure in his bespoke broadcloth coat and tricorne beaver, came; and here they were in a coach bound for Grattan, and he carried his dueling-pistols.

Nothing happened to them on the journey from highwaymen, accidents, or the like. Early next morning, with the sun gilding the empty road, they clattered into the village where the Fleece still slept across its cobbled yard, and drew up there, Morven instantly yelling for a groom. When the latter came out, rubbing the sleep from his eyes, he bade him go and wake his master. "Tell Abel I want a shave, and some breakfast," he said, grinning like a boy. "Do it before you take off the horses; then come back."

The groom's demeanour, which had been truculent, changed; this was a man who could call the landlord by his Christian name, and must be a respected person; perhaps much more. His faculties slowly recovering with the morning air, the young groom climbed to Abel's bedchamber, and shook him awake where he slept with his wife. Abel pulled on his breeches and came down, grumbling and still in his tasselled nightcap; when he saw who it was, with Morven by now stretching his legs in the yard, his expression was comical.

"It—it can never be Morven Doon?" And he pulled off the cap and stood turning it about between his hands, with the early sun shining on his black-fringed pate. Morven stood still, smiling. "How is it with you, Abel?" he said. "Do I disturb you too early? But I was always an inconvenient fellow, you know, though Aaron and Bart suffered more from me than you did."

"I—I—" Still Abel seemed devoid of words; then they burst out of him. "Morven, I can't but feel the heart glad in me to see you stand there again . . . I let the wife sleep on, not knowing who had come. She—she works hard, and it's not yet five of the clock. Have you told them what you'll eat? I have eggs, always, and a bite of home-cured ham and . . ." He bustled away to get the fire lit; Morven could hear him shortly, roaring for the maids to get up; what was it Abel had said about a wife? He could, despite his state, have been assumed to have married again by now, Morven thought out of the void which had been his, regarding any news. A cautious, slow, safe remarriage to some plump widow with a comfortable tocher; that would be Abel, and he wished him joy. His own face hardened with determination. As soon as Devenham's signature endorsed the lease, with Malvie visited, and he himself set down in the Mains for the time with Samson, and what they could scratch together for fare and fire, after the journey; after that, he'd set out, and if it took the rest of his days would find out what had become of Livia Millarch and her child. He had a notion Livia would have contrived some means of not being left abandoned, or roofless; unless—and this was his greatest fear —she'd perhaps found her mother's people, and would be stravaiging with them now up and down the country, so that it might take years to find her again. But he'd find her; and when he'd found her, he'd take her away with him. Most likely the good lass was in service somewhere, though with a child at her hip it would have been hard to find a situation. The devil had been in it that he hadn't been able to write, or she to read; since blindness had fallen upon him like a pall and he'd been sent, more dead than alive, in a stinking hulk chained beside Tom Neilson to the Antipodes, it had been like taking a new skin, painfully.

But now he was himself again, except for the eyes; and he had his plans.

He had breakfasted, hungrily and well, on Abel's ham and eggs and coffee; and shaved with the hot water the awakened maid-servant brought. Afterwards, when not the maid but a talkative urchin came to carry away the shaving-bowl, Morven, feeling better, reached out a hand and ruffled the boy's thick hair, and asked his name idly. He'd be about seven years old.

"William, sir," said the boy, fascinated by the sight of the brown man rather than the blind, whose disability he hadn't noticed. He had heard of Negroes, but had never seen one before. "Are you from Africa?"

"No, further off," said Morven. The question had amused him and released, with the well-being the food and the shave had brought, a sense of power. The joy of returning life, hardly circumscribed by blindness—had his will not hardened to meet it, and his fingers and ears grown cunning?—filled him with the awareness of being in his own country again, with Malvie a stone's throw off, or little more. He tossed the child sixpence.

"Have you any other name, my urchin?" He heard the boy catch the coin, and bite it providently with his teeth; the amusement grew in him. "William Judd, sir," the name's owner said.

"Indeed?" Had Abel lost no time in extracting an earnest from his widow? Old Aaron, if he had known of that, would be surprised. Aaron had always said Abel would never father a child; he'd had an injury to the testicles in boyhood. Everyone knew of that. The puzzle grew in Morven's mind, and he detained the boy a moment. "Who is your mother?" he asked him.

"Mistress Judd," said William, wriggling to be gone. He was disappointed in the question; this customer had looked as if he would have other things to say than most folk had. It was like the kirk elders, who'd come by now and again with their long faces and black coats, and lay a damp hand on his hair and bid him mind his letters and his Bible, for he had a kind father now to tend him. William disliked letters and the Bible bored him. He repressed a derisive noise; Abel, or possibly his mother, would beat him, he knew, if he caused trouble with the customers, and this one had a coach.

But the gentleman who'd given him sixpence and who had a face like one of the carved stone saints they hadn't managed to hack off the wall in church, as it was part of the pillar, kept asking questions. William was certain now there was something queer about his eyes; they looked at and yet through one. The man asked what his mother's name had been before she married. William was looking round for a way of escape; just then he saw the maid Tib come out wiping her hands on her apron. She might have been sent to look for him. He shouted, and at once Tib called, as he'd hoped she would do, "William! You're to come in, your father says, at once; who told you to wait about there? They can't keep him abed, and it's best to let him help," she said cheerfully to Morven, in the way Grattan maids had of caring for no man's rank, even should he be the Provost. And thinking of that, there'd been a terrible to-do a week or two back at Maddon Magna, where the Provost's brother-in-law there, a sour-faced elder named Priddy, had lost his position, and had been fined and publicly disgraced, for pestering young girls at Emmett's orphanage. Imagine it! Mistress Judd, she'd smiled when she heard, and said, "Ay, I know," but that was all.

She was about to lead William away by the hand now, dragging back again, as he kept doing, to look at the gentleman about to step again into his coach; the horses had been fed and watered, and wouldn't need changing as they said they weren't going far. But the blackfellow stepped in the way, and Tib drew a breath like a squeal; what did that one want? "Doon asked you for a name," he said to the boy. "You did not give it."

Tib giggled; she was enjoying the episode. Perhaps Samson, as she'd heard the other call him, would be along one day for ale; that'd bring customers in, for a sight . . . She heard William call out the name Morven had waited to hear; as children do, he made a song of it, repeating it again and again as he followed Tib across the sunlit cobbles. He was no longer unwilling to go in.

"Livia," he was saying. "Livia."

And the name Morven had waited to hear echoed about the yard of the Fleece, which he could no longer see; but joy lit up his face so that it would have seemed to William, had he been looking, that the stone saint saw celestial visions.

But Morven Doon said nothing, and stepped, still smiling, into the coach.

After he had heard the coach drive away Abel went upstairs again; Livia had got up already and was dressing, seated now in stays and undergown, brushing her hair. The swishing sound filled the room with rhythm and scent; the loose hair lay about her shoulders, black and thick. He went to the window, no longer trusting himself to look at Livia with her hair loose, and her taut fine body with arms upraised, brushing at it. He stared out of the window; one couldn't see the yard from here, only the corner where the alleyway jutted.

"You were up early," she said to him. "Was it a customer?"

"Ay." He ought to tell her, he knew, who it had been. Perhaps in a moment he'd do so; but now, as if for the last time, he was conscious of the comfort and cleanly intimacy of the room behind him, and of his wife seated therein. If he told her, would things ever be the same again? Yet she'd be bound to know soon; he'd be back, would Morven.

"Livia—" He turned to look at her; she'd twisted up her shining hair now in a knot; presently she'd put a little cap on it, then shrug into her overgown and apron. Neat and clean, she always looked, a worthy helpmeet, a good worker, Livia; but it hadn't been only that.

"Did Tib do all they wanted? I thought I'd come down and see."

"Ay." Why couldn't he tell her? But the words wouldn't come easily. This plan of Morven's that he'd heard the other day; this storing up in warehouses in Leith instead of under stones and about the moor, and employing packmen; it was risky, maybe. They'd all get rich, Tom Neilson said. But he himself had doubts—Ah, that! It wasn't that that exercised him now; it was that he, a stoutening middle-aged publican with a bald head, was in agony lest his wife leave him for Morven Doon. It wasn't loving a woman, he knew, to force her to stay if she'd sooner not. But for all they'd built here together—

A sound came in the doorway; William. He'd left it too late. He turned away, knowing he couldn't prevent whatever might happen now. It had always been like that, and he was

177

one of those who couldn't stop the world from going its way. Poor Abel, they'd always called him; his father and everyone. He knew. Poor Abel. And now—

"A man gave me sixpence," said William. "His name was Doon."

Afterwards she said to Abel, "You knew, didn't you, love, that he was coming back? You knew the other night." And she bent to tidy the place at the mirror, and he couldn't see her face.

"Ay." There seemed no more to say. The name she'd used had been from habit.

"You didn't tell me," she said now, as if to herself. Then, "Has he changed much, now he's blind?"

He said suddenly, bitterly, "Morven won't ever change in a hundred years," and turned and pushed his way, blind as Morven, out of the room, past William who was still turning his sixpence about in his hands, and downstairs. Later he heard Livia come down as usual and the sounds of the housework commence, as if nothing had happened.

IV

Morven went first to Malvie.

As his coach drew up at the door others were drawing away, the grooms and coachmen who had come with them preparing to lead the horses round to Malvie stables, for an hour or two; it was the day of young Mrs. Devenham's rout-party, and the gentry could be relied upon to be occupied till the early afternoon at cards, and thereafter for tea-drinking, no doubt in the garden if it did not rain. The house had grounds which were swept and immaculate, the shaven lawns smooth, the flowers well-tended. Morven saw none of them, and had asked no questions of his companion since last saying to him on their drive, "Is this the iron gate?" It was seven and a half years since he had seen it.

He dismounted at the door and, going in after others, gave his name to the footman who asked for it; Samson kept behind him, as usual. The servant offered to divest Morven of his cloak, but he shook his head impatiently, and the Negro signalled that he should be left alone. "I will not stay long," said Morven. The footman, who was new, thought he was one of the guests. He stood at the door of the room and announced in a lull that had come over the assembly.

"Mr. Morven Doon!"

And Morven, in the midst of the hush that had fallen, made his way across the expanse of carpet, unerringly, towards the hearth where the Doon escutcheon was carved, and where the portrait of Philip and Grace hung waiting. His tapping staff, which he used to guide himself, made the only sound in the room. All about him were guests, fallen silent at the sound of his name; they waited foolishly, like bright, vapid fish at the approach of an adverse tide, with news of enemies, so that they hold themselves stock-still before suddenly turning and vanishing with a flicker of fins, leaving untenanted weeds and empty water.

And at the end, in her place, the hostess rose, her cheeks white as paper, a hand to her breast; and out of the grave, where she had placed him, that other came on, and nearby somewhere was Godfrey in his invalid's chair, maintaining silence.

Morven found the fireplace, and took up his stance in front of it; turning and facing the assembly, and standing directly beneath the portrait of Philip Doon, whom he somewhat resembled. His lips smiled and his eyes as always, were bright like those of a wary animal. He gave a short laugh and said. "Well, my cousins; do you bid me welcome home?"

It had been a mild social triumph for Annabel, today's rout-party. In the beginning, perhaps for the first year after her marriage to Godfrey, local society had been a trifle wary; not openly showing discourtesy, but in the normal manner of the county waiting to see which way the cat will jump; it was known Agnes Retford had laid herself out in an unseemly way for this match. Certainly there was money enough at Malvie to make such a course almost excusable for an impoverished family like the Doons; equally certainly, their name was ancient. But even that advantage had been sullied by the disgraceful doings of Morven Doon, culminating in his trial for murder of a common customs-officer; and there had been the hasty indiscreet manner of the Devenham marriage itself, and the birth of little Sybilla had happened very promptly. And Kitty Bowes was, as always, a vulgarian, and her young daughter Clairette not a girl one would want to encourage at any time. The balance, in short, had been fairly evenly weighted; and it had taken much patience, and imperceptible climbing which must seem to be effortless, and a resolve not to notice snubs, and much giving without return, for young Mrs. Devenham. By now, two things were in her favour, in addition; the genuine respect everyone in the place, both men and women, had acquired for Godfrey, whose shyness no longer disguised his worth; and, in addition, the natural curiosity everyone displayed to see the improvements which had been made to Malvie. Gradually, gatherings had been caused to include the Devenhams; the Master of the Hunt asked them to dinner; such things helped, and cards were left, and Annabel later gave a small reception. There had not, or not yet, been a ball; that might, with regard to her own and Godfrey's indifferent health, wait till much later, possibly till Sybilla was old enough to be the reason for it. Today, however, Annabel had hit on the notion of bringing down the beautiful little creature, with her governess, and making Sybilla proffer, with a pretty curtsy to each female guest, a small nosegay picked from the garden early that morning. The innovation was a success; nobody could resist Sybilla, and the mingled scents of rosebuds and southernwood, clove-pink and lavender, made the room smell like a flower-garden and would refresh everyone, no doubt, in the growing heat of the card-games. Sybilla was removed upstairs, having played her part admirably and without a fault; she was quite perfect, Mrs. Lagardie of Instone said. And Mrs. Lagardie, who had at last been prevailed upon to leave cards and to come today, and bring her two elder daughters, was, with Colonel Cazalet and the Stuart-Neils and the Walmers, one of the people it was essential to know; her presence was an accolade. There had only been a minor hitch today in that George Oakes, the footman who so lovingly and knowledgeably tended Godfrey, had received word that his father in England was dying and had asked permission to go at once to the old man's bedside. Replacing him at short notice with one of the younger footmen had not, as matters were to turn out, been entirely satisfactory.

For if Oakes had been here, he would never have made the mistake of admitting Morven to the assembly, without first enquiring if he should do so. But for the raw new recruit, overburdened with his duties, it was no doubt the expected thing to do.

It was additionally unfortunate that Annabel's partner at that moment in the whist-round should have been none other than Mrs. Lagardie herself. Charity Lagardie, who of necessity made a career of always knowing the right place to be, and the proper thing to say and do—she had the immense handicap of a stupid husband and three unhopeful and, to date, single daughters, the youngest not out of the schoolroom —Charity dared let no standards slip, in an area almost devoid of single young men. Her aspect, after Morven's entry, changed in swift and guarded succession from, perhaps kidskin to quartz. Her fine grey eyes hardened; she laid down, in unhurried fashion, her hand of cards, and rose; curtsied towards the host and hostess, and swept to the door. Not a word was said; the daughters, two of whom had been playing somewhat uninspiredly at a further table, rose and hurried after their parent like obedient goslings. A flurry announced the ordering of the Instone carriage. The two young Berrys who had shared it, had no choice but to withdraw likewise, shambling in Charity's wake with a murmured lame excuse to Annabel from a scarlet-faced Edgar Berry. The rout began to resemble an ebb tide with the figure of Morven standing like a rock among it, the waters foaming and receding about his feet. No one had addressed him or acknowledged his presence.

The withdrawal took in all about seven minutes. When there was no one left in the long room except Godfrey, his wife, his mama and young half-sister, and old Colonel Cazalet, who had fought at Culloden and was deaf and half-blind, and had seen and heard nothing of what went on, Morven moved. The Colonel said to no one in particular, "Why don't they call trumps? Eh? Eh?" and reached for his ear-trumpet.

Someone, possibly Kitty, hissed an explanation into it; no one could afterwards recall when and how the Colonel left, except that he had had the grace to apologise to Godfrey, left seated in his chair. The room now resembled a littered abandoned shore, with the idle hands of cards lying brightly about the tables, and a deserted nosegay or two making sad, nostalgic scent. The sound of carriages bowling down the drive made the only sound. Annabel stared at Morven, her face still drained of colour. She supported herself with a hand gripping her chair.

"You have come back," she said presently. "You have come back." It seemed the only thing to say.

Morven tapped with his staff, and went across to where

a nosegay lay and picked it up, and sniffed at it. "This is pleasant," he said. "We used not to grow flowers."

He drew the lawyer's papers from his pocket and Godfrey took it. "Do you care to implement your offer to rent me the Mains for five years, cousin?"

Annabel gasped; Morven's aspect was almost sneering. She made a little movement forward; how dared he, how dared he address Godfrey so, with an emphasis on the word 'cousin' that was an insult as things were . . . And to move into the Mains! Of course it must not be permitted! But Godfrey, seeing her intention, shook his head gently. He fixed his eyes on Morven; in their prominent gaze there showed both gravity and kindness.

"I did not then know the identity of the enquirer," he said. The even tone he used angered Morven, who flushed a little.

"If you had known, you would have refused, eh? A returned convict, a rogue who escaped the gallows-end by your kind offices and my uncle's . . . pah! You expect, in gratitude, that I'll hide myself forever from your sight? You still have that, Devenham, at any rate."

"Oh God." Annabel laid her face in her hands and broke down into sobbing. Presently Kitty Bowes went to her and ushered her quietly from the room. She returned presently, her red and white paint glistening like the brave varnish on a Thames barge. "Our darling has gone upstairs to her room," she told Godfrey. "She was—it is understandable, sirs— overcome at sight of her cousin, returned after so long. Will you not be solitary at the dower house, Mr. Doon?" She smiled brightly; for Kitty, a disaster was best larded over. Morven grew rigid with offence; a common woman, Devenham's mother! He answered coldly.

"I shall have enough company, I assure you, madam." Poor Kitty subsided, used to such rejections as her daily lot; afterwards, she realised what a fool she'd been. They couldn't ask Morven Doon here; not a soul in the place would call, and after the trouble Annabel had been at, and for the sake of little Sybilla—

"Godfrey has refused to accept any rent," said young Clairette. Her eyes were shining and she looked from one to the other of the men; her mother scolded her.

"Be silent, what do you know of such things?" But she was pleased with Godfrey, for that act of swift generosity, concluded no doubt while they'd been upstairs. It would have been almost improper for a Doon—after all, they were the old family, had sent knights on crusade from Malvie—to live nearby as a paying tenant. "I hope that you will find everything to your comfort, Mr. Doon," she told Morven, forgiving his unkindness. "There have, I know, been fires lit in the house now and again, and it's furnished after a manner, I daresay; when will you move in?"

"At once," said Morven. He bowed briefly, in a kind of capitulation of courtesy, to where Godfrey sat; Godfrey was smiling a little uncertainly. "I must ask you," he said hesitantly, "to forgive my wife. She is upset, and—"

"Never fear." The blind man spoke harshly. "A roof over my head is all I need, from which I can be near known places. I'll not trouble your social occasions, Devenham." He turned on his heel and left the house, Samson following. None of the party left behind in the deserted drawing-room said anything at once. There was, after all, very little left to say.

Annabel was not placated; when Godfrey went to her at last she was still weeping, pounding her fists on the softness of the bedcovers and the victim of harsh angry sobs, such as he had never before heard from her.

"My darling, my darling, you need not trouble about the guests. They will return, once they have seen the folly of their own behaviour." His lips tightened; he himself had assessed Mrs. Lagardie long ago for what she was, but if it pleased Annabel to have her at these affairs—

"You do not understand. How can you? How could you—in any case—let *him* come to live at Mains? Nobody in the county will know us, or will send invitations—and Sybilla, it isn't fair to her—and in any case, Morven, of all people! You don't know him, what a devil he can be; he will destroy us, and our marriage. He has come here resolved—" She sat up, her face swollen, her eyes bloodshot with weeping. Godfrey's heart turned over with pity for her; he still tried to use reason, thinking she was hysterical.

"My dearest, how could I turn your kinsman from the door without shelter? I could not ask him to stay with us, as you say, for the sake of Sybilla; but, after all, if he had not been permitted to stay at Mains he'd have made do for himself, I doubt not, in the ruined cottage Aaron left him, I hear, rather than leave the vicinity. It's—it's his native place," and Godfrey faltered, for he, a southerner, could not fully understand the fierce need Morven had for Malvie, Malvie which he could no longer even see or hope to inherit. After he and Annabel were dead, Godfrey knew, the place would belong to Sybilla and the man she would marry. He tried, as time passed, to comfort his wife on this head, and the other she had mentioned; but she would not be comforted, and it was some days before Godfrey felt that she had forgiven him for letting Morven into Mains, after wrecking her rout-party.

Morven moved in to the dower house at once, setting Samson to light a fire and bring out and air the bedding; the house was somewhat damp with lack of being lived in since aunt Retford's death. They cracked a bottle between them that they had brought from the Fleece, that night to keep them warm; and sat by the fire reminiscing till near morning. It seemed to Samson that his master never grew weary, for even he was beginning to feel the need of repose; tomorrow, Morven promised him, they should go again to the village and fetch necessaries. He was smiling as he said this, and Samson felt the delight of a small boy who has been promised a treat, but will not be told more till he sees what it is; he often had this experience with Morven.

The evening after moving into Mains, Morven returned to the inn.

Livia Judd was behind the bar-counter, looking as folk always saw her now; a comely young woman in sad-coloured kirtle and snowy apron, with her famed skill in laundering, which she also taught her maids, well shown in the neat goffering of her cap. The fine bosom her tight-laced bodice displayed was the occasion, sometimes, with new customers for lewd advances, ogling its owner as they sat across the counter at their ale; but no man who behaved so would be made welcome at the Fleece, and as her older customers knew, Livia was chaste and faithful to Abel. She was respected nowadays, as tonight's talk showed; it was pleasant and not bawdy, and men kept their consumption of ale at a decent level. Some smoked long pipes at a table nearby the door, and the blue-grey smoke rose, rivalling the cheerful blaze of the fire on the hearth, which sent reflected lights out on to the well-sanded irons. It was a kindly scene, made more so by the increasing contrast of the wind rising outside, which made the flames dip and sway, like bright-clad ladies curtsying.

Doon came in at the door, borne on this wind.

He stood for instants, the dark caped cloak he always wore swirling about him into stillness. He was like a thing of the

184

night, of the devil; the pale eyes, unerring, focussed on Livia as though they could see. There might have been no one else in the room for either of them. She made one slow, hesitant movement with her hand to her bosom, then set down the flagon she was filling.

The ale at the tap brimmed over. Livia was still aware that the flow, which she had not yet turned off, was dripping over the floor and would stain it and her skirts. But there was nothing she could do, nothing; it was as though she were already bewitched. She heard Morven's voice, across the sudden silence that had fallen in the taproom. It was as though she had known what he would say.

"I have come for you, Livia; and our son."

In after years it would become a legend, what happened that night. Those who witnessed it perhaps said less, later on, than those who did not, but imagination could not in any case gild the truth. And the truth was this; that the chaste, comely tavern-wife of the Fleece, still wearing her snowy cap and apron, left the counter, and the ale still brimming over at its tap; and walked across the floor to where the blind man stood. To most of them here he was still the heir of Malvie, young Doon to whom a cruel lot had denied his heritage, not a criminal, as the gentry regarded him; but tonight he put a chill in men's hearts. He himself said nothing to anyone, only caught his cloak about Livia as if to protect her from the night outside. Then they went out together, and for a long moment there was nothing heard but the sound of the wind, and of a coach driving away.

Then—it had taken as long as that—someone remembered to go and turn off the ale-tap, and somebody else said they'd better go for Abel. But no one in the end, did that; and when he came down, and found the counter unattended, nobody for a long time answered when he asked where his wife had gone.

The coach must have been ready and waiting; Morven had helped her in at once, and himself after her. He must have had it planned at all points, because the mulatto, carrying William wrapped in his greatcoat, sat already up beside the driver on the box, and she couldn't see more because of the night. It could have been no easy task to drag William from his bed, to go off with a strange blackamoor, and she . . .

The horses drew away and were making all speed through the night, and Morven's hands had found her.

"Not here," she tried to say, "not until we . . ."

"Livia, Livia."

"Not until . . . ah, Morven, Morven . . ."

Afterwards, he asked her if she'd expected him to wait one moment longer, having waited all these years? And it was as it had always been between them, a living fire. She felt the coach swaying on the road to Mains, and even heard the driver's whip crack over the heads of the horses, and they drove on and on; and she, held in Morven's arms so tightly that it did not seem that she could live till journey's end, knew ecstasy; to live again, when she'd thought of herself as dead. To live . . . for Doon. He was unaltered. She loved him. It didn't matter whether or not he was blind.

"You were always mine," he told her afterwards. "Did you doubt I'd come for you? Why didn't you wait for me?"

But she'd waited, she'd waited. She couldn't find the words to say that Abel didn't matter, had never mattered in any case, poor Abel. Later she would perhaps regret it more. But now . . .

They drew up at last by Mains gate; she saw the hedge in the light of the carriage-lamps. "There's a fire lit already, though the chimney smokes damnably," he told her. "Come in."

Next day, Abel came for her on foot, walking up the path from the gate and tirling the door-pin. It was Livia who opened to him; there wasn't anyone else, save the blackamoor who was drawing water and had already served their meal. She herself was in disarray, her hair hanging down like a girl's; she looked, no doubt, like anyone would after the night they'd had, she and Morven, together in a half-aired bed, not finishing till noon. There would be a thousand and one things to do at Mains to make it habitable again, she'd get busy with it, she told herself, as soon as Abel was dealt with. Already she knew she would not go back to Abel, for the kirk folk or anyone.

Morven came then, and the two men said the things to one another which had to be said. They finished it together indoors, beside the fire. At one point Livia bent forward and put on more sawn logs, her black hair slipping over her shoulders like a veil. She put it back, and caught the expression on Abel's face as she did so; and felt sorry for him.

"I've listened to what you have to say, Morven," replied Abel slowly, "but I haven't yet heard what Livia has to."

"Livia has nothing to say."

"Speak up, lass, and don't be afraid of either of us . . . the kirk elders may come, you know, and order you to the stool again." For Abel knew, for she'd told him, at the beginning, of her past; and hadn't judged her for it, and wouldn't judge her either, it was evident, for this. She began to cry quietly; it was worse, much worse, than if he'd been angry with her.

"Abel—" she began, but Morven again forestalled her. He slid an arm about her waist in a swift, possessive gesture; for the first time since coming, Abel's face flushed to his hair-fringe.

"Samson will kick the elders down the path," said Morven brutally. "Don't say you can see me perched on a stool by Livia in kirk, lad? It wouldn't do for either of us." He laughed; the kirk folk wouldn't come here, it was, he thought, too far out of town.

"Is it your wish to stay with him?" Abel said, as though there were only the two of them in the room. "If that's so I'll not hinder you; you know well it's always been, from the beginning, what you wanted, only that. But if you come back with me, as I hope you will, I'd as soon Morven kept away from us at the Fleece." He turned to Morven. "And there's this also," he said slowly. "I don't know for certain, Morven, what it is you mean to do with your warehouses, and your packmen across country, and the rest; but you can leave me out as a customer; from now on I'll pay dues on what I buy openly."

"Poor business, Abel: no other publican can afford it." Morven was smiling openly. "Don't let pique throw you into the arms of Billy Pitt in London: he's cold company, they say, and never cheap."

"Billy Pitt may well perceive before long that lower tax will bring him bigger profit. But that's not for me to say. All I know is that I'm done with you, Morven."

"As Livia is with you, from this day."

"Is it true, lass?" said Abel.

Her eyes were full of tears. "You've been good to me, Abel; well I know that. But—but it isn't enough for me. I'm a bad bargain, come of bad gipsy stock; you're well rid of me."

He did not answer this. He jerked his head, in the peasant's immemorial gesture, towards Morven, standing by the smoking fire. "You're staying with him, then?"

"Yes. I'm staying. I'm sorry, Abel."

He turned without another word, and left the house. She heard the door close and the bolt, shot to by Samson, slide into place behind it; outside the rain was beginning to patter down. "He won't have a dry walk," she said. The habit of years, of seeing Abel warm, dry, fed, and comforted, was strong again in her; she felt miserable and ashamed. For an instant she made as if to go after Abel; she saw the massive dark shape of the mulatto go upstairs to his own place, then felt Morven move at her side.

He took hold of her, unlacing her gown. His hands were sure and confident and she felt, seeing the near glow of the flames glinting on the surface of his eyes, as if he could see her and the room; she recoiled a little. Was he to make a whore of her, openly and so soon again here by the hearth? That that was what he would do she knew; a puppet, an obedient thing on strings, she was now, without mind or conscience. Still, if she thought hard enough, she could picture Abel in his soaked clothes, walking back alone to Grattan, with nobody to get him dry gear when he got there, or make his supper. Then the gaspings of ecstasy came to her, above the faint sound of the rain; they were her own, and Morven was within her, already having his way with here as he had always done. He was so quick, so sure, was Morven Doon. Soon she forgot Abel. The dark came down early and the fire died in the hearth.

She was kept busy, those early days of their together, by day with the work of the dower house; there was a great deal to do, almost as much as there'd been at the Fleece when she first went there. Lacking a woman, any house suffers neglect, and she found the passages were all to scrub, the beds to air, the crockery and linen to see to. It was worse than it had been when she went first to Mrs. Retford, long ago; but she knew where everything was at Mains. Perhaps later, when the scandal had died down a bit, she'd be able to hire a scrubbing-woman or a maid, from somewhere other than Grattan; Morven had let her take the coach there one day to buy necessaries for herself and the house, and had given her enough money. But she'd come home early, with mud on her gown that the women had thrown, and they'd called after her for a harlot. No doubt that's what she must be now; but search her mind as she might, she couldn't bring herself to go back to Abel at the Fleece again, or even let William go to him; and Abel hadn't, come to that, asked her to part with William.

By night, often, men came to the Mains now asking for Morven. She supposed they were in the contraband-trade, and asked nothing more.

The buzz of gossip which followed the unheralded return

of Morven Doon, his taking up residence at the Mains dower house, and his abduction of Abel Judd's scarcely unwilling wife, brought no direct repercussions to Morven. For this, the protection and strength of his coloured servant, and the known fact that Samson owned a pair of duelling-pistols with which at present he shot birds, was responsible more than the fact of Morven's blindness. The zeal of certain officiating elders who made the morals of the community their affair— one was a blood relative of the recently disgraced Governor Priddy of Emmett's—would not have been quelled by physical limitations in a suspect fallen from grace.

They called, in the end, upon Godfrey as the reprobate's landlord. Annabel was not present; they were admitted to him alone. Godfrey's asthma had troubled him all summer, and made him short with the visitors; he disliked, in any case, what he regarded as the lack of charity shown by the kirk authorities here, differing greatly from conditions as he remembered them in the more tolerant south. He received the two men lying, as was his custom nowadays, in his long-chair nearby the window, his eyes watching the sunlight as it glinted on his leaves of Solomon's Seal beyond the glass.

"Well, gentlemen? How can I aid you today?" They usually came for money. Godfrey bade them be seated, and pressed them to pour themselves wine. This they did, relishing its quality, for it was from France, and some time passed in talking of the iniquitous taxes. Godfrey however paid his tithes handsomely, and they were studious not to offend him. At last one, whose name was Mathew Jarvie and who was a butcher by trade in Grattan, found the opening he needed.

"You have made of your garden a glory unto Zion," he told his host in the archaic language it pleased chosen vessels to employ. "It is a pity, sir, that less than a mile away—" he flung out a great red hand—"Babylon swells; ay, fornication and adultery, a reproach unto Israel—"

"In the broad light of day," echoed the lesser Priddy. "And there is other ungodly company." He had heard, as Godfrey had not, of the gatherings at Mains of pack-carriers.

"Is it consonant with your own position here, sir, that these abominations should persist unchecked? The woman of Babylon, the man of blood, in filthy unrighteousness one with the other—"

"My kinsman has expiated his sentence. In common law he is now a free man."

"But, sir, the woman is an adulteress! She—"

Godfrey held up a wasted hand, watched by the pin-point

pupils which are somehow peculiar to the elect; his own expression showed displeasure.

"Mr. Doon, who, as I have told you already, is kin to me, is under my protection, being blind," he told them. "Moreover at his age, which is one of discretion, he may order his way of life, I believe, in any manner he chooses. Is there not a saying among the many you employ—" he smiled somewhat maliciously—"concerning who may first cast a stone?" He watched Priddy's kinsman flush, for news of that scandal must by now, he knew well, have reached Malvie. The man stared straight before him above his dark cloth coat; why were these folk dressed to resemble crows? Godfrey thought. And even a crow, come to that, minded its own affairs. He knew, though they had not discussed it together, that Annabel would have taken it badly had she heard of Livia Judd's presence at the Mains with Morven; he was uncertain whether or not she had; God knew! thought Godfrey, other company didn't press itself, and the man had been seven long years alone and blind in Botany Bay. He himself was, it was true, in some discomfort about poor Abel Judd, and had Morven been any other man, and with his eyesight, he'd have said a word to him by now. But he wasn't going to be put to it by these soberly-clad persons who wore out not only their wives—Jarvie had married his fourth—but got behind cupboard doors at some poor little servant or orphan who dared not refuse them, and seldom later admitted their due blame.

The other Priddy took up the cudgels now, using thunderings from the Old Testament as, no doubt, an antidote to the single mention there had been of the New. Godfrey had not, Silas Priddy took it upon himself to remind him, been assiduous in his own church-attendance of late.

"Sirs, you may see for yourselves the way I am," smiled Godfrey, discounting the impertinence. He moved his hand again, seeing the transparency of the flesh and fingers against the light. Fear caught at him, as it sometimes did by night, or during one of his attacks, concerning the possibility of his own early death, or that his mind should become affected by the creeping of his disease. He closed his eyes briefly, forgetting the two watching men; the former fate, he thought, was preferable, except for Annabel and Sybilla who would be left alone. But what good would a paralytic, mindless hulk be to them?

His eyes opened again and fell upon Sybilla herself, newly come into the garden with the governess, Jane Glover, nearby. The child was chasing a butterfly. Godfrey continued to smile, with a lightening of his heart; whatever befell him now, he'd had Annabel and Sybilla to love, and love was what lasted after one's body decayed even while still living. He returned to the watchful, tight-mouthed faces of the two elders again. "You are satisfied, I hope?" he asked them patiently.

They conferred together, and nodded; their prying was, he knew, part of their office, and had Malvie been nearer a town there would have been incessant surveillance of a kind he did not believe he could have endured. "And Mrs. Devenham?" Priddy said presently. "She has likewise been remiss, all this year, in attendance. It does not set an example to her servants or her child." His voice gritted; Godfrey was aware of the rare springing of anger in himself. How dared they criticise Annabel?

"Mrs. Devenham's health has not been good for some time," he told them coldly. This was true; Annabel's headaches had returned in frequent severity, since . . . since when? Since the return of Morven Doon and the rout-party's failure, he remembered, she was often ill.

He called for the servant, and had the two elders shown out, with no pressing invitation to come again. He guessed their carriage would drive past the turn to the dower house, without stopping; but he did not see Morven, and would have no opportunity of asking if he had cared to do so concerning the matter. He called now to Sybilla from the garden, and she came running in, and put up her flower-like face for him to kiss her. "At least you are high on the approved list of the gentlemen who have just visited me," he told Jane Glover with solemnity. Jane, a devoutly reared young woman, never missed her church-attendance, and as a rule the child went in the carriage with her.

The setback to her social life suffered by young Mrs. Devenham following the collapse of her rout-party was, after all, minimal except for Mrs. Lagardie, whose sense of the proprieties had been permanently offended. They could afford to ignore her; invitations continued to arrive at intervals for Annabel and Godfrey, who went out less and less; sometimes for Kitty and Clairette, and rarely all four. In the summer after Morven's return to the dower house, though they had not seen him again, Godfrey called the physician in for Annabel. He was the same who had presided at her confinement, and put most of her ills down to the results of that difficult birth and also—and about this he kept his own

191

counsel—her marriage. In any other society, in the south perhaps, a young woman tied to an impotent invalid would have taken a lover by now; the headaches alone were a sign, to the cynically informed physician. One could not, however, in this circumscribed and polite northern group, prescribe any such relief. The doctor prescribed, instead, clysters and sea-bathing. The latter benefit was after all at Mrs. Devenham's own doorstep.

Annabel therefore, after a week spent in bed following the clysters, which had left her shockingly weak, ventured out, in the very early morning, to where the little beach lay at the foot of stone steps cut out of the rock, which Godfrey, while he could still get about the garden grounds, had caused to be planted delightfully with scarlet valerian, pink and white thrift, and sea-lavender. The dry leaves rustled in the stillness of dawn as Annabel walked down barefoot with her hair loose, clad only in a wrapper. There would of course be no watchers at this hour to espy the elegant Mrs. Devenham, arbiter of all that was tasteful, forget herself so far as to plunge in the sea and bathe. The water was still opaque, with a sea-mist rising from it whitely. Later in the day it would be hot.

She set foot on the narrow strip of sand and disrobed, leaving her wrapper on the lowest steps; the beach was screened on two sides with cliffs, on one of which Aaron's cottage still stood, a ruin. This was unseen now in the thick mist; and the sea, like glass, lay invitingly, with its horizon invisible, and the tide scarcely thrusting at the shore. As Annabel stepped into the shallows, a slight, cool breeze arose and stirred her loose hair. Seen thus, she was Aphrodite, if anyone had been watching; the pleasure of standing naked, letting the breeze and water play upon her, filled her with sudden, glad elation, not entirely by reason of the absence of tight-lacing and formal attire in what would, later, be enervating heat. For this hour, Annabel was an animal; a high-bred, nervous, but still physical creature, and her trials of the flesh slipped from her like a discarded garment and she became young again.

She closed her eyes, unthinkingly laving the warm water over her thighs and breasts. How clear one's thoughts became at this time of day, at this pastime, unwatched, unhurried! Now, she could assure herself that it was no disloyalty to Godfrey that his poor, flabby, stoutening body had become a trial to her and to himself, so that she could not endure the touch of his fingers. She could esteem Godfrey, now that

192

they no longer made even the pretence of marriage, the more, and have a deep regard for the qualities of his mind. The old, hot longing for Morven which she had once known, which had overcome her again briefly at the renewed sight of him, and had since troubled her in the night hours, could be locked away once more in that part of her recollection which must never, never again let it out. Not even in her inmost soul did Annabel now admit that Godfrey was not Sybilla's father. The girl's golden hair was the colour of Kitty's, of Godfrey's own when a boy. He loved the child dearly, was educating her after his own pattern, helped by Jane Glover, and told her facts of natural history as well as myths, legends and fairy-stories. When Sybilla went away to school next year there would be a gap in Godfrey's life, which she herself must fill by being more than ever attentive to him . . .

She would not let herself admit the fact that, perhaps, by next year, Godfrey would not be there; or would have grown so much worse that he would be confined to bed, a huddled mass of unresponsive flesh, perhaps no longer with the ability even to make known his wishes. That it might happen in this manner some day the physician had already tried to make clear to her and to Kitty, gently underplaying the progress of a disease whose cause no one knew and for which there was no cure. One must be prepared; but until it had happened, there was perhaps hope that it would not, or would be less severe than they feared.

Godfrey. How much did he suffer in his mind?

She frowned with uncertainty and pain; looked up and stiffened in fear. A man was standing above her on the cliff, with the mist clearing about him, so that he seemed carved out of the rock. She had no means of knowing how long he had been there; he stood quite still. It was Morven. She crouched to cover herself with her hands, still knowing he was blind and could see nothing; no longer Aphrodite, but Leda, outraged and betrayed by the true identity of the swan.

She drew a sobbing breath, and turned and fled out of the water; found her robe, seized it and huddled it on. Then she ran, stumbling and bruising herself, quickly up the flight of stone steps, and back to Malvie. She did not turn again to see if the figure of Morven was still there, or had moved; Morven, who could not have seen her nakedness, but in some way, she was certain, had known she was down there in the water: had known it, and had said nothing. given no sign. As always, his blind eyes had been turned upon Malvie,

Malvie with its ancient tower rising beyond the mist across the bay with the early light behind it; Malvie, which he desired always and would never with his physical eyes see again.

She knew she was not a woman to him but a means to Malvie. This was, in the end, what frightened her. The days passed in an access of shimmering, unaccustomed heat, but there was no more seabathing by order of the physician for Annabel that summer.

It was about that same time that Morven purchased his boat. He had bought it through the offices of some of the known men down the coast, who came to Mains by night regarding the pack-carrying over to the east. It was a sizeable craft, almost rivalling a cutter in size, and made of seasoned timber, with a cabin and space for a galley. Morven and the mulatto went out in it a good deal, mostly when the weather was fine; there was a certain place on Malvie tower where one could look down and see the blue bay, and the running keel and, above, a blind man's white intent face at the tiller. Morven would know the tides that ran between here and Man, blindfold, as he'd once stated; Morven could avoid the rocks and shoals, the sudden shallow places nearby the shore, and sail his boat safely, anchoring now and again in the innumerable small bays and inlets, transacting his business, loading and unloading bales, having a word with the men who came, wading out from the shallows to where they could hail him where he sat, or rowing out in smallboats, and going aboard.

A woman sometimes watched from the tower; it was Annabel. Godfrey's illness left her with a good deal of time to herself, and she found solace of a kind in watching the sea, and looking for the boat when it passed by.

Down at the Mains, young William Judd was finding himself unwanted.

The fact of his enquiring presence tended to raise difficulties; at first, he would keep coming upstairs to look for his mother as he had always done at the Fleece. "Where's father?" had ceased to be asked at the same time, roughly, as his other favourite question about when they might be going back to the inn; he missed the comings and goings there, and no doubt the occasional sixpence. He had been told, in answer to one question, that Morven was his father. "Because he sleeps with mother?" he asked. He asked other questions also. Morven began to find him an irritation; he had taken the child less out of any personal interest in him than by reason of the fact that he was his property, as Malvie should be. But he was not prepared to show patience over such matters as having his privacy with Livia invaded.

William would take no telling, however; he could get away from the blind man fast enough. He would run along the passage and finding their door locked, would listen for a while and then rattle at the fastening; on the third or fourth occasion he did this, and refused to go away, Morven opened the door, white-faced and angry in his shirt, and called for Samson.

William had meantime looked into the room, and saw his mother lying on the bed, naked, which was extraordinary as it was afternoon; her eyes were shut, and she was smiling. William decided she must be dead, gave a roar and tried to push past Morven; but the latter caught him and, seizing him by the waistband and the collar of his shirt, held him, kicking and writhing, till Samson came. Livia had meantime, to William's great relief, sat up and put up a hand to cover herself. She would have flung on a wrap and come to the boy, but Morven cut in coldly.

"Take him downstairs, take down his breeches and give him a flogging, and tell him it'll happen each time he comes up here," he said, and shut the door fast. It was done, accordingly; and William, still howling, betook his sore buttocks to Malvie stables, which he had early discovered for himself, and lay four hours on his stomach in the straw. The warm, friendly smell of the stamping horses was all about him, and reminded him of the Fleece; in company with the beasts' companionable silence, his sobs ceased.

Aitken the groom found him there later, and took him under his wing. It was a good time for help to have come; he himself felt unwell, and he knew he had a growth which troubled him, but would say naught about it yet. The small black-haired boy was willing, good with beasts, ready and able to carry pails and help with the mucking out and feeding; if he went home with a whiff of manure about him by the day's end, who should complain after the way he said they'd used him? For William, like most of his tribe, had made a good story of it all; his stepfather, he said, beat him thrice daily.

As time passed, William became more at home in the great house stables than ever at Mains, nor did he seek the company of Samson after the latter had whipped him. Once, munching a fair-sized slice of bread and cheese the cook had given him from Malvie kitchens, William encountered a golden-haired little girl, clad in a riding-habit and hat with a long feather. She was going to mount her pony, and Aitken brought it out, and obsequiously stood with his hand beneath her boot-sole while she got up. William jeered. "I can do it without that," he said, "and without a saddle."

Aitken told him not to speak in that way to Miss Sybilla, and as if in extenuation of the bread and cheese told her a tale. "He's had no breakfast, miss, where he comes from," he said, and William, who had in fact eaten like a prince that morning on devilled ham and kidneys, said nothing; the girl was like all girls, he thought; soft, with all that fair hair blowing about, and couldn't mount a pony. A doll, she looked like. Often after that he saw her, but less often her mother; one day, however, Mrs. Annabel came out dressed to ride with her daughter, and surveyed the wild-haired, untidy little boy.

"What is your name?" she asked, as they'd done in the Fleece yard; but when he told her she closed her eyes, as if it hurt her, and turned white, as though she'd faint. She turned back to the house and didn't go out that day, though Aitken had got her mount all ready for her and had groomed it till its chestnut coat shone like satin. Next day she came again; but that time Aitken got William to make himself scarce, hiding him in the hay-loft till the two fine ladies had gone.

"*She* says you're not to come here, varmint," said Sam, who was English-trained. "But I've got used to havin' you, see? You can come here any time, provided they don't notice," and so William became an adept at hiding himself in time, and otherwise life went on as before. He was happy enough, like a small unthinking animal, and as time passed he grew wilder and more intractable, except for Aitken the groom. By the time Livia found out what was happening to her son it was too late to hope that he'd be the scholar, preacher or physician she and Abel had once planned for. But most of the plans she and Abel had made together had gone down the wind long ago; it seemed another life she'd led as the wife at the Fleece, and now she was a wanton again. She was well aware that the kirk folk, if they could have got hold of her, would have seen her whipped as the mulatto had whipped William. Gipsies they were, the pair, no doubt, and a gipsy William was fast becoming, to remain that way to the end. He never again showed dependent affection for anyone after his mother had, so to speak, betrayed him with Morven; he

196

would eat and generally sleep at the house, and Morven paid for the clothes he outgrew, and Aitken doused him sometimes under the pump in Malvie yard, when the stable-odour grew too pronounced about him.

This was, as it happened, how Annabel discovered the presence of Livia with Morven at the Mains. She had not hitherto known, and nobody had told her.

Another indication of the way things were going came from Tib Willock, the serving-maid who had used to work for Abel and Livia at the Fleece. One day that winter she came to the back door of the Mains, and asked to see Mistress Judd; Livia, by then having grown used to the treatment meted out to her by the housewives of Grattan, went unwillingly. But Tib was as usual, if a trifle more subdued; the master, she said, was drinking heavily, and few of the other servants had renewed their term of service. "He doesn't get violent, m'm, or noisy, or lay hands on any of us; he just sits lookin' in front of him, and that's more than flesh and blood can stand, when he mostly don't answer, or eat his food; as for the customers, they can come or go for all he cares." She'd done her best, she said, as most of them had, but she wouldn't go back with Abel for another term if there were anywhere better to go; she wondered, hearing that Mrs. Judd was now at the Mains, if she could maybe use a maid to scrub? "You taught me floors yourself, m'm, and to make the chalk patterns." She smiled: there was no alteration in her manner now that her former mistress was a light woman and frowned on by the authorities. These things happened to folk.

Livia hired Tib, and was glad she had done so, not only because Tib was a good worker and these were hard to find, or because she herself was now relieved of the rough work, and could keep the rest of the house as it should be done, with the two of them and Samson's occasional help. Tib's company was welcome, even though they talked together seldom at first; but as the year went on, and Morven's business already begun with the men who carried bales increased, so that he was often most of the night conferring with them down by Malvie cave, and said little of what they'd all been at and Livia never asked—as the year went on she was increasingly alone, and it wouldn't have been pleasant listening to the wind outside, and thinking of what she'd done to Abel, by herself; often by winter she would make her way down to the kitchen where Tib sat, and they'd brew a posset together, and talk of old times at the inn. Samson seldom joined them; he kept himself to himself, and although, Tib said, she'd been chaffed by some of the other girls, who'd hired themselves out on the nearby farms, about her black swain, there was naught of that; she'd not be one to fancy a blackamoor atop her. It was Tib, also, who told Livia where William now spent his days, for the maid had been in charge of the little boy a good deal while they all lived at the inn: but it was too late to retrieve or alter William now.

V

There was one member of the family at Malvie in whom Morven Doon's appearance in Annabel's drawing-room on that fateful visit did not induce either contempt, pity or despair; Clairette Bowes, Godfrey's young half-sister, conceived a passionate admiration for Morven. This brought him no pleasure.

Miss Bowes was given to enthusiasms. From the beginnings, almost, of her conception in humdrum course, the Bowes couple living at that time prudently in France, she had been a storm-centre and bone of contention, or object of embarrassment, whichever way one cared to look at it. She had arrived prematurely, when Kitty was in a carriage between Dijon and Paris, after having caused the latter every imaginable ill in course of pregnancy. She was not an attractive baby; poor Kitty, sickened by that time with her new marriage, never loved her as she had loved Godfrey or even Cecily, the placid earlier result of those hot, illicit couplings in Bloomsbury with Mr. Bowes, then newly Kitty's lover. His excesses by now had donated to his younger offspring, as well as his wife, permanent ill-health; Clairette was always ailing, and grew up subject to chest-colds, perhaps for a time even phthisical. This gave her a narrow rib-cage, a depressed stoop, and a snivel, manifest as permanent by the time she was sent away to school. She also, unfortunately, had a strong body-odour which neither civet and musk, ambergris, nor any other medicament, could quell. Kitty saw her off to boarding-school with vague relief, and hoped for invitations from the young ladies' parents, in course, to Clairette for the holidays. But these were not forthcoming; she made no friends, less on account of the odour—it was, alas, not uncommon even in second-best circles, which described the school and other schools well enough—but because, in some way, unpleasantness was suspected in the child. This had never been made openly evident; perhaps if it had, Clairette would have been less disliked. The young ladies' parents could not know, for the young ladies themselves did not, that Clairette early became, with the clashing inheritance in her own blood, a prey to furtive desire for sexual enlightenment.

This was not, in course of the upbringing accorded to polite young females of the day, easily forthcoming; the girls were constantly chaperoned at school, met no young gentlemen during the term, and in any case these would doubtfully have been attracted to Miss Clairette. She burned in deprivation, therefore, all through her teens, furtively assessing Cecily's betrothal and the probable doings on the bridal-night, but coming no nearer direct information. Her brother's marriage, on the other, baffled her totally. She was unable to become intimate with Annabel, and as a result, out of a kind of personal vengeance, evolved a theory that Sybilla could not possibly be Godfrey's daughter; she folded the suggestion away for future contemplation.

The years passed. Twice Clairette had a passionate involvement with an assistant minister, and in each case the candidate in question had made off shortly to other parishes, leaving Clairette encumbered by much knitting to be finished for the poor and a list of visiting-rounds for jelly and soup. She had begun the visits gladly, in the days when, on initial journeys, Mr. Setoun or Mr. McIntyre might be beside her, steadying her arm and showing her the way; now, she could hardly give the patronage up. She might, accordingly, have shrunk unremembered into the average spinster of her unhappy kind, with the passions of hell broiling beneath an exterior unchanging, calmly mittened, through half a lifetime. But before that, she saw Morven.

She had of course seen him before, notably the time he came to Malvie on the first day they'd all arrived; his unaltered appearance now gave him an elfin, magical quality for Clairette. Any blind man, moreover, was unfortunate; and how brave this blind man was! He'd dared, without assistance or guidance of any kind from the dark acolyte behind him, the whole expanse of Annabel's Chinese carpet, peopled on every square with Annabel's critical, unkind county guests (they had often over the years snubbed Clairette also). Morven had held, despite the moneyed pomp and blue-blooded certainty of the guests, the stage at its centre. While remote from the Noble Savage—Clairette these days had time for much reading—he maintained an air of breeding as well as tragedy, and Clairette's heart, as from one solitary to another, yearned towards his. By the time she discovered he kept a mistress it was of no lasting importance; in the fantasy Clairette already nourished in the narrow caverns of her half-instructed mind, Livia played no part.

She went as soon as possible to call on Morven at the Mains, riding her grey pony, and choosing a moment when she knew Annabel and her mother were separately occupied. Socially, she knew they would say, Morven Doon was not acceptable, and in any case it was not correct for Clairette, a young unmarried lady, to visit him. Such taboos hedged conventional society about that it was more like living in a savage tribe than an informed Christian country, Clairette assured herself; and rode on.

She met Morven as he came down the path from the door, while she was in the act of dismounting; thus unprepared, Clairette lapsed into the cheerful, unfortunate, aggressive manner she used with the visiting poor. "I was passing," she told him, and accorded him a vigorous handshake. It must be made evident from the beginning, she told herself, that she could view the situation in intelligent terms. Her small eyes flickered briefly towards the house-windows; there was no sign of the mistress.

Morven, who had had no idea who Clairette might be until informed, could have told her already that he would know her again; she stank. He muttered some courtesy, and did his best to entertain so unexpected and eccentric a visitor. He could not, however, apart from anything else, be cordial to Godfrey Devenham's half-sister; and when Clairette called a second time, made it clear to her that her visits were unwelcome. To his extreme displeasure and discomfort, she received the rebuke with loud laughter, and a kind of coyness that made his skin rise.

Thereafter there was hardly a week when Morven was free of her. It would have seemed incredible to Annabel Devenham, herself in former days so often flayed by her cousin's bitter tongue, that he should want to be rid of anyone and yet be unable to contrive it. To Annabel, the delicate, fragile image of the woman she had been reared to resemble would not endure the roughness of denial; a rejected female shrank, in confused virginity, back like a snail inside its shell. But on Morven's first tentative and, later, open rudeness Clairette thrived, robust as a mutton-chop; like some form of life that flourishes best under the knife, flame, or whip she would writhe, and presently give her loud laugh and come on again; she brushed herself against him frequently, so that, as he confessed to Livia later, he was fain to have his clothes sponged down and hung out in the air. But nothing he could say or do would dissuade Miss Bowes, now consumed by the abiding fire of true love.

During the course of their acquaintance she obtained, by some means which evaded Kitty's vigilance, a copy of the writings of Mary Wollstonecraft. This brought about a revolution, or perhaps modification, in the thought-processes of Clairette herself; women were no longer born to be slaves, to marry or be old maids only. Every woman had a right to her chosen lover; Mary herself had demonstrated this. That Mary had borne her Godwin a child in the process did not concern Clairette meantime; she was obsessed by theories, never facts. She lectured Morven on the rights of woman till he was almost physically sick of her; if, he was beginning to think, laying the little bitch on her back would get rid of her, he'd do it, perhaps, and be quit of the affair. But he suspected that this would not, in female reckoning, be the end; and he had in any case no appetite for Clairette Bowes's seduction.

The family at Malvie could not, by now, be ignorant of the rides Clairette continued to make each day; they had, she told Morven, got Godfrey to speak to her, and as a rule she could deny poor Godfrey nothing, but this time she'd told him, firmly, that her life was henceforth her own. "Mama is one of those females brought up in a sheltered, ignorant fashion, by an earlier generation, and has no notion of reality or breadth of thought," she told Morven, and he, caught between a yawn and a laugh, told her not to be a goose; she could have no idea, he said, what she was talking about. Had she not been as unattractive, and as persistent, he could, he was aware, have treated her as a brother might have done, and laughed her out of it; but Clairette was impossible, a being for whom there was an unprintable word in ancient Greek.

She was cruel also, and snobbish in her narrow way; once while she was there, Livia had come out, thinking there was nobody; she didn't as a rule show herself when anyone came.

Morven himself had spoken naturally to her, and asked her something; Clairette had thrust in, addressed Livia like a servant, and sent her hurrying back to the house. Morven was deeply angry. The man Samson's appearance elicited no such direct response from Clairette; she saw him once or twice going about their daily concerns. Once, however, when she and Morven were alone again, she made it clear that Samson's dark skin disgusted her.

"Why that?" he said, wryly determined to let her trip herself up over her often-expressed themes of equality and freedom for all men and, presumably, women. "He is a member of the human family of whom, you say, you have a high opinion." She was stuffed with Rousseau at the time.

"Oh," pouted Clairette, "they're different, somehow. They're nearer the brute creation," and it was thereafter that Morven decided how greatly he loathed her; she had not even the courage of her blue-stocking convictions.

Besides, she was Devenham's sister; and he had sworn revenge on Devenham. The generous freedom of the dower house had made his own grudge deepen; to have to be beholden to a cripple for charity, as though he himself were a beggar! To have to mind his ways—there had, by some means he had himself forgotten, come a trickle of informed comment about the two elders' Malvie visit, and their complaint about Livia. It was begging the question to say that Devenham had taken no action; he'd been given the right to. To wither his prosperity, deface his honour, drag his parvenu name in the dust; father his heirs, ruin his undeserved contentment, his smug English security!

Such thoughts had often come to Morven since the time he was alone, staring out sightlessly beyond the brazen sky and sea of the Antipodes, thinking of Malvie.

About that time Samson, who had been away for a few days to purchase necessaries in town, returned, with braggart stories of himself in the whorehouses.

He sat by the fire quaffing small-ale, regaling Morven, who never took him at such times with full seriousness, with ribald tales impossible of reality, or at least well larded with lies. To Samson he himself was Casanova, Hercules, the god of love and his own namesake. The whores, he stated as he always did, had shown him to one another, marvelling at the great size and potency of his parts. "And to think the French would have taken them!" Samson reminded himself happily. He was, at such times, the small boy he had once been; much about him was indestructibly childlike, despite the subject. He continued to relate, with the artless pleasure of his Irish ancestors and of a long line of negro forebears from the Ivory Coast, other adventures he said had been his while he was away. Morven continued smiling, but had ceased fully to listen. What Samson kept inside his breeches, even if it were all only half true, should quell Clairette if such an outcome were ever possible.

He tensed suddenly. Why not? he thought, and began to grin, so that Samson thought it was with pleasure at his tales. By evening, the plan Morven had felt growing in his head was almost perfected. It would take time, more than a day or two, perhaps even a week or two; but, in the meantime, he himself could become almost resigned to the inevitable sessions with Clairette.

"You quote the writings of Mary Wollstonecraft; you say all women should take a lover. Yet you yourself would never have the courage so to flout your upbringing. You are a coward, for all your fine words."

Clairette maintained her catlike rubbing against his sleeve; she enjoyed the contact. "I'd take you," she told him, using the boldness of an emancipated woman; the world was changing, soon women like herself would be pioneers, and not—"Would you?" he said, smiling and half aiding her. "Where and how?" It was like, he thought, some sickly game played by children, for their diversion; how he wished she would go!

"You could show me a time and place." The secretive eyes gazed possessively at him. How handsome he looked, in his familiar shabby cloak! Dear Morven, he always wore it. A time and place; not here, where at any moment somebody might come down the path, that dreadful blackamoor or even somebody looking for her from Malvie. So Mary Wollstonecraft would have spoken, calm and unafraid, to her lover; how else were poor women to indicate an understanding of such matters? At the same time, a tingling excitement was mounting in Clairette's veins; Mr. Setoun, let alone Mr. McIntyre, had been far from eliciting it. But Morven Doon, seated there in pale wrapped mystery and asking her to be his lover! This was life as it should be lived, grasped at with both hands. What did Mama and Godfrey matter? They'd done it themselves, hadn't they? Ah, to love like the great lovers of the world, like Abélard and Héloïse, Catullus and Lesbia—

When the conditions he outlined were made clear to her, however, she pouted. To go to the old hayshed, up there on the hill, by night, and lie down like a milkmaid? To do that, and keep silent, as he said, and afterwards go back to Malvie by the side postern, like a servant-girl on an assignation? For the first time, Clairette wondered if the Wollstonecraft precepts were entirely consonant with dignity; her lip trembled.

"If it's so dark, how will I know—" There were only the stars to light the night sky now, no moon; she mustn't bring a lantern, of course, for fear of being stopped. But all the same—

She heard Morven answer smoothly. "I will wear my white wig, so that you'll see it, and this cloak. You know the cloak, don't you?" He smiled, and she could have sworn his bright eyes watched her; the expression in them was, she suddenly thought, like a triumphing devil's. She shivered, and heard him laugh.

"Won't that suffice? I declare, you are only half in earnest about wanting a lover."

"I am not—I am not!" She clung to his cloak, twining her fingers in it like a child in search of familiar certainty. She raised her face to him. "You will—truly—be there?"

He mocked her. "I will wager you a sixpence that when I come tomorrow night, and put out my hand into the hay, I find it empty. You will not have the courage to come."

That fired her, and she remembered the dark would be the same to him as day. They would love, then, together tomorrow. Tomorrow would begin a new life.

Samson grinned, and assented readily; any orders of Morven's were for him to obey, without question; he did not even ask if there would be trouble. This, as Morven already knew, seemed unlikely; if Clairette had so far forgotten herself as to come by stealth and lie waiting in the hay, in the dark of a moonless night, it was unlikely that even a magistrate would take a serious view of the offender; it was more likely that a private word of advice in the average parents' ears would guarantee a sound whipping for the young lady in the case, except that Kitty Bowes was as big a fool as her daughter. Morven left the matter, weary of Clairette and her unquenchable fires; except that he said a further word to Samson, perhaps attempting, by a kind of outward bravado, to quiet his own conscience, which troubled him.

"A guinea for the maidenhead, my friend, and five guineas if you get her in calf. Agreed? Then you had better take my cloak. We are much of a height; practise casting it about you, and walking the way I do. You have till tomorrow; see that nothing happens to it, it's the warmest I have."

He did not trouble, next night, to ensure that Samson left at the time arranged. He knew that the mulatto, obedient as any janissary, would obey his orders to the letter, as far as it could be done. Morven knew, in his usual way, that dark had now fallen; he felt the warmth of lit candles on his cheek. He stretched out a hand to the peg where his cloak by custom hung, and stroked the bare wall, and smiled. The cloak was gone. He sat down by the fire, and waited till Samson should return.

As the hours passed a strange sensation reached Morven; he told himself he knew nothing of regret, of pity. In the darkness which now encompassed him, that unalterable night into which he had been plunged after the fracas with the customs-officer, years back, it was as though he had come to terms with the darkness, had become in himself what darkness was. That he had engendered evil, that evil was by now, at this moment, through his agency being done, should mean nothing to him, he told himself, any more than his early treatment of Annabel should have meant anything, except as a step towards the achievement of his goal. That Clairette's shame, her destruction possibly, might in turn destroy her brother, his name, his estate, had already occurred to Morven; coldly, he had made it part of the plan. Yet now, as at times in the lonely darkness, without Livia by him, he felt deceived; as though an agency greater in evil than anything he himself might contemplate, or invent, directed him; screened him from human feeling, so that the very urge to own Malvie itself had been transformed into something grotesque, unmentionable. Morven moved where he sat, felt for the fire-irons, found the long poker, and viciously jabbed at the dying ashes in the hearth. He must keep a fire for Samson when at last he came home; came home, with his tale to tell. Why should he himself, Morven Doon, sit here, almost regretting Clairette's ruin?

When Samson returned it was near morning; upstairs, Livia was asleep long ago. Morven had not gone up to her. The ashes still glowed with his long care of them; he raised his head, and forced a smile. "Well? Did you have her?" The mulatto, he sensed, had acquired a slight swagger, an air perhaps of social as well as physical satisfaction. He made an elaborate business of removing the wig and cloak.

"I had her, as instructed. She was a virgin."

"You altered that, I don't doubt. Is my cloak back on its peg?"

"The mantle of Elijah has been returned," said Samson unexpectedly; he had, in common with most malingerers in the Bay, been flogged to church on occasion by search-officers. They laughed together. "Or," Morven ventured, "Jacob's kidskins. You may borrow the cloak again tomorrow night, my friend; do you go back?" His smile mocked the other. It would depend on the dark of the moon, no doubt; otherwise, Miss Clairette might be duped for long enough. But Samson queried it.

"I will go again, perhaps; but she may not come." Without more words on the subject, he went and cut himself a manchet of bread, and bit into it cautiously with his teeth, which as usual pained him.

But Clairette did not return next night; she had been badly frightened. It was one thing to hold Mary Wollstonecraft's advanced theories; another to be the prey, out of pervading darkness, of the malefic, tearing force which had invaded and half destroyed her: to feel a hand over her mouth, and a foetid warm breath, like a dog's, against her cheek; and to have no further answer. She had left later in fear and bewildered pain; next day, she found she could neither stand nor walk without difficulty, and, evading Kitty's sharp eye and questioning, she stayed in bed, with some tale to her mother of delayed courses. These remained suspended: and as the days passed Clairette came to realise that the queasy, changed young person who was herself had something physically far wrong. In due course, pale, red-eyed and subdued, she came again to Morven. He turned his head coldly.

"What is it?" he asked her. "Why are you here again?"

She burst into tears. "You frightened me," she sobbed. "That night in the shed—you were so unkind, so—so brutal. I think I'm pregnant, oh, oh, oh," and she collapsed into wailing.

"Not by me," said Morven, and stood up from where he had been seated by the wall. He could sense, rather than know, of Clairette's mouth dropped witlessly open, as she stared at him from where she stood. He made himself be hard with her, of full intent; to be rid of her for all time was a less unthinkable alternative to having her with him always.

"It was Samson who got you pregnant," he told her. "The child however may not be black." He smiled, and reached for his staff, ready to take himself off. "It may be a quadroon, a little coffee-and-milk coloured creature, quite charming in fact; but, even so, my dear, will Godfrey be pleased?"

He had grasped his staff, and was feeling his way along the wall with it. He knew the Mains less well than Malvie, and must go carefully. His concentration, however, was not so close as to prevent him from hearing Clairette's departure. She had begun to emit shrill cries of fear, horror and disgust; he heard her run away down the path that led to Malvie.

Clairette went home and tried to kill herself. There was, lying in the garden-shed, a new substance Godfrey had had sent from Kew, made mainly of arsenic to prevent rats eating plants. Kitty and Annabel had returned from their evening stroll and were about to change for supper before they found Clairette: she was lying on the floor of her bed-chamber vomiting blood, the empty container of chemical nearby. They sent for the physician, who when he could be found came and worked knowledgeably on Clairette, with milk possets, enemas, finally a rival mild emetic. In the end, when he had saved her, he made a certain examination. The facts, as he could later tell them to Kitty Bowes, should have remained veiled; but the poor woman had hysterics, the truth leaked out, and the girl's brother at least, by devious ways, heard it. Clairette had been with a man; but that there had been more, much more, was evident also in course of the poor child's delirium, when she raved a good deal. At last, between renewed vomiting and purges, this time for a different reason, the embryo Samson had lodged in her was voided, which was the best anyone could do for her. Clairette after all was alive, and, though it was probable she would be affected mentally, no longer pregnant. She was removed shortly, and Kitty accompanied her meantime, for a prolonged stay at Maddon, to help Cecily with the children.

Godfrey grieved for his young half-sister, whom almost alone among everyone, he had loved. Love to him was a well-spring in himself, abundant, to be given freely. He never fully recovered from the episode of Clairette's disgrace; weakened and discouraged to an extent which only those who believe that the mind has an influence on the body can understand, he withdrew into himself, growing steadily less accessible after Clairette had left Malvie. The pain in his chest recurred more often; but he still took no action against Morven Doon, or demanded that he should find other living-quarters, though Annabel constantly urged that this should be done.

Fear had come to Malvie; it ate and slept with them. Annabel herself felt it, aware that, no matter what must follow as a result, she herself could do nothing to avert the triumph of fear. By night she would feel fear choke her, like a miasma from the nearby sea; after an hour or two of sleepless tossing on her bed, she would get up and go to the casement, and open it and feel the night wind blow her hair, the stone of the sill strike her flesh, as she had once done long ago when Morven stood below her window, at Mains, ready to come up. She had no lover now; her flesh was hungry, thin and dry with desire; at time she would writhe uselessly against the stone. At other times she would go back to bed and try to sleep, and wake screaming that he pressed upon her. And always the sea sounded, sounded in her ears, as it had done when both she and Morven had been born; both she and Morven.

VI

Godfrey's health improved with the clear, cold weather they had that spring, and by the end of April he was again able to be lifted into his calèche and to drive it about the grounds a little, to see to his gardens.

It was his pride to have Sybilla with him, now that the child had learned to master her second pony; when she was a toddling thing she had used to sit by him in the carriage, pretending to guide the reins; now she rode alongside him. He was, however, compelled to go too slowly for a spirited young rider on her mount, and lately had encouraged Sybilla and Annabel to ride out together, gallop to stretch the ponies' legs along the bridle paths in the planted forest, and return later when if it was fine enough they would all three breakfast al fresco on food out of a hamper Godfrey brought, packed by the kitchens.

This year, he was anxious to see his larches.

The slopes where they now grew had always been roughly wooded, with thorns and other wild low-growing trees swept always by the off-shore wind, so that they grew with a list to landward. Godfrey had had windbreaks planted, quick-growing fir and poplar; then five years ago had set, on the cleared dug land, the new light-green conifers from Scandinavia, scarcely known anywhere in Scotland as yet. Their pale feathery appearance was, he understood, very beautiful, the red trunks contrasting with the springlike foliage. By now they should be at their best.

Annabel set out that day alone. Sybilla would join them later; her daily lessons with Jane Glover were becoming important, for though Godfrey could not bear the thought of parting with the little girl it was time, at any rate, to think about sending Sybilla in due course to school. Annabel remembered her own lonely childhood, and was resolved that such should not be her daughter's fate, lacking brothers and sisters. Sybilla should make the right friends—Annabel was never free of mild ambition—and the best way to achieve this was by putting her name down for the right establishment for young ladies, already suggested by Jane Glover. It was probable, though nothing definite had been said in this way, that when Annabel no longer required her at Malvie, Jane would be offered a place on the school's staff. This would be of great benefit to Sybilla, who would feel less strange, in her first long absence from her home and parents, if her former governess were with her. "And so, my love, you must work hard each day till then, for there is—" Annabel smiled at the innovation—"an entrance examination, and those who are stupid, or lazy, will not be admitted. Think of the shame of that!"

But Sybilla would not be too stupid, she was convinced; Godfrey had taught her from an early age to use her mind, to look about her and to cultivate memory. Annabel walked her pony, surveying the new forest and thinking how tall the trees had grown in under six years. The light filtered between the delicately traced branches was the colour of dry sherry-wine; something of the tonic quality of wine, too, was in the air from the sea, and she herself felt better than she had of late, even glad Godfrey had persuaded her to come out for the ride and al fresco today. She stayed indoors too much, he told her; and now that he was about again, she must make, she told herself, more effort to accompany him.

He had not appeared yet, and Sybilla also would ride down later, when the lessons were done, like a grown-up young lady in her habit. Annabel meantime cantered her mount along the coast-road, seeing again the well-known vistas of sea and rocks, caves and the distant bulk of Man she had known from a child. The remains of invalid weariness, of doubt, fell away from her with the speed of the ride; with their health, now that she and Godfrey had begun to regain it, they could not be content with their lot? A good horse, a daily ride before breakfast; a beloved child, enough money to satisfy every whim, and Godfrey himself, a saint and scholar; what did she lack?

She turned the pony's head at last, and the beast trotted docilely back the way they had come. As the underwater shadows of the forest closed again about her, Annabel drew a sharp breath. Standing on the bridle-path, straight in her way, on Godfrey's land, was Morven Doon, a long staff in his hand on which he was meantime leaning. He did not move or alter his stance as he heard her come; there was no escape between the interlacing tree-branches, and she reined in her pony.

He smiled, and she knew well that he was aware of her as the rider. She said severely, "Morven, you should not be here," and waited for him to bow, apologise, and allow her to pass before removing himself. He must use, she realised, the long staff to tap his way among the trees; they would be new since his earlier sojourn here. Pity for his blindness claimed her, and she slid from the saddle. He had not moved and she saw, too late, that he had in fact been waiting for her to dismount; taking charge of the reins, he tied them to a branch with strangely expert fingers.

"Morven." She smiled, and decided to try to charm him into going; it would be unpleasant, she thought, if Godfrey came upon them here; it would spoil Godfrey's day. "Morven, why do you act always as if we were enemies, and try to embarrass us? Can the past not be forgotten, so that we can both of us wish you well? I am happy, you know, with my husband and child; I—I would wish to see you happy also. Godfrey, I am sure, would feel as I do, were you to act in a friendly way to him, and show a little gratitude for all he has permitted you. It is at least ungrateful," she finished gently, "to trespass in his forest." She did not mention, indeed hardly thought of, Clairette: that matter was done with.

"There were silver birches here once, among the thorns," said Morven inconsequentially. "I remember them from a boy. I carved my name on one."

210

He took his staff and viciously, as if he wanted to wound it, slashed this against the trunk of one of the evenly planted young larches, then laid the staff down. A weal showed on the assaulted bark: Annabel drew a breath of anger. How mean, how needlessly destructive Morven could be, like a small boy whose will has been crossed and who pulls the wings off flies! As though to prove that he was by now more of a child, or savage, than he had ever been, Morven himself broke into sudden laughter.

"Happy, eh? With your husband and your child?"

He mimicked her tones cruelly, stressing each syllable to convey a hidden meaning in the outwardly harmless words, stripping her of pretence. "Was he ever in truth your husband, my dear? And the child is mine."

"Be quiet, you will be heard—"

"And that would be a pity," he mocked. "That'd prick your genteel soap-bubble, would it not? Are you happy in it, Annabel? Poor Annabel; your tail's ill served nowadays!"

She had drawn away from him, in disgust; he was coarse, she thought, and lewd; the low company he affected had altered him from what he had once been. She would tell him again to go, and—"Shall I solace it?" he whispered, drawing neared. "Shall I rouse it to life again, my dear, your little tail?"

Still laughing, he pulled her to him; and on the gasp of outrage she had given at the words he used, he kissed her; her mouth was open, and he put his tongue in it, and held her thus for moments; she could feel his laughter.

She had struggled against him, striking out until he pinioned her hands, easily in one of his own; then he began to handle her with the other. Her senses reeled, and she grew dizzy; this couldn't be real, it was a dream; an evil dream, Morven couldn't be here with her, his fingers thrusting down inside her bodice, his mouth on her mouth. He knew, had always known, how to rouse her, where to touch; he did so now, at the same time talking, talking always against her imprisoned mouth.

"Do you remember how I came below your window, then climbed up, and into your little bed . . . a virgin, a chaste little maiden nun, you were . . . but not by the time I'd done . . . do you remember how you would leap, and cling afterwards, and not want me to go? Do you remember, Madam Gentility, eh? Do you, do you?"

And he caressed and teased her; and presently her thighs, her knees, had become like melting wax, and he would have drawn her then into the privacy of the trees, and she could not prevent him, no, she could no more prevent him from anything than the moon from rising . . .

"Ah . . ."

And the shameful flood, the hot unbidden surge of desire, welled in her as it had used to do, and the thing was as it had used to be, and she—

Then she tore herself away and raised the arm which held her small silver-handled riding-whip, and slashed and slashed so that the blood ran down Morven's face.

She must have been screaming, although she had not heard herself make any sound. She was aware, at some time, of an answering shout in the distance, and at the same moment the tension in all her body eased and she turned and ran, one hand still clenched over the whip, and saw Godfrey in his chair, coming down the path to where they were, so that he must have heard and seen her strike and strike at a blind man, who couldn't defend himself. What had come over her? What had she become?

She reached Godfrey. He had stopped the calèche, and was at the reins still, staring down to where Morven stood. Annabel flung her arms about him; in the terror Morven had aroused in her, it seemed as if he could do them both harm, as if they were here unprotected together. But Morven was blind.

He came then. He began to walk towards where they were, without his staff which he had left lying by the tree. The whip had cut four weals across his face and the blood had welled up in these and now ran down, disfiguring his cheeks and chin and staining his clothing. The light, blind eyes were fixed on Godfrey; he must have heard the latter call out.

"Are you there, Devenham?" they heard him say as he came. "Are you there, eunuch, protector of other men's women? Do you know, my usurper, that she—" and he pointed at Annabel, again as though he could see her, for her breaths were loud and rasping now with the horrified sobbing that would soon overcome, and she clung to Godfrey as if in fear that Morven would strike. "Do you know that she was *my* bedfellow, Devenham, in the days when you were collecting shells on the shore together? That was a pretty spectacle, I declare; but the nights were mine. I climbed up to her window, as you could not."

"Stop, stop," screamed Annabel, "can't you see—" Then the impossibility of what she had said, had tried to say, in such a situation overcame her, and she gave way to crazed

212

laughter. Morven was blind, blind. She'd asked a blind man if he could see. She'd slashed a blind man till the blood ran down his face. She'd—

Then she saw Godfrey; and her laughter died.

He had half risen from his place, in a way he had not been able to do for years. The effort had caused his whole body to quiver, as though at any moment it would collapse, in ignominy, back again in the upholstered seat. His face was the colour of tallow, the brow glistening with sweat; below it, the eyes were glazed like a calf's which is dying. He surveyed the blind man. When they came, his words were mild.

"Will you go from here?" was all he said. Morven laughed, and his teeth showed white through the drying blood.

"Go? Oh, ay," he said, "but I'll return. Maybe your lady wife—" he gave the word vicious emphasis— "will remember more kindly, another time, how she gave me earlier welcome; it was warmer than your own has ever been. Do you suppose, you moon-calf, that she would ever have married you save for Malvie? Malvie's ours, Doon heritage, for no interloper. Sybilla—"

"No!" Sybilla's mother screamed then. She heard her screams echoing down the forest paths, at the top of which, surely, a small girl on a pony must be riding soon, riding now. The child mustn't hear this, mustn't see. But above all Godfrey must be prevented from hearing, from knowing the truth, the brutal, undeniable truth about Sybilla. If her own scream could invade his hearing and prevent other entry, she would scream on deliberately till her throat was dry . . .

"Sybilla is my daughter. Did you suppose you could get a child?" said Morven clearly, and turned away. Godfrey had heard. She knew, and suddenly silent and in tears flung herself across his knees where he sat, so that he sagged upon her.

"Oh God," she heard herself moaning, and presently felt him somehow drag her up to him; she felt his poor hands caress her hair; had she ever resented his touch? Still she could say nothing but, "Oh, God, oh God," and knew a sudden fear that Godfrey was dying. His face, as with one near death, had acquired a serenity, a smoothness about it; he smiled, and kept his hand on her hair.

"Don't cry," she heard him say, and then "I . . . knew."

His breaths, as though they were someone's who has been running a long way, were growing shorter; a gasp of pain came, and his whole body grew rigid. She could see, as if in a nightmare, his teeth clench against the fierceness of the pain; that he should forget her, forget or fail to hear the thing she must tell him, was intolerable. She almost shouted at him, holding him fast about the body.

"I love you, I love you—my darling, my own darling—"

But he smiled, the face having relaxed and changed to an expression of great serenity and sweetness; perhaps he had not heard her. That he should not have done so possessed Annabel's mind all through the hours and days that followed; after help came, after they took him away, after they laid him out for burial.

For he was dead. He had perhaps died doubting her.

Later, after she had gone away for help, the child Sybilla had come, having ridden down at speed on her pony as soon as the lessons were over. She saw her father's body slumped sideways, found him glassy-eyed and silent, not answering her kiss; and then she screamed, and looked about her for help at last; a blind man with a bleeding face stood nearby.

"Do not cry, my child," he said, "he was never your father. I am."

Sybilla fell again to screaming.

Godfrey's will was read by the lawyer Fosse, who had come down from Edinburgh for the funeral. He read it in presence of the widow, Kitty Bowes, Sir Hubert Melrose and his son Paul, who had arrived with Kitty. Clairette Bowes was not present. Neither was the child Sybilla, who was, it was stated, under physician's orders and distracted with grief. So, Mr. Fosse thought, unexpectedly, was the widow; she twisted her mourning-kerchief in her hands throughout the reading, and appeared to understand very little he had to say.

The will was straightforward. The house and estate of Malvie, with a large jointure, went to Annabel direct, without provisions or clauses. Fosse looked at her, cleared his throat, and kept silent concerning his own thoughts on the matter; it was, he decided, no time to mention that, if she chose to marry again, the property was hers to leave or dispose as she chose. But as things were, no doubt, she herself would will Malvie directly to Miss Sybilla. He would discuss that matter with her, perhaps before he left.

Sybilla herself was generously provided for; Kitty and Clairette received life-annuities. The trusteeship of Sybilla's fortune was, as was prudent, under Sir Hubert's care as well as that of the child's mother. There were one or two benefits

214

to servants, in particular to the footman George Oakes. "Nothing and no one was forgotten by him," said Sir Hubert afterwards, gruffly to disguise the emotion he felt. He was compelled to add that if Annabel cared to make her home with them at Maddon, and to bring Sybilla with her—

Annabel shook her head; she was, the old man thought, in a state of shock, and could not rightly decide her course of present action. He tried to persuade her; would she, perhaps, desire him to remain here for a day or two with her, till she might have had leisure to think what her future arrangements might be? "It will be solitary for you here, niece," he said kindly.

"Mama Bowes has offered to stay," said Annabel dully. Kitty's choice had surprised her, for with her two daughters now at Maddon one would have thought that she preferred to remain there, now Godfrey was gone; but she would, she said, like best to remain with Annabel and little Sybilla. Clairette refused to return. It might not be long, everyone thought, till Kitty herself would need the attentions due to an invalid; her painted face sagged, and she seemed to have aged ten years since Godfrey's death; she was still given to uncontrolled outbursts of weeping. But Annabel did not weep; not even at night, when she was alone on her pillows. She had, after all, been for some years alone in such a way.

Her solitude was like a wall about her; nobody, she resolved should break it down. After Sir Hubert and Paul and the lawyer had gone she walked restlessly about the house, the great empty house of Malvie. Godfrey had filled it with beautiful and rare things, and his garden; she must always tend his garden, though not as he—

"Let me keep it worthily, as he would have wished. Let it be a memorial to him."

Outside, she already knew, Morven would be coasting about, waiting; it was like the onslaught of a chess-army, red against white. If she'd think for herself, think what she was doing, Godfrey had once told her, she'd sometimes win. She'd win this game. Godfrey had left Malvie to her; she herself had signed a will, lately before Fosse rode away, leaving everything to Sybilla. Morven, who had killed her saint, her love, Godfrey, should not have Malvie. She and Kitty and Sybilla, three women together, should resist him alone.

She clenched her white hands, and felt the stiff ridged stuff of her mourning-gown yield under them; but she herself would be unyielding, in this war. With every one of the resources left to her starved and lonely body, Annabel made ready to fight Morven Doon. She had already sent, the day after Godfrey's funeral, a request to him to vacate the Mains at the earliest opportunity.

PART THREE

I

Sybilla had been having nightmares since her father's death. She would wake in trembling silence, bathed in sweat; what the form of the dream had been she could not, she said, remember, except that it had brought with it the sound of the sea, pounding against rock. Often those who waited with her would come by with a shaded candle, and find the child wide-eyed watching the vibrations of the wall-lamp which floated in oil and gave off a tiny flame from a wick fashioned of rushes. Annabel had hung it nearby Sybilla's bed so that she should not wake and find it dark. She was afraid of the dark, nowadays; and afraid of her mother.

"What is it, my darling?" Annabel would say, bending over her, and would receive no answer; Sybilla would turn her head away. Only to the governess, Jane Glover, who now shared her room, she would sometimes say, "The lamp. It shakes when they move." And her eyes held terror; in the dream, which she could not remember now, she had heard those who hammered and cut, hammered and cut at the rock deep under Malvie. With each blow, the lamp flickered. But why should they always come in the dark?

Papa was underground. Papa was where they had buried him, in a coffin covered by a stone slab, in the new tomb dug in the grounds. He would be lonely, Sybilla thought; only, of course, he wasn't there. Mama, crying, had tried to persuade her of that; but she wouldn't listen, or yet believe that Papa was now where he could walk and run, and pick the flowers he had loved to grow. Papa wasn't anywhere, except in the tomb and the coffin: lying in it with glazed eyes. Without him, the house was empty.

Cousin Paul had come, with his father, and had tried to comfort Sybilla. She liked Paul; he was so solid and calm and strong, like Papa would have wanted to be, able to ride a horse and shoot and stride about, like other people. Paul and Uncle Hubert had wanted Mama to come and bring Sybilla with her, and live always at Maddon. But Mama wouldn't go. She spent all day, Sybilla supposed, walking from room to room, or going alone into the garden, always in her black dress. Sometimes she would go to the room where Papa had kept his shell-collection, and would lock the door and, Sybilla knew, give way to bursts of dreadful crying, which could be heard beyond. It made one, almost, sorry for Mama, though it had been all her fault. Her fault, and the blind man's.

He had come again once. Sybilla knew about it, having glimpsed him from the schoolroom window when Miss Glover had been sent for to go down to Mama. He'd come walking up the drive as if he could see, striding firmly, with a tall staff in his hand and his cloak swinging round him. He didn't seem afraid to come alone. But they hadn't let him enter Malvie; Mama had sent word to the footman who replaced George, and he had shown Morven Doon the door and he had gone away as he had come, but quite untroubled; he was smiling. Sybilla had seen that, and it had increased her fear and horror; to smile, after everything that had happened . . .

He had not come again. Miss Glover had told Sybilla that he had been asked to leave the Mains, and would soon be going. "He says he has found another house to live in," said the young governess, wrinkling her brow. "I wonder where it can be? It will be better, far better, once he has gone from here."

Sybilla nodded and traced the answers to her sums, and let one finger stray inside the golden curl which could be coaxed now to fall on her shoulder, like a grown-up lady's. It would be better, far better, as Miss Glover had said, once the blind man had gone.

Annabel had herself tried to forget that visit of Morven's. She had tried to forget his very existence, making herself, as day followed day, pass her hours as Godfrey would have had her do, if Godfrey had still been able to speak. Often she would find herself talking to Godfrey in her own mind, though never aloud; she would roam the rooms of the house, seeing that the maids had left everything as he had been used to have it left. The garden also she tried to tend. But his gardener had already left her.

He had been the first of the servants to go; he had been waiting for Annabel one day when she came out, his ancient half-beaver in his hand; he had always been a personage of some pretensions, having trained at Kew. "But why?" she had cried, when he signified his formal intention of leaving at

219

the end of his term. "The garden will not be the same with anyone else." She tried to smile. "I'm not knowledgeable, as your master was. But I had hoped we might, between us, at least keep it as it has become." She turned to look over at the glory of flowers and rare shrubs and trees in high summer; some of them would perish in the cold seawind of autumn without expert treatment. Tears sprang to her eyes; did everything have to be made harder for her? To have kept the Malvie garden as it was, a memorial—

The gardener cut in regretfully. He had, he said, the instant Mr. Devenham's death was known, been besieged by requests from other estate-owners, some rich, others fanciful, all in the south. "I've a notion to better myself, madam, by going back," he said stiffly; he had never been on the terms with Annabel that he had with her husband. A gardener born, Mr. Godfrey had been; knew in advance what to do with every leaf and root, not that he ever ordered one against one's ingrained ways, and they'd both kept learning as they went. But a lady, now, who hadn't the business at heart, no matter how she might sigh and weep nowadays, was different. "I'm going down to Richmond again, madam," the man said firmly. He added that it wouldn't have happened so soon, maybe, but that the gentleman who'd spoken for him—he was newly home from the East, with a consignment of rare bulbs worth a fortune, and other things—he wanted everything well begun before the autumn. "I'm sorry, madam." The second footman was sorry also; that had happened in the following week. One couldn't expect them to stay on here, in so remote a place, no doubt, with a widow and a child, and poor Kitty as she now was. There was no company and nowhere to go in their free time.

She sighed. Kitty—her stroke had come upon Godfrey's mother while she slept, and by the morning she had been found lying without the power of speech, and with half her limbs useless—Kitty must be looked after. Clairette had announced, indirectly by way of Paul, that under no circumstances would she return to Malvie. It was not, accordingly, a kindness to Cecily Melrose to ask her to add to the burdens she had already, and look after an old invalid mother as well as the five young girls; and Kitty had, in the ways in which she could still manifest meaning, declared her intention of staying on in the place where her son had died, so that she could be buried with him. All things centred as always on Godfrey, lying in the new tomb.

Annabel herself knew she would not leave here. A kind of

mulishness, standing in the way of what, she knew, others intended for her good, had entered her soon after the death. She refused both Sir Hubert's offer of a home for herself, Sybilla and Kitty, and a later circumstance which, by itself, might have given rise to kindly laughter in everyone: Colonel Cazalet had, pompously and correctly, aided by his ear-trumpet, proposed marriage. "Wouldn't have been as pre-cipitate, m'dear, with poor Devenham hardly cold! But your own situation here, it's—it's damned solitary! No state for a woman!" He added that he had always admired her. Anna-bel, had declined, kindly and formally: she would never, she assured him, marry again. Her heart—the good Colonel would, no doubt, have understood this trite assumption more easily than subtler metaphors, for his was an uncomplicated intelligence—her heart was in the tomb with Godfrey. Hav-ing understood this fact, the Colonel left her with, she doubted not, a certain well-concealed relief; to change one's single state at sixty-odd would have taken a good deal of resolution and courage. He stumped off to his coach which waited, assuring her of his continued esteem.

Other than that, few people had come to Malvie since the funeral.

Sybilla's continued dreams troubled Annabel, and one day she caused Sam Aitken, the groom, to go down to the base of the ancient tower where, she remembered from childhood, there had been a legend of an old entrance, leading down by a shaft to the caves. She had not gone with Sam, saying to herself that she did not care to soil her gown; but truth to tell she had no wish to look at the trap-door, or what lay beneath. The groom came back, avoiding her eyes.

"Well, Sam?" She had known him from childhood; it was he who had—what a lifetime ago it seemed!—boxed Morven's ears for scaring her by making her walk along the haunted ledge. She asked him if the entry below the tower was visible.

"Not now—ma'am." He had always to think before remem-bering that she wasn't Miss Annabel these days. The thought struck her that he looked thin and somewhat yellow. "Are you well, Sam?" She had already forgotten about the trap-door.

"Well enough," growled the old groom. He did not add that he'd got young William Judd, whom he knew she didn't like to see about the place, to help him roll two boulders in from the outside, and batten down the door. The dust had been disturbed lately; looking down at last through the yawning opening, one could see a dark receding shaft, and steps cut, with stanchions. There'd been someone there, that was evident, working at it since *he* was a boy; he remembered that shaft well enough as smooth and difficult to climb. With all one heard—but, the Lord bless poor Miss Annabel, *she* wouldn't hear it!—about the packmen calling in almost daily at Mains, and the boats there were lying in about the coast, far more by night now than in the old days, and the rumours of some great and mighty business of Mr. Morven's stretching from here to Leith, so that the excisemen hardly dared come near—what wise man but would keep his mouth shut? But he'd put the boulders across, for *her* safety; didn't want rough entrants into Malvie, while she lay asleep in her bed. As for her question about did he feel well, he didn't; he had a growth in him as big as an apple, all this year; but it was better to die in harness, for what was left, except the alms-houses, maybe? Mr. Godfrey would have seen him right; but one could never tell with a woman.

For Sam's wife had left him thirty years back, and he was accordingly a misogynist, apart from his devotion to the members of the family, whom Aitkens had served for three generations.

Annabel was troubled about Sybilla's distrust of her, and had discussed it with the governess. Here however she found herself at a loss; Jane Glover was a wise, cold, provident young woman, a credit to her profession; she could by no means be informed of the full progress of events leading to Godfrey's death, or, hence, be brought to understand Sybilla's changed feelings towards her mother. The solution she put forward was simple enough; Sybilla missed her father; Anna-bel herself must spend more time with the child.

By now the spring and the height of summer were over, and there were already cool days with a hint of mist or early frost. On one of these, Annabel wrapped herself in a shawl, shod herself stoutly, and called to take Sybilla for a walk through the woods. These had changed in colour from that other fateful, too-bright day when their foliage had been virgin green; they would avoid the larch woods today, and would make for the brakes, where Godfrey had latterly stocked young pheasants. In May the place had been a mass of bluebells; by now, the bracken had grown up, and was already dulled over pending October changes to yellow, brown and flame. They followed a path above it, at first in silence. Then Sybilla said, a trifle primly, as if speaking to a stranger, "Papa and I found scarlet toadstools last year, down there," and she pointed, taking a hand out of her muff. "May I go down Mama, and see if I can still find them?"

She turned her face, rosy with the walk, to Annabel; the eyes were still wide and remote, but perhaps with time the constraint might lessen; so her mother thought, and watched the small dark-clad figure in its neat hood venture down the slope, beyond which pines reared blackly. Watching, Annabel thought sadly that all of her own life now revolved round that young, tentative one; if anything befell Sybilla, what would be left to her of Godfrey? "Can you see the toadstools, darling?" she called. "Do not go too far; there may be adders in the bracken." Sam Aitken, she recalled, had killed one hereabouts when she was a child; it had been as long as one's arm, marked with diamonds as big as a rajah's; an old one, Sam had said. Since then she herself had been afraid to go down there; how many things there were to be afraid of! If one were to give way completely to folly, life would be no more than a waking round of fear upon fear.

Sybilla's answering cry came soon; she had found the toadstools. She bent down among the fronds, and presently emerged carrying the garish, deceptive fungi in the overskirt of her gown; she began to clamber up towards the path again, and Annabel kept silent about the danger of poison. Godfrey had reared Sybilla to have both enough knowledge and enough sense not to put her fingers in her mouth after touching any unknown object, or to try to taste it because of its colour.

The child turned her enchanting face up and briefly, trustfully smiled. Annabel felt her own heart fill with joy; and it was then that the thing happened. She could remember afterwards hearing a small *ping,* an alien sudden sound, from among the trees. She then saw Sybilla fling up both hands to cover her face, while the forgotten toadstools scattered among the bracken like bright beads. The child was screaming. Annabel picked up her skirts and ran, stumbling down over the rough slope of unseen ground between bracken-stems and dwarf sloe, catching and tearing her clothes on thorns. At last she knelt by her daughter.

"Sybilla, darling, darling, let me see . . ."

When she could bring the child's rigid hands down free of her face, a great wave of relief took Annabel; there was only a weal, a bright weal where something, a stone, had lately struck the smooth, rounded cheek below the eye. The flesh was already swelling; but the eye itself was safe.

"Come. Quickly, my darling; we must take you home."

Fear rose in her now for more attacks upon them both, by whoever waited still among the nearby pines; she was ignorant of what precise means had been used to launch the stone. She seized the child, now crying with fright and pain, by the hand and half dragged, half carried Sybilla up the bank; on the way back to the house she tried, vainly, to comfort her.

"It was a stone, my love. Only a little stone. We will bathe your face and it will be well tomorrow." All the time, through her desperate talk, she was thanking God the eye was saved; an inch higher and Sybilla might have been disfigured for life.

Who would do such a thing to a child, an innocent child? Evil was pressing closer about the house of Malvie, waiting already in the nearer trees. She felt such evil everywhere, rolling towards them now like a great cloud; soon she herself would not be able to stir hand or foot abroad without risk of danger. For Annabel knew well it was herself against whom the evil moved for Malvie's sake, and not Sybilla; they had victimised her daughter as a means of weakening herself. They would know that, filled as she would be by now with fear for Sybilla, a particle of her own resistance would have flaked away, like stone from a corroded wall; that gradually the wall itself would grow so weak as to be fit in the end to destroy with a thrust, a motion of purposeful hands. What would they do next to herself, to Sybilla, to obtain Malvie?

But on no account would she leave here. They should never drive her out.

Young William Judd, after they had both gone, slid back again between the trunks of the pines, stowing his newly acquired catapult away in his pocket. He was not yet perfectly expert with it; it had been the woman, Mrs. Devenham, he had in fact hoped to hit. He owed her a grudge for trying to keep him away from Malvie stables, and denying him the familiar company of the horses and of Sam. But William still went there in any case, mostly after dark when she'd be indoors; and meantime it had at least been something to have hit, even by mistaken timing, the dressed-up doll of a little fair-haired girl. Honour satisfied, William took himself off to where four or five packmen, who came to Mains regularly nowadays, would be assembled ready to leave again by dusk. They'd promised to let him ride a Welsh pony he fancied, and felt a yearning for, at least part of the way, till its chargeman joined them as arranged by night, four miles beyond Grattan. William would go any distance to have dealings with horseflesh, even though it meant he'd have to walk back. Afterwards, when he returned to Mains, it was likely enough, the boy thought without sentiment, that nobody there would even notice he'd been away. The blind man—William was beginning to feel a curious fascination for Morven, despite what he'd done to him, and wished that, like Samson the negro, he could go with Morven Doon to his boat on which both men spent most of their time nowadays. As for William's mother, she sat by the fire looking into it, hour after hour, and took no heed of William.

Sybilla fell ill with fever following the shock of that experience, though her eye took no harm; by the end of it all she was pale and thin, and had grown two inches. She had never, until recent months, encountered grief, shock or violence in the whole of her short life, and now all three worked upon her to make of her a changed, silent, alien being. Only to the governess would she give any trust; it was as much as to say, "Mama persuaded me to go for a walk with her, and that happened; I must take as little as possible, apart from politeness, from now on to do with Mama." The politeness was heartbreaking; it was after the third or fourth exercise of question and answer, the formal presentation after dinner of a quiet, pale little girl in a plain muslin gown tied with ribbons, but with no spark of life or joy in her, that Annabel began to consider a measure Jane Glover had been urging, gently but persistently, for some time; although it was so early, and she was young, Sybilla must be sent away to school. To stay here would kill her. Annabel was convinced of this; the governess only smiled slightly.

"Kill her? Oh, my dear Mrs. Devenham, not quite that, perhaps; but she is melancholy, and everything here reminds her of her Papa, and perhaps new friends and new faces—and the school is very well spoken of." Jane Glover lowered her lashes, and Annabel surveyed the quiet, mittened creature wordlessly, knowing very well that Jane had been repeatedly pressed to join the staff of the school in question, but had remained here out of, no doubt, a sense of duty. Well, her life and Sybilla's must not be further spoilt; they must go together, in time for the new term. She herself would not accompany them; there had grown in her a fixed determination not to leave Malvie, as though if she did so, it would be surrendered and closed to her forever: a citadel left open to the enemy who already encircled it unseen. She knew Morven was there, watching and waiting, in his darkness that to him was light; only her presence, she felt, could keep him out.

Sybilla went, and her roped bandboxes with her on the coach beside Jane's modest covered hamper. The school had demanded two alpaca gowns, four gowns of Paris muslin, several wide sashes of a blue colour, three pairs of shoes, house-slippers and shifts and hose, and a pelisse for walking. Sybilla had been sent off dowered like a little princess, in half-mourning only, so that her velvet pelisse was of a pretty, subdued dove-colour, enhancing the brightness of her hair. "The other girls will love her, and will make a pet of one so much younger than they," Jane Glover had assured Annabel, who was already fighting back her tears. The governess went on to add that she had so arranged matters with the headmistress—"she is a school-friend of my own, a great advantage, you will admit, Mrs. Devenham!" that Sybilla, for the first few weeks till she no longer felt strange, should sleep with Jane in her own bed, not in a dormitory. The governess could not have done more, though doubtless it would be to her own advantage to show zeal over a new pupil's welfare. Annabel felt this wry certainty come to her even as she waved farewell, from the steps of Malvie, to her child seated docilely by Jane's side in the carriage. After it had bowled down the drive, and the little face in the new, school-approved bonnet could no longer be seen behind the glass of the window, Annabel turned away, feeling already that a part of her life, her heart, had been cut out with scissors. However it all turned out—and no doubt she would be excellently cared for at the school, and out of danger—Sybilla would never again be Annabel's carefree delightful child; Annabel herself never, never any more the respected, idolised, pampered Mama of Godfrey's day, whose least whim was law and in whose presence nothing unforeseen, nothing frightening could happen. "There will always be doubt in her mind about me now, and soon, as she must be so often elsewhere, I will have become a stranger," Annabel thought. How little she had heeded the happiness of those carefree days when they were all three together, Godfrey, herself, Sybilla! How short a time she had had, by the end, to enjoy the real worth of Godfrey himself before he was taken away so cruelly!

Tears fell, remembering Godfrey's death and the manner of it. And now, when dark fell tonight on Malvie, she would for the first time be quite alone.

Annabel walked about the house that night. As soon as dusk fell she had lit a taper, and carried it about with her through the great empty rooms until, by the time darkness had fallen and the shadows flung themselves about beyond its flame as she moved, she found that she has carried it up to the height of the old Flodden tower. She had not meant to come here; but as she had, she made herself down the terrors that rose, and stand deliberately with the slender light in her hand, looking out to sea. Tonight she felt that the sea fashioned monsters, and so had made Morven; that a sea-beast, not Richard Doon, had visited his Highland mother as the god long ago visited Danaë, alone in her tower. Morven was of the sea; its eternal crying reminded her of his presence, somewhere below; from it, tonight, a light mist had again risen, so that her vision was limited to a region of swirling, pallid wreaths in the gathered dark. It was like the last time she herself had gone down to the little beach to bathe and had seen him standing, above on the cliff, his blind eyes staring across to herself, towards Malvie. Was it her fancy that tonight, through the flung veil of mist, there could be seen the dim shape of a boat? "There is a lanthorn burning at sea," she thought, "he is out there now." She withdrew quickly from the window, and shaded her taper with her hand; he mustn't know she was up here, waiting, watching. But he was blind, Annabel again remembered; Morven wouldn't see a taper, even on any other night so clear one could count the stars.

Perhaps she should have agreed to see Morven that time he came, and she'd ordered the servants to send him away. Perhaps, if she'd received him reasonably, he—they—

She writhed a little, biting her lips. It had happened again; she tried not to let it happen. The fire that was resolutely forbidden, the old physical longing for Morven, flickered in her, despite her will; again, now, staring out at enveloping mist which might hold him, she had disobeyed herself, and she wanted, she wanted . . . Her hand sought her own breasts, the free hand that wasn't holding the taper. She pressed and solaced her own body, as if it wanted hardness, pain, touch. They mustn't see her, no one must see her do such things, she must occupy her waking time with tasks, unremitting tasks, small things, charities, anything; visiting old Ellen, still alive in the almshouse at eighty-three in recalcitrant pride; or doing embroidery, or visiting, perhaps, except that she didn't dare leave the house and grounds, in case Morven might be waiting. There were surely things about the place she could do . . . tomorrow, she'd tidy the roses. They needed training, pruning perhaps, and the withered blossoms could be cut off. Their petals already littered the ground of that part of the garden, like mingled snow and blood.

Next day, Annabel went to visit Kitty Bowes in her rooms as usual. The poor old woman was endeavouring to walk, balancing on two sticks. A paid attendant stayed with her. Kitty, as the old will do, noticed this and resented it, and the fact that the woman was not her daughter Clairette. She often asked where Clairette was, and why the girl wouldn't come to her, her own mother. It was impossible now to do other than murmur some palliative gentle reply. Clairette had again refused when asked to come back to Malvie and bear Kitty company; but how could one remind this poor soul of that, and the underlying reason?

Annabel kissed her mother-in-law, as she did daily on greeting her. It was a discipline of the kind she had at first had to impose on herself in the early months of her marriage to Godfrey. She still found it difficult not to feel revulsion at the eager caresses of the slobbering, unaffected side of Kitty's mouth; the other side was powerless. She tried to think of caressing an old, devoted, half-paralysed dog. She continued to smile at Godfrey's mother, and sat down at her side afterwards, and talked gently to her, often answering her own unimportant, trivial queries aloud, as Kitty could not speak clearly and one often mistook what she said. It was better to make one's own conversation. Annabel said, among other things, that she was going out today to cut the roses.

"Godfrey tended them so carefully." She often, and deliberately, mentioned Godfrey aloud; she wanted Kitty to feel, as she herself did, that he was not forgotten with burial; not a memory but a living inspiration, almost a companion. "I do not want them to revert to ramblers for lack of care, but I know so little!" she said of the roses. The new gardener whom she had, with some difficulty, at last, found was untutored, a rough stranger; he hoed and weeded carelessly, but did nothing else, and had already destroyed, through ignorance and lack of interest, many of the more delicate plants at Malvie. Annabel did not inform Kitty of this. She let only such news escape her as would not further distress the sick old creature.

She smiled; how fixed and bright her daily smile had become! "Perhaps soon you will be able to walk again in the garden, Mama Bowes, when the weather is warm," she said, and this made the tears course weakly down Kitty's face. Whether the thought of feeling pleasure again was emotionally too much, or whether she had already convinced herself that she would never again walk in any garden, no one would ever know. Kitty had her own courage; each day, still she made the attendant rouge her, and put a freshly curled bright wig over her own shaven, defeated, thin grey hair. The garish unlikely gold made the painted, lop-sided mask beneath bizarre. But Kitty never looked clearly at herself; all mirrors had been taken from the room or left in shadow.

Annabel kissed her mother-in-law again, and felt the jewelled hands, like claws, clinging. "I shall be back again in a little while, Mama Bowes," she said gently, "only a little while." She reminded Kitty again that she was going down to the roses. It would not matter, she knew well, once she was beyond the door; Kitty would retreat then into a world of her own, a world of trifling annoyances, shutting out the recollection of Annabel's visits. Memory of long ago was sharper than more recent memory in the mind of the old, and Annabel often wondered if Godfrey's mother remembered he was dead. If she did not, so much the better, perhaps. How must it feel to be too weak to walk, too blind to look in a mirror, too confused to speak or remember clearly?

Annabel went down to the garden with her own resolution strong in her. She must devote her life to Kitty, to old Ellen, to Sam Aitken the groom who grew daily more ill and less active, and would not have a physician. Later she would look in at the stable-quarters to visit Sam. That boy, she knew, might be again with him despite her orders, but no doubt he ran Sam's errands, and she'd turned a blind eye. She hadn't the heart to forbid Morven and Livia's son the premises when Sam, her childhood's friend and ally, relied on the black-haired urchin almost solely. And Sam himself was not the only servant to disobey her.

Her mouth tightened a little as she bent at last over the roses. The housekeeper, only this week, had said she was leaving; they didn't, she assured Annabel, accord her proper respect any longer in the servants' hall. "I don't know who the half of them are nowadays, madam, or where they came from or what they think they're here for, and that's the truth," the woman had said respectfully. Her words aroused an inner, long recognised dread in Annabel; could it be that all the servants who came to Malvie now had been sent, chosen deliberately by Morven who drove others out? Sometimes she thought it might be so . . . but such imaginings were idle, impossible. Even Morven wouldn't plan so meticulous and fiendish a siege against a lone woman, and yet . . .

And she herself was helpless, almost as helpless as poor Kitty. She hadn't tried to persuade the housekeeper to stay. All Godfrey's English servants had come here for his sake, and were anxious now to get back to the south where they belonged. She herself must interview new women for the situation, no doubt, and her heart failed her; would it not be better to withdraw to live in the tower, and close the main part of the house, and contrive with a maid or two for herself and Kitty? No one now came to Malvie, and all the faces of the servants were closed and strange, for she had lately had to employ whom she could find, and at times it seemed that the place was becoming filled with strangers, faintly hostile, not making haste to carry out her orders, sometimes failing to obey these at all. Her dream of keeping Malvie as it had been in Godfrey's day was fading; but here were the roses and she would make a task of them for herself.

She snipped fading heads, placing these in a flat basket to dry out later with lavender and salt, for laying between the linen. The dying scents rose to her nostrils enhanced by the hint of frost and damp there had been; presently the sun came out, and she moved among the blossoms, busied among them, almost happy, immersed meantime in what she did; sometimes she would bend and sniff the varied scents. The shadows grew longer.

There was a place nearby the hedge where a climbing Dutch rose grew. Annabel spent some time in ordering the trusses, snipping here and there with her gloved hands where the petals, of an apricot colour with hearts of yellow gold, showed signs of fading and curling back; this flower was scentless. There were so many varieties Godfrey had imported from as far away as Persia, descended from the flowers among which kings' favourites had walked, and by contrast there were simpler native roses and the bizarre, almost foreign striped red-and-white of Lancaster-and-York. One could take pleasure in the very names and memories; one could bury oneself here, perhaps in a smaller garden. She would conserve, possibly allow certain parts to revert to wildness, and here, where roses grew, bring herself daily to find peace.

A shadow moved then. In the instant that it took her to know alarm she had no time even to cry out; a sack was flung over her head, she felt herself lifted bodily after a brief, useless, terrified struggle. Then darkness came, and a certainty that she could no longer breathe; her hands flailed helplessly, and were pinioned. She was aware that her senses were leaving her, that she was powerless to stop their departure, to do anything to resist; she remembered nothing more except being still unable to breathe and falling, falling accordingly through red darkness, like the shaft she had lately failed to see, except in her own mind, below the tower of Malvie where it led out at last to the caves and the limitless sea. By the time the pressure of the hands against her mouth and nose slackened, easing the sack's muffling weight, she felt nothing; not the forced pouring, to make her too drunk either to resist or call out, of brandy down her throat, later reviving and then again submerging her. It all took a very few minutes; men endured amputations on less than Annabel was forced to drink in that time. She became pliant, silenced; they might do with her now as they would.

Samson the mulatto, who had waited two hours behind the rose-garden hedge, grunted with satisfaction. The woman wouldn't give further trouble till he'd got her to the boat, and not for a long time thereafter. They could be well out to sea before she came round, and then it was his master's concern what befell.

Cautiously, he wrapped Annabel's now lolling head in the sack again, more loosely than before; and moving with a care proportionate to his burden's light but valuable weight made his way down the slope towards the shore and the small-boat, already moored unobtrusively below. It was a better method than that of the shaft, which they had at one time, before William said Sam Aitken had made him place boulders on it, intended to use to convey Mrs. Annabel by force at night from her bed. But even with the steps and iron stanchions, carrying a woman down that way would not have been easy. Doon, however, thought everything was possible. Perhaps he had reason. Samson glanced once, over his shoulder and the weight still lying on it, back at the house of Malvie, disappearing now as he descended the slope. "It will not be long before it is yours, my master," he thought. "Will you be content then?" For Morven's happiness was of great moment to Samson; had Doon not once saved his life?

231

II

Annabel awoke to an awareness of three things; she was in a bed; under the roughness of a single blanket she was naked; and when she opened her eyes, which she did with reluctance, the world rocked and heaved. It was not only that they were at sea, and that this was the cabin of Morven's boat; so much she knew, and also that she was tipsy. They—Annabel blushed as she realised the significance of the word; it would have been the coloured servant who did Morven's bidding like a familiar of the devil—they had undressed her. Where were her clothes?

She looked about, aware of rising misery, anger and shame. They had taken her clothes, even her shift, away. Without them, how could she escape? She knew, as if she could read his mind, that Morven had long since planned every detail of her capture; that he would come, and that she had not—had never had—protection from him. He had always intended to have her. Why had she thought, even briefly, that it could be worth while to resist? No one could resist Morven.

He came soon. She lay and looked at him in sick silence, not moving or protesting as the cabin door opened, revealing him as he stooped briefly below the lintel. He closed the door but did not trouble to bolt it. What need has he? she thought bitterly. It's his boat. Everyone on it does his bidding. The cabin, she knew, reeked of brandy: her senses still swam, and her head ached badly.

He showed no embarrassment, staring down as though he could see her. "You are awake," he said, though she had not spoken. "Does your head hurt?"

"I wonder that you trouble to ask," she replied unsteadily. She was assailed, at sight of him, by a creeping cold fear, a deadly lack of feeling. It was as though she were already a corpse, and whether or not he now ravished her had no meaning as it would once have done had she been still alive. Like the dead must, she felt her flesh shrink back against the bones; she could neither shudder, withdraw nor protest. This was the final outrage, that Morven could have his way, and she feel nothing; she, the widow of Godfrey whom he had lately killed, could feel nothing. Morven . . . The faint, half-forgotten memory of the magical young lover and seducer of that early time at Mains, till now invested with some of the warmth and colour of youth, left her. This was a stranger, to whom she must yield because he permitted her no choice.

He made no haste to take her; she could feel the coldness in him also. He leaned for some time against the wall by the bed. "You know," he told her, staring past the sloping wooden walls which he could not see, and out to the unseen water sliding past, meantime empty of ships, "you know that I must compromise you to obtain Malvie. There seemed no other way. I had to force it, Annabel."

"You do not flatter me, at any rate," she said grimly. She closed her eyes, and heard him talk on, to himself rather than to her. "Leave you there, queening it; while I took my place on the list as a possible suitor among others? I, an ex-convict? The time I called, your servants showed me the door by your order; had I persisted, the county would have had me removed in some way, as obstructive to their unchanging social pattern." The pale, compelling eyes turned on her, forcing her to open her own. "There is no limit to what your gentry may achieve in the way of thoughtless cruelty. Have I not suffered from it all my life?"

"My own father treated you with kindness—and you reward him thus—"

"Ah, do not beg the question," he said, smiling. "Uncle Philip meant me to have you, and to have Malvie, which is mine by right. Now I shall carry out his will—and mine." He laid a hand on her, pulling down the blanket from her naked shoulder and breast. She writhed away.

"I loathe you, Morven," she said clearly. "Nothing is real to you except Malvie, a pile of stones. It is an insult to my husband's memory to name him here, but *he* did more for Malvie than you ever, with your idle dreams and boasting, could do in a hundred years—you brutal, lying, murdering, ravishing criminal—do not touch me, now or ever, I will not, I will not—"

"Ah, but you will," he said, still smiling, and seized her; and subduing in the end her struggles, coldly as he had done all things regarding Annabel till now, he raped her, while the water ran smoothly under the boat's keel. He was aware, through it all, of the constant sound of the water, heard latterly beyond Annabel's defeated sobbing. He could almost

233

picture their location at sea. They must be somewhere within sight of Invale; could the Berrys see the vessel from the shore? He had given orders to Samson to hoist Annabel's mourning-gown, as a sign of what had taken place, from the mast. There would then be no doubt in the minds of the county, not even the most diehard among them, that Morven Doon must marry the publicly compromised widow of Malvie; anything else would be unthinkable.

In his place on deck, Samson the mulatto went about his tasks. His stripping of Annabel recently had aroused no undue lasciviousness in him; she was his master's woman. He glanced briefly up at the masthead, where the purloined black gown already flew; then down again as sounds came faintly, as they had done for some time at first, from the cabin below. The woman had struggled, resisted, wept; but there could have been, Samson knew, in the end only one outcome. By now, the sounds had changed; his master was giving his woman pleasure. That was as it should be. Samson's mind, always detached, harked back to their years together in Port Jackson, when it had never, during all the latter period of the sentence when rules were less strict, been possible to interest Doon in a woman. Prostitutes, of the kind Samson's own mother had been, abounded in variety in Sydney Cove, since the released consignment of some years earlier; most had chosen not to return home. But Doon had been adamant. "Go down for yourself," he had told Samson on such occasions, and it had begun to be said of Doon that he was a frigid man, a man perhaps secretly interested in men and boys; but Samson knew his tastes had never tended that way. Now—the coloured man smiled—his master had redeemed himself fully, first with Livia Judd and now this captive woman. Seated here at this moment, gazing past the Berry acres to Malvie which still, beyond the intervening inlets, reared its towered head, Samson found that the renewed silence had a sated quality, not altered by the faintly commenced lapping of the tide about the great boat's sides. It was almost as if he had lain with the woman himself. Loving Doon as he did, they were no doubt in constant sympathy.

He stretched himself, and watched the evening fall gradually on the sea. No sign of protest had yet come from the shore about the boat, with its hoisted garment; someone must have seen it by now; it meant they were either afraid, or bribed. As for the latter, all arrangements were long ago made at Malvie, with some of their people working there already. Samson had, under previous orders from Doon himself, strictly instructed the men and women who had gradually been chosen to replace all original house-servants about the place. The stables themselves would now be in charge of young William, aided meantime by grooms: the sick old man himself could go out to the almshouses. Samson smiled; the little boy would be happy enough, thinking himself of importance. Doon had stated that the other servants formerly in the house, including Sam, were each one to receive forty days' pay, as was the custom here, and to be out by the day after tomorrow, when Doon would bring home his bride. He was generous enough. Everything else had been thought of. "I don't want any of Devenham's servants about me," Doon had said, and it had been ensured that, of such as were still left, there would remain not one to welcome the bride. Samson was certain that he had carried out his own orders well.

He cast a line into the sea, having baited it with several tied hooks. The fish rose well and he was soon able to light a brazier in the sheltered place on deck, and cook enough for their supper, and the woman's too if she would eat. Presently Doon emerged, buttoning himself, tempted by the smell of baking fish, and ate his fill; he seemed cheerful and certain that, as he had foreseen, they would soon be in Malvie, and he the laird of it. He indicated that the woman in the cabin would not eat yet; tomorrow, perhaps. He brought wine, and together they drank to Malvie. Later, when Doon had drunk a good deal, he went back to the woman again; he would sleep with her, he said. Samson cleared away the remains of their meal and while doing so listened without lasting interest as regarded what passed again in the cabin; there were fewer of the sounds on this occasion, and no doubt the woman had decided not to resist longer. Women always acted so; they were predictable, manageable once their desires had been satisfied. Samson yawned, and having made all ready for the morning, settled down to his night's watch, with a single lanthorn burning.

Annabel irritated Morven by delaying his plans, a state of affairs he could seldom forgive. With her continued obstinacy, moreover, as the days went by, the possibility of a rescue grew. Morven had never discounted this, but had assumed that long before now Annabel, the pliable, the adoring of old days, would yield to his wishes, and marry him that he might own Malvie and so redeem her reputation. But wax in his hands as she might still be, or had lately become, she would afterwards turn stubborn. He had never encountered so stubborn a woman. He used her, as Samson had heard him do and as he himself had foreseen and deliberately intended; he even beat her once, overcome with impatience lest her prolonged resistance prove the undoing of all of them, and a rope's end for himself instead of Malvie. But still Annabel refused the marriage.

Could it be, Morven wondered, that she hoped certainly for aid? Was it possible that she expected the sparse, effete neighbours—old Cazalet, for instance, having hummed and hawed as he did a generation since the Hanoverian vanguard at Prestonpans, driving over at length to consult the Berrys, and together with them, maybe, and a spyglass, examining the appalling, revealing spectacle of Annabel's purloined mourning-gown flying from his, Morven's, masthead, tutting at what must without doubt be taking place on the boat at that moment, and sending at last for law-officers? Even so, Annabel's reputation would be ruined. But ruined or not, and silenced again and again as Morven forced her under him and repeatedly ravished her, she would never yet, in her inward spirit, yield. He had not expected so much strength of mind in her.

Bodily she was conquered. Morven knew well enough that he had again, of intent while plying her, released the well-spring of physical delight which lay always in her, and gushed readily at the last, unbidden. She could not control it; and the damage it caused her gentility amused Morven. It diverted him to force her, knowing the trembling, initially resistant limbs were no longer truly unwilling (in fact, he thought, they never had been; even in Devenham's day he could have lain with Annabel to her pleasure, had he then taken the opportunity) but that she felt, due no doubt to her position in the county and as Godfrey's widow, that she must make a pretence of reluctance. Such prudishness—he called it by other names—was in itself a reason for sustained punishment, Morven thought. He heard her transports, at the same time reminding himself how she must look now, after four days at sea; without paint or other aids, with washing-water, food and slop-buckets carried in and out by Samson, at sight of whom, no doubt, she'd pull the coverlet up over her naked body like a rudely disturbed nun. Morven had kept her naked, not for his pleasure—he reminded himself, each time he lay with her, that there was no personal aspect whatever in his relations with Annabel, though as a source of animal satisfaction she was adequate enough, like any woman —but because so genteel a creature as Mrs. Devenham— Morven grinned—would never, never struggle out of a boat into the water in such a state, and perhaps be seen. And Annabel couldn't swim, aunt Retford not having considered such an accomplishment necessary in the list of educational attainments prescribed for eligible young females. If Annabel tried to escape, she'd sink like a plummet: but help arriving from an outside source by sea was another matter.

He took leisure to think, once again lying in possession of her body. As often when he had otherwise relieved himself physically, a notion came; he smiled at the analogy.

"There may be a cutter approaching," he told Annabel. Samson had in fact lately sighted one, cruising well out beyond Man. Whether it was looking for them or not he could not say. Morven felt Annabel's breasts tauten as he spoke: it was as if her whole body surged hopefully with the news.

"So you think your friends are aboard, eh?" he said, adding, "It will make small difference to you, my dear; here you stay with me, until—"

He quelled her. While her trembling increased, and small cries at last came from her, he rode her with purpose, remaining hard within her till victory was assured: he could break her, he knew, in time. He handled her breasts and limbs, savagely at the end again, to show her—it was time she learned, he thought—who was her master. He made it clear to her once more that help would not avail her.

"One single cry for aid, if they could come near," he said, "one ladylike flutter from the porthole, any such thing, and I'll have Samson rape you till you can't walk. It can happen while they board us." He laughed aloud at her horrified recoil, her loud revolted cry of sheer animal terror. Morven followed up his advantage. "You know, eh, what happened that time to Clairette? Do you doubt it can happen again, and to yourself? Then grant me my inheritance of Malvie."

Her changed state from then on—he had made her almost imbecile with fear—in itself reassured Morven as to the uselessness of any attempt at rescue. It was unlikely in any case that the vessel had been more than a revenue-cutter; shortly, it passed beyond view and they themselves made in again towards the shore. Afterwards, when night had fallen, Morven betook himself to Annabel. She fought, sobbing and crying like a child, afraid in the darkness it was Samson, come for her. Morven comforted her, aware that he himself was perhaps now regarded as her only saviour from the mulatto; the possible situation amused him. He used such means as he would in other ways have done on a half-trained, almost broken, valuable animal. Provided she would do his will, he assured her repeatedly, he would not let the mulatto touch her.

"Promise, promise." She was stupid with fear, she seemed to hear nothing he said, or if she heard would not believe. Thereafter, at nights when he slept with her, she would waken him often in screaming nightmare, clinging wildly to him once he had convinced her he was himself, Morven Doon. The transformation of his presence into necessity even touched him now he felt that the original plan he had made would proceed; in a few days, no more, he would certainly own Malvie as her husband. He contained his impatience, cozening and almost nursing Annabel. But he still lay frequently with her. The condition of mind in which he desired her to stay, for the time, till his wishes were fully accomplished, was one which he knew could only be obtained in her by repeated coupling, constant pleasuring; a turgid state, in which neither she nor any woman could think or reason clearly. In such a condition, finally exhausted in body and mind, Annabel gave way.

"I will marry you, as you wish it," she said one day. Her face was swollen with tears.

He kissed her, and made her rise and dress at once, though her only gown was sodden. He then took her ashore, still with Samson by them to ensure Annabel's continued obedience, if she should try to elude his purpose. There, in a place where they were not known, in a riverside manse, he and Annabel were married. Morven paid the minister well, he himself recalled afterwards. The less gossip arising later about all this the better: the bride seemed dazed, and could hardly even make the replies that indicated they were man and wife.

Afterwards, he put her in a hired coach and drove her straight to Malvie. He had already left word that the great bed in the main chamber on the first floor, where Doons were born and begotten, was to be kept ready, and a fire lit nightly in the hearth, against their return.

"I am married to Morven. We are back again at Malvie. He is giving me wine."

The separate, allied facts spelt themselves out in Annabel's tired mind as if she had been a child still, and was being taught her lessons. Hadn't there been, long, long ago, another time when Morven told her she was married to him? A hand-fasting; then afterwards memory failed; she was recalled now, by a wavering brightness in front of her eyes, to the present. It was the blaze of applewood logs in the fireplace in the great hall. Someone had put on a great many; but she was glad of the fire, she was cold, cold . . . Beyond the blaze, there were the waiting shapes of servants; motionless, grouped self-consciously, fidgeting a little as her eyes at last focused on them. They'd formed a line of honour, doubtless, on hearing the arrival of the carriage, in traditional fashion to welcome the new-wedded master home. The master . . . Morven was now the laird of Malvie.

"That will please him," she thought. For a reason she could not presently remember, it had become imperative always to please Morven. In every least thing he must be obeyed and pleased, or, or . . .

She had forgotten again: her mind, she knew, had made itself forget. She was still tired and afraid.

She watched the fire glow redly through the wine-glass Morven handed her. He had poured out the ruby liquid himself unerringly, without spilling it, and had then replaced the flagon on the table. How precise his fingers were! Morven's fingers . . . she could remember now . . . she felt her limbs sink with shame, as though they were still together on the boat. He'd left the boat beached. Why did her mind dwell only on such things? Why was it that the servants looked strange, almost furtive, and that she recognised few of their faces, and that none would look at her? Even the new gardener, with whom she'd after all talked at times, looked at the floor tonight, as though he'd never known her.

The familiar housekeeper had gone. Where was her own good maid? "I'm tired," she thought. "I want to go to my room."

She must have said it aloud, because she heard Morven laugh. "You shall do so, but first we must drink a toast to Malvie," he told her. She couldn't swallow the wine; she tried, but could drink nothing. It made Morven angry, when she said that; he tilted her head back, and poured some of the wine from his own glass down her throat.

"Drink to the lady of Malvie," she heard him say, to all the servants. "To Malvie's mistress! A toast, a toast!"

During all of it—she didn't know where they had found their drink, or had dispersed, and were meantime obeying Morven, and lifting their glasses in their hands, and shouting and applauding—during it, he seized and kissed her; hard

239

thorough kisses, such as the common folk used. She didn't like having to endure such things in public, in front of his servants—*his* servants, that he'd gradually chosen, she knew it now, had known, perhaps, in her own mind, impossible as it seemed, for some time. She sensed their grinning; she felt on her own mouth the flavour of the wine Morven had drunk, and shivered wretchedly. "I want to go to my room," she said again. "I want my maid." She might, she thought, be going to be ill. Her head ached already. "Please, Morven—"

He looked down at her; she could have sworn that the pale triumphant eyes could see. His own cheeks were flushed slightly. "Eh, my love?" She might, she thought with distaste, have been a stranger he had somehow brought home. Perhaps she should speak more loudly; he had drunk a great deal of wine.

Morven, I beseech you . . . I am so very tired I must go to bed, and I want my woman so that she can undress me." She spoke quietly, nevertheless aware that each word she said seemed to make manifold echoes through the hall, where the drinking progressed. A young woman in cap and apron came forward.

"This," said Morven, "is—what is your name, girl?"

The girl bobbed. It was Samson's voice that answered. "Christian, sir. Polly Christian." The new steward of Malvie himself cast an appreciative glance over the maid's trim figure and light, sandy hair and eyelashes. Like many coloured men Samson preferred a pallid woman. He would test Polly later. "Live up to your name, then, my good girl, and get your mistress to bed as quickly as may be," he heard Morven say. Everyone smiled at the new laird's jest. Annabel alone did not. She said nothing more, and ascended the stairs, followed by Polly Christian, carrying a candle. When she was shown into the great bedchamber Annabel felt weariness cover her like a pall. If Morven would only leave her alone tonight!

She felt herself being undressed somewhat roughly by Polly. Annabel disliked the girl and the faint, acrid odour which came from her; she disliked even more the familiar way her own limbs and clothes were being handled. "Here's your shift," said Polly carelessly at last, and pulled it over Annabel's shivering body; try as she might, she couldn't control her shivering; the room was cold. "Got bruises, haven't you?" said Polly, eyes knowing between her light, sparse eyelashes. Annabel dismissed her coldly, and the girl shrugged and went out of the room.

Such a maid was intolerable, Annabel decided; whether or

not a replacement could be found, the girl must leave Malvie as soon as possible. When she saw Morven again . . . perhaps he wouldn't come in tonight . . . she prayed he wouldn't, she was so tired . . . she would speak about the maid in the morning.

But he came. Nor did he spare her. Afterwards she found that she had forgotten Polly altogether. Despite exhaustion she was dimly able to understand what this wedding-night meant to Morven; that to himself, he was no devil who ravished her despite all weariness. He was the laird of Malvie, come into his own by whatever means; the descendant by blood of crusaders and near-kings, taking his bride in the ancestral bed above which the great escutcheon wavered, growing faintly gilt at last with dawn. She herself might have been a high-born, stubborn virgin, a stranger brought with her dowry to Malvie to enhance its land, to make its heirs. Annabel shivered then, and Morven did not ask why. Unaware of her as a person, sated with her body and his own dreams, Doon of Malvie slept at last, content with his inheritance.

The following day Morven went by himself about his house, feeling for everything. There were, he said afterwards, many changes which must be removed; Malvie must be made, again, as much as possible as it had been in his father's time; he would direct all of it. Annabel closed her eyes against the dust and neglect which had become evident, with even a few days away, and the new, careless servants. No doubt they thought that having a blind master meant less trouble to be taken than must be done for someone with eyes. She was still too much afraid to speak to the man Samson directly about anything; though he now called himself the steward. Later she found an opportunity to tell Morven himself about the girl Polly Christian, and that she herself was not pleased with her as a maid. He promised that the woman should go, and that another should be found if possible: but weeks later Polly was still in the house, although no longer about Annabel. By then the latter could say very little; all power had been taken from her regarding the dismissal of servants, and young William Judd himself lived now above the stables, smoking and spitting like a man. Her own days were filled with increasing leisure to notice such things; Morven went off alone, mostly in the afternoons, and had forbidden her to follow him. She recalled that a blind man would be sensitive to any feeling that he was being watched or supervised, and tried to obey her husband. For this reason she was the last person at Malvie, or immediately beyond, to know that Morven still visited Livia Judd daily, and had recommenced visits on the afternoon following his wedding.

He had not lain again with Livia. Had Annabel known what passed between them, even she might have felt small hurt; it was little more than what might take place between a child and its mother, as though he had run to Livia in his own way; he laid his head on her breast. Later he opened her bodice and felt the warm velvety globes, burying his mouth and hands in their softness, savouring her. That was all the love he made; he stayed against Livia, while she held him, a long time in silence. Then he spoke, in a whisper as though someone else might hear.

"I've needed you . . . needed you . . . ah, if you knew!" He raised his head; the face was haggard. "You've heard of the marriage?"

"Ay." She continued her rhythmical stroking of his hair; at such times she was laconic, often thought mistakenly to be sullen. But Morven knew her, and that for the moment he was her own bairn. "Lie still," she said, "lie still a while."

But it was as though he must talk, and stride up and down the room, at the same time, as if the energy infused into him had returned; as if, she liked to think, her own brief holding of him, the nearness of her flesh, had already revived him in spirit. He seemed younger, filled again with the devil's power Annabel had lately known; he related the cause of it, his voice trembling, his cheeks unusually flushed.

"You know I'm master of Malvie? My life's wish, and I—"

"You'll be happy, then." She spoke so drily that she sounded like an old woman; it was difficult to convey the joy she had felt at seeing him come to her again, so soon, although—

"Happy? What's happiness? I feel that only when I'm with you. You know it, and that I've had to jettison happiness for more than a part of both our lives, so that I could win my —my inheritance." He stammered, still with the unwanted tremor in his voice; he was like a man who has seen visions. "All my life I've been the outcast, the penniless scorned fool, the convicted criminal. Now I'm Doon of Malvie, and I have you. A spin of fortune's wheel, eh? But *I* intended it; *I* worked towards it from the beginning." He struck his hands together, eyes shining. It was impossible to remember that he was blind; a stranger, she thought, would have guessed nothing.

"You have one other thing," she said, looking down at her hands. What was it that she really wanted to say to him? she wondered. Morven laughed; he thought she meant money. "Malvie, riches—almost all I covet; and yourself, waiting for me here—"

"And your wife, waiting for you at Malvie."

"Annabel?" He frowned; it was a subject that should not have arisen between them. "She occupies herself," he said coldly.

III

Sir Hubert Melrose called at Malvie two days later. It was made clear from the beginning that he had ridden over from a sense of duty only, and because he had been Annabel's guardian and wished to find out if in truth the marriage had been forced. His aspect was more disapproving than Annabel had ever seen it; her heart failed in her as she came downstairs to receive him, having been informed he was already in the great hall.

Morven had gone out. Already it struck her as strange that she should regret the lack of his support in the matter, although all she would have had to do was pour into her uncle's ears the tale of how she had been forcibly abducted, and he might have taken steps to have the marriage annulled. But how could she ever live through the shame? She was in either case ruined, lost; no one having heard, or—Annabel blushed —seen her poor black gown flying from the masthead for days on end but would know that, forced or not, Morven had certainly had her body. And last night again—how could she relate all of it to anyone, or deny the increasing knowledge in herself, which was made clear to her nightly, that her body, however shamefully, now more than ever craved Morven? If they were to take him away, imprison him again, so that she was left quite alone—ah, he'd been cruel, wicked, but now, particularly as he had Malvie by right if she was still his wife, he would become more loving, perhaps, as he'd almost been last night, except that he always fulfilled himself upon her at the last so coldly, while she—

A remembrance of herself, still sobbing with unslaked desire as he withdrew from her, merged into the present image of Sir Hubert, looking as he must often do on the bench; flushed and trembling, Annabel greeted him and offered him wine, which he refused stiffly. He'd judged her already, no doubt; he thought she'd run off with Morven, perhaps, although the matter of the gown surely argued that she could not have foreseen or approved all that would happen.

"Will you not be seated, uncle?" she said timidly. If only Morven were with them! Annabel turned her head distractedly as if hoping to hear sounds of his return, anything rather than meet Sir Hubert's eyes, which never left her. He had not accepted her invitation to seat himself, and throughout the interview stood looking sternly down on her; there was nothing for Annabel to do but stand before him, she felt like a little girl again, ready to be scolded.

Sir Hubert wasted no time, but asked her roundly if the marriage to Morven had been forced or not, and if she were content with it. Tears sprang to Annabel's eyes as he spoke; it would have been pleasant, a reminder of former days, if he had at least shown he wished her well. She recalled, when poor Peter took a calf-love for her, Uncle Hubert had put an end to her visits to them at Maddon, and the suggestion that she live there instead of with aunt Retford. No doubt, by this, he was more than ever thankful that so wanton a young woman had not been drawn into the closer circle of his family.

She lowered her lashes, so that he should not see the tears on them. What she said to him she could not afterwards in detail remember; she kept control of herself, however, and assured Sir Hubert that the marriage had been of her free will. "It wasn't at Gretna, uncle," she said, and in her nervous uncertainty laughed, a trifle shrilly, so that no doubt he put her down as a heartless woman as well as a light one. It was scarcely two months since they had buried Godfrey, his expression was saying. The memory of Godfrey struck at her again, almost with terror. How could she so soon have forgotten! But Sir Hubert was giving vein to his contempt, and she must listen.

"A trifle of patience would have procured you a more

seemly bridal, both on this occasion and the first." She recalled, as if it had happened to someone else, the hurried marriage to Godfrey, and now this; what must everyone think of her? And that was not the worst part; a returned convict, Uncle Hubert's expression said, was hardly a person whom one knew. Annabel had made her bed; she must lie on it. A fit of hysterical laughter almost took her if he knew what it meant, to lie in bed with Morven!

She suddenly flung her head up, proudly.

"He is my husband," she said, "and I love him."

A shadow crossed the threshold; had Morven himself heard what she said? She bit her lip; to have been discovered in course of a declaration of love for him didn't suit, at present, their relationship. She felt an uprush of misery, not helped by the fact that Sir Hubert, after the coldest of nods to Morven, stated the other reason why he had come. If Annabel could not be prevailed upon to leave her husband, Cecily was desirous, as he was himself, that Sybilla should be sent to them to Maddon, to be brought up.

Annabel's cheeks burned. So he thought of her as an unsuitable mother! Before she could reply, she saw Morven ease himself forward a little; when his voice came it was like silk.

"I, more than anyone, am in the best position to be a parent to Sybilla, sir."

Annabel covered her face with her hands. Would he say it? If he did, she thought she would die of shame—she would never forgive Morven—Sybilla's future, ruined, her fortune . . .

Annabel solved the problem herself; she burst into tears. Considerations of etiquette thereafter set everything else aside. Sir Hubert had to make a show of consoling her, as did Morven; between them they contrived to maintain appearances. Morven was smiling in the way he had. Annabel dabbed at her eyes, and heard him say, good-naturedly on the surface of it,

"If you will not take wine I'll not detain you; you seem a cursed unwilling guest."

He turned away, after casting at Sir Hubert's empurpled countenance a final *congé*. "I've come a fair way without your guinea, uncle," he said, slewing round on his heel so that the pale face showed itself, turned back over his shoulder. "Do you recall how I threw it back at you on the steps of Mains? You meant it kindly, no doubt."

Sir Hubert did not reply, and went away much mortified.

Later Annabel was able to indicate a certain degree of contrition to him, and they regained enough mutual civility to enable her to send Sybilla, when she could, to Maddon in the school holidays. There were other reasons by then. But now, watching the hurt old man ride off again on his long journey home, her heart smote her; how many such friends must be offended and lost!

"We did not betray one another, after all," said Morven, his face and voice without expression. She was never certain whether or not he would have betrayed Sybilla by boasting that he was her father; the child and her fate did not seem to arouse any interest in him, and Annabel dreaded the school holidays, when her daughter would have to come home and witness the changes that had been . . . Could Uncle Hubert perhaps, in some way, be later placated, so that Sybilla could at least sometimes take refuge with them all at Maddon? It was extraordinary, unnatural, not to want to see her own child again yet; was she herself changing so greatly, day by day? There had been a time when she would never willingly have parted from Sybilla. "But it is for her good," the mother told herself desperately, repeatedly. Then she turned from Sybilla's good to her own ills again.

Morven had, Annabel was already certain, overheard her own statement to Sir Hubert defending her husband and her marriage. That he must know, therefore, that she loved him would add one more weapon to Morven's armoury. He used it, telling her once—perhaps it was after the one and only quarrel they had openly about Livia—that she didn't understand the meaning of the words she used; she didn't understand love. Was it because—as she hardly dared remind herself, let alone think of telling Morven—that since Sybilla's terrible birth she was barren? Could that be the reason?

It was about that time that Annabel found out that her husband still visited Livia Judd daily. Everyone else, besides the servants, no doubt, had known about it all from the beginning. Annabel astonished herself by the strength of the resentment and betrayal she felt; afterwards, trying through her own wretchedness to view the matter sanely, she supposed that she should have guessed in any case. There was no reason why, because he had now married herself, Morven should forsake his mistress; many men, especially in fashionable circles, she knew, maintained both a mistress and a wife.

She had found out, in fact, one day when she's overheard

him order the coach outside; it was blowing a gale. "I'll drive
down to the Mains for today's visit," she heard him call, as
she herself was descending the stairs. "The path'll be high
with mud; no need to risk it on such an afternoon."

He hadn't known she heard him, or watched the coach later
drive away, then still later walked back upstairs alone to
their room. Once there, she felt her limbs begin to shake
with uncontrollable anger; going to a mirror she saw her
cheeks already bright as carnations. She stood there, staring
at her own reflection, while the enraged blood gradually
suffused her face and neck, and tears stood in her eyes. She
wasn't, despite all that he'd done to her, so ugly . . . and
never, never again should he have her body. To have to share
Morven a second time with his kitchen-wench!

Annabel's anger stayed. She remembered to down it somewhat while she visited poor Kitty, who had lately had another stroke and was by now imbecile, almost helpless; she
still tried sometimes to sit up and walk. But afterwards rage
rose again in Annabel. Tonight, and every other, she thought,
she'd forbid Morven her bed. Anger gave her strength to do
it. She'd tell him so, when he came in; before he began to
fortify himself with wine. The joy poor old Mama Bowes
had shown today at seeing her made her realise that perhaps,
of late, she'd neglected other responsibilities in her anxiety
to please Morven.

He came back early, and was for once talkative. It was
some time before he noticed his wife's silence. She had been,
when he came in, standing in the drawing-room, near the
long windows, watching the rain which still dripped down
outside, though the storm had long subsided. Inside, the room
had been stripped; the only familiar things left were Philip
and Grace Doon's hung portrait, and the Turkish sofa.

Morven walked in, accordingly, with the assured stride he
could use when at Malvie, having arranged the furniture to
his own convenience as at Mains. Each object in the room
was precisely where he had placed it. His blind eyes gleamed
with catlike power. He was like, she told herself, a thin white
cat; a tom, mating more than one queen. She need trouble
no more with him. She heard him curse the rain, and did not
answer.

"You are there, I know," he said. He always knew when
anyone was in a room. He raised an eyebrow at Annabel's
continued silence, and she rounded on him.

"I did not know you had been going between me and your

tavern-wife all this time, Morven. It surprises me that you can serve both of us; what a man you must be!"

His eyes narrowed but he said nothing. Annabel heard the icy, continued steadiness of her own voice. "There is no necessity to tax your strength doubly, night and day. From tonight—" The words trembled, and she realised that her whole body now was shaking; she must get out of the room, she thought, before she lost control of herself. "From tonight, Doon of Malvie, I'll sleep alone, and lock my door. Go to your whore by nights also if you must."

She had picked up her skirts to run, and the warning rustle of satin gave Morven the time he needed, and the direction. He barred her way, and seized her by the hair with one hand. She stood there, pinioned and helpless. He had pulled her head slightly back.

Morven began to slap her face. He slapped, hard and repeatedly, with his free hand; he had chosen her mouth for preference. A weal shortly rose and spread there, over the flesh. When he had punished her enough in this way he stopped, and told her coldly, "That's to silence your tongue. Next time it'll be your backside, with your skirts up."

She did not reply, only swayed as if she would faint: but her eyes stayed open. Morven began to smile with closed lips; a sign she dreaded.

"I will not chastise you further, my dear. Go and lie down on the sofa."

He gave then, with the hand that had already struck her repeatedly on the mouth, a small, vicious downward tug at her bodice. Annabel's hands flew protectively upwards; he'd almost exposed her nipples. Her face was a morass of raging pain. She tried to readjust the bodice.

She could hardly speak. She heard herself mumble at him, through swollen lips,

"Morven, it's afternoon—and we are in the drawing-room." He threw back his head and laughed, and jerked at her hair.

"All the better; have you not lately informed me you will lock your bedroom door tonight? Come, do as you're bid; I'll soon show you whose strength is taxed."

She resisted still: this was unspeakable. "I beg you—if the servants should see, or anyone come in—"

"They will see—and hear—if so, nothing which concerns any one of them. Do you mean to obey me, my dear wife, or shall I strip you down to your garters? Lie down; do as I say."

And he compelled her. Terrified, shamed, her knees turning

to water after the briefest of struggles, she had to end by doing his will; crimson-cheeked, closing her eyes as he unbuttoned himself and, with an unfaltering movement, lifted at the same time her petticoats and exposed her: it was all of it appalling, sordid. Cry out she dared not; someone might come in. They would snigger about this in the kitchens, the taverns; how dared Morven do this to her, how dared he?

Morven deliberately prolonged the act. He stayed within Annabel long enough to divert himself, knowing every moment increased her affronted, helpless gentility; that presently the response, which when they were in private always made her cry out, would have to be endured by her today behind bruised and bitten lips, in disciplined silence. It came; he felt her mounting distress, and his anger lessened and amusement grew. He'd served her as she well merited, the bitch; how dare she despise and rail at Livia?

Annabel had been accordingly forced into an abject withdrawal of her already declared intention to lock her chamber-door; in any case, Morven told her, he'd have had the servants break it open. To remove her initial reason for anger did not however suit him, and he never told Annabel about the actual continence, these days, of his visits to Livia. He'd found—but in any case how could Annabel, or any wife, understand this or condone it?—that Livia's very presence and touch, arousing his deepest, most intimate desires, made him the readier to lie with Annabel by night if he intentionally had not satisfied them. Otherwise the dreary, crying creature his wife was rapidly becoming would not, Morven told himself have interested him enough to sustain an erection. He discounted the many years Annabel had lived as a wife in name only to Devenham, for Morven could consider no one but himself; he realised that she benefited in some way from the powerful urges the recent handling of Livia had roused in him; but his intention was not to please Annabel, but to get an heir. It was as before, in the days when he climbed the pear tree, he told himself; Annabel was again damnably slow to conceive, and there must, to make his own ambition complete, be a son and heir soon for Malvie.

Sir Hubert's visit was to be one of few from Annabel's former friends and social equals. The news that Godfrey Devenham's widow had married her disgraced and unacceptable cousin Morven Doon, and had returned with him openly to live at Malvie, was manna to the county-gossips, who had been provided with nothing like it since the news of Culloden. So recently widowed as she was! The relict of so fine a man!

Being, no doubt, as Godfrey latterly had, despite his excellencies of character and temper, there could not have been full marriage between them since, no doubt, the birth of poor little Sybilla or shortly after. But they had seemed, in spite of everything, a most devoted couple, nor had there been any breath of scandal concerning infidelity of Annabel's, though many wives, alas, nowadays in the degenerate south, were taking lovers almost in the way Italians did, as soon as the ring was safely on their finger. But this! It was too soon, by far, to think of remarriage; and if such a step should ever have been contemplated it would have been, one expected, to a person of the widow's own class and upbringing, perhaps to an elderly widower or someone of that kind (hadn't Colonel Cazalet proposed, the first time it had ever been known to happen after a lifetime's angling for his hand and fortune by every unattached female of whatever age in the county, and been refused?)

Yes, she was a sly one; there had been no question of unwillingness or force, Sir Hubert had had it from her own mouth. No doubt the pair had been lovers in secret before poor Godfrey's death. And the brazen behaviour on the man's boat for several days before the ceremony, as everyone could have seen from the shore by reason of . . . "An ancient name like the Doons!" said one old dowager. "She has unclassed herself," and then remembered, too late, that Morven was a Doon also. But his father, after all, had been a Jacobite, and that was no longer considered an asset in elevated circles. They lived on it, most of them; others kept their counsel.

IV

The matter of the county's acceptance, or otherwise, of Annabel's remarriage was put to the test in a few days after the return. It was Sunday, and everyone had turned out for church. The great came in their carriages, with the servants sometimes walking, sometimes crowded together on the box; some carried food to eat, to stay over for the afternoon sermon. Silk bonnets and braided hats vied with one another to bow and acknowledge acquaintance; all were dressed in their best, old Mrs. Fawcett, Charity Lagardie's mother, in her famous Paisley shawl of many colours, which had cost a hundred pounds and made her wizened, yellow face look like that of a Chinaman beneath her narrow bonnet; Eliza Berry and her goodman were alike in green. There was a flurrying of silk furbelows and petticoats, a tossing aside of panniers and deep frills to step out of the carriages, assisted down carefully on to the raked surround and, at leisure, going up the path to the door in order to be well seen. Everyone played this game; nobody found it absurd, and the servants were doing the same as their masters in comparing best coats and furbished bonnets. It was almost towards the end, and the final bell had just sounded, when the Malvie carriage drew up by the gate. Inside were Morven Doon, his bride, and the mulatto. Annabel sat bolt upright in a wine-coloured pelisse, and did not turn her head. Her bonnet was one that had been often seen before. The company fell silent, in one of these sudden cessations of all sound which make the grass almost heard to be growing: and the bell in the tower, having pealed its last note, trembled into a silence of its own as blind Morven Doon climbed out unaided, and assisted his bride down from their carriage.

They walked up the path to the gate in silence, Samson following; Annabel's face wore a fixed, waxen smile. The company had by now gone in, and were seated in the pews. Everyone watched as Doon of Malvie walked down the aisle, his new wife on his arm, and turned into the Malvie pew without groping or fumbling, as if, they said afterwards, and as many folk had done, he had eyes to see. Pursing its lips, the congregation turned to its business, and the precentor intoned the note of the first psalm.

When the Malvie party came out again, not a soul greeted them. The company—including many who had enjoyed the hospitality of Annabel's drawing-room, in former days—stood in silence, or with averted heads supposedly talking to one another, as they walked, Morven's wife again on his arm, back to the carriage. The horses were whipped up and the carriage drove off. The buzz of talk after they had gone was like a midden of aroused flies; everyone in the county, who did not wait for the second sermon, was, accordingly, late for dinner.

Morven was not defeated. Each Sunday thereafter, no matter how inclement the weather or how desperate his own affairs, or pressing his business, he would bring his wife and Samson to church, sometimes with servants, oftener alone, the three of them; he himself invariably clad in dark velvet edged with silver braid, and a chapeau-bras, a trifle old-fashioned now; the mulatto echoing him; Annabel herself— the gossips fastened on this with malicious delight—increasingly dowdy, as if she could not even afford a new gown. But she always came. Of her full bravery they were not aware; they thought, no doubt, that she was insensitive, abandoned, shameless, so to show herself, with regularity, in the front pew, so that everyone could see her, her ex-convict, and the coloured servant whose debaucheries were by now a byword in three counties. What they did not know of, and Annabel would never tell them, was the constant sinking of mortification, fear, regret and shame she felt at the hostile pricking of eyes on her slim back, as she stood by Morven's side in the pew pretending to join in the psalms intoned, or listen to the minister's long sermon, to which she could hardly ever in fact bring herself to attend.

Among those few who had little to say about the happenings at Malvie in those days was William Judd, but he was not in the habit of talking very much; as a rule, there was nothing worth the effort it took to string words together. William was not bright; his early urchin sharpness with the sixpence, which had initially interested Morven in him, had not survived puberty, which occurred early and left William mature in body and somewhat slow in mind. He was, accordingly, given orders as a rule like one of the servants, and obeyed them because he lacked the imagination to do anything else, even to toss his thick, rebellious black hair out of his eyes.

He had however certain stubborn affections; one was for Sam Aitken the groom. Sam had been good to him when he lay howling in the straw with a sore, skinned bottom, that time all those years ago; Sam had taken William and fed and trained him, so that now he could do anything with horses if not with folk. But Sam had lately been turned out to the almshouses, and William, from his promotion to the stable-quarters at Malvie where he now slept upstairs in Sam's old sagging bed, would trudge down the road almost every day, when his work was over, and take the sick old man a bite of mutton pie, or some home-brewed ale in a stoppered flagon William had, for the food they issued at the almshouses was poor. He would go on from there sometimes to visit Abel at the Fleece, to see how he did and bring the news to his mother. William said little, for he was not a young man of many words, but he kept his ears open, and knew everyone had been saying for a while how low Abel was fallen at first, drinking more heavily than any of his customers, and letting the Fleece itself sink into neglect, leaving the slatterns of maids to get on in an idle way with their brooms, and not change the bed-linen often enough. It was all since Abel's wife went off with Morven Doon, they said in Grattan; they'd be licking their lips now, swearing Livia would regret her folly; no doubt, now Morven had got himself a lady-wife, he'd turn Livia out on the road, and Abel wouldn't take her back again. But it hadn't happened yet; and meantime William himself noted a change in Abel. He had stopped drinking—he said himself he could see the way he was going, and that he wasn't getting any less miserable for all the ale he drank, nor whisky either. "There was only one thing to do, and that was stop," he said; and like the man he was he had stopped, as quick as that, and hadn't touched a drop since; and now although his hair was white, and he'd lost weight a bit, he was the orderly, reliable soul he had been formerly, and the inn was seemly again, though not what it had been in Livia's day.

William had been returning across the fields to his stable-quarters one night late, having come on foot from the Fleece; he'd had a drink or two of ale; that might account for the thing that happened, or rather what he felt about it; as a rule, nowadays he wasn't given to much feeling, or thinking either; he liked a horse, a drink and, in a year or so, he'd probably like a girl. He'd got a bit unsteady on his feet, and going across the rough grass he'd stopped to look up, and rest a minute, and his glance had roved across to the main Malvie front, which could be seen clearly by day. Now it was nothing but a black rearing bulk in the darkness, with not a light showing, except in one place. That was from the window on the first floor, directly under the wide pediment, where the great bedchamber would be. A man stood there holding a lit sconce, motionless, apparently looking out over the dark field; it was Morven Doon. William said afterwards it gave him a turn, as though he'd seen a ghost up there; what was a blind man doing carrying candles, and holding them to look out as though he could see? "He didn't look like a newly-wed," he said afterwards to Livia.

Livia said nothing.

Morven in fact suffered less than did Annabel at the behaviour of the county folk, perhaps because he was used to ostracism from them. Now that he was master of Malvie he in any case considered himself, if he had not always done so, above them by reason of birth and blood. Aware that Annabel spent much of her time alone in useless, resentful tears over the matter, he mocked at her.

"What are they worth, when all's said?" He spoke with an assurance which sprang from his complete confidence concerning himself. "The Lagardies have foreign blood, not from the Conquest, as a part of our own is from an English bride, you remember, of the Doons before Bruce's time. Charity Lagardie's husband's grandfather was a pimp of King James's, brought out of France. The Berry's? No one heard of them before the Union; they say old Berry aided the vote that sent the Parliament south, and was given a package of land for it by interested parties. They sing for their supper nowadays, it's said; there's nothing in their coffers. The rest? Never a one with blood as ancient as ours, Annabel."

He looked at her with that pale, incredibly piercing gaze from the eyes which had been so long dead to sight; and as always she felt her bones weaken and yield, as if she failed Morven in all ways nowadays, as if soon, at any time, he would speak of it to her. Fear was her companion so constantly now that she had almost forgotten what it was to feel free and unafraid; so she did not answer, merely sitting still in her place; she was like an automaton, which moves only when moved. She had given up her former pursuits, her gardening and riding and embroidery; her days and nights were wholly spent awaiting Morven's pleasure.

She had tried to help him, though it half broke her heart, at first to carry out his wishes regarding Malvie. She was, after all, she thought, his wife now by whatever means: his desires should be hers; she should be glad, no doubt, and in a way was so, that he had accomplished his dream. But the furtherance of it involved more than the initial fingering of every object in the house, familiarising Morven's blindness with Malvie as it had now become; his expressed ambition to restore it as it had been in Richard's and Philip's time had begun to be set about also. Morven could not see the havoc he wrought, the bleak empty spaces where there had been cherished things, a picture, a piece of Persian silver, a subtly tinted wall-panel showing the portrayed history of jewelled Indian princes. Most of these he packed away for sale; they were worth money, he said. Annabel's horror mounted when he sat down and, allowing neither herself nor the servants near him, felt and assessed every separate article for its value, remembering in his own mind without lists what each should fetch; his obsession with money seemed to her both tragic and needless, now that he had her own as well as his. What need was there to let his impoverished childhood, still after all this time, warp him in such a way? But money had become a god to Morven, for it would ensure that never, never need he part with Malvie again. He himself packed the articles, in the end, with the precise skilled movements of the blind. "You forget that the Governor trusted me alone with his silver at Port Jackson," he told her, courteously as if they exchanged idle words at a rout-party. She shuddered, watching the valued things which had belonged to Godfrey and herself wrapped, crated and sent south at last by carrier; there were, Morven assured her, no markets in Edinburgh which would give him full value for such things. She found the sight of the blind laird of Malvie doing his own packing moreover degrading, but the new servants no doubt were not to be trusted; and on the one occasion she herself had for some reason been permitted to help Morven she had found her hands trembling so much that she had dropped and broken a cup from Dresden. Morven had been angry.

"If you're so butter-fingered, leave me alone; that's a set ruined, no doubt, by being made incomplete? What a careless little fool you are! Go to your own concerns, and leave me to mine."

She rose without more words and left him, trying to restrain her tears at the memory of his narrow, furious face. To be blind would no doubt mean that small things came increasingly to matter, but had she been less in subjection she could have replied, with truth, that Godfrey had made Malvie his concern also, and had loved it better in such ways than Morven. Godfrey had made Malvie a place of beauty and peace. Morven—but of what use to say anything of the deterioration already beginning, even if she dared do so? He only mocked at her, and never failed to dishonour Godfrey in every way. That dear dead man she had come so slowly to respect and love must become her strength hereafter in memory as in life; she had no other source of it now; even God seemed mocked in that weekly, deliberate Sabbath parade of ill-wishing and spiteful pride, their own as well as others'; what made Morven so determined that they should always show themselves at church, without respite either for her or himself? What good did it do him to have to prove to everyone, week after week and year after year, that no matter what befell the county would never relax its condemnation of him, would never accept him in fact as Doon of Malvie?

"It is in his own mind he is that, however," she thought, "and nothing else matters to him."

She tied on a chip-hat and, as the day was fine, went out into the garden and made her way to where the lilacs, planted by Godfrey in the year before their marriage, bloomed now in a riot of wine-colour and bridal white; the scent came delicately. A desire overcame her to take some of the blossoms to Godfrey, lay them on his grave where he could perhaps, from where he now was, smell their scent; the very folly of such a notion brought tears to her eyes. Godfrey was perhaps nowhere any more; but it would solace her to do this for him, like Andromache at Hector's pillar. The tears overflowed, as she recalled how Godfrey himself had taught her the little-known end of that sad story; before she married Godfrey, she'd been ignorant of all such things. She broke off a great armful of the flowers and leaves, and made her way to the graveyard. The tomb there was still new and clean, as yet without a memorial inscribed on the stone.

She laid the lilacs carefully down on the turned earth and saw their heads already droop; they would be dead soon, one couldn't keep cut lilacs more than an hour or two, even in water. She sat by the grave for a long time and thought of her dead husband; how happy they'd been, she realised now! He had never disregarded a single wish of hers, never over-ridden her will; he had set himself, at all times, to consider her, as she had, she knew, tried from the beginning, and latterly with love, to consider him. The facts of their marriage were already overlaid, for Annabel, with unreality like a golden veil.

She cried for a long time by the grave, and still red-eyed and desolate went back to the house as it grew dark. Morven, she thought, would not have missed her; he never took tea, and in the absence of any company she herself had given up the pleasant sociable custom. Perhaps when Sybilla was at home again, at some time, she must exert herself to—

Morven was standing in the hall, a glass in his hand and bottle by him. "Where have you been?" he asked her. He used the right he had to question her movements, though now there were seldom occasions when Annabel gave him cause; she answered reticently, and he laughed, as though the uncanny knowledge he applied to most things had informed him accurately, already, as to where she must have been.

"Mooning over the grave again, eh? Why trouble with a man who was half dead before they buried him? Women attach themselves to such customs, no doubt, when they're idle all day."

His eyes narrowed; there came the look in them that Annabel dreaded. "There should be a certain duty for you to fulfill by now," he said. "Why are you not yet pregnant?" His tone was cold, but he smiled. "You can't deny I have given you cause, eh?" He awaited her answer, going over to the flask meantime and pouring himself more wine.

She trembled, hearing her own stumbling, stammered reply; she dreaded telling him the truth, and yet perhaps—"Sybilla," she began. She bit her lip; what had she been about to say? That Sybilla was the only child she would ever be able to bear? That he himself had ruined her for further childbearing when she was little more than a child herself? Fear drained her bones; she felt her knees grow weak, as always, and cast a glance about to ensure that none of the servants were listening; that girl Polly Christian, whom she'd surprised, last week, again with Samson on one of the beds—they mustn't overhear, Morven should not have asked her concerning such things in the hall, their talk should be private.

"You do not answer me."

"Morven—"

"If I find that you've been taking preventive herbs, I'll have you whipped."

The humiliation of it made Annabel burst into outraged sobbing; she fled upstairs, leaving him no doubt with the notion that what he'd suggested was correct, as though no insult could be too cruel to fling at her now that he knew she couldn't do without him, she couldn't do without what he did . . . to her body . . . she remembered the sight and sound of the coupling servants, the negro's thrusting buttocks seen uppermost on the bed, and below him the sounds that came of Polly's groans of pleasure; it must have happened often. She herself was being reduced to an animal, like Polly; she knew it in herself, and the oftener Morven served her the worse it got, and she wanted it increasingly, wanted it and wanted Morven, and if she told him she was barren she was afraid he would leave her, and go to Livia Judd or some other woman.

Morven, left behind in the hall, drained his glass. He was

257

not unduly concerned about Annabel, nor did he genuinely believe she'd been taking ergot or any other abortive drug; she had neither the courage, he thought, nor any means of obtaining it. For the present, as his own chief anxiety was to get her pregnant, which meant keeping her content in some ways, he had yielded a point, and had given his permission for the girl Sybilla to go, meantime, for her holidays to Maddon rather than returning to pass them here at Malvie. Morven had no interest in Sybilla; his interest was in her successor, but in the meantime it would, among other things, prevent Annabel from going out on companionable pony-gallops with her daughter. Such things were said to be unsettling to breeding women. And if Annabel wasn't breeding yet, why the devil wasn't she. If, after last night and this, her lunar periods followed yet again, he'd better take her to a physician.

He fingered his empty glass, and at last set it down on the long oak table once brought home by Richard Doon. There was a film of dust on it, which the blind man's sensitive touch duly noted; he frowned. The slight, fine overlay would no doubt thicken with time for as long at Samson was too greatly taken up with Polly Christian to remember his supervisory duties as steward of Morven's household. But Samson, as Morven knew well, was essential to him; he'd let the affair run its course, for as long as it lasted. He smiled; Samson must be allowed to use that famous instrument of his. Someone had told Morven there was an increase already in the number of dark-skinned babies born in the area, and perhaps Samson's facility in such matters would somehow, with the affinity there was between them, improve his own.

Morven went in with such thoughts to his dinner, pleased enough. Annabel did not come down and he dined in solitude.

Later, as he had intended, he went up as usual to her. That night he used her hard, determined to open, by brute force if need be, the withdrawn, difficult womb. It seemed in the end, with the familiar short sharp animal cries she at last emitted, that he had possessed Annabel finally, utterly; that she could not fail, after so determined a further mating, to be proved with child.

Annabel lay quite still. She had heard herself, again lately, making the harsh inhuman sounds. The way she was made to behave at such times had ceased to astonish her, but still filled her with distress, confusion and shame after it was done; she knew it made her seem like Polly. Since the wedding-night she had envisaged Morven's own demanding body as a demon's. There was nothing it couldn't make her own body do; except one thing. Pain, beatings, punishment, possession; they were all of them a part of her revived need for Morven, which she no longer denied, could no longer perhaps do without. Morven had however told her often now, himself, it wasn't, had never been love.

Annabel began to cry again, thinking of how Morven would stop coming to her at all once he knew she was barren. She would dry up and wither, she thought, if he didn't come; she didn't think she could bear to tell him quite yet. Perhaps in a little while, if she could summon the courage, and had a door ready through which to escape . . .

She lay silent, sleepless as often, with the tears running down her face and soaking the pillow. Morven noticed nothing of any of it. He was already asleep.

V

There were other visitors at Malvie now, when the carriages of the genteel no longer drew up at the door. Most came by night, sidling up in ones and twos from the shore, where they would have run in their small boats between the rocks, or fastened them to iron rings sunk in the wall of the cave below tide-level. Morven had had the underground passage widened and excavated, though the manner of its entry was still concealed; one end, as before, was in the cave itself, and the other below the Flodden tower, where the men could ascend now easily enough by gripping the stanchions, and go out again by the tower-door, leaving their bales. In this way Morven transacted much profitable business, unseen either by the revenue-collectors or the excisemen; the latter may have had their suspicions, but dared do nothing; their numbers were too small. For the men who came up from the sea, or the packmen who would vanish at once with their goods across land, Morven would himself be waiting, seeing, as though he had eyes, that they were made welcome, warm, and fed. Some, like Pieter Van Hooghen the Dutchman, he entertained privately to dinner; the pair would sit far into the night to discuss events in Europe, and particularly France, where shortly a general who had sprung from nowhere would make his impact felt on freebooters and all others, for all time. Dutch Pete was a bearded giant of a man, descended, as he made out, from a Utrecht family as ancient as Morven's, but he was an engaging liar and his robust sense of the ridiculous would have led him on to mock the white devil, as well as the black, though no one else dared to do so. Dutch Pete was high in the hierarchy, but even those less well-known, or lower-born, might find lodging at Malvie, good food and drink in the kitchens and for their ponies, if they were packmen, devoted care from William Judd. William soon became a familiar, ageless figure, like a dark primitive cave-man, seen mostly by night, caring constantly for the horses; the yellow light of the stable-lanthorn would shine down on his rumpled thatch of black hair, and his face, with the vacant dark eyes intent on the beasts, nothing else, as William fed, looked after, befriended and watered them. If a pony had a stone under its shoe, which made it limp, or a sore beneath the saddle which festered, it was William who saw to it, and fomented the troubled part or put on unguents, so that the beast could travel comfortably by the night following; if it could not, it did not leave Malvie until it could, and a substitute was meantime found for the packman. No one in the length and breadth of the land had so well-schooled a team of workers as Doon of Malvie; no one, in its smooth-running exercise between the west coast and Leith, grew richer, but he paid his men fairly.

They respected him, but to say they loved Morven or were familiar with him, or with the man Samson either, was untrue. They regarded the pair, and this may have been the reason for such long and faithful service to Morven as many of them put in, for after all there were certain benefits in being free—as two different aspects of the devil. Some, and Dutch Pete amused Morven by telling of this, made the sign against the evil eye when they came up to the house. Pete himself had no religion and such things did not trouble him. "Whatever you are, you and I grow rich together," he said in his guttural growl, and slapped his thigh, giving a yowl of laughter. "How did you begin to be rich, Mynheer? They say many things of you, but I believe only what I hear from your own mouth."

"I began in Australia."

Suddenly Morven smiled, not in his usual narrow fashion

260

but gaily, as if he were a boy again. He told Pete the whole of the story, or nearly so; how, when he himself was convicted and transported abroad, the news of Aaron's legacy had come in time to let Morven purchase a tract of land, nearby the river, cheaply. Many convicts did this, cleared it of yams and farmed it. "It's good, fertile land," Morven said. "Some stay on, when their sentence is finished; others sell out at a profit. I sold, in the end."

He told Pete about finding Samson in the corn-bin, and the way in which, as his foreman able to control and speak with the unpredictable natives of the region, he had been worth a great deal to Morven. "He made them work. He could speak their tongue, and he knew that as long as they were kept from starving—that's what they are afraid of, since the whites came—they'd work hard on a low wage. It was better than others paid, though." Morven drew at his pipe. "In four years, a strip of wilderness was a productive arable farm. By then, it was time for us both to come home."

"So you sold."

"Land, implements, goodwill, everything. No doubt it still goes well. Soon land will cost more, out there. I went out at the right time, no doubt, though I hardly chose my fate."

"You will do all things at the right time, no doubt. But with this government of yours in London, why London? It is a long way off. They cannot, it is evident, know what happens here."

But Morven did not continue in discussion of the Union and its doubtful benefits. Instead he allowed his mind to open, as he seldom did with anyone but Livia, Pete and sometimes, more rarely, Samson into talk. He had said nothing—there was no need, the Dutchman would assume it—of all the money formerly left behind under stones, on the moor, among thatch, in double-floored cellars at the cottage, which Aaron had also left to him, and elsewhere. All of that, and the Australian purchase-money, were safely now in an Edinburgh bank, earning interest, and the profits from Leith came in also, so that shortly he was thinking of purchasing more ships to fetch the goods direct from sources in Holland and France, instead of employing middlemen like Van Hooghen himself. He wouldn't say all of that yet . . . best break it gently. Pete and he would remain good friends, no doubt, in any case. He felt, in his own private darkness, a ray of warmth from the big Dutchman, as from Livia also, and Malvie . . . his house for which he must beget a son.

How he returned to that theme again and again! It was

as if he could never be free of the necessity, even here, in a room free of women's presence, filled with men's talk, and the scent of pipe-smoke and taste of fine Hollands, French brandy, Indies rum. Pete liked rum. But a son . . . a son to inherit . . . without that, all would have been for nothing, and when he himself died Malvie would fall into hands, with no Doon left to own it; whoever young Sybilla might marry, he wouldn't bear the name of Doon.

Pieter van Hooghen wondered why his host, lately so expansive and genial, looked suddenly like the devil again, pale, narrow and angry, with his long powerful fingers clenching on the table's edge as though he would dint the very oak. What a strange fellow he was! A man never knew where he stood with him, except for business.

Livia for a long time now had been less of a mistress to Morven than his plaything.

Their afternoons together were almost always the same. It was seldom that Morven did not visit her. He had his days and nights divided, she knew, into the three separate parts which made up his life; Malvie, which included Annabel, and was an aspect still closed to Livia, by her own unspoken wish as well as Morven's; the men who came by night and whom he governed and controlled, like a spider at the heart of a giant busy web; and herself. Without her, she still felt, Morven would become inhuman.

She would hear the firm unafraid tread with which he always entered the house, and swiftly ascended the stairs. She would wait, not rising from her chair, till he had entered the room, and then would go to him. He would take her by the shoulders and kiss and fondle her tenderly, ask her concerning any news she had of other folk, perhaps give her his own. Neither of them, she thought wryly, was concerned for long except with one another. Morven would presently start to undress her with his deft fingers, while they still talked, and take the pins out of her hair. With it fallen at last like a warm, fragrant veil about them both—she washed it frequently with herbs for his delight, he'd always loved her hair and still often played with it, burying his face in it to savour the softness and scent—with it like that he would carry Livia to the bed, blind as he was; and lay her upon it carefully, and then kneel down. After that it was as though she were a doll, a toy with limbs that he, a boy, could move and handle. He would commence a kind of progress, while they laughed and murmured together like two children, of delight upon her body, without ever taking it. The hands, Morven's strong, shapely hands that could cozen Livia's flesh, roved in fondling it, probing, caressing, stroking, like a sculptor's who has made a statue of a beautiful, recumbent woman and wants to enjoy it before it sells elsewhere. But she, Livia would remind herself, wasn't a statue and never had been. She was flesh and blood, and under his touch her very womb throbbed with open longing; but Morven wouldn't make love. Sometimes, it was true, as if he himself could no longer endure the nearness of Livia's body without some contact, he would lie and writhe upon her, even perhaps enter briefly, but not remaining to satisfy her or himself. He seemed to prefer merely to caress, to feel, the contours of magnificent breasts and shoulders, the flat belly and long shapely thighs and calves. Once he kissed her feet. After an hour or so of it he would rise and leave her. When he had gone Livia would get up off the bed and go and dress and tidy herself, twisting her hair up again in its great piled knot. The urges his hands had raised in her were another matter; they wouldn't tidy. Sometimes it would take all night for them to die down. She tried to forget herself, and Morven, till he came back next day; then it all started over again. It wasn't a life for a woman, but for a long time Livia said nothing.

Sometimes, she would think bitterly of Annabel. After Morven had left her most days he would go, she knew well, full of roused desire, to his wife's bed, no doubt, and empty himself into her. "Maybe that's why he still comes here: maybe he does it better after he's been with me." It was all very fine; but worse, in almost all ways, than when she herself had been a serving-maid here at Mains, and he'd come to her as a man, not, not—

What was Morven Doon turning himself into?

Sometimes although it took a lot to make her afraid, Livia would feel fear for Morven; not for herself. She was Morven Doon's woman, he was her man; nothing could alter that, or what had been between them. The change in Morven, she knew without being told, would be somehow connected with Malvie. Malvie was, after all was said, what he'd wanted more than he would ever want any woman, and in the end he'd got it, his house. "He can keep it for all of me," Livia muttered. She herself disliked, had done from the beginning, the great ghostly place, redolent of departed Doons. As soon live in a tomb; and that's what she would tell Morven, she thought, if he ever, by reason of some change or other in his plans, asked her to leave Mains and come to live at Malvie. Many a man kept his mistress nowadays under the same roof as his wife; but Livia liked her own little house, and would tell him so, if he ever gave her the chance. She'd loved Mains since first setting eyes on it that day long ago, when she first came into service with Mrs. Retford, pretending to be Mary Reid. It had always been her home, as though she knew from the start she'd come back to it some time; more so than the Fleece had ever been, it was home. Here, as at the inn, she kept everything in the place clean and shining, the curtains fresh and blowing at the casements, a good fire blazing in the hearth when it grew chilly with the first frosts; a different sight, if he could only see it, from the shambles it had all been that night Morven brought her back here, before his marriage, having caused her to walk out of the taproom and leave the beer running, and poor Abel. Abel . . . he was a good man. She'd used him very ill.

Her own inner fires burned high, troubling her, increasingly after Morven had departed, and she couldn't down them at last by any means; sometimes she would try to solace herself by remembering that journey in the coach uphill, when Morven first came back after seven years in Australia. He hadn't been able to keep himself from making love right away, like a half-starved man falling on food; they'd coupled before she'd even got her feet on ground again, with young William and the mullato still perched up on the box. There hadn't been any hand-strokings or ladylike undressing then; he'd got right down to the business, had Morven. But now, for all the good she seemed to be doing him these days, it seemed a pity he'd ever made her leave poor Abel.

She tried, after thinking it over for a very long time, to say something of the kind one day to Morven when he came. He was angry.

"Leave?" he said, when she'd half suggested it. "Leave me? What would I do? Where would you go?" He'd thrust Abel, that was evident, back into the place in his own mind he kept for everyone and everything unsuited to his convenience; or perhaps he thought Abel wouldn't take her back. Livia thought queerly of how she'd never doubted he would, in spite of everything. There was no vengeance, no lack of understanding in Abel: he didn't seem to have the faults of ordinary humanity, as she remembered.

But Morven had meantime acquired his look of a lost child in the dark, and Livia went to him and put her arms about him, and rubbed her head lovingly against his shoulder;

264

he was wearing his old dark velvet coat; she could savour its rich pile.

"I'd manage," she told him, "and so would you. We're neither of us folk who can't shift for ourselves when we have to, Morven, you and me. Maybe nobody is when they're put to it. But I love you as a woman loves her man, not like a toy or an ell of silk to handle and feel how fine it is, and remember how much it cost, and never even cut it up to wear it."

"Livia—"

"Either you need me, or you don't," she said, and drew away from him. He heard her controlled voice, low-pitched for a woman's, holding no slur like the locals generally used, pronouncing each word clearly. It was partly because she did such things that he loved Livia; she would naturally discard, he thought, what was out of keeping, and he could turn her into a fine lady with ease at any time in a strange land, not here, where they were known. "Here everybody has their place," he thought, "and one can't change it," and thought of himself, and how he was now the laird, whom nobody visited by day. He cared little for that; he wished now, though, that he could even for moments again see Livia, with her white neck bent, her back towards him, and the glossy hair he'd admired that first day in the church-line jet-black still, or were there perhaps threads of grey in it? He had no way of knowing, except to ask; and he wouldn't. He didn't want to know if Livia had changed or not. Her shape, the glorious body and inviting quality of the rich flesh, hadn't; nor, as she said, had he used it lately. A surge of desire for her caught at him and he seized her, pulling her round against him, and kissed her hard on the mouth, then when she clung to him shoved her, almost roughly, away.

"You know who I need," he said, his voice still thick with emotion. "It's yourself and always has been. When I'm without you I'm like a man without his guts; but I must have a son who's a Doon."

"What's to prevent you in any case?"

"If I—" he spoke with difficulty, and as always her heart melted. "If I were to leave in you, as I'd like well to do, the very seed which might, which should, make Annabel conceive—"

"Men have enough to spare. Ask Samson of it." She spoke sullenly; they said the mullato had bulled every woman in the countryside who hadn't a husband of more than five foot four. It was a tale, of course, most of it, but—

"Don't mock. This means everything to me, Livia. The Doon heritage—the name of my ancestors, which should stay with the house—"

The house, always the house, thought Livia. Everything goes back to that damned barrack of Malvie, in the end. She said, "So I nourish your seed, Morven, when you handle me. Is that it? But my name's not Doon, so you can't waste it in me. There was a time when you'd plenty to give us both." She didn't, now she could see his face, say one word about the kind of life he was at present leading her; he himself looked like a creature in torment. "Livia, when my son is born it will have been worth it, all of it," he told her, adding, "Afterwards, again, we'll—"

"I myself gave you a son." She knew it was irrelevant to mention William. Morven spoke coldly again. "You couldn't bring me Malvie. Do not you yet understand, woman? Malvie is a part of myself, of my life. Without the hope of the continued inheritance, I'm nothing."

After he had gone Livia found herself crying. They'd made it up but only in a way; until Annabel's womb opened, however tardily, her own might cry in vain for physical release. Nothing she could have said on that head would ever move Morven. Well, she hadn't said much; and she'd do the moving for herself. She dried her eyes and then, putting on her hooded cloak, went down to the kitchen to find the girl Tib already peeling potatoes. Tib looked up.

"You're going out?" she said. "I was getting ready your supper. It's minced collops."

"I won't need any; eat them yourself. I'll be back tomorrow, maybe, if not before: anyhow, in time for the afternoon."

Abel had aged greatly; she hadn't realised, last time she saw him briefly on the road, in his dray, while she was in Morven's carriage driving to a further town for a bit of shopping, how white his hair had grown. It made her sad and yet humble; he was like, she thought, an old patriarch; not with a beard—God forbid Abel should ever grow one, it would choke the taps—but like Isaac, perhaps, whom she'd always thought of as clean shaven, although the others, Moses for example, were hairy.

They drank ale together; he talked with her. It was as she'd expected, and he'd got over, as far as anyone could see, her shameful abandoning of him. "Who launders your shirts?"

she asked, unable to keep some envy out of her voice; no one could blame Abel if he'd taken a woman.

"I do them myself," he said, "but I'm never the hand you were at it, Livia."

He was looking at her; the gentle admiration in his eyes was far, far from what she should have expected, could have been led to expect from anyone less than a saint. She broke down suddenly and howled and cried like a baby. "You—I—he." No sense came from her, and the harder she cried the worse it got; but Abel didn't come over and paw her, or take advantage.

At the end he said, still gently, "Is it Morven? Is something not as it should be between you both?" as if Morven were her husband, and he himself only a bystander. Livia gave a great final shuddering sob, and blew her nose. The kerchief was of Holland linen.

"I shouldn't have left you, Abel, as I did," she said, "but now it's done, and I—I couldn't leave Morven, not now, you know that. If I did, he'd come for me and I'd go back again. I couldn't help myself. That's how bad I am."

"You were never that," he said. "Tell me what's amiss with you and Morven," and, with a sense of walls broken down between them, she told him, leaving nothing out. After it was all said she felt better.

Abel made no reply. They were sitting upstairs to drink their ale; it was an hour when there were no customers, and the maids were in the downstairs rooms, never in any case private. Livia told herself she'd known all that, had no doubt worked it out in her mind from the beginning. In her way, she was as bad as Morven. She didn't deserve either that Abel should love her now, or that he should ever have loved her. She knew that. He knew she knew it. There weren't many like Abel.

He laid down his ale-glass and she noticed he'd hardly touched the contents, only having poured one out to bear her company while she took hers. She remembered hearing how he'd conquered his own drinking too much, at one time; and remembered its cause. She watched him go over to the door and bolt it. Then, gently, respectfully, he laid her down on the bed.

He solaced her need. All the time they lay locked together she was thinking, as if treating Abel already as a substitute, how his silence differed from Morven's silences at such times. The one demanded, brooding over something, or wanted something always, and took it; the other gave instead of

267

taking, was considerate, gentle, kind; and the release of her pent-up urges was a grateful thing; but—

At the end she said, "You're like a draught of good fresh water, Abel." Her eyes were still closed. She heard him laugh.

"Home-brewed, maybe," he said, "water's cold stuff."

"You've had to take to it, though, Abel, a good deal; because of me."

Abel smiled at her. It had been good to hold her in his arms again, he was thinking. In her way—always in her own way—Livia needed him as much as ever. It wasn't only for this. There would be other things.

"I know you couldn't help going off with him that time, Livia," he said; he did not want to name Morven again, but later had to. "Nobody does aught but what Morven wants them to," he told her presently. "Father knew that well enough, and Bart. I held out for a while; I like to stand back and think for myself a bit. And so do you, love."

"Maybe. But you know well enough I have to go back. He needs me, Abel; queer as things are by now he still needs me; and he's blind. I don't know it all yet, but he's like— like—" she sought for words, and fell back on the ones she'd chosen already, in her own mind, looking lately at Morven. "Although he's so sure of himself, sure as the devil, as they say, he's wide open to hurt; no one would think it of him, even the way they maybe see he is, like a child in the dark sometimes, like—" She fell silent, unable to express the pity Morven must never know she felt for his blindness, lest he be unmanned; never again to see a ray of sun, a flower, a colour, a known face!

She began to cry again. Abel listened; instead of comforting her, as most men would have tried to do after what had just befallen, he silently brought her his own ale. That made Livia laugh. She sat there hiccupping and laughing and drinking Abel's ale. "You've made me tipsy instead of yourself," she told him. "It's one cure, maybe."

"It isn't that," said Abel, who had tried it. "You've needs of your own in plenty, Livia. Don't let Morven make a sorry jennet of a good, honest mare. There's only one life of the body, whatever the preachers say; and no woman was ever like you are."

"Like a mare, you've just told me I am. There's flattery for you."

"I'm glad you came back, Livia," said Abel quietly. "Even if it's only for a while; even the once; even that." He seemed content, she thought. She blinked back tears again; what the devil ailed her that she couldn't love such a man as he deserved to be loved? But she made herself express pleasure at any rate; he'd given her some, in relieving her.

"Then I can come back, the times when I need home-brewed?" The tears made her eyes bright. "It's making use of you, you know, Abel; and you're too good for it."

"You can come whenever you need, for as long as you want," he said. "Whenever you need, my dear."

At Malvie, an end came to the reign of Polly Christian.

If Annabel had known, the sight of Samson with Polly on a bed, which in the old days would have caused her to dismiss both servants instantly with their money in lieu of forty days' service (in England, she understood from Kitty, they could be turned from the door without a penny, at the master's or mistress's whim,) was no indication that he was besotted. In fact, of late the steward of Malvie had grown weary of Polly, who, in her elevated position as his mistress, gave herself airs; she had, once or twice, attempted even to order him. Her days were, accordingly, numbered; Samson was, had she known it, wating only for a suitable successor, who must be biddable, with a comely body. He had cast his eye already about the markets and farms, but it was becoming difficult—and as a good servant he noted it—to persuade even abandoned, very poor, and unsuitable young women to come into service at Malvie. The place had a bad name, they said; one hussy told him so to his face.

"There are two devils in it, they say, a black one and a white. No woman's safe there in her bed. And there's more goes on, they tell it about, than women, and that by far."

She spat, and walked off; and whether she had made a veiled reference to the doings of the smuggling-fraternity in the tower, or to supposed darker things, Samson neither knew nor cared. He returned to Polly, and recalled her idly to her chief duty meantime; but he was beginning to wonder why he had ever been attracted by her; she reminded him now of a white rabbit; an aggressive overfed doe. She tried that time to make him buy her a necklace.

"There's pedlars comes round, green beads they have and red. They come from Spain," she said afterwards. Samson was silent, busied by now in fastening up his breeches. It wasn't beads he'd give her, he thought, if she didn't hold her tongue. And it wasn't Spain they came from, those pedlars; it was Birmingham.

The pedlar came, in course, and Samson bought Polly

nothing. This made her sulk, and whether or not it resulted in the behaviour which led to his finally getting rid of her he did not afterwards know; nobody asked Polly. But she was found by Annabel, one day when the latter walked unexpectedly into her own bedchamber, at an hour when she was understood to be out, and found Polly parading before the mirror in one of her gowns, with a pair of filigree earrings Godfrey had once given her, as a birthday-gift, dangling from the girl's narrow ears. Annabel slapped her, bade her take the things off instantly, and herself went straight to Morven, her creeks burning with anger. It wasn't the gown she minded about, though she'd never wear it again; it was the earrings, Godfrey's gift decorating that little slut. "She must go," she told Morven, with a force which these days was, for her, no longer customary. He turned his head wordlessly from where he sat; she could never predict, from any revealed expression of his what he would do.

On this occasion, he took her side in the matter. Not only— as Morven knew, he knew all such things—was Samson weary of his mistress, but that mistress by her behaviour lately had insulted Doon's wife, the lady of Malvie, aping her position however briefly. This was no doubt the reason why Morven roused himself, and issued orders to Samson— a thing he seldom did regarding the servants, whose appointment and dismissal he left entirely in the mulatto steward's hands. The woman Christian must go, he said. Some guilt assailed Morven; he'd promised, he remembered, long ago at the beginning to Annabel that he'd have the girl got rid of, and had never done so. "Have her whipped, and tell her it will happen twice weekly in public while she remains here; otherwise, she can take her money afterwards now in lieu of service."

Polly was recalcitrant at first. She knew her rights, she said. "They can't turn me out of here without bite or sup; I want my time; I'll find another situation." She would not, or not easily, she knew; her doings with Samson would prevent anyone but a brothel-keeper from taking her in, and her position at Malvie had, besides, been comfortable; nobody made her work hard in the house, and the food was tolerable, and— But after the first public whipping, Polly changed her tune. It was not, for he was not interested enough, Samson who exercised this privilege, but the cook; and that lady had endured so much over so long from Polly Christian that, given her chance and Polly bared over a chair, with the grinning servants brought in in rows to watch, she laid into her with a will. It was a howling, snuffling, flayed creature who that same night left Malvie, saying she didn't care if she had to sleep in a ditch; give her her money, and she'd leave the accursed damned place as fast as anyone liked. And so she went, limping off down the road with her bundle of clothes and forty days' money; nobody ever heard what happened to her.

Morven had forced Annabel to witness Polly's whipping. At first she thought this was merely to distress her or, perhaps, though it seemed unlike Morven, to imagine he was thereby satisfying certain notions of vengeance she was presumed still to nurse over the gown. But when he came to her that night, she knew that it was neither of those things. He lay with her. This was usual enough, but of late she had felt, and knew, with terror, Morven noted it also, that her response to him was growing flat, as though she were exhausted, incapable even of simulating passion. Perhaps she was so; she felt like a dried leaf. She'd grown thin, but it wasn't with pregnancy; he had felt her loss of weight, and had asked her, and she'd told him, and experienced for the first time, perhaps, a shiver of dislike, a hope that she might evade Morven's lovemaking for a little while till she grew better; but the only means of doing so was by raising his hopes, and she dared not, she dared not, he'd kill her afterwards if he found that she'd deceived him on such an issue. No; she must endure it at nights. But to give the word endurance to what she'd once needed, and told herself she could never live without, showed how much she'd changed.

Was she in fact ceasing to be a woman? Her signs were as usual; but there was nobody to ask, and Annabel was uncertain when that particular change should happen. Perhaps she'd grown—she had heard someone use the word of Charity Lagardie, long ago—frigid. Charity, they said—but they always said something of such people—had never truly enjoyed the relations with her husband which had presumably resulted nevertheless in the birth of three daughters. So it didn't, evidently, alter that.

Frigid. Dry, empty. A worn-out, barren woman; of no further use to Morven. She felt his contempt of her, bartered on every count except the last, that he didn't as yet know about. When he did . . . ah, she must still go on with it! But had he perhaps hoped the sight of Polly and the whipping would make her, Annabel, responsive again in bed? It had, that night, a little . . .

This gave Annabel a notion of her own as bizarre as Morven's; when she thought of it at first she shuddered away from the idea; it would mean she'd become abandoned, hopeless as poor old Kitty had become with her damnable second spouse Bowes. It was from Kitty she'd learned about it at all, the existence of the green powders. Aunt Retford would never have permitted, or known of, such things. Annabel recalled how angry she herself had been when Kitty put them in Godfrey's wine.

After Polly had gone Samson combed the countryside without avail, for a successor, and in the end he found a little hunchback, who agreed to come into service at Malvie. As she had been literally all Samson was able to find, he resented at first having to take her, in every sense; she was not in any case of a shape he could readily use in the event of persuasion. But he constantly needed a woman, and the hunchback girl had come from a poor home and needed the money, and dared neither deny Samson, nor leave Malvie. They went on for some time accordingly together, but Samson himself got little pleasure of it, and when a new apple-cheeked, straight-backed wench came to the home farm that quarter he would be found in the dairy there, and no one troubled them. The twisted creature at Malvie, relieved, got on with her housework; for a while, and in places, the house was swept clean again. Annabel brought herself to contemplate the hunchback without shuddering, and gave her a gown and shoes, but could not bear to let the girl act as her own maid, or touch her. As it had grown difficult to persuade young women into Malvie nowadays, its mistress gave up the lifetime's habit of a personal maid; in any case, she told herself, Morven never saw her.

VI

It was some years later. The laird of Malvie sat at his meat, clad in puce satin and Mechlin ruffles as befitted his station and the hour. Although he dined only with the family tonight—the meal generally begun at four, had prolonged itself by habit though talk now was sparse—he wore powder as was his custom at dinner. It heightened the saturnine quality of his face and the air he had of having been transported from a somewhat earlier age, perhaps a generation back. The blind eyes' pale gleam was enhanced by candle-light; the candles themselves burned high still, in sconces of heavy silver, wrought by London craftsmen of the time of Queen Anne. Morven's great-grandfather had brought them home. They were well-cleaned now, done by the little hunch-back with a care that the laird, once responsible for keeping Governor's silver bright in the penal settlement at Port Jackson, would have approved had he known of it; but nobody troubled to tell him.

Down Richard Doon's oak table the sconces reflected both themselves and one another, striking a subdued gleam from the oak, a brighter one from rival silver. The scene they revealed might have used less tallow with more kindness; half-way down sat old Kitty Bowes, whom the last seizure of all had rendered senile and half helpless, but she still lived on. Tonight—a certain obstinacy made Kitty endeavour to come down for meals, and she would still appear at times, and other times not—tonight she again shovelled the food into her mouth with difficulty, and dribbled and slopped it all about her; the attendant was not present, and the audible, distressing animal sounds offended Morven, intent within his own dream of dignity and splendour at Malvie, amid silver and candle-light. Coldly, he decided to give orders that in future Kitty must always be fed in her rooms; an old woman, an encumbrance of Devenham's, unable longer to converse intelligently, to add wit or sparkle to the meal. He pictured, leaving the matter of Kitty meantime, the other aspects of tonight's scene he could imagine, carrying out to the letter, he knew, his youth's dream of long ago. His servants, better drilled than when he first came, would be going silently about their business, handing French sauces to pour on the fish and meat; because of Morven's blindness this was ready cut, carved and apportioned on the silver plates. Morven had withheld the seventeenth-century service from nightly use for some time, intending to have it used for the first time in generations at his son's christening, with the county present and toasting the heir in wine. But it hadn't befallen yet; Morven refused even yet to admit to himself that it might not now do so, that such a ceremony was peopled with the folk of dreams, and the heir a dream also. His will was to be done; the heir must be conceived. But he'd begun to use the silver plates. He ate his food off them now with precise, bird-like delicacy, subtly assisted by Samson who stood as always behind his master's chair, and never sat down to the meal with him, although he remained later for wine and chess. He still watched over Morven in a thousand ways, each night making certain that what his master wanted was ready to his hand, as he ate, without rousing his resentment. Morven would have been made coldly angry by solicitous aid; this his steward knew.

The wife Morven Doon had long ago promised himself sat, as he had planned, at the further end of the long table, dressed like Morven himself in powder, satin and lace. This was his expressed wish, and such was her fear of him that Annabel spent long hours of each lonely day attiring herself for dinner; she'd grown adept, she told herself, at curling and powdering her own hair, tying and disposing the folds of her gown, with its Malines lace elbow-cuffs a trifle yellowed with the years; the lace had belonged to her mother. She herself, despite the candlelight which supposedly flattered women by casting a soft glow over aging or unclean skin, seemed older by many years, more so than she was; the innocent, flowerlike quality had long fled from cheeks and throat, as though there were nothing now between the taut skin and the sinews; she tried to disguise her haggard appearance with red and white paint, and in the end was like a thin, daubed clown; the cosmetic failed to conceal the hollows beneath the cheekbones, and enhanced them and the skeleton thrust of the clavicles between shoulders too prominent without their former flesh. She was like a woman who has been for long afflicted with some wasting illness, but she was not ill. Nor, this time yet again, as Morven had already ascertained, was she pregnant.

She closed her eyes an instant, shutting out the sudden dazzle of the candles against her tired eyes. She had for a time found one haven again in the morass of fear which was now her life; the garden. During the earlier part of the day she had repaired there, while Morven would be with Livia; and covering only a small part at a time had begun to try to retrieve a very little, no more, of what she and Godfrey had once started together; she had weeded out the encroaching nettles, dandelions and bishopweed, finding, when she could, a remaining clump of irises or such perennials as had remained. So much had gone; many even of the roses had died with the winter frosts, or else had reverted to ramblers over the years, but she had done what she could; a thing, in the former rose-garden, that she had come upon while weeding had made her feel faint, for moments, kneeling by them; her pruning-shears, that she'd left on the ground that time Samson abducted her and carried her down to Morven's boat, making her drunk on the way. That time . . . the shears were rusty, no one had looked for them since. She'd picked them up carefully and tried to close them, and make them fit to use again; but both she and they were useless, she and they . . . But now, with the passing of winter, already the young shoots had opened out again from bud to leaf, and soon there would perhaps be blossom; by the time Sybilla came home, in summer, the pair of them would surely be able to sit out there, talking and hearing the subdued murmur of the wild bees who had never in all these years left their place in a wall; they had been used to rifle tall spires of Aaron's-rod for nectar, and also a bush with tiny white flowers which gave berries in autumn, but it had died long ago.

Annabel still thought of her daughter as Godfrey's. The remembrance of Godfrey himself never left her, in the garden when she was alone; as she worked, she could sometimes pretend to herself that when she turned round for a moment, he would be seated there in his chair, ready to advise her on, perhaps, a suitable direction for planting clematis; some kinds liked to face south, others east and north. There was in the garden, by day, and alone; but lately, even here, it had seemed as though in his sky way Godfrey were edging nearer, not liking to come uninvited into a room, but knowing she needed him there; to support her, from somewhere in the candlelit silence, so that at no time need she, perhaps, ever again feel quite alone. As time passed, he and she might even become wrapped together in a separate, jewelled enclosure of the mind, while the body itself . . .

The body. Morven, if he knew of her present preoccupation, and its cause, would shatter the content it brought her with some mocking, cruel saying, as he had done that last day of Godfrey's earthly life. How he had smashed her tranquil happiness then, leaving destruction and misery in its place! And by night, still, in the dark together, it would be only Morven who was with her, not Godfrey any more. It made her so tired always now, she wished . . .

She had, accordingly, tried the green powders. She plucked now with a nervous, uncertain motion at the grapes and filberts set out nearby her own place at table, selecting a few and even conveying them one by one to her mouth. They tasted harsh and unripe. The effort of pretending to eat, though she wasn't hungry, would make her, perhaps, contrive to forget, to forget . . . But she couldn't. No woman, not even the most degraded and abandoned, could forget such things as Morven had said and done to her, or wonder by the hour, in lonely fear, if he'd meant it, or had merely been jesting. It was the kind of jest he preferred to make more than ever against her nowadays, so heartless, so grotesquely cruel . . .

Kitty had come down for dinner today. Annabel stared over at the wrecked, kindly, often mistaken creature who had been her mother-in-law, marvelling that, in the chaos of recent invalid arrangements, she had been able to lay her own hands on Kitty's carved box. The powders were still there. There were enough left to . . . to do some good, perhaps, if that was the term one must use. To Annabel herself as she had once used to be it was evil to use such things, even to dream of using them. But circumstances changed people. She, who'd been so angry with Kitty once long ago for slipping the powders into Godfrey's wine, was now using them herself. Poor kind foolish Kitty. The world had used her ill, when all was said, despite the money. Palsy made her mouth sag sideways; saliva dribbled out of it always, and particularly when she expected food. Annabel, afraid of retching, could not look that way; she kept her eyes on her plate, and fingered nutshells.

She had already seen Morven's blind gaze avoid Kitty's direction also; she knew that, again after tonight, he would probably give orders that the old woman must be made to eat alone in her rooms. Instead, Morven kept the sightless stare fixed on herself, his wife. What was it about him that made her feel now that all of herself, her very hands, trembling and too thin with the flesh hollowed out between the small, delicate carpal bones, were being studied by him, examined for some fault? What would he say if he guessed she had begun taking the powders? Perhaps he knew . . . perhaps, having no respect left for her at all, it had given rise in itself to the thing he'd said to her about Samson; the fearful thing he'd lately threatened. She couldn't bear even to think of it, to look at the steward or speak to him; Samson's huge hands, powerful as a blacksmith's, hung by his sides now, the palms showing pinkish edges, the nails also. For them even to touch her flesh—

She clung to the table's edge, to avoid fainting, even that, as she thought perforce of the thing that Morven had said. It was, a very little, like his earlier threat to her that time on the boat, but in ways much worse; unnatural, degrading, horrible.

She tried, while they still ate together and Kitty sucked her food in audibly, to school herself to remember the other, lesser horror that still loomed between herself and Morven. If she wasn't pregnant this time, he said, he would take her to a doctor. That was sane enough; but a doctor would certainly tell Morven the truth. Annabel's whole body melted with fear.

That was why, after finding what they could do, she'd continued taking the green powders. They couldn't afford any lasting relief to her situation, she knew, and yet . . . and yet they would stave off Samson. She couldn't endure the thought of Samson's hands holding down her bare flesh, spanking her, as they did to worn-out whores, before she went to bed with Morven.

At a different time, but for the same reason, they must have discussed Sybilla.

She herself had been querulous, as often now, she remembered. She had told Morven, sometimes, again, that she felt tired nowadays, too tired to make such constant love.

"You have no reason to feel tired. You have little to do, and you are not yet pregnant." He was inexorable with her. He kept as strict an account of her lunar periods, she knew, as if she'd been a mare or greyhound bitch. At such times, and only then, he left her alone. Otherwise her vapourings, as he chose to call them, met with little sympathy from Morven. He reminded her, as he often did, preparing, that she was in better health now than she'd been for years; his assiduous lovemaking had at least put an end to her migraines. "All that was wrong with you was what was wrong with Godfrey," he smiled. "Now, I give you enough of what a woman needs. It's time you repaid me, Annabel."

"Let me rest," she begged miserably. It seemed all she was able to ask nowadays; even the rage that still rose in her at this invariable mockery of Godfrey seemed feeble, as though the exhausted state to which Morven had reduced her had invaded every faculty and feeling. Godfrey was dead. What would he say if he saw her now, used almost nightly. She wanted both to sob and laugh during it; by the end, worn out, she sometimes cried aloud to Morven of Sybilla.

"She is a Doon, and your own daughter." He knew that

and had always known, but it seemed to matter nothing, Sybilla's mother thought; her own agony in bearing Morven the only child she would ever bear, with a parturition that had finally ripped her womb apart, mattered nothing. Nothing mattered, nothing, but what Morven wanted now; a son, a son, and Sybilla might for all he cared spend the rest of her life with the Melroses at Maddon.

She gave a final sob, and said. "I'm not fashioned for bearing others." It was the nearest she dared go towards the truth. But he only made a coarse rejoinder about her fashioning, and presently entered her again. Annabel heard her own outraged weeping, felt Morven's needless usage of her, knew that she was almost shouting by now, despite deadly tiredness, as though he were both deaf and blind. "Make Sybilla's husband take the Doon name, when she marries. What's to hinder it? Your blood would still inherit; leave me now, Morven, I'm so tired, so tired . . ."

But he would not leave her, she knew, now or ever, till he had his will. During the completion of the marital act Annabel again heard the precise, cold words he used as though they came from a stranger; a stranger who could demand the ultimate rights of intimacy as a due, as though in failing, time and again, to meet his requirements she was failing in her duty. He had answered her briefly, curtly about Sybilla.

"Devenham acknowledged her." It was enough reason, for Morven Doon; but Annabel clung to the notion lately come to her, as though it were her salvation.

"What does that matter, when you know the truth, yourself, as to who was her father?" Even yet, though, she was unwilling in her own mind to break the remembered link between Sybilla and Godfrey. How he'd doted on the child, loved and laughed at the engaging things she said, delighted in teaching her, and taking the angelic, beautiful little girl about with him in his calèche, at his side, steering the reins, when Sybilla was very small indeed . . . So long ago; so many things had altered. Morven and she lay now in surcease.

"There is an obstacle to Sybilla's adopting the name Doon," said Morven idly. "No doubt in the prosperity to which you have grown accustomed, my dear, it hadn't occurred to you; but Godfrey left a fortune to his daughter, not mine. I have no doubt that Cecily and Clairette—" he laughed—"would contest the will, if I were to say that, from the beginning, she was my child and not his. Had she been a son—" he fondled Annabel's thin limbs, as though still hoping to elicit

278

a response that would make her bear— "I would have deemed it worth the price. But a girl has no place in the Malvie inheritance."

She felt, through her utter weariness, anger struggle up again; he'd sold every movable article of Godfrey's choosing out of Malvie, and kept the money; but the Devenham fortune bequeathed to Sybilla, and her own generous portion, he'd deign, no doubt, to enjoy. If she could but dare to say so, and make it evident how she loathed Morven at such moments! But she could not.

Morven said, as though he had read her thoughts, "For a male heir of my blood nothing would be too dearly bought —or parted with." And she felt the brutal force still lying within her quicken; he served her yet again, and she, by now wailing, no longer resisting for very exhaustion, felt at last a sad flicker, a ghostly remembrance of the eager, passionate response she had been used to feel. He withdrew from her.

"You displease me of calculated intent," he said coldly. As her sobbing mounted again he turned on his back. Staring up in his private darkness to where the Doon escutcheon would be sewn in gold on the canopy, he said, as though to himself and not to her,

"Our marriage bed is growing cold. I believe we must warm it."

The tears were running down Annabel's face and she did not answer, thinking he meant by that to couple with her tonight yet again; but Morven leaned over and slapped her.

"Do you suppose—spineless, useless thing that you are, a very dish without salt—do you flatter yourself I'd have a renewed appetite tonight for a woman who can't even hold what I put in her? But if I must lie with you each night till cock-crow, my genteel, fine bitch of a wife, you shall conceive by me in the end. Tomorrow we will try again; see that you do better."

"Morven, I—"

"Keep your damned mouth shut; if you'd open as wide elsewhere it'd serve you better. I swear by God, Annabel, that if you continue as cold, I'll have Samson smack your bottom each night till it warms to its duty. That works well enough, I believe; they tried it at St. Petersburg, on their jaded Empress, at her own request. I forgot who told me that. But I doubt if Godfrey can have left you in such a state."

He turned over on his back, and through the maelstrom

of horror and shame, the unbelief—surely even Morven would never order such a thing to be done!—she heard herself say "You shall not insult Godfrey. He was kind to me." Then she burst into abject, terrified weeping; he was already weary of that, and drew the covers finally over himself, to hear no more of it. He had no shred of pity for Annabel; the entire dedication he had to his own plans, his own ambitions, for Malvie, obscured the fact that, as other men might long ago have begun to suspect, a force stronger than Morven Doon existed, and might cause them to alter.

Thereafter, Annabel became like a thing half-crazed.

She spent her days in a state of cowering submission, not finding any longer that even working in the privacy of her garden brought her relief. It was here the mulatto had once come and silently flung a sack over her head and carried her off; he could have raped her, that time, on the way down to Morven's boat, easily enough, having made her drunk before he stripped her; that he hadn't done more was, she knew, because she was Morven's property, his master's own. Livia Judd would likewise be untouched by Samson. Apart from the two of them, almost no woman in the countryside was safe. Samson himself could come upon her here, each time a shadow moved; shortly Annabel abandoned the garden. If Morven carried out his threat—of a kind with his behaviour, that early time, with her on the drawing-room sofa, forcing her to behave in a whore's fashion and worse, almost in public—if he ordered the mulatto even to touch her, she'd die of degradation and horror. One could die so. Morven would have made an animal of her, and less. The alternative was better. She'd begun that day to take Kitty's green powders.

At first they'd worked. If poor old Kitty had been able to speak, Annabel would have asked her advice about how much to take; no doubt also for other advice. As it was, perhaps in her anxiety she took too much; when Morven came to her that night in bed she found herself doing things which filled her, next day, remembering, with confusion and deep shame. She recalled his jeering laughter; his saying she was trying harder. Trying harder . . . and never, never, Annabel knew, would there be a pregnancy no matter how many green powders she took. Sometimes she wondered if it would be better to make an end to herself. But she was afraid even of that, and there was Sybilla.

The powders themself were no doubt foreign, made of little

iridescent crushed insects, still recognizable. She didn't know where to get any more. That was another fear; and moreover, the oftener one took the powders the less effect they seemed to have, so that she found she must take more and more each time, and soon they'd be finished. What would he do to her then? Samson, the physician, both? And he didn't even respect her any more, the way she was behaving; she couldn't, she admitted, expect it: Morven used her, and spoke to her nowadays, like a whore. She couldn't, he had said once lately, control herself. He used words and did things she'd never formerly thought of or imagined, as though she . . .

"Oh, Godfrey, Godfrey," said Annabel aloud suddenly, and burst into bitter tears. It occurred to her that what she was giving Morven now he could get in any case more readily from his mistress. Some time, soon, when the powders were all finished, she would have to tell him the truth . . . and then he'd kill her.

Morven still went to Livia Judd daily. Could she, dared she, ask Morven's mistress for advice? Morven—Annabel had no means of knowing how she felt certain of this—Morven respected Livia.

The candles had burned low along the dinner-table. For some time now the meal had been finished, and Annabel realised that they were waiting for her to withdraw. She rose, taking Kitty on her arm to escort her back to her rooms, and knew that as soon as they had left Morven would reach for the wine-flask, and gesture to Samson to seat himself and join him. When the women had gone the two men became no longer servant and master, but boon-companions as they had been at Port Jackson. They'd play chess, not with the delicate Eastern set she and Godfrey had used together long ago—it had been sent to the salesroom—but with a chipped set of her father's, resurrected despite its missing pawn from somewhere, since Morven had come home. They would play till they could no longer do so for the wine they'd drunk, till even Morven's fingers fumbled over the pieces; then, Annabel knew with dreary certainty, he'd come, with Samson gone off to his mistress, to her bed. Love? What travesty of the word involved the things Morven did to her? He had never genuinely loved her, Annabel knew, but he might, she thought, have hated her less if she hadn't owned Malvie. Lust for Malvie had long ago driven him mad.

"I myself am perhaps so by now," she thought. To save

281

Morven's sanity and her own, and her life, her wretched life, if only for the sake of little Sybilla, she must pursue her own latest plan, and go to Livia. Livia could tell Morven the truth.

Next day Annabel had a pony saddled. She had given no such order to the stables for long; William Judd, to whom she gave it, said he didn't know if he should, the master had said, one time, he thought . . .

"I know of that. Do as you're bid," said Annabel coldly. She knew well enough that Morven had issued orders forbidding her to be given a mount, having himself informed her she must no longer ride. It might disturb an implanted foetus. The meticulous nature of such orders to his servants almost amused her now, when she need no longer heed them. She watched William, who never had the wit to question much, go and saddle the pony. It was a grey beast, with a blaze on the forehead. Once mounted, and having ridden off, Annabel felt the weariness and terror of the past months slide from her like a garment; soon Livia, good unafraid Livia, would put the whole matter right. How extraordinary to have to rely on Morven's mistress for such a thing! How strange their life was altogether at Malvie!

She let the grey pony carry her in docile fashion across to the dower house. Between aunt Retford's death and Livia's occupancy the latter had not been constantly inhabited. Sometimes, for the shooting or at other times when there was a concourse of folk at Malvie, guests of her own and Godfrey's had slept there once the great house had grown overcrowded.

Godfrey! She would have all the leisure in the world to think again of his kindly ghost, she thought, once she'd seen Livia, and Livia had told Morven she, his wife, was barren. Annabel's thin hands tightened on the reins a little, as the pony ambled on.

VII

The high autumn winds had already made havoc of the dower house garden, beating down the Michaelmas daisies and yellow spires of golden-rod which appeared, year after year, without any tending. Livia had picked her way down the still glistening path after the rain, and had gone to lean over the field hedge to watch William breaking in a pony. She had for some time tried, with Abel's help lately, to atone to William for her neglect of him in childhood, and show him interest and care; but it was too late. William could look after himself; he needed no one but his beasts, and, possibly, Morven.

Livia had accepted that strange situation. She stood for a while now, idly watching the almost unknown creature who was her son; he was almost a part of the pony as it curvetted and bucked, held by the strong grip of William's powerful thighs. The lad's black hair, the beast's black mane, seemed to mingle flying as the wind caught at them both; hadn't there been creatures once that were part horse, part man? "The men'll pretend anything, and in their cups say they've seen 'em, if I should ask," thought Livia, who was humble about her own lack of learning. But William today seemed as much centaur as gipsy. He trotted the now docile, obedient pony once around the field, slid off its back, gave it a pat and briefly caressed its proud, trembling neck and was off, with a comradely wave to herself; William had no enemies, she thought, any more than he had friends now Sam was dead. Perhaps she hadn't many friends herself now either.

The wind stirred her own hair, in which a white lock showed lately at the temple. She'd put on a shawl and no cap today, and had troubled little about herself till the afternoon, when Morven should come. She stood now in the immemorial attitude of gipsy women, arms folded beneath her shawl, wrapping it thereby tight round her. Her eyes brooded.

A sound of patient hooves plodding came across the near distance, and Livia turned her head idly; it couldn't yet be

Doon. A thin woman sat on a walking pony, and at first Livia did not know her at all; the likelihood of Mrs. Annabel's visiting herself was so remote that the possible identity of the changed face and figure had not even struck Livia. Then she knew who it was.

She did not move. It had been a while since Annabel, the fortunate, the rich, the married bedfellow of Doon of Malvie, had disturbed her days. The nights, at least till Abel aided her lately, had been different. No one would ever know what she'd endured through those nights, knowing they were at Malvie together, Morven and his wife. But there was no doubt Mrs. Annabel had changed, aged. She looked like a ghost of herself. She looked— "What's he done to her?" Livia heard her own mind ask itself, suddenly. It was an echo from the old protective days, herself forever protecting Miss Annabel.

The two women had stared at one another for instants, like two statues; then Annabel loosed the reins, and slid down out of the saddle. She walked forward, leading the pony. He's an old one, Livia thought. Why was Morven's wife riding an old broken down pony? "She could afford the finest beast in any stable," Morven's mistress thought. But she did not grudge Annabel her money. It didn't make her happy, from the looks of her. She seemed almost as broken as the old pony.

"May I speak with you, Livia?"

She sounded humble. Morven's wife shouldn't be as humble as that, Livia thought. The Doons, who'd lived in Malvie since God knew when, were themselves; whereas she herself was half gipsy. "But my mother's folk were Kings of Little Egypt, and my father they say was a lord's son. I can better the Doons, maybe." So Livia thought, but she still could say nothing of it aloud; she only nodded.

"Come in," she said curtly. "Tie your reins to the gate."

Annabel tied them, and her fingers fumbled over the knot; a kind of impatience rose in Livia. Couldn't the creature do anything, tie a knot or bear a child? If the child were only born, then she herself and Morven, again—

Suddenly, the cruelty of Annabel's situation was borne fully in upon Livia. It wasn't too difficult to think for other folk if one had to, and Miss Annabel's face had always been a mirror. Now, it reflected a soul in terror and grief.

They had gone into the house. When they were inside Livia shut the door and waited awkwardly. Should she or should she not offer tea, or wine? "Morven hasn't made a

284

lady of me," she thought, "I don't know what I should do."
And the other stood there with her drawn face working, her once pretty face that had been like a flower, innocent and never needing any paint. She was painted now. She was worn thin as a lathe as well, and unhappy, and—

"It's Morven, isn't it?" said Livia suddenly. Why waste time, as the gentry always did, skirting round and round the point? One had to get to it, in the end. And it could only be Morven's business that had brought Mrs. Annabel here at all, some matter concerning Morven, Livia's own lover. Her own man, that she'd lent to this frail stick of a thing to her own hurt and no one's good, evidently. If Morven's wife began now to tell her some matter she didn't want to hear, such as to beg her to leave Mains, or the like, she'd soon show Miss Annabel who had Morven's heart. She'd endured enough, herself, to—

But Annabel did not even form her lips round Morven's name. Her face continued its strange working for moments; then suddenly she broke down into wild, lost, abandoned crying, like a child. She stood there with tears running down; they splashed unheeded on her bodice, which the breasts now hardly raised.

Livia went over and took her in her arms.

After it was all said, all of it, Annabel felt better. She had begun to cry again—she had hardly ceased from the beginning, Livia thought, and the appalling story had had to be wrenched out of her between sobs, like someone racked by torture to a final confession—but her crying was different now; less elemental, healing rather than destroying. She'd been almost destroyed, had Miss Annabel, Livia told herself.

She had said, on her own account, meantime, very little; it hadn't, she thought with wry certainty, been to hear her talk that Mrs. Annabel had come here. She stroked the still-bright head of Morven's wife, now in her lap; the curls were tousled, and it was time the poor dear washed her hair with herbs; her clothes, too, were somewhat soiled; the chemise showing at the nape of the bent neck, bordered with neglected lace, was yesterday's. Miss Annabel hadn't used to be like that. Was it true what they said, that she no longer even had a maid about her?

"She'll never manage," Livia thought. Miss Annabel had never been a manager. The great jerking sobs had begun again and Livia said, soothingly, feeling by now old and tired, "What is it, love? What else is it?" and Annabel told her;

some matter or other, some new fear she had concerning the mulatto, and Morven. Everything came back to Morven.

"Godfrey never used me so," sobbed Annabel.

"It's not the dead we're speaking of now, it's the living." Livia felt a second, fierce protectiveness rise in her also for Morven, blind Morven hungry for his son. She had not ceased her stroking of Annabel's hair. It seemed to be what she was here for, to listen to them both. She did so, saying little more.

"And now he'll leave me," wailed Annabel. She relapsed into her weak, gentle everyday crying again. Livia found herself smiling at the irrational, childish creature who was Morven's wife.

"Now, love, you can't have it all ways, any more than anything else in this life. You've told me already how cruelly Morven uses you and that you're frightened of him, and want him to leave you alone; and in the next breath you're greeting again, because he may leave you."

"I—I—ah, Livia, I'm foolish today, I'm tired—"

"And I'm thinking of Morven," said Livia sternly. "If I'm to tell him what you ask, it's likely enough he'll leave you, Miss Annabel, and that's the truth. I couldn't make him stay, could I? And if I could I wouldn't, would I?"

She found herself unable to say more; she turned away almost in tears, overcome with the longing she had for Morven. Lord, she thought, blinking her eyelashes, that'd make two of us creating Noah's flood here; what use is it?

She heard Annabel babble on. She seemed happier; that was something. Her face looked brighter and younger already, as though the sweet unsullied girl who'd lived at Mains long ago was showing through the paint. But it wouldn't ever be the same for Miss Annabel as those days had been, once the truth was made clear to Morven. That much Livia foresaw; Annabel still talked as if everything would be simple thereafter, all problems solved. She smiled up at Livia, the tears already dry on her raddled cheeks; they had smeared the rouge.

"You will tell him for me, and see to it that he doesn't—doesn't grow angry, and harm me when he knows I can't have another child? I've been so afraid, even of things and people I knew: I was afraid of coming here today, afraid even of ordering them to saddle the pony."

She smiled a little, as though a pale sun had wavered through cloud. To be friends once more with Livia, to hear

Livia forget not to call her Miss Annabel again! But Livia was frowning.

The Doons, she was thinking drily; they'd charm a bird off a tree. Even this woman sitting here in her soiled linen had such charm no one could refuse her what she asked for, except Morven. She herself would have to remember to send William down to Abel at the Fleece, to say she wouldn't be coming to see him again for a while, perhaps for a long while. Abel would understand; but the way she'd used him made her ashamed, despite all he'd said. He was too good for her, and there it was. A woman couldn't love a saint, such as Abel had become, in the way she, Livia, loved Morven.

She sat up very straight, and spoke slowly. "You must know I'd want to tell Morven this for my own sake, Miss Annabel, as well as yours; you know that?"

"I know that." Annabel was resigned, even docile. She'd grown used long ago to the notion that Morven loved Livia; at first it had shocked her, then embittered her, and latterly it hadn't mattered as much. And it had made her marry Godfrey. "Godfrey, Godfrey," she thought now, and closed her fingers over his ghostly ones; he was not, she knew, far off.

"Then listen," said Morven's mistress. "After I tell him, it won't be easy for you; I doubt, though, if it'll be harder than it has been. But the thing I am saying is this; what Doon bids me I must do. It's always been that way, and the Lord knows it's got me into queer places and queer ways. But I must do as he tells me, for I can't refuse."

"No one can," said poor Annabel. How taut and hard Livia seemed suddenly, as if she were a drawn sword! But she herself was different also. Instead of resenting Morven's woman, as in her position she should certainly do, in particular for a former serving-maid, she felt she was talking to a queen, perhaps of ancient times. A queen with black hair, and a way of bearing herself that was royal in an old gown and shawl, with her hair uncombed after being out in the wind. "The white in it suits her," thought Annabel. She must be thinking in this way today because she was so very tired, but it was all of it a relief and she was glad she had come to Livia.

"You want Morven told when he comes this afternoon, then?" said Livia baldly. "You're sure of that?"

"Oh yes, yes." A great weight seemed lifted from Annabel's mind. She felt already like a child again, a happy enough, bullied but protected child. If only Morven ceased to trouble her about a child of their own, and—and had Livia, she herself could work in the garden, and do the things she enjoyed and had been used to, such as riding daily, and perhaps when Sybilla came home—

"Please tell him," she said, already in the tone of one ordering a servant. But it was a respected, trusted servant on whom Annabel could rely. Livia, she knew, had never shirked anything.

For Livia to tell Morven what Annabel had asked was easy enough in one way; she never made any bones about anything. She told herself that, and that she'd say it, when he came, straight out, before he'd even undressed her. For her own sake, as well no doubt as Miss Annabel's, that was as it should be; she herself wanted Morven, wanted him with all of her body and heart, the sooner the better. But for Morven's own sake, she trembled.

It had meant so much to him, she knew, the thought of his son, that he'd even denied himself her body.

How did it happen she hadn't heard at the time, as one did hear such things about Miss Annabel not being fit to bear other children? She'd heard, it was true, about the unduly prolonged labour, the terrible birth; it had been bad enough to give the gossips plenty to occupy them, till the next untoward thing occurred about the countryside, whatever it was. But as for the rest, it hadn't been allowed to be made known, that was all: no doubt Miss Annabel herself, poor Mr. Godfrey, the physician, and maybe old Mrs. Bowes herself, were the only folk to know of it: the midwife would leave too early. And the physician they had had died three years since, on his brown cob's back returning from yet another confinement; the good beast had brought the old man's dead body home, still in the saddle, tilted forward. Now they had a new doctor at Grattan.

But Morven . . . surely even his obsessed mind could have allowed such a doubt to enter it?

He thought he was God at such times, as Livia knew. In any matter concerning Malvie and the inheritance, Morven assumed that because he said a thing was to be, it must be. It was like, she recalled the Ten Commandments they'd taught at Emmett's, with the bit about the graven image dwelt on at length by Priddy. Morven had made himself a graven image of Malvie. He'd bowed down to it. Although he might never bow down to anything else, and thought

288

he could mould every living creature to fit his notions, there
it was; even to make a barren woman bear, and a pas-
sionately aroused woman, herself, remain continent while
he—

"Thank God there'll be an end to that," Livia thought,
"and now he's coming up."

She could hear the sounds of Morven's expected daily
arrival, the familiar, confident step on the stairs, his voice
calling her. She felt calm. Miss Annabel had done right to
come to her at last. She herself, Livia Judd, and no other,
knew how to tell Morven whatever he had to know.

When he had entered the room and had not yet reached her
she stood waiting, not eagerly hurrying into his arms as she
was used to do. Morven had already held them out, and stood
waiting. Livia saw them drop again to his sides when she
did not move.

Before he could ask any questions, she thought, she must
get it out. She said, "Morven, stay a moment. I have a
thing to tell you."

Then she told him. It was as simple as that.

Afterwards the thing she chiefly remembered was, among
other things, what had chanced amiss. It might have seemed
a small thing; but Livia knew it wasn't small. It was of more
importance than the first cry Morven gave, when he understood; a loud incredulous, outraged cry like a man suddenly
castrated. Then he'd launched himself towards Livia. He'd
tried to reach her and strangle her, not knowing, doubtless,
for the moment, even who she was; he might even have done
it, if his hands had finally gripped her throat. That didn't
matter. What mattered was that as he came towards her,
Morven tripped, for a footstool lay unexpectedly in the way,
and he sprawled his full length on the floor. Morven, the all-
seeing without eyes, fell on the floor; and lay there sobbing,
his head laid on his arm; Morven Doon the undefeatable,
who'd thought he was God.

She'd gone straight to him, of course; he wouldn't kill her
now. She had knelt down by him as if he were William himself as a child, and had taken his head, very gently, in her
lap. Then she'd soothed Morven: kissing his still averted
neck, drying his sobs, stroking his hair. A while back, she
was telling herself, she'd been stroking Miss Annabel's. It
looked as if the Doons couldn't do without her easily; in
one day, stroking them both like bairns till their crying
stopped, and she— But Morven's sobbing, she still knew, was

that of a soul cast alone into the uttermost wastes of hell, the frozen part where they'd already left Judas Iscariot and a few special other folk. Why recall Emmett's twice in one day, where they'd stuffed the Bible into her ears with one hand and gone up her skirts with the other? Since then, she'd had no time for kirk-folk.

She was still kissing and murmuring to Morven. Small, comforting sounds came from her. Some of them were hardly words; others were. "There, lad, there. There, there. There, there. There, my own love. There, my own dear love Morven." She said it all over and over and by the end the word love prevailed; she began then saying, "Love me, love me," and presently opened her own bodice, and gave him her breasts. He turned suddenly and she eased herself down by him on the floor, drawing him on top of her; cozening, whispering.

"Give me your seed, love. Sow the good seed in me, Morven, now. I'll hold, lad, I'll hold the seed, never fear."

And he heard; and by the end turned a face so white and lost towards her that she feared he'd been driven crazed, but soon she was able to match his frenzy in their loving; they loved at last like Titans, gods, matching thrust for thrust, mouth hard against impassioned mouth, as Livia received Morven again and again in royal splendour; afterwards, she remembered they'd trembled together enough to shake the floor, the very house of Mains, as he filled her at last with himself, his seed.

Somehow later she got him on the bed with her. When they came to themselves it was dark, they were naked, had had no dinner, and were still coupling. It went on like that for the rest of the night. During it at times he slept in Livia's arms, then awoke again crying for her; it was as though he could never again leave her body for long. It was as though she herself could never let him do so.

VIII

Morven did not return that night or the next to Malvie. Towards dusk of the first night the wind had increased, and by midnight had risen to hurricane; it hurled itself about the walls of the old house, shrieking and rattling the casements. On pretence of ensuring that all of these were fastened Annabel made a journey up and down the house, not daring to ask any servants she met if they had seen Morven. That he was at the dower house she knew; that he had not come back signified some dire change at the reception of the news Livia would by now have given him. Morven's wife felt her limbs tremble; what would happen? Would he kill her, now that he knew?

But he did not come. For a time she went back and lay on her bed, keeping the candles lit against his return in order that she might see him come, see his face and what it might tell her. She was in cold fear. For him to know that she was barren, had been barren since the birth of Sybilla, that she could never further the design he had to breed sons of his line for Malvie . . . Malvie! Its great age tonight made it groan like a woman in labour, Annabel thought; every rafter and board sounded and whined in the force of the storm. Towards morning it had abated; still he had not come, and she rose stiffly in the cold dawn and dressed herself, flinging a shawl over her shoulders, and went out.

The ground was littered with the fallen branches of trees; in many places Godfrey's remaining saplings had been uprooted. She felt tears prick her eyelids; it would take more strength than she herself had to replace them, and the careless folk here would let them die. She went on, past the muddied pond, down to the place where, between pines, one could see across to Mains and the further bay. On the shore, by now, there would be piled driftwood, perhaps the wreckage of boats.

It was very calm by now; the wind had died. Annabel climbed to an eminence between the trees from where one could look down towards Mains; in the tearing away of branches and leaves by the late storm, it was possible to see clearly. A man and woman were standing together below there, looking over towards the shore. The woman's head lay on the man's shoulder, his arm about her, and his cloak; it was Morven and Livia, in the immemorial attitude of spent lovers; in such a stance they would have been carved in stone or marble, signifying the eternal personal surrender of deep love. They did not move for the instants she watched them.

Annabel turned and went away. She took herself up to a place between the higher pines and there flung herself down on the wet ground and clawed it, and daubed her face; she was like a mad woman, with the tears running down her cheeks making runnels in mud, and her hair dishevelled; great dry sobs came from her. Later, when she had composed herself, she returned to the house without meeting anyone, and tidied herself and somehow got through the day. Morven still did not come. Nor did he come the next night. But by then, Samson had already been in her room, rummaging in the clothes-closets.

She did not herself come upon him at once; the place where she saw him was the same where she had often gone, and went up now, to pass the time somehow in solitude; the Flodden tower. She was in the small bleak room there when a sound made her turn and behold the mulatto, his arms piled high with her gowns and gear, standing in the doorway. She shuddered, and could hardly speak; the sight of him, here or anywhere, filled her with horror. And he had touched her gowns. She stared at the floor, and Samson went and flung the gowns down on the bed-frame in the room.

"You are to stay here," he told her. "Doon has sent word that you are no longer to be with him in the great chamber."

She lifted her head to watch his retreating back, feeling unable to speak yet or move. Later he came back with more of her gear, though not all, and directed a servant to make up the bed with feather-ticking, blankets and linen. That night she lay in it along like a dead thing, waiting for the sounds to come which would show that Morven had returned. But nothing disturbed Malvie night or day, and it was not till the following evening that Annabel received some word; she was expected downstairs at dinner. She put on a gown of grey satin, dressed her hair herself and went down. She was still not aware of any particular emotion; perhaps it had been wrung out of her that time among the pines, and now she could feel hardly anything any more.

The food was already on the table when she went in; an air of disarray still prevailed, as it had not done in Godfrey's time; the meat was carved in great chunks, and served carelessly, littering the surface of the table already with crumbs and fragments. The candles guttered unevenly; the shadows they flung picked out objects in the room, the thrust-back chairs, old Kitty who had already come in despite Morven's banishment and had lurched to her place, and was shovelling some mutton into her mouth with her good hand, for she could no longer hold implements. She appeared oblivious of anyone else at the table, conscious only of her food, like a greedy child. At the table also, at its head, was Morven; and by him Livia, dressed grandly with her hair *à la marquise*. She raised a quick grey deprecating glance as Annabel entered, and took her place lower down; it was as much as to say, "Forgive me. I must obey him, as I told you."

Throughout the meal Morven did not address his wife, or Kitty; occasionally he would turn to Livia, and fondle her or signal that wine be poured into her glass. Annabel found she could not swallow food; after making a vain pretence to eat, she drank a little wine and sat for the remainder of the meal in silence, head lowered. This is how it will be from now on, she told herself; I may share a table with him and his mistress, but never his bed. Her resentment already surprised her.

Afterwards, she went alone back to the tower room, knowing Kitty also had gone to her quarters. The polite custom of withdrawing for the ladies, wine for the men, and tea together afterwards for everyone, had long fallen into disuse. It seemed in another life that music had ever sounded from the harpsichord at Malvie, heard by a polished assembly in the drawing-room, while talk tossed courteously back and forth like a gentle game of battledore. Now, the great rooms were all fallen into disuse, as they had been in her own father's time; and dust lay thick, and she herself wandered through the house like a ghost. If Sybilla could only come home!

PART FOUR

I

Livia had conceived a child on the night of the storm, when she comforted Morven. Afterwards, and ironically, she was to find that the course of this pregnancy caused her, for the first time, discomfort and upset. From the time she set foot in Malvie she was never well.

She had not ever wanted to go to live there with Morven; she remembered telling herself, long before such an arrangement seemed probable, that she would never agree, would tell him he could come down as he always had to her when she abode at the Mains; her own little house, where she could be happy now Morven was again her lover.

But all he would say was, "You must be with me. I need you always," and so Livia had come to Malvie; there was no further argument about it; Morven, she knew, always got his own way. And once there, Livia found how true it was that he could not, indeed, do without her; he would come to her night and day. It was not always to make love; it would often be for some small thing, such as a blind creature needed, that his wife, had he been any other man or Miss Annabel another woman, would have seen to for him. But now she, Livia, was as a wife to Morven, and more; companion, mother, mistress, friend.

She would have been glad of all this, overcoming by its means perhaps, the shadows that lurked in Malvie, so that she herself seldom ventured now beyond their bedchamber and the stairs leading to the hall. But at the same time change came to Morven; swiftly, so that by the year's end he was a man constantly the worse for drink; disappointment, Livia already knew, could do such things to men. Morven could not have his Doon heir; the great inheritance would end for the Doons, with his death. In other words he might never have lived; it would have been the same, would be so by next century, had there never been a man born named Morven Doon. This hurt him more than anything, Livia knew; and he turned increasingly to the bottle, and to her arms.

She would not refuse him; she was strong enough, she thought, to endure his constant demands on her in the great bed, where the tester and coverlet had been changed—Livia did not know of this till a year or more had passed—from the heriditary device of the Doons of Malvie to boast, by now, intertwining pomegranates, flowers and leaves. Had she been told that poor Annabel had sewn them, long ago in the garden of Mains itself, Livia would have felt the more discomfort in Morven's arms, where she sometimes lay, behind the drawn curtains, till noon. But no one told her, and Annabel lived now always in the old tower; and so their love-making could take place unhindered. By the end, and in particular after the Leith venture no longer claimed his attention, Morven had come to pass his days almost entirely between the bottle, the mulatto steward, and Livia herself. And, more and more, his need of Livia seemed to mean the flesh, always and increasingly; by the end he could hardly leave her alone. She suffered it, though she often felt ill, tired, queasy; at other times she saw what Morven must become in such ways by the end, and the uselessness of it all overcame her, and she would give way to silent weariness and a need, impossible of fulfillment nowadays, to talk again with Abel. But with Morven's constant craving for her she could not now go to Grattan; and would even Abel welcome her as gladly when she was, again by now, big with another man's child? She must stay on at Malvie, she knew, until the birth. Perhaps this time, as he'd be here for its arrival, the child she bore would mean something to Morven.

William she hardly saw. He had settled amiably enough into the role of Doon's servant about the stables, now old Sam Aitken had died in his almshouse. After that William had gone off by himself for a while, and when he returned he was a man. It had happened so swiftly that Livia marvelled at the coming of maturity to her son; he was a stocky, thick-set slow, peasant of a creature, with a down of dark hair already on his upper lip and an eye for the girls, though he still preferred horseflesh to anything. He had little to say to Livia or she to him; at times she found it difficult to credit that she had borne him, least of all to Morven. But Morven himself William obeyed, without question. It was as though the blind man filled the place in his understanding that Sam had left empty by death. William's mind could encompass little more.

Sometimes, in the earlier days while she was still active, Livia would venture down again to the Mains, which now stood empty. As soon as she was inside the door the lethargy, the discontent, which weighed her down at Malvie left her, as if a heavy uncomfortable cloak had been shrugged off her shoulders. She would become the old Livia again, if only for an hour; would take a cloth and wipe the dust from the furniture; even clean the sills and casements; sometimes she would scour the empty hearth, where it had always been her pride to have limewash frequently, to keep it white and fresh. There wasn't time to light a fire, though she left logs ready laid; by the time an hour or so had passed, she had to hurry back to Malvie, to dress for dinner. "Set me up!" she told herself, having no illusions; like a dressed-up turkey for Hogmanay, she was, she decided, in the gowns Morven bought her. Some of them came from foreign parts, from places with names he told her, but she'd forgotten in an hour; outlandish places, and there was one robe of China silk with a high round neck and a button to it, and dragons and clouds all over, and the lining was silk also and the colour of flame. It was too grand for Livia Judd; so were the velvets, figured and plain, and the French gown of lace one could see through, as though she were a harlot; no doubt that's what she was. Caps and cloaks he bought her, and gloves, like a lady, and a painted fan, and a carriage for her own use, but she never had much fancy to ride in it. Oh, he was generous, was Morven; he could be as open-handed as he could be mean, when the mood took him. She understood him, and the way his strange mind worked; the bond that joined them held as fast as it had down that first day of all, at the cave, on the shore. She didn't mind what she did to please Morven, not even aping a fine lady for his sake, though it didn't come from the heart, not that part of it. The thing she minded most was hurting Miss Annabel.

"Night after night we sit at the same table," she thought, "me like a peacock, and her like a sparrow; one at the head, t'other at the foot, like a dependent. It's not right."

She had spoken to Morven of it; not that Miss Annabel would ever look less than a lady however shabbily she was dressed; her head was set on her slender neck too proudly. "Send me a bite of food to the room, love; you can come to me after, when you've drunk your wine and had your chess-game with Samson. I don't like to sit above Miss Annabel at her own table, and that's truth." And she herself in her gewgaws, mutton dressed as lamb; sometimes, when Morven had men to dinner, they'd eye Livia and, no doubt, make jests afterwards among themselves. But never in Morven's hearing, she thought; never that.

But he refused to hear of Livia's eating anywhere but by his side at table. "What'd I do without you, eh? I like to have you near me," he said again. He began to thumb her flesh, drawing a hand proudly across the swelling of pregnancy which had already begun to show; he was glad, Livia knew, that she'd proved him fertile again so promptly after everything that had happened amiss.

"Annabel?" he said, for he no longer refused to discuss his wife with Livia. "Why should I consider a woman who hasn't done her duty and never can?" The changed, vicious face turned towards the wine-bottle again; his hand reached out, trembling a little, and refilled his own glass and hers. Livia pretended to drink. For the first time, pregnant, tired and sick as she was, she wanted to draw away from Morven. She closed her eyes, swallowing a drop, no more, of the wine. It steadied her somewhat; the thing she must say now always made him angry; well, she'd risk it.

"She's your wife, Morven, and this house itself came to you by her. And she's done her duty, poor soul, as well as she can. That time the baby was born, when you were in Australia—"

"A mewling girl! What odds does that make to Malvie? But for the house itself—" he nuzzled Livia's shoulder— "why, her whey-faced ladyship may bide here; why else do you suppose I endure her under my roof? Go up to bed, love; I'll soon follow."

It wasn't his roof, Livia thought; it was Miss Annabel's, but of what use to say so? She held fast to the table's edge for instants, easing her heavy body to its feet; then swept to the door like a duchess, and kicked aside her train ready to mount the stairs. Miss Annabel had gone, by now, to old Mrs. Bowes, no doubt, or to her tower. She was kind to poor old Kitty, whose attendant lately had been found dead, sitting in her chair. Who'd have thought the old lady would have outlasted her sick-nurse?

The matter of Kitty perhaps rendered Annabel a slight service in passing her days, after the unexpected death of the attendant. Morven announced that he would engage no more women, and that if the cripple's mother wanted paid nursing she could go back to Maddon. "Why not empty her slops yourself?" he sneered. "It'd give you a purpose in life, as you seem idle."

So Annabel nursed Kitty. She had never previously done such work, and to anyone—there was no one now—who had seen her in the old, pampered days of the salon and the music-makers, it would have seemed incredible that she, of the white useless hands and frail sensibilities, should now do such things as she must. For Kitty by this time was incontinent, and must be held at stool like a young child, and have her wet linen changed, and the beds dried out. Later, with lying on feathers night and day, she developed sores; these had to be cleansed, and latterly they also stank, as the poison of decay mounted in poor Kitty. The winter passed, and spring came, and in the summer, Annabel told her again, she should be taken out soon, to see the garden; but there was now no garden to see; the weeds had claimed it, and it was no one's concern to ensure that they did not conquer, Annabel herself having now no heart. She would sometimes stare beyond the window to where the wilderness of docken, nettle and at last willow-herb blew; it was astonishing with what speed destruction could claim its hold, as though no one had ever turned a spade at Malvie.

But she never told Kitty this; hoping that by some mercy the wordless creature in the bed could remember things as they had once been, the clear avenues of wisteria and lilac and the gentle pool, where strange fish swam, and the planted pergolas and rose-garden. She herself had come to neglect the rose-garden early . . . how could she even bear to remember? And Godfrey had died so long ago.

Kitty herself died in the second winter; but by then there had been another call made on Annabel. She had been seated by the old woman on one of the nights when sleep would not come, and the useless lips formed words which were meaningless; sometimes Annabel would lean forward and speak to her of Godfrey, and remind Kitty of something Godfrey had said, or that he had liked or had done. It seemed to bring the dead man nearer; but Kitty gave no sign of having understood, and Annabel's own loneliness pressed in with the night, beyond their single candle. She had not seen Livia for some days, even at dinner; the mistress's body now was so large with the coming child that she could not lace herself any more into her fine gowns, and Morven had at last permitted her to eat in her room. At eleven at night the hunchback serving girl came for Annabel.

"She says will you come." There was no title given nowadays; the women who were all that Samson could employ knew very well who was mistress at Malvie. Annabel closed her eyes; she could endure, she thought, very little more. Kitty's sickroom, with its stenches, often made her head ache, though she was not, as a rule aware of the closeness of it till she had gone out briefly into fresher air. "Where is your master?" she asked the woman.

"Gone with Samson for the physician. He's been gone this hour and more. She calls always for you." A gleam of humanity showed in the obliquely set face, lightening the hunchback's dull eyes for an instant. "She's in a bad way, I'd say," she told Annabel. The other rose at once, and followed her down the corridors, down the twisting staircase, to the room where Livia lay.

The bed was devoid of the escutcheon on tester and coverlet, but apart from this the great room was unchanged. Afterwards it was to astonish Annabel how little change there had been, as though the difference between herself and Livia should somehow have shown more in the furnishings. Here, in this bedchamber, heirs of Malvie had been begotten and died. Here there had been wedding-nights other than her own; her father Philip's, with her mother Grace; and others before them, meek Doon brides who had done as was expected of them, until the day came for strange Helen in her high tower to give birth to Morven. Ah, Morven . . . but all the other women had been duly brought to bed here, beneath the canopy, of Doon sons and Doon daughters. Now, from above the great carved hearth, on the panelled walls of oak, hung tapestries, portraits of Doon ancestors, coats of arms. The faces in the portraits stared down coldly on Morven's mistress, labouring hour after hour in the historic bed. What was she doing here, a gipsy halfbreed servant, not the laird's wife?

But the laird's wife went to her.

"Livia," Annabel said. "Poor Livia," and put her arms round the woman, remembering how, in her own dire need less than a year ago, Livia had done the same. The sweat made great pearls now on the mistress's brow and cheeks. She seemed to have neither colour nor strength left, as if she had strained already to exhaustion. Her eyes looked up at Annabel as a sick animal's will, without recognition, light or hope; then she knew her. "You came," she said: and gave a little sigh. Presently her eyes closed. Annabel wiped the sweat from the poor face with a kerchief, and Livia smiled a little. "You came," she said again. It was as though she had not believed that Morven's wife would do so.

301

"Will you take a little wine?" said Annabel timidly. Within her own mind was the uselessness of having sent for her, who of all people knew so little of the practical side of childbirth; she remembered hardly anything of Sybilla's except the pain or what anyone had done to ease it. She only knew she had been surrounded with care of every kind, burnt feathers in a shovel, spices thrown on the fire to make an aromatic scent in the hot room, and Godfrey, waiting behind a screen where her cries of agony had torn him also apart through the long night.

Afterwards, he'd held her in his arms to tell her the physician had said there could be no more children. But that must have been long after . . .

The wine had come. Annabel held it to Livia's lips.

"Ahhh . . ."

Spasms again, and lastingly; the poor exhausted body endured them. Hours seemed to pass with no further sign, and then again there would come the contractions, the spasms, growing ever fainter. "She is almost done," thought Annabel, culling her knowledge from a source she herself could not remember: had someone said that, when Sybilla delayed in being born? She laid her ear close to the bed; Livia was trying to speak, her lips forming the words almost in silence, as though no sound would come.

"It's bad," she said faintly, "worse than it's ever been, Miss Annabel."

She knows me still, Annabel thought. Aloud she said, "I know, Livia. I'm here. I won't leave you."

At intervals she sponged the other's brow. She did not know what else to do. All resentment, if there had been any in her, for the state of affairs nowadays at Malvie had been purged at sight of the appalling, patient suffering on the bed. Annabel thought of Livia, again by now, as the friendly, taciturn creature with grey eyes who'd been the only companion of her own age years ago at the Mains. That Livia might die now before the physician came occurred to Annabel, who at the same time realised that she herself ought to feel afraid. But she couldn't feel for anyone or anything but Livia. What was keeping Morven and the physician?

"When did they leave?" she asked the hunchback servant. The girl shrugged; they'd left when things got bad, she said. How long ago? She didn't know. Maybe, she added more helpfully, the physician had gone already to another confinement and couldn't be found in time. And the old woman who came in most such cases had an ague, and was in her bed. There was nobody. "Have you hot water?" said Anna-bel. "We must do the best we can."

She tried, in case it should be needed, to remember the things that had been done to her that time, with Sybilla. On the bed, Livia still strained and cried weakly. It had seemed for some time that she was beyond feeling even pain; her body almost a mindless thing, hardly any longer a vehicle for sensation; weakness had claimed her wholly.

Annabel sat down by the bed; she herself felt very tired. That she should be here at all was strange, she told herself; she, Morven's wife. But she was as anxious that the baby should be born unharmed as though it were her own; only he wouldn't ever believe that. He would think, if anything went amiss with Livia, that she, Annabel, had—

"Ahhh," screamed Livia, at last, with the tears coursing down her face.

Suddenly and unaided, the child shot out of her. It was a girl, with dark hair. The birth-cord lay about its neck, like a halter. It lay quite still.

"There's the carriage now," the hunchback said.

Annabel wanted to laugh and cry; the child, the carriage, Morven and the physician, all coming at once, and Livia—But Livia was alive. She turned her head restlessly from side to side as if at once relieved to be free of the birth and to hear Morven. There were sounds of arrival in the hall below; presently he came into the room, with the physician.

"We had to search far beyond Grattan for him up in the hills," he called to Livia. "How are you, love?" Then he raised his head, and smelled blood. "What—is she—?"

"The child is born," said Annabel quietly. She saw the physician, an unknown man who had only lately come to the district, bend at once over Livia, the curls of his old-fashioned wig falling forward. Presently he straightened.

"She must have a posset," he said. The hunchback girl disappeared. The physician turned back to Livia. "A hard time, my lass, eh? But it's all over now." He laid hands on her, to hasten the afterbirth.

"The child?" asked Morven; he looked haggard and old. He had not seemed aware that Annabel was even in the room and she prepared, like the servant, to leave it quietly. "The child is dead," she heard the physician say. He wrapped the dead baby in a linen sheet, having vainly tried to warm it into life by the fire. Afterwards he stated that it had been strangled by the cord; it would never, even with the best of care, have lived.

He added a word at the time about the weakness of the mother, in a low voice so that Livia might not hear. Annabel, waiting beyond the open door, saw Morven fling himself across the bed where his mistress lay, and break into uncontrolled weeping. She saw Livia's hand, her weak tired hand, reach out then and stroke Morven's hair.

II

That was the worst of the labours. During the years that followed, Livia was to have three miscarriages and a further stillbirth; she never bore another living child. The answer, though she did not state it, was evident; Morven could not leave her alone. She had become a drug to him; his disappointments, any aspect of his life, his thwarted ambition, that could not bear the clear light of reality could be forgotten, blurred and evaded in Livia's arms. They were kind arms. If she felt tired—and, as the years passed and her womb failed again and again, she would feel weary, feel the sadness of death, both for herself and Morven and the children—if she felt unduly so, she would tell herself the women of her mother's tribe fared no better, very often. A woman had her man, was faithful to him, took the good and the bad with him, whichever befell; she'd do likewise herself. She made no complaint to anyone; she never sent for Annabel to a birth again. It wasn't fair, she thought, to Miss Annabel.

The brief, single occasion they had again come to one another's aid was shelved, therefore, much as Annabel's earlier expedition to the Mains was never alluded to again by either of them. Annabel, in any case, had other matters on her mind; alone in her tower, except for the times she nursed old Kitty, she pined increasingly for Sybilla. She hadn't seen her daughter since she was a child; it was not considered suitable, either by the Melroses, the school authorities, or Annabel herself, that a young girl should spend her holidays yet at Malvie as it was. Morven made no difficulty. And so time went on, and Sybilla continued to regard Maddon as her home, rather than Malvie. She wrote short, correct, polite weekly letters to her Mama with school-news, but with nothing personal in them; and Annabel, a trifle guardedly as they would be read by Jane Glover and others, sent duly loving replies. It was all she knew of her daughter; she herself was not yet, she knew well, welcome even for a brief visit to the Melroses at Maddon, to see Sybilla.

Kitty died at last in her sleep at that time of year which is hardest on the old and weak, February month, when the ground outside was iron-hard with frost and the sea moaned coldly. Annabel was glad that, as she thought, there would be no need to dig a grave in the frozen ground; Kitty had always expressed a wish to lie beside Godfrey in his tomb.

But Morven only said he had spoken to the sexton, who had allotted a space among others in the churchyard. Annabel pled with him. "May she not be with Godfrey?" she said. How dreadful a thing it was, she was thinking, to have to plead with this stranger regarding the disposal of a helpless old woman's dead body; did he even yet grudge Kitty room?

He did, as was made evident; there should be no more damned intruders buried at Malvie, he said. His speech had slurred by the end and he poured himself copious wine, slopping over the glass a little. Annabel drowned revulsion at the sight of him; he drained the glass and then smiled, showing his teeth.

"If she must lie by Devenham, he may go to her, not she to him," said he. "I'll expedite it," and he began to mumble, as a drunken man will. Why should Devenham's bones be housed here? It was Doon ground, for the Doon dead only in such tombs. "There's space enough in the churchyard for a foreign cripple's bones." He leered at her. "They can go in there together."

She felt her mind and body swaying, as if madness overtook both. "Do you deny his very bones their rest?" she cried, "and here?" It was Doon ground, for the Doon dead only in such tombs. Morven might at any time desecrate it. There was no predicting what he might do. A sudden eagerness came to her to guard Godfrey's body, take it after all beyond the reach of Morven's power: the thought came to her to write on the matter to Sir Hubert at Maddon. She left Morven as soon as she could contrive it, and wrote at once, sending word that very day by one of the servants. She seldom commanded these as urgently; she made the man swear to ride straight to Maddon, deliver the letter and bring back a reply.

It came, before they had lowered Kitty into the hard ground. There was room, it said, and more for both coffins in the family vault at Maddon. Annabel mounted to the room where Kitty still lay in her open coffin, her face brave and garish with paint in death as in life. "Have I done kindly by you both?" she whispered. "Have I? At the least, you will be together."

It seemed that the rouged lips smiled a little where the wrinkles of the years were already smoothed away; but it might have been only the flicker of the candles placed at the bier's head. She herself felt, nevertheless, that the best had been done that could now be, for Godfrey and Kitty.

The cortège set out two days later, along the upper road called Corse of Slakes, used always for funerals. In the way that such things will happen word had got about of Godfrey Devenham's uplifting and reburial, and many of those who had not exchanged a word with Annabel for years, and who would not invite Morven Doon over their thresholds, came mounted or in carriages to escort the two lead coffins to Maddon. A flurry of snow fell as the hearse swayed forwards, making the sky leaden above the coffins, which lay side by side in the carriage drawn by four plainly accoutred horses; in these parts no one troubled with sable plumes. But the woman who had been Godfrey's wife sat veiled in black, in her carriage; as they had passed by Malvie gate, and Godfrey's neglected water-garden, she gave way to tears. It was not as a rule seemly for women to attend funerals; glances were cast at the shrouded figure from time to time, and a few spoke awkwardly to her when they reached Maddon at last and Sir Hubert, with his son and another, met them on the great house-steps. They were given spiced wine to warm them after the journey, then proceeded to the tomb. Morven was not present.

The minister of Maddon read the words of the burial-service, and the bodies of Godfrey and his mother were lowered side by side into the waiting vault. When the stone was replaced, closing the burial-place, Annabel felt a great thankfulness rise in her. Godfrey was safe; whatever befell at Malvie, he was safe forever from malice and destructiveness, and she herself must look for solace elsewhere than an empty tomb . . .

The other figure on the steps had not been Clairette—she did not show herself even for her brother's funeral—but a slender dark-clad young girl, exquisite as an angel. Annabel knew shyness at the sight of her own daughter; they had embraced as strangers. Sybilla was more at home here in Maddon of late years than at Malvie, with its unhappy memories and changed state. She spent most of the school holidays as Annabel had wished, with Cecily and Hubert and their family. Annabel saw young Paul draw close to the girl, protectively, as Godfrey's coffin was lowered and covered again with the stone. Sybilla was in control of herself and did not weep; her conduct, in fact, Annabel thought, was correct to perfection, too self-contained perhaps, like a well-trained whippet or greyhound; but for what other purpose had the child been sent away to school? She would have grown wild and strange at Malvie, and later it would no doubt have been hard for her to learn to behave in a manner which would conform with the demands of the society into which she must one day marry.

On the return journey Annabel felt the memory of young Paul Melrose, and his kindness to the child, linger with her; would not he make Sybilla a suitable husband, and one of whom she could be fond?

Fosse the lawyer had ridden down from Edinburgh, following on the news of Kitty's death. He had not been in time for the funeral.

The jointure Kitty had received by means of Godfrey's will would now revert to the estate, and it was for this reason that Fosse had called to see both Annabel and Morven. He thought, privately, that Doon's wife looked unhappy and much aged; did the blind man treat her well? There was no help for this one way or the other, however; the marriage laws, and Devenham's generous provision, entitled Doon to his due ownership, by reason of the marriage, to Malvie estate. Fosse put the matter of a fresh will forward; it was necessary in view of the naming of heirs. He leaned forward eagerly, his wig slightly out of curl with the journey, his myopic lawyer's gaze shrewd.

"You, madam—" he addressed the wife of Doon, who sat with them in silence, her hands idle in her lap; she had, he thought now, the air of a woman who has long ago lost interest in herself, becoming almost a sloven. A pity, when a year or two back she'd been a pretty creature! But such things occurred— "Madam, you should make a will," he urged her. At the same time he was conscious of Morven Doon, lounging in his chair with a bottle by him. "The question of heirs—"

"Do I own this property?" Doon asked suddenly. He retched a little; the lawyer sat back, offended. It was unpleasant to watch the degeneration of a client, and he could see a difference in Doon from the modestly elegant, incisive man who had called at his Edinburgh office with his coloured servant all those years ago; could it be the matter of continued childlessness that troubled this couple? "You own it, sir, by right of your wife," he said, smiling. Doon then made a statement which shocked him.

"If anything should happen to my wife?" He spoke as if Annabel were not present. Fosse felt the hair on his own neck rise with a presage of danger; he was swift however to cover up the fissure that had appeared in their smooth talk.

"At present, unless Mrs. Doon should make a will to the contrary, the estate on her death devolves on Miss Sybilla. Should Mrs. Doon care to alter arrangements, which have been left at her discretion . . ." ay, and by the dead man whose bones you have sent away, rather than house them here; the countryside was full of that.

"I will leave the will as it stands for the benefit of my daughter," said Annabel dully. Fosse let himself smile again.

"Or legal heir, madam. The phraseology of the will at present allows a loophole, so that should you have a son—"

Morven laughed coarsely. "Have more wine, attorney," he said. "Sybilla—"

"Miss Devenham, as Mr. Godfrey's daughter, is the ultimate legatee."

"As Mr. Godfrey's daughter. It shall be as though she were my own. My dear—" he bowed to Annabel with a travesty of courtesy as though they all three performed at a pull of unseen strings, revealing only prescribed emotions— "my dear, it is certainly time Sybilla was sent home to us. She has trespassed on the hospitality of Maddon too long. You must write tomorrow."

Annabel bowed her head, and did not answer. Stronger than any other feeling, than warning or disgust, was her own need again to see and know Sybilla, to have her daily company. Surely they could not now continue as strangers when the child was older, and the shock of Godfrey's death and the later happenings glossed over, as was always the case, with time, and her experiences at school and among other friends? "And she is so beautiful," the mother thought. "Perhaps even

Morven in his blindness can be brought to understand how beautiful she is, and will be kind to her."

And for the first time, clear in her mind, the admission she had long ago denied herself, over the early years, rose strongly. "She is his own daughter, his own!"

"We must bring the heir to Malvie home," said Morven. He emptied the last of the bottle into his glass, and drank. The blind eyes surveyed them both unreadably.

III

It was accordingly decided that Sybilla should leave school at the end of the current term, and come home. Jane Glover, by now deputy-head, wrote to Annabel in profound disappointment. Sybilla's proficiency at Italian, Jane hinted, and the harp, would delight her mama and stepfather with only a trifle more of finishing, by the summer. Might not permission be after all granted for her to stay?

Morven grunted on hearing the contents of Jane's letter; he was unacquainted with the former governess, and the undoubted fact that Sybilla was her especial pride and joy did not interest him. "She needs no Italian here," was all he would say. As for the harp, there was old Susannah Doon's. It hadn't been played since her day, seventy-odd years since, and the strings were broken. Morven knew everything, every last detail, of what had happened to each remaining item in the house.

Annabel went one day alone upstairs to the attic and cast her glance over Susannah's harp, with its peeling gilt and frayed strings, long banished even by Morven. But hope rose in her heart at sight of the instrument, now that the German harpsichord Godfrey had once purchased was gone. Perhaps if Sybilla were to play the harp here at Malvie of an evening, the sound of the sweet notes might soften Morven towards his daughter, towards herself; there might even be, for all of them, a new way of life at last, a late contentment.

She ordered the harp to be re-strung, therefore, and brought downstairs; and with that, began to grow more critical of other matters; the dust on the carpets and furniture, the change in Morven, the change in herself. One day she looked at her husband almost coldly, as though she had seen him for the first time; was this slovenly man, with the narrow, lined white face and disordered greying hair, and stains on his waistcoat, Doon of Malvie, proud Morven for whom only the best had been worth ambition? And she herself had grown defeated, dowdy, old; when had she last ordered a new gown, in the altered fashion of nowadays, high-waisted, with one's hair cut shorter and brought forward, to display the neck and shoulders? Sybilla would be young, would have scanned the latest fashion-sheets, seen sketches of what they were wearing in London. She would be a carefully-educated young lady, expected to marry according to her fortune and upbringing, and she—

"A young female needs accomplishments nowadays, if she is to find a suitable husband," she said half in apology over the mention of Sybilla's Italian. If one thought of it, why should a knowledge of Italian increase one's eligibility? It was probable that once Sybilla was married she would never be called upon to speak another word of any foreign tongue; with the troubles there, one no longer even visited France as formerly. So an expensive education was, perhaps, less necessary than everyone supposed; but it had been given to Sybilla. Yet who was there, hereabouts, for Sybilla to meet who would be eligible, unless she herself—Annabel's shyness recoiled at the thought—took her daughter to the south, or to Edinburgh for a season? "One must be careful of fortune-hunters," the mother thought. Not for the first time, the kindly, conventional memory of young Paul Melrose at Maddon occurred to her. Paul was well enough endowed with this world's goods not to have to marry his bride for her money; she herself would perhaps sound Morven on that matter at some time, when her husband's temper seemed favourable to any such project. His reply to her statement about accomplishments had boded ill.

"Sybilla needs no accomplisment but one, that she bears sons," he said, and took himself off to Livia. Annabel stayed where he had left her, conscious both of distress and disquiet. Was she perhaps doing a disservice to Sybilla in yielding to her own hungry desire for her daughter's company at Malvie? Would it have been better to risk Morven's wrath, and herself write to Sir Hubert—he was a magistrate, and would know how such matters were arranged—to ensure that, until Sybilla was married, he remained in charge of the girl at Maddon even though he were not her legal guardian?

How hard such a decision would be! "I have hardly set eyes on Sybilla since she was a little child," thought Annabel, and wept. "She hardly knows me, her own mother."

Jane Glover's wishes were disregarded: Sybilla came home to Malvie at the end of that term, dressed faultlessly in a watchet-blue pelisse and matching bonnet, and a gown sewn all over with white daisies. The sight was in itself a delight to Annabel; she tried to describe their daughter's appearance to Morven. Sybilla's conduct was also faultless, perhaps too much so; she displayed no emotion at all, neither joy at seeing her mother again—Annabel had taken trouble with her own gear, and had dressed her hair carefully and applied a little rouge, for the first time in years, to her worn face—nor, which was surprising, any disappointment at not having been permitted to spend even a part of the time at Maddon this summer. It had been made clear, by Morven's expressed wish, that Sybilla's home was now Malvie, and at Malvie she must stay. Any other young creature might have wept, or pleaded; Sybilla did neither. She was like, in fact, a pretty wax doll with some unseen power of correct, graceful motion, as though a clockwork key were regularly wound inside her. This, Annabel thought rather sadly, was after all a correct young lady; the final exquisite product she, the Melroses, and Jane Glover's school had paid and laboured long to achieve. She should be proud of such a daughter; it should not matter that she herself felt a stranger to Sybilla. But a stranger Annabel still felt; and had been—she could be honest with herself in the night hours—since the day of Godfrey's death, when all their lives had altered as though by the downward stroke of a sword.

Sir Hubert himself rode over within a week of Sybilla's arrival at Malvie. It was his first visit to the great house since Annabel's remarriage; undoubtedly he regarded Sybilla almost as one of his own daughters, and was prepared to forget the past for the young girl's sake. Sybilla herself, for the first time, behaved impulsively, and ran straight to the old man and kissed him; her mother had, on hearing his name announced, come down at once to receive Sir Hubert. As he bowed over her hand in his customary grave, old-fashioned, courtly manner, Annabel thought how well he still carried his years. "Cecily and he have in some way grown nearer of an age," she thought, remembering the unusual disparity there had been between the middle-aged bride-groom and his young second wife. In a quiet, unassuming way they had been happy together at Maddon, despite the lack of sons, thought Annabel bitterly. How different her own fate had been! Had she, in fact, at one time despised Cecily Melrose slightly, as a mother-hen, interested only in her daughters and her preserves? Now she envied her. She enquired courteously for Cecily, for the children, and for Paul.

"Paul is as you have always known him," replied Paul's father. "He does not change greatly, either in duty or affection."

The shrewd old eyes regarded her; Annabel knew the thoughts they had were shared. Sir Hubert then transferred his gaze to where the portrait of Philip and Grace Doon hung over the hearth.

"My sister was a good and gentle soul," he said. "It is your misfortune, my dear niece, that in the nature of events you can hardly remember your mother."

Annabel did not answer. They both stared up at the portrayed face of the fair-haired young woman in her yellow gown. "It would give me pleasure if Grace's grandchild might one day marry Paul," said the magistrate in a low voice. Annabel smiled a little; a load had been lifted from her heart, she thought, and yet—

"Would it give Paul pleasure also?" The question was needless, she knew; perhaps she was staving off other queries, to be asked only of herself in the silence of the night. Sir Hubert returned her smile.

"They are fond of one another, and know one another well; more than many young couples starting married life together. Such a state of affairs could conclude very happily." His smile faded and he frowned. "Annabel, could it not be permitted that Sybilla make her home with us now at Maddon? I have heard . . ."

He fell silent. The whole county, she knew well, would have heard long ago that Morven maintained his low-born mistress at Malvie. It was not a place for a gently reared young girl to remain pending her marriage into the Melrose family. "Yet I," thought Annabel, "would like to keep her with me for a while."

She demurred; later, after Sir Hubert had ridden away, the other notion recurred that had disquieted Annabel. Although for her own sake Sybilla would be welcome to the Melroses as one of them, it was as Godfrey's daughter, never Morven's. Was she, the mother, erring in failing to

312

reveal the child's true parentage? Yet to whom would the truth do anything but harm? Sybilla's marriage might be ruined, her dowry sequestered, her fortune placed in jeopardy, her very name perhaps uncertain. She would be a bastard; not even decidedly the heir of Malvie, though that might be overcome in law, owing to her, Annabel's, own subsequent marriage to Sybilla's father.

"What should I do?" she asked herself. The question was to give her many cruel and sleepless nights; least of all could she expect help from Morven himself concerning it. He had never forgotten the grudge he had held all his life against Sir Hubert Mclrose, from the time he flung him the guinea and long before; a mere word of the suggested betrothal between Sybilla and Paul sent Morven into a white rage.

"Who the devil gave permission?" he shouted. "Not myself; and I'm her father."

"Morven, when Uncle Hubert came I didn't say—"

"He came here, eh? Damn his impudence; I'd have shown him the door." He himself had been with Livia, had heard nothing of any arrival. Annabel had known this; it had not, as it never did at such times, occurred to her to disturb her husband. How could she have sent for him from his mistress's bed? Yet he seemed, now, to blame her for leaving him uninformed till now, to have asked no permission of any kind regarding Sybilla.

"She has her portion as Godfrey's daughter. You yourself said so," Annabel reminded him, but he blazed out; as usual nowadays, he was the worse for drink.

"That old hoodie-crow, riding over . . . spry for his years, I don't doubt. Tell him I have other plans for Sybilla."

"Morven—"

"You hear me? Tell him she's not for Maddon. Our gilded lily shall be plucked elsewhere. You thought it was all of it settled, eh? You thought there was no need to consult me, of all people? I tell you, Annabel, you gutless, useless bitch, I'll—"

"I beg of you lower your voice; the servants—"

"The servants," he mocked. "Always those; but they're my servants, and Sybilla is my daughter. My daughter, a Doon; you hear? Send her to me."

"A little later, I beg; you will see her in any case at dinner." He was drunk, she was thinking; he would disgust Sybilla, with his slovenly clothes and stale odour of wine. At night, they would all of them have changed, and—

"Send her to me this instant, or I'll warm her backside as

well as yours. Who are you that you should decide the future of my daughter?"

When Sybilla came he began to handle her, assessing her arms and bosom with exploratory fingers. "You're a young lady, my dear, eh? You're a woman now."

Sybilla stiffened, flushed, and endured it. One must always, they had assured her at school, be courteous to older persons, in particular gentlemen, who were often unreasonable. The members of one's own family must always be treated with particular respect, and—

But the members of one's family surely seldom behaved in this fashion? At Maddon, they hadn't. At Maddon, everything was orderly, affectionate, calm, and Uncle Hubert and Aunt Cecily, and Cousin Paul . . .

Cousin Paul. Sybilla made herself think of him, his kind, familiar face, shy ways, and gentle manners; Paul would never, never use her like this, and this man who was now her stepfather, and also, she knew, Mama's own cousin, was the same who had been present that day long ago in the larch wood, blind then as now and with blood running down his face, and Papa lying dead . . . Papa. He was buried now at Maddon. There was nothing any longer at Malvie left to love; they'd taken even his body from the tomb.

Samson entered the room, and Morven released Sybilla. The girl's blue eyes surveyed both men unreadably. Morven's treatment had not ruffled her impeccable outward reserve; not a single cry had escaped from her.

The days passed. Sometimes Morven would take it into his head to send for Sybilla, and break down her impudence, as he put it; she withstood his treatment icily, infuriating him still further. When she could, Annabel would rescue her daughter, or stay with her; as often as might be she would take the girl up to the Flodden tower, and together they would sit at pieces of stitchery, and perhaps talk of unrelated matters. Their talk was never intimate. Intimacy was impossible, Annabel had begun to feel, with Sybilla; the girl was surrounded by an adequate, polite, protective armour, alike impervious to bodily assault or affectionate, tender prying. Annabel endeavoured in any case not to pry; whatever feelings Sybilla entertained for Paul Melrose, for anyone, must remain her own, leaving her at least such right to privacy. At any moment Morven might send for the girl, or lurch in, and fondle Sybilla, or force her to kiss him, as though she had been a much younger child in his power; but he knew well enough, from his first touching of her, that Sybilla was nubile. The sewing-sessions took place increasingly in silence; there was less confidence that ever between the mother and daughter.

Sometimes, if it were fine, Annabel would take Sybilla out walking with her in the grounds. "Do you remember," she said one day, "how we used to ride ponies together each morning, and often go down by the shore road, or towards Grattan?"

As soon as it was said she could have bitten it back; it was too closely allied with Godfrey's death, too painful. And she herself had not the strength nowadays to consider riding; she was tired, old, ill.

"Yes, Mama, I remember," said Sybilla. She said nothing more.

At dinner she would sit calmly unobtrusive, eating with delicate manners, her eyelashes lowered, not speaking unless addressed. Livia, seated at the table's head with Morven's chair drawn close to hers, might as well not have been present. The mistress seemed somehow tawdry nowadays in her finery, her whitening hair piled up *à la marquise* in a fashion dead with the last king. The firm, queenly flesh had begun to grow blurred with fondling, using, unsuccessful childbearing. There was little talk at the table. William Judd, who by now joined them at meals, ate silently, shovelling the food into his heavy mouth and chewing it slowly. He had lately got a farm-wench somewhere nearby with child. Annabel said nothing to anyone, picking at her food like a bird. Sybilla a disdainful, icy little princess, ignored everything except her own slim fingers and her plate. Outwardly cool, perhaps at such times, Annabel thought, her daughter was recalling Maddon; the friendly, natural talk and laughter, the tales of the day's doings in covert and hunting-field and still-room; the placid golden presence of Cecily and her daughters, Sir Hubert in powder, young Paul in velvet coat and plain-tied stock. How different from everything here at Malvie, the child would be thinking: how heartily she would wish herself back again at Maddon, in security, decency, peace!

So the time went by at Malvie. Meantime certain changes taking place in His Majesty's Government affected, indirectly, events there also.

One day Samson came to Morven saying there was bad

news. The blind man raised his head.

"What is it?" he said dully. Nothing these days had savour; he could smell the perfume of civit Samson used on himself, like a woman, and hear the jangling of his watch-fob and eyeglass chain. He hung himself with such things, spending the money they had made in course of the Leith venture on that and fine clothes, more than women. He wore, now, a coat of fine smooth broadcloth, with his hair cut *à la brosse*. He had agad a little. He consulted his watch with an air of importance. "It is Pitt," he said, "young Billy Pitt in London. They say he will bring in a law to lower excise-tax. That will, perhaps, be the end for us; though not for some years."

Doon did not reply for several moments; he himself had already heard rumours of the youthful Prime Minister's foresight. A government of imagination would, he knew, have made contraband redundant in this way long before; it had taken that young man, who they said was himself often drunk as a lord by day in the Commons, to see the necessity. "Where did you learn this?" he asked Samson. The latter let fall his watch, which swung for moments against his violet brocade waistcoat. "From the news-sheets," he said modestly.

Morven grinned. They both knew Samson couldn't read a line; nevertheless his gleaning from other sources would be accurate enough, and his predictions more so. "You're a canny creature," Morven said to the mulatto. "It was a good day for me when I picked you out of the corn-crock."

"I have been your eyes. I am glad."

Morven rose from where he sat, and went and swung his cloak on his shoulders. "I also," he told the other. "What do you think I shall do now I have heard your news, eh? What would a wise man do with it?"

"Sell the warehouse, perhaps. It will fetch a good price now; the people here, *les gens,* will take some time to find out that they will in the end lose their money."

"We agree in all things," Morven told him, smiling. He made ready to ride to Edinburgh in the coach, taking Samson with him.

Morven sold the warehouse, and the train of packmen and fleet of boats, as a made concern to one of four eager buyers. With the money safe in his bank, he was by the end a very rich man; before leaving the capital, he visited a jeweller's and bought a pair of earrings and a neckllace for Livia, the latter of twenty-four perfectly matched pearls. She gasped when he hung it on her. "Morven, love, these aren't for me."

"Who else?" He kissed her neck; she would look beautiful, he was thinking, like a queen, in the milky stones, with her fine bosom reflecting and echoing their quality. But she drew away from him as she often did now: he frowned. She'd said she hadn't been well of late. Perhaps she should see a physician. She—

"Give them to your wife."

He laughed. "Give them to Annabel? They'd weigh her down; she's a bag of bones and takes no heed to such things." But he felt guilt rise, unaccountably, in that he brought back no gift for his wife, or for Sybilla. And odd life they led here at Malvie, with his heart entirely given to a servant woman! Nobody else mattered. He nuzzled Livia's shoulder.

"Give them to whom you choose; but give me what I ask, tonight." For some time she had denied him.

"I've got a flux. No, I won't see a physician, Morven. What can they do? Later, maybe."

Later. Morven spent the night alone, in increasing discontent; what had his life been for? Malvie was his—the blind man's fingers sought and found known surfaces, intricate carved panels, shuttered casements—but only by virtue of his marriage to a woman who could bear him no son. Later, it was true, his blood would still own it through Sybilla and her children, but secretly, no more; stemming in any case from the hated name of Devenham!

If Annabel had only borne him an heir in wedlock! The boy would have been growing now, learning to ride a pony, running about chattering by his father's side, his small fingers clinging to the skirts of Morven's coat. His name would have been Richard Doon, one day to be Doon of Malvie. He—

Morven gave a groan like a sob. All Livia's children, who might have consoled him in part had died in the womb. He knew why; he'd misused Livia, because he so loved her; why did love do harm? And now, with the increasing idleness his sale of the warehouses would bring, with nights forever empty of landing bales for stowage, men and boats and a murmur of talk in foreign tongues at the base of the Fodden tower, in the quiet hours, he had leisure to brood the more. Black brooding, it was, such as he'd often known when a young man, penniless and despised by everyone except Aaron and Bart and Abel Judd: Abel, who'd given his name, and kindness, to Livia and Morven's only surviving son.

William Judd. "He's thick as a cave-monster," Morven

thought. William had got a farm-wench with child this year, he recalled: the farmer had come irate to Malvie and Morven had bought him off, saying the wench would be as good as ever within nine months, to milk a cow and for every other reason. Within himself, he had felt a kind of pride at the early virility of William. Perhaps . . .

Morven grinned. The notion that had lately come to him was so shocking, in the reckoning of such folk as Madam Annabel, that it would be far worse in her estimation than the time he'd up-ended her petticoats for her in the drawing-room, in broad daylight. This . . . it was incest, she'd tell herself if not him. Her gentility would never allow her to utter such a word. It was perhaps doubtful if she even knew it, but she would know its implication if he, Morven, suggested that Sybilla and William should marry.

He laughed aloud in the night. For the first time since the sale of the warehouses he had some creative, constructive plan in his mind to lighten the darkness, the surrounding unvarying darkness, out of which he must project himself if he were not to sink down to the level of a mindless hopeless thing, a vegetable, a mere existence other men called, by courtesy, a man. The Doon name, after such a marriage, could be adopted without hindrance; everyone knew William's name was no more Judd than any other. They might know, or they might not, already that he was Morven's son. "Let them think what they choose," the blind man thought, while his thin lips curled. "They take no heed of our existence; at that rate they cannot expect to criticise it." His fate, the very fate of Malvie, was his own, in no one else's hands. He would cause an heir to be fashioned, in due wedlock, between William and Sybilla: Livia's and Annabel's blood and his own should merge in the new heir of Malvie. Doubly a Doon, this child Sybilla should in time bear to William; and, by God, he himself would see that he was obeyed and that her megrims in the matter met with short shrift . . .

They must wait till Sybilla's fifteenth birthday in a few weeks. Morven frowned; the niceties of the law delayed somewhat the desired consummation, but meantime he would educate Sybilla—he grinned, for the education Annabel had had instilled into her daughter had been somewhat different, he knew—to tolerate William, his hands upon her, his company, perhaps his kisses. It would all need his Morven's, constant connivance; it would be the mating of an Arabian filly to a coarse, plodding shire-horse, but it should be done; and shire-horses had in their blood the ancient heritage of the stallions who, centuries since, rode armoured to war beneath their armoured riders, and were not meanly regarded by the knights in course of battle . . . The battle! It lightened Morven's darkness to look forward to a further brush, if only of words, with his lady-wife Annabel.

IV

Paul Melrose rode over once again to Malvie, mounted on a safe brown cob. He himself had more assurance than on that previous visit, when, as he himself remembered, he had been little more than a boy. His mouth was set somewhat grimly in his blunt-featured, honest young face; he was perturbed about Sybilla, and despite the fact that he knew his father and stepmother did not approve this visit today, he had come; after all, he was of age now and his own master.

He missed Sybilla, who in school-holidays, for several years now, had been his constant companion at Maddon. He had sought her out at first from a kind of unacknowledged loneliness; Cecily, kind as she was, was not Paul's own mother, and the brood of young half-sisters could never replace his dead brother Peter. He had soon come to seek out the company of the beautiful golden-haired child who had, still, an air of quiet withdrawal, a certain sad restraint, about her; Paul believed that Sybilla had never recovered from Cousin Godfrey's death, which he understood she had witnessed. He remembered, always, the brief sight he had had of the happy family circle that time at Malvie, the day Scots songs had been sung about the harpsichord and Sybilla had run out unbidden afterwards to feed his horse with cake; and as far as he could, had ensured that that time, with its remembered security and unthinking happiness, should not be lost to the girl. There had been nothing noteworthy, nothing spectacular, about his own growing devotion for Sybilla over the ensuing summers at Maddon; perhaps Paul had not himself known till she left how necessary the young girl had become to his own completion. At any rate, he rode now to Malvie, to ask how Sybilla fared; it was some months since anyone at Maddon had heard from her.

There was nobody at home when he was announced, however; on asking for his cousin Annabel, he was told, casually enough, that he might find her in the tower. He left his cob with the stable-boy, and went round unannounced.

He was shocked at the weeds, which grew knee-high about the space of clear grass he remembered; dockens and nettles impeded his progress; it seemed that no one had any care to Malvie nowadays. The tower brooded darkly as always; he called up, then, receiving no answer, pushed open the outer door and went in, and up the stone stairs. These twisted in corkscrew-fashion, lit now and again by small inset windows in the centuries-old tower wall; the stone struck coldly. Paul mounted, and presently came to a door on which he knocked, and a woman's voice answered.

"Who is it?"

Steps sounded; and presently an old woman looked out. Paul's first impression had been of this, and of the way her greying hair straggled unkempt about her face. Then shock slowed the blood in his veins, later sending it racing; this was Annabel. How she had changed!

He let her embrace him; let her draw him into the room. It was simply furnished, with a low fire lit by custom in the hearth; a smaller room opened off beyond. "That is Sybilla's" Annabel told Paul. "I expect that you would have liked to see her today; but she is out riding—with—"

Suddenly she flung her thin hands up over her face and said "Oh Paul! Oh Paul!" and collapsed into sobbing. He stood a little helplessly at first, unused to this even in women; at home, everything was placid and orderly, the worst thing that could happen being when Marian cut her finger, or Cissie misliked the colour of her new pelisse which must be worn on Sundays till she had outgrown it, or—

But Annabel's distress was dreadful, unlike anything he had ever imagined. Did people, one's own people, suffer so? And she cried still; her tears, like the tears of a helpless child, flowed out between her raised fingers and down her shabby gown, staining her bodice, and he—Belatedly, Paul produced a clean linen kerchief, and thrust it at her.

"Won't you dry your eyes, and come and sit down?" he said gently. "Cousin Annabel—you are in great distress. If I can help, or Father—" His words trailed off lamely.

"No one can help me." She had let her hands fall from her face, and oblivious, or perhaps uncaring, of its blotched tear-stained appearance trailed over to a chair, and sat down on it, clasping her hands in her lap. She tried to smile at him. "Ah, Paul, such a welcome for you; not what you had last time, if I remember! I wish we could see you more often; but as we are situated, as I am——"

She looked at him suddenly, squarely, with bloodshot eyes. "Does Uncle Hubert know you are here? Does he approve it? He told me, I recall, when I married Morven, that he could not consider himself as able to visit here any longer, except, of course, in straits. He came once afterwards." She put up a hand to her bodice, fiddled with the laces that held it together over her thin frame; she was like a skeleton, he thought. What had Morven done to her to make her like this?

"Is it straits now, Cousin Annabel?" he asked her calmly. Within himself he felt secure, competent, much older than his years; he could assuredly help this poor ill-used woman. Where was Sybilla? At all costs he must see Sybilla, arrange to get her immediately away from here; it was not a seemly place for a young girl, alone in this tower, or—where was she?

"Sybilla is out, riding with William," Sybilla's mother told him more evenly. "William Judd."

"A groom?" The reaction was instantaneous, not deliberate; Paul's fair eyebrows raised themselves slightly. There were no Judds on the county-list, his expression stated. Annabel spread her hands out, then began to talk; already, since he had come, she seemed more at ease. Her solitude must be driving her crazy, he decided; what was to be done about her? Could she leave the husband, and come to Maddon? Would Father permit such a thing? "He will have to," the young man thought grimly. "She will run mad if she stays here, in solitude; mad and old before her time." And Sybilla——

Suddenly Annabel told him everything that had already transpired between William and Sybilla, and Sybilla and Morven. He listened, while the time went by and, beyond the window, there was as yet no sound of riders returning.

"He took a crop and flogged the pony today," said Annabel dully. "Sybilla was mounted and she—she didn't want to go with William; he——" How to describe William himself to Paul, to underline the loathing and fear Sybilla felt, the necessity, perhaps, of yielding in the end to one who was after all no more than a stable-hand, a gipsy halfbreed, with thick black hair falling over his eyes and a way with farm-maids, one of whom he'd got with child? And William, too, was aware, inasmuch as such a creature could be, of the social difference between them. Doon had told him that he must do this thing, and he'd do it, if he might; nobody disobeyed Doon. But Sybilla was a young lady, and William had no real appetite for the marriage; he grinned at Doon's jests, did his best, rode out by Sybilla's side when the horses were saddled, steadied her with an arm about her when Doon, from his blindness, let go with a cut from the crop against her pony's buttocks, as today, so that it reared and galloped off, neighing, into the forest, with William knee to knee with the terrified girl, and God knew what might happen later among the pines. "But Morven wants it," Annabel said, still speaking as if in her sleep. "He has them down to the hall nightly to dine together, and teases Sybilla and makes her laugh, and handles her in a way he oughtn't and makes William do so also. He's coarsened Sybilla already, though she loathes it; in a little while she won't be able to resist . . . Paul, will you marry Sybilla and take her away? It would have to be to Gretna Green, she's still under age and though you have my consent and perhaps Uncle Hubert's, Morven would never give his. Would you do it? She's fond of you, and you could save her, and— there's the money."

He stared at her. It wasn't, he thought at first, what he was used to, what any of them were accustomed to, at Maddon. Then he found himself flushing and trembling. "Marry Sybilla?" he said. "If she will have me . . . it isn't for the money, you know well." Sybilla was young, he thought; himself, he wouldn't have thought of marriage for her yet; but as an alternative to such as William Judd . . . by God, if he came across the fellow he'd horsewhip him, damn his eyes! Let him show his face at Maddon!

"Go home and tell Uncle Hubert," Annabel was saying. "Don't be seen here by them now."

"You will give my love to her?" He was still flushed, eager; already the conventional betrothed. He would, she knew, do what he could. "I will give it," said Annabel, "and I will let you know. When I send, will you come without fail?"

"Without fail; you may rely on me."

She watched him ride off; a clean, well-bred, suitable young man, the right husband for Sybilla. The money, as he had himself said, didn't matter; there was enough at Maddon, Sybilla would be well looked after, would find happiness of a safe, approved predictable kind. But meantime, there was danger, which grew worse each night. Annabel had not told Paul, but by now Morven, irritated by the child's impervious

322

calm, would come up to her chamber by night, ostensibly to kiss her goodnight where she lay in bed, and once or twice he had brought William . . .

If only she could save Sybilla while there was still time! And the worst thing of all, the unnatural thing, she hadn't, of course, told Paul. For that conventional lad to know that Sybilla was William's half-sister might deter him from the marriage, the suitable, desirable marriage, which must happen soon now, as the child was almost fifteen . . .

Annabel waited at the window till the riders should come home; each day she did this, anxious to be quite certain that, to date, nothing untoward had happened. Sybilla could spur her horse well forward; she was aware by now of the danger. One must pray that everything would be as it should . . . as it still should be. When had a proper state of affairs last pertained at Malvie? She herself hadn't been permitted to go with them, Morven had said that, even were she fit to ride, there wasn't a horse to spare. Soon there would be no room to spare, doubtless, for her here at all, in the place where she had been born; in her marriage which was now no marriage, so that of all she had once owned, there was only this tower left, with the sea sounding beneath, always the sea.

She turned away from the window. Soon the riders would reappear over the crest of the hill, Sybilla still foremost, the wind tugging at the golden curls beneath her hat; William Judd lagging behind. That wasn't the way it would be if he had already had success as a lover. A rapist . . . it couldn't ever, between those two, be love. When Sybilla mounted the stairs, she herself would tell the child at once, today, about Paul. It was certain they would be happy enough once married, two of a kind, those children; and then she herself could accept whatever might be her own fate; it would matter very little, by then, what happened to her.

But the return that day was to be different. Annabel was not, this time, to see her daughter come safe home, contained, obedient, outwardly calm except for cheeks bright with the wind of the ride. She did not hear the cry Paul heard, by chance, as he rode down towards the iron gate of Malvie; or see, as Paul saw, two dismounted figures struggle together among the trees. They were not far off; Paul flung himself from the saddle, and left his obedient cob standing to await his return. The figures were those of William Judd and Sybilla.

The girl was resisting, hatless, screaming; the lout—Paul

thought of him so, with his leathern waistcoat, the odour of the stables that came from him, his tousled gipsy-dark hair, his face loose-lipped and lustful as a beast's, the hands with their stubby, grimy fingers gripping the girl's slim body, while he tried to kiss her, fondle her, perhaps more—the lout had left their horses ready tied to a branch, cropping grass; what had persuaded Sybilla to leave the saddle, to put herself in such danger? For danger it would be, with such a creature; he wouldn't stop at kisses, and—

Paul thought no further. For the first time in his life, he acted swiftly, instantly, brutally. His fist shot out, hitting William Judd full on the side of the jaw; William staggered, and Paul took his other fist and hit from that side also. He found himself punching William, till William's face looked like black-currant jelly; till William, taken by surprise, at last went down.

He lay there for instants, drawing deep ugly breaths, his tongue lolling in a mouth from which blood seeped, then he got himself up; and like a game cockerel, like a good honest fighter in the ring, squared up to Paul, both fists at the ready. Paul would have met him; he himself was the taller, he was thinking. He could give this so-called groom as good as he got, as good as William Judd deserved and had asked for; he—

"William," said Sybilla. Her cool voice astonished both men; they looked round; she had tidied herself and had already put on her hat. "William, please take both horses back to the stables at once, and bathe your face under the pump. You understand me? At once, if you please, William. Do as you're bid."

And William went. As soon as he had gone the girl's courage—what courage she had, Paul was thinking, what cool, undeterred bravery! "She is braver than I am," he thought, "she is wonderful, she—"

But Sybilla had cast herself already into his arms, sobbing "Paul! Paul! Paul!"

If it had not been for Morven Doon, Paul knew afterwards, he would have carried Sybilla away with him there and then, on his saddle-bow, to Maddon. Afterwards he knew that it would not have served. There would have been legalities, feuds, unpleasantness, and she, his love, returned to her stepfather in the end despite all agony. It was better as things turned out. But at the time Paul was angry; angry, foolish and wretched. To be dismissed at last by a blind man, a man standing with his ashwood staff in the driveway, and made to return ignominiously home alone, while she, Sybilla, went back with the white devil to Malvie . . .

That was how it had happened; he himself had been comforting Sybilla, murmuring to her. "We will be married sweetheart. You would like, would you not, to come back to live at Maddon? You could tolerate me as a husband?"

"Oh, yes, Paul—oh, yes, Paul!"

And they had kissed one another; gentle, respectful kisses, such as a brother and sister might also have given; he would make Sybilla endure no more of what had happened lately, Paul thought, for a long time till she had forgotten the horror, till she was content and settled at Maddon as his wife. But she needed him, he found with pleasure; she clung to him. Then she stiffened in his arms, and he had looked up and seen, above her golden head, the blind man standing beyond them. He was not alone; the other, his familiar, was with him, standing as always a pace behind. The black devil and the white. Together, Paul knew, they could overpower him and Sybilla.

He himself spoke first. "Sir, I would have your permission, as Sybilla's guardian, to make her my wife." He would say more, he thought, as soon as he might, about the treatment to which she'd lately been subjected. He would say much more when the blaze of rage had subsided in his mind and he could control his tongue, let alone his temper. He'd already made a sorry mess of Doon's head groom. Damn the groom! Damn Morven Doon! And the mulatto, who . . .

Then Morven spoke.

"Take yourself off my land," he said. He stood unmoving, like a figure carved in stone. Paul answered civilly; perhaps, he thought at first, Morven imagined he was a stranger.

"Cousin Morven, it is Paul Melrose of Maddon, Sir Hubert's son. You know me, I think; we are some kin, and I have asked you, therefore, although it's early, to consider me for Sybilla. I know I—"

"Get off my land. You heard me? If I must say it a third time, I'll set the dogs on you. Sybilla, come over here and stand by me."

Sybilla was trembling. The sensation of the quiet, controlled tremors of her slight body roused more anger in Paul than he had ever known he could feel. He controlled himself also; the man, the blind man, was dangerously mad. That was evident, and Father, if consulted about this whole matter, would— "Do as he says meantime, sweetheart," he whispered to Sybilla. He kissed her, and caressed her briefly as one might do a puppy, or a scared child. To watch her go back to that brute and his minion were almost more than he himself could stomach, and yet for her sake— He would save Sybilla in the end, she herself must know that; he would save her if it meant giving his own life.

Meantime, he bowed to Morven Doon; somehow a necessity, although the man could not see him.

"Sir," he said, "I cannot remain on your land, as you do not wish it; but, I beg you, have respect for the wishes of others, and allow me to—to see Sybilla at times, and write to her. May I not do so?"

Morven jerked his head to the mulatto, who began to move slowly forward. His hands, powerful as hams, were tensed ready to do harm.

"Paul," said Sybilla's young voice, "Paul please go."

"He went; as William had done, retreating under orders. He felt, he afterwards admitted, foolish; the last memory he had of Malvie was not even the slender figure of the girl standing there, but the sound of Morven Doon's mocking laughter.

Sybilla returned to her mother's rooms later. She was silent, and seemed more subdued than usual.

Annabel looked up from her sewing. "My darling, did you have a pleasant ride?"

She smiled, but as always on such occasions, her heart beat loud with dread. One never knew when the thing might have been done, the devilish intention perpetrated. Morven had neither conscience nor heart nowadays. She watched Sybilla remove her hat and, taking a comb, run it through her shining hair. With it about her like a veil, concealing her face, she said,

"Mama, I am going to marry Paul."

That night, as every night lately, Morven came in to bid Sybilla sound sleep. He would go into the girl's room, often taking William with him. They would close the door and draw the bolt; Annabel was not allowed to follow. What took place on such occasions she had never dared ask Sybilla, knowing the girl a stranger to her, not liking to pry . . . to pry! Herself, the child's mother! And Morven's hands, knowing too well how to go where they should not, how to destroy and corrupt a young girl's innocence gradually, to prepare the way. It had happened to herself, with no mother waiting in agony beyond the locked door. It had happened. More had done so, soon enough alone as she had been left with Morven.

She went later to Sybilla, as she would always do after they had gone. The bedclothes were smooth enough, but Sybilla's cheeks were flushed; her eyes avoided her mother's.

"Sybilla—" She herself, fool that she was, could keep less rigid control than this girl not yet fifteen! She herself, who dared not, for the tears in her voice, even ask—

"It was nothing, Mama. They—he did nothing, except kiss me goodnight."

Relief flooded Annabel; she began to smooth the covers, plump up the pillows. It was better, in all such circumstances, to occupy oneself with practical things; either than in weeping or laughter which could not be controlled. Shortly she found she could speak. "Soon you'll be gone," she said, "to Paul."

Surprisingly, Sybilla's eyes filled with tears. "Yes, Mama," She flung her hands up to hide her face. "Please, please make it soon . . . I'm afraid."

Annabel left her daughter to sleep if she could, and that night wrote to Maddon. Uncle Hubert must not, could not withhold his blessing even for a hurried wedding, an elopement unsuited to Melrose dignity. Without a word to Morven, Paul must be allowed to come and take Sybilla away. Afterwards . . .

"That will be my cross to bear, not Sybilla's," Annabel thought. What Morven would do on discovery of the success of such a plot she dared not try to foresee; nor must the plot fail. What did it matter about herself, or about Morven's insane insistence on maintaining, at all costs, Doon blood in possession of Malvie? Sybilla should have her happiness, if it cost her mother's reason; if—as Paul had also sworn for himself, had Annabel known it—it took her life.

V

Morven thought no more of the meeting with Paul at the gate following William's mumbled message; the Melrose cub, he assured himself, would trouble them no further. The impudence of attempting to forestall his plan—like all Morven's notions regarding the future of Malvie, this also seemed dictated by his inward spirit, of habit, unaffected either by considerations of right and wrong or of law—the impudence latterly amused him; then he ignored the Melrose offer as the Melroses had, for years, ignored him and his marriage. Silence, as a weapon, was effective, he knew well.

Forgetting Paul, and with his conscious mind still filled with the prospect, now imminent, of marrying William to Sybilla, Morven groped his way about the house and grounds, as always, daily. It was, had been from the first day at Malvie after his marriage, as though he could see without eyes, know without assistance; even Samson never accompanied him at such times. Morven's mind dwelt on his own death and after, when now—with his plan perfected, this time, it should be certain—his blood, Doon blood, would own Malvie forever. Doubly Doons, the unborn children of William and Sybilla; a race of young gods soon to walk the earth. Good would come from both parents, Morven decided; it was a mating of bloodstock, not only involving his love for Livia, her dear flesh, his need for Annabel, her descent, the final threefold pattern. There was also the physical appearance of Sybilla herself, which Samson had described to Morven. Golden hair, fair skin, graceful slim body, tiny hands and feet; a brain, inasmuch as a woman could have it; all the signs of breeding. Her accomplishments in this way would offset William's lack of social graces, enhancing perhaps only his dark gipsy strength, his physical maturity. With William to provide the stamina and courage, Sybilla the beauty and intelligence of the race, Doons would, once again, become a force to reckon with in the county; he himself would not have lived in vain. That was the pattern. Morven thought again, and smiled as he made his unseeing rounds of Malvie; only he himself, no other, could nurse such a plan to completion.

The Doons! Moneyed, numerous, strong—all this his doing —they should be sought out, again, in marriage by the best blood in the land. Royal blood had mingled earlier; in the days of James the Fourth, a Doon beauty had intrigued that amorous king, had borne him a son, whom her legal lord acknowledged; later their kin had intermarried, keeping the descent pure. Then Charles the Second, on his weary journey north to be crowned King at Scone, had met Isabel Doon, and—But why dwell on myths, legends, the past? The future lay before them with its hope; centring about Morven, where he moved through darkness now, were rainbow dreams of the years ahead. Sybilla would settle down as William's wife, contentedly enough once the thing was accomplished. Half-brother and half-sister? Who was to prove that, or would dare speak of it? "The Pharoahs of old made brother and sister marriages, to preserve the line," he reminded himself, as though a ghost of conscience rose in him.

He never for a moment questioned the righteousness of his cause. Much of the day, now the contraband-men no longer came, he would spend in finding out where William and Sybilla were, commanding that they ride out together, that the girl sit by William at the fireside in the evenings, teaching the young man chess. He would make them walk by day about the grounds, sometimes accompanying them; his confidence in his own ability to make the marriage never faltered by reason of William's slow answers, Sybilla's cold formal replies. Sybilla knew well enough he'd flog her to her wedding, if he had to; as yet, he hadn't laid a finger on her. The birthday was in ten days.

Morven permitted himself a jest. "Soon it'll be one pillow for the pair of you, one pair of sheets; no more parting after a goodnight kiss, only the curtains close drawn about you both till morning." He was remembering, himself, how he and William's mother long ago had lain in a hayshed, never feeling the wind or winter cold, so warm they lay together. If only he could infuse some of his own remembered eagerness, his hot desire, into this young pair! But they were damnably slow. Even William showed little interest.

It so happened that Morven had to absent himself for the best part of a day on some business, taking Samson with him; it was seldom that the house was free of them both. Annabel was in the tower room, without Sybilla who had gone down into the main part of the building; she would sometimes amuse herself by going over the things Godfrey had collected and which were still left there, odd shells, unusual stones, folios of pressed plants; they kept her occupied, and William Judd, who seldom entered the house except at Morven's bidding, would not trouble the girl there. Annabel sat idle, at a loss what to do with her day; these passed, as by custom. She seldom read, and had no heart nowadays to do her embroidery or even—she was aware of her shabby appearance—to mend her clothes. No maid had been allotted to her since the dismissal of Polly Christian some years ago after the quarrel the servant had had with Samson. It was less distressing to contrive for herself, without such women. She was solitary, in any case, and saw nobody; what did her appearance matter? Sybilla, now, was all of her life; to furbish the child with pretty gowns, even if these were often made down from some of her own, had become a pastime, and perhaps if she were to search, today, among her chests and cupboards, and find something, an old paduasoy or Spanish shawl . . .

The door opened and Livia stood there, in her hooded cloak.

Annabel stared; astonishment had taken away her speech, even her courtesy. Although they had lived under the same roof for years, and met nightly at dinner, Morven's mistress and she, his wife, did not ever in these days exchange a word; there was nothing to say, and at the end of the meal Annabel would excuse herself, and go back again to her own place, and seldom nowadays even think of the pair of them, together afterwards in the bed she and Morven had once shared. Those days were dead; why had Livia come? She stood, now, like a figure in a dream, unmoving, even the draught from the staircase hardly stirring the heavy folds of her cloak; beneath the drawn-up hood, the grey eyes looked out almost, one thought, with shyness, almost apology. It was the same look as when she had first come to Malvie with Morven himself, all those years back, after Annabel had bidden her make clear to him that she herself was barren . . . Why had she come tonight? To mock, to reassure herself of her own continued triumph? But one could not be discourteous. Annabel rose, and the two women stood confronting one another. "Come in," Morven's wife said presently, "and close the door."

When they were together in the room she drew forward a chair, but Livia shook her head. "I can't stay," she said, and looked round helplessly. "This place—it's bare enough . . . oh, Miss Annabel!" She stretched out her hands, in an uncertain, tentative gesture; Annabel did not take them. "What do you want? she said. "Why have you come tonight?" There had been many a year, she was thinking, when she had sat here solitary, and neither Livia nor Morven had come near.

"Because *he* is away, and Samson also. Samson spies on us both, always; you know that. I came because—you know, do you not, what Morven plans for Sybilla and William? How can you be a mother and not know? I, the Lord knows, have been a careless enough guardian to my boy, but *I* know; and I'd save him from himself, and Sybilla also." She struck her

330

hands together, and began to walk about the room. "I do know it," said Annabel.

"What can we do? What can either of us do, to prevent this—devilment? He's never been a natural parent, not for either child. I can remember when William was a little boy, he had him whipped till he couldn't sit for a week, and drove him out to Malvie stables. My son was lost to me from that day, only I—I was mad with love, and in that way, you know, I still love Morven. No woman but can help loving him, when he—" She looked at the other, and remembered who she was. "How can I say all this to you—I, who've robbed you?"

"You have taken nothing that was mine. He never cared for me except as a means to Malvie." Their talk was, she knew, not that which should be between a wife and mistress; but when had their relationship ever been other than strange? She had always felt it impossible, within herself, to hate Livia. Now, despite everything, she felt inclined to trust her; before the other woman left tonight, she knew already that she would do so.

She hardly debated with herself whether or not to reveal her plan that Sybilla should be married as soon as possible to Paul Melrose, and that Paul was willing and would help them, even despite his father. Sir Hubert had replied to her, it was true; but his letter had committed him to nothing, had promised nothing, was the statement of a cautious, legal-minded man who would put no simple word on paper that might later be used against him to his detriment. To rely on Uncle Hubert would be impossible, as things were; but Paul . . . and with Livia's help. . .

"What can you do in the matter?" she asked the other woman, after telling her, very briefly, of Paul's recent visit, and of the arrangement they had both made. "Sybilla's very young . . . and if I were to go away with her, Morven would follow at once. I know well enough; he watches like a hawk, eyes or none, when he thinks any plan of his own is being crossed." She closed her eyes, remembering the boat that had waited below the shores of Malvie, cruising and biding its time till she herself, forgetting for an hour, should have come out alone to the rose-garden. And before that he had watched and planned the downfall of Godfrey, striking through his young sister, through herself, through every means available to his mind, even through years of enforced absence.

"We must prevent him," said Livia. "I—I believe I can help."

"How? Samson's about, remember; he will tell him if—"

"I do not mean that. I think you yourself should stay here; let me—if you will—take Sybilla to her husband. It will not be noted if *I* go away, for an evening." Livia smiled wryly. "Lately I've told him—oh, it has sometimes been true—that I need the physician, and am not well. I don't, truth to tell, need physic as often as I say I do; but since this last whim of Morven's I find I cannot readily be his bedfellow. He thinks I have a flux, that it's the change that comes to women. He won't think anything if I go away with the carriage, and if Sybilla joins me at a certain place, say the dower-house, then—"

"What about William? William comes up here, with his father, at times. Together they . . ." But she could not bring herself to say what it was that William and Morven contrived together in Sybilla's room and, no doubt, elsewhere; made ready, with an unwilling bridegroom and an unwilling bride, for the consummation as soon as might be? If William himself had not been so unwilling and had not had to be cajoled, accustomed perhaps, the thing would have happened by now, not stopping at a goodnight kiss.

"Take her away," she found herself saying desperately to Morven's mistress. "Take her . . . I will send Paul a message, and he will come."

"You are sure he will come? He will come without fail? If not, what will become of us, and of her? *He* can be ruthless; there is nothing, even that he thinks he loves, that will stand in his way. I doubt if even Malvie itself would survive if it interfered in some manner with the pattern he has planned for his own life, for all our lives." Livia shivered, and where she stood nearby the firelight Annabel saw, for she seldom looked directly at the other woman, that the flesh of her face nowadays was puffed and slackened, that of her body also; a woman too much used, night after night, so that every living child she should have borne Morven had died before birth, except one.

"What about William?" she asked, having assured the other that Paul would not fail. If that happened, if some accident had occurred meantime to Paul, the alternative was to send Sybilla on to Maddon, to ask them to shelter her there, and later perhaps herself join the child, but not yet; her own life, despite herself, was still bound up with Morven and with Malvie, like some poor lichen clinging to familiar rock. She could not summon the will to leave it, or him. What kind of creature was she? To endure, as she had always endured; and with more, no doubt, to come.

"I will engage that William is elsewhere that night," said William's mother. "There is still one thing that can move him," and she smiled a little. "You yourself . . . what of you? It will be your part to stay here . . . and if Morven comes he will be angry—and if he follows at once, how can we escape him? Maybe it'd be better if I did not take the carriage, if you told Mr. Paul to meet us near at hand, and then all that is to be done is for me to get back on foot, and pretend I know nothing." The grey eyes looked at Annabel with panic in their depths. "It's a queer thing how a blind man can make two women afraid," said Livia. She had stopped her walking up and down. "What should we do, what's the best to do? I'm in fear for you, and more for Miss Sybilla; but she's young, and her life must not be ruined for his whims; all else should go by the board for that, no doubt."

"I will contrive that he does not follow, till there is time for you to have got her safe to Paul," said Annabel. An access of strength rose in her that she had not known in all the years since Godfrey's death, perhaps even since. In the early days of her first marriage she had struggled against the physical distaste which must be overcome, in the search to give Godfrey happiness. Now Godfrey's daughter—she still thought of Sybilla as his—was in danger. She owed it to Godfrey, he would have wished it, that this thing should be brought about. She'd contrive it somehow; when Morven came up, as he always did, to look for Sybilla at night before she slept, he must be prevented, in some way, from knowing that the child was no longer there. The time between the ending of dinner and the bedtime visit was all they would have, Livia and Sybilla between them, to slip away; on foot would be best, she'd send word to Paul, by reliable means, some means she could trust, to be ready.

"I will arrange it," she said to Livia. As the other prepared to leave Annabel held out her slender hand. "It's been an odd coil, has it not, between us both? Yet I do not believe that one of us would ever refuse to aid the other, in dire need."

"You aided me at a time I well remember," said Morven's mistress, "and if you ever again need aid, in your turn, I'll give it if I can."

Not of the sort I gave, thought Annabel wryly. She held the light so that the other could walk down the twisting stairs without stumbling. Then she went back to the room to await Sybilla. There was always anxiety in her mind until

333

she heard the girl's footsteps and her voice. Once Sybilla was Paul's wife, he would guard her well. There would be an end to that gnawing of malaise, at least.

VI

To say that William Judd felt affection for his true father would have been inaccurate. He feared Doon, obeying him as everyone did. Since the flogging William had had administered in his boyhood—it hadn't been the last, but for some reason it had changed him from the child he had been to the man he became—since that, he had trusted no man and loved only one, Sam Aitken the groom who was now dead. Sam had taught William, besides horse-lore, his own peculiar qualities of self-sufficiency and distrust, particularly of women. William's needs for women were therefore entirely physical. He still recalled, with mild pleasure, the ready and willing young farmworker he had got with child; but if anyone had suggested that he must marry her he would have made off, for a while, beyond the county-boundary till all the fuss was over; he wanted nobody as a lifetime's companion.

Still less did he want Sybilla. This latest command of Morven Doon's, that he must go up her—William in his own mind thought of the matter as simply as that, and the marriage-service itself was beyond his reckoning and the prospect filled him with disquiet—was the most difficult yet. William had performed many feats for Morven which most young men would have found hard, if not impossible; he had thought nothing of ascending and descending the steep shaft below Malvie tower, frequently with bales balanced on his shoulder, agile as an ape. He had seen to stowing, unloading, under the very eye of a customs-officer looking out to sea, while William laboured quietly under his feet at the cave-mouth; other times he'd taken out a small boat in the dark of the moon, to guide Dutch Pete and others ashore, without any light. He would do all such things, without complaint and without fear, for he had none. But to go up Sybilla herself was a different matter. She was, William knew, a young lady;

334

she made him feel uncomfortable. He wasn't used to such folk, or to their talk. Talk was hardly ever necessary to William; it was the unnatural quality of the silence during one of his enforced pony-rides with Sybilla that had caused him, the day Paul Melrose came, to drag her at last out of the saddle, and start to use her as he had, at the beginning, used the farm-wench. He hadn't been able to put up with the continued silence, and young Miss looking down her nose above the sound of ponies trotting; by the end, it was his own nose that had suffered, but he didn't bear Mr. Paul any grudge. Such folk—through a haze of blood William had already been able to assess the situation for himself—such folk as Mr. Paul and Miss Sybilla would be happier together by far, in church or out of it, than the likes of himself. He'd gone away to bathe his face under the pump, as Miss Sybilla had told him to; it was the best thing, and saved further argument.

But Doon had been very angry.

"It's a laggard lover you are!" he had taunted William, having heard from the mulatto steward about William's black eye and swollen jaw, and thereafter dragged the full story out of his son. After that, William had been made to accompany Doon upstairs to the tower most nights, to bid good-night to Miss Sybilla as she lay in bed. Doon was right in that the sight of her disrobed, the familiar handling of her soft flesh through her shift and the feel of her cheek beneath his lips, would banish Willam's shyness enough to make the male part of him, never laggard, eager to do more. But always the thought—and when William had a thought at all it was deliberate, slow, and eradicable—the thought of all his life as Miss Sybilla's husband, cooped up here at Malvie, never getting away again to the packmen or the tinkers or the horse-dealers or Dutch Pete—Pete had promised to take him on a voyage, and show him the flat canals and the islands, and the fine big breasts of the women of Holland and their backsides, in seven petticoats—all this, and the thought of being, as Doon said, the laird of Malvie in time, with the county calling daily in their carriages, depressed William more and more.

But he did not dare say any of it to Doon. He helped him, as best he might, to initiate Sybilla in part; unmoved by the girl's flushed cheeks, her averted eyes, her loathing.

As for his mother, William had half forgotten her; she no longer meant anything to him, except as Doon's whore. Everything centred on Doon; nobody had wishes, intentions, which conflicted with the blind man's. Even Samson, who was omnipotent, whose eyes were everywhere, who appointed and dismissed the servants, who knew every least thing that went on at Malvie, obeyed Doon. Doon, in his way, was like a god; a silent, moody, sightless and frequently drunken god, but one whom no one would think of circumventing, certainly not of disobeying.

Therefore when Livia took her son aside and told him a thing he must do, and that Doon must not on any account know of it, he could hardly credit his hearing. When he did, he stared at her, his mother. Those days at the Fleece, that William could still remember, seemed far off now, in another life. She spoke more like the mistress of the Fleece again at this moment, with independence and assurance. She had a purse of money, which she gave William.

"Take yourself off," she said, "tomorrow night and the night after, and spend it as you choose; don't be seen here, or return here, till the day following. Beat you? Ay, he well may—" for Morven had not, by way of Samson, spared the rod on occasion, even now that William Judd was grown to full man's stature and could, if it had occurred to him, have given blow for blow, but he had never done so. "You'll need to risk it," said Livia. "There's enough in there to be worth a beating." William opened the purse and looked, carefully as he had once bitten sixpence; it was true, there was enough.

"There's more where that came from, unless you show yourself again too soon. Remember, William lad, nobody must set eyes on you; make yourself scarce, and never tell a soul it was I who said it." She waited motionless where they had stood talking; for once, with rare imagination, it occurred to him that she was a witch, with fire behind her eyes. "Where am I to go?" he said sullenly; but he had taken the purse, and stowed it away in a pocket of his leather coat.

Livia laughed wildly. "You're a grown man, aren't you? Go where you please; go to a whore, to a tavern, to a horse-fair, to hell. What do I care where you go, as long as I don't set eyes on you for the next two days, or better still for three? Go your way," and she gave him a little thrust, and vanished inside the house again. William stood gaping after her for a moment, then shambled off before Samson should take note of him, and want to know where he'd got the money. Samson wanted to know everything. The sky had turned leaden meantime and it was growing cold; he himself could have used better weather for being thrust outdoors. He'd take one of the horses from the stables for his journey; as well be hanged for a sheep.

VII

The cold hardened to intensity and the roads were rimed with frost. Annabel was filled with apprehension about Sybilla's journey in the carriage Livia had after all decided to take, stopping for them outside Mains later that night in order that Morven might know nothing. They themelsves would have to hasten down, after dinner when it was already growing dark, through the woods to the lane, then along it to meet the carriage. What if the wheels slid on the icy road to Gretna, along which Paul would of necessity come? She herself never doubted Paul; the danger was chiefly at this end, in getting the child away from Malvie. If Paul failed, for any reason, Livia would take Sybilla on to sanctuary at Maddon. But it would have been better to have the knot already tied so fast that even Morven could not unravel it; that meant a consummation at an inn. She herself must stay here, to keep him from following; how this was to be done was not yet clear; she must work such matters out as they came. She prayed, meantime, that all would go as it should, and the Gretna smith would marry Paul and Sybilla as he had married a hundred eloping couples, and afterwards they would stay overnight at the public inn before returning to Maddon. Was Uncle Hubert apprised? Annabel could not tell; but it was unlikely so dutiful a son as Paul had failed to give some inkling to his father.

Dinner passed unbearably slowly. It seemed as if Morven would sit forever at his meat, conveying it slowly to his mouth and turning, often and at length, to the mulatto steward who waited as always behind his master's chair, ready with wine, ready to listen, ready to advise while, at the same time, making it clear that the decision had been Morven's own. Samson, Annabel thought again, was less of a servant than a familiar spirit, like the genie of the old tale. Where he slept, where he ate, she had no notion; it was not in the servants' hall: the servants went in fear of him, even when he selected a mistress from among the maids. Possibly he took a collation in his rooms. He was, as far as could be, his own master; any wish of his was law at Malvie.

"Where is William?" asked Morven suddenly. No one answered, and shortly he turned to talk of other things. It was not notable for William to absent himself without warning; he had the roving instinct of his strain of gipsy blood; when he chose to go off, he would go, and ask nobody; later he would return, not saying where he had been. Even his mother was assumed to know nothing of his movements. The moment of danger passed; the candles burned lower.

Annabel had closed her eyes, unwilling to look any longer at the scene which had grown so familiar night after night. The fact that Morven had known William was not at table did not surprise her: Morven by some means never failed to be aware of such things. She found herself unable to watch the inevitable figure of Samson, the blind figure of Morven. She dared not even stare towards Sybilla's young, bright fairness in the light of the candles; it might betray, by some emotion she herself showed, that it might be long, very long, before she saw her child again. Could the plan even yet fail? By tomorrow, she prayed and hoped, Sybilla would be Paul's wife. The child would have her own establishment at Maddon; there could be no fear or uncertainty for her future, her happiness, in a house where she was already so well loved. It was the best thing for Sybilla, and yet, and yet! "I have known her so little," the mother thought. Since Godfrey's death there had never been complete trust between them.

But Sybilla must trust her mother now. An hour later, when it was dark, they stole together out of the tower-entrance, both wrapped warmly in furred cloaks and hoods, with a single valise only for Sybilla; the night embraced them, and almost at once Annabel felt herself stumble, for the ground was rough and she dared not yet light the lanthorn. She suppressed a gasp of pain; her ankle was twisted. "It is nothing," she whispered, as Sybilla turned; "go on."

She made herself forget the pain as they made their way down among the trees; this was the place where, long ago as it seemed, she'd stood one day and had seen Morven stand with Livia, after their night's loving. What would become of Livia for this coming night's work? Would the carriage certainly be waiting? A thousand fears crept in on Annabel,

making her catlike with nervous tension on the walk; she
held Sybilla by the arm, but made no attempt to speak. As
they caused the distance to widen between the great house
and themselves relief came, a little, and it was as if her own
breaths could draw more easily; Sybilla, she felt, was calm.
There was nothing to say between them that had not already
been said, those times in the tower when they were left alone;
she had prepared Sybilla to become the wife of Paul, and
knew the girl was ready, though she was so young. This was,
in its way, as it should have been long ago between herself and
Morven, had Morven been different, had circumstances been
different, and he himself not eaten up with hatred and love,
not for herself but for her inheritance . . .

"Write to me sometimes, my darling." She found to her
surprise that tears were pouring down her cheeks; she had
not felt them come, or willed them, nor could she stop
them.

"Yes, Mama. There are the carriage-lamps." They were
dimmed, in order not to be too clearly seen; but it was true,
they were gleaming a short way off, outside the Mains, and
Annabel's heart lifted in thankfulness. This part, then, was
safely accomplished. The rest she would not herself see;
perhaps Livia, when she returned later, would find an opportunity to tell her of the marriage, and of how things had
fared. She almost ran to the carriage-door stood already
opened, and the veiled figure of a woman appeared within.

"Livia?" In the access of fears which troubled Annabel it
seemed as if some other woman, somehow, might have
usurped the place, might be a party to the plot, to upset it;
but Livia put back her veil.

"I'm glad you are warmly wrapped," she said to Sybilla.
"It will be cold on the journey; I've brought blankets, to cover
our knees, and—" she smiled—"a good flask of whisky."
For the bride to arrive reeking of spirits might give a genuine
air to an abduction, rather than an elopement; but nothing
was said, and Sybilla embraced her mother, then without
saying a further word climbed into the waiting place in the
carriage. The coachman was Morven's; but Sybilla and
Paul would meet at a changing house on the road, and the
man would know nothing except that he must return with
Livia alone. The horses drew away now; Annabel stood in
silence, watching her daughter's face as the coach moved
off. Then it was gone, and the night closed round her. The
pain in her twisted ankle stabbed as she turned away; she
had made herself forget about it in the urgency of conveying

Sybilla to the carriage. If only everything now would go well!

She regained the tower some time later, limping slightly; she doused the lanthorn some way before regaining the house. Once in her rooms, she slipped out of her clothes and put on a bedgown over her loose nightshift, and eased her feet into sheepskin slippers. A fire burned in the hearth. Annabel sat down by it, unwilling yet to go to bed, though she was weary and could have lain down. Perhaps Morven would not come up tonight, as William was away.

The resolution which had sustained her began to seep away as an hour passed; by the end of it, she was in much fear. Was it true that she had contrived this thing, and that Sybilla was no longer in her room next door, being by now, if all had gone well, at Gretna, a married woman? And now she, she herself, was quite alone, and if Morven came had no defence against his anger when he found Sybilla gone. What should she do, what could she say. He might even kill her.

If he killed her, it would perhaps atone . . .

"Godfrey," she said aloud. Often in these solitary hours she would think or speak of Godfrey, when she was alone feeling him at times near her. Godfrey would sustain her, would guide her in what she must do.

For the footsteps sounded now on the stairs. Morven's blind steps, ascending; Morven alone, come to visit Sybilla as he always did, as if in his mind, already sown, there lay suspicion that in some way she would escape him, evade the planned marriage to William.

Morven. Morven, the enemy. And suddenly in that moment, Annabel knew what she must say and do, as if a voice had told her. Her trembling stopped and she was calm. She called out to her husband; why receive him as a stranger? He must be made to feel welcome; time was important; by now, surely, the carriage would have met Paul's own. An hour, half-hour, would make all the difference in the world to the uselessness of pursuit; if no one could persuade her meantime to say where Sybilla had gone, if the child could be thought to be still in her room, for some time, as long a time as possible . . .

"Come in, Morven."

He came, closing the door after him; looking over at him in the light of the fire, she could see how greatly he had aged. His hair was grey, though still fine and thick; he wore his clothes as if they had been thrown on in any fashion, the neckcloth awry, the coat-buttons wrongly fastened. At another time, in another life, Annabel would have felt a motherly desire to set them right, to straighten his cloth, smooth the hair about the thin wild face; but now she hated what he stood for, what he would have done to Sybilla. Triumph rose in her; no matter what he might do, William Judd should never have Sybilla now. At worst, they would shelter her un-wed at Maddon.

Morven had not replied to her greeting; he lurched towards Sybilla's door. He was three parts drunk, Annabel saw, as was customary after dinner. What else could a blind man do but drink? And he was solitary . . . "She cannot see you quite yet," she heard herself saying. Her voice was coy, the voice of a genteelly reared mother observing the conventions; in-wardly she despised herself. "She has taken a purge; it will be a little time before she is ready. Sit by me, Morven, mean-time; will you take wine?"

She heard him laugh, coarsely commenting on Miss Ele-gance farting on a night-stool like other folk. "We'll give her leisure," he said. He turned and, sensing the warmth from the fire, made towards it; fear rose in Annabel again and made her bold. "Will you not spend a part of the leisure with me, your wife?" she said. "I see little of you, Morven, nowadays." She reached out a hand and stroked his sleeve. He felt the touch, light as it was; blind men were sensitive to such things. He laughed again.

"You don't desire to see more of me than you do, m'dear." The speech was slurred; she made herself sigh. "Ah, when do I have the opportunity? You are always surrounded by others; you never come to me of your own will." She remembered, and used the knowledge, that his mistress had denied him over the past weeks; exerting all her own forces, she set out to charm Morven. It was for Sybilla; of all things, it would pass the night.

"Morven, Morven." She sighed again, and rubbed herself against him; her body, soft and without tight-lacing under the gown, she knew, would excite him, flown as he already was with wine. Presently his hand came out and fondled her thigh. "You're a bag of bones," he sneered. "I've always said that; no flesh on you to speak of."

"You could cover my bones, if you chose. Try me." she heard herself speaking like a whore.

"Eh?" He was confused, still part drunk. knowing only that a woman's willing body was beneath his hand, that a woman rubbed herself caressingly, unceasingly against him.

341

The soft mass of her hair touched his face; he could not picture the grey in it. Annabel; who'd have thought it? But she had used, when she was young, to be a hot piece, by the end; he'd taught her well. Did she still remember? It would be amusing, perhaps, to find out; remembering all the years she'd spent up here, a no-wife, alone in her tower, seeing no one. "So your little tail remembers me, eh?" he said thickly. He made ready to take her, not displeased at the prospect. As she had suspected, it was some time since he had had a woman.

He had already begun the business coarsely, contemptuously, meaning to finish soon; but to his surprise he found he had unleashed a tigress. The passionate woman beneath him—he no longer thought of her as Annabel, his meek downtrodden wife—clung and demanded; she would not let him go. He responded, finding excitement rise in him as it had not done, perhaps, since he was a young man; the late years with Livia had been like man and wife, an easy accustoming; not this unpredicted storm, this whirlwind; it was as if his very bones were turned to water, only his member itself remaining hard and urgent; he thrust into her, and the woman received him, and demanded more, and again more, and he gave her what she asked. Together they made one flesh, and the flesh melted presently to a rushing, merging torrent; he took Annabel again and again, and he himself was by now no longer a person but transformed, translated beyond himself. Afterwards he would remember it as if it could not have happened so between them; it was incredible, a dream without substance, and he and she no longer their everyday selves, but changed in some manner beyond all understanding. He was no longer even aware of time. She herself was obsessed with the growing need to give to him, and give.

It had started when they first lay together, stemming no doubt from the early need to protect Sybilla, perhaps even to serve Godfrey himself in such a way. But before the end she had forgotten everyone but Morven, Morven whom she had once loved physically as she would never again love any man. Her body now was Morven's, the opened crying womb discrete from her known, humdrum daily life, her assumed passivity. She received Morven Doon as never before, never again, any being. Afterwards she remembered nothing further, and sank into a healing sleep.

"Where is she? Where is she?"

She could hear the voice calling, then felt Morven's hands

342

on her again. She awoke from the sleep she had been in, a sleep where there had been darkness and peace; now, waking to the cold hearth, the grey light of dawn, she remembered many things, among them the fact that he must have gone, at last, to look for Sybilla, and would have found an empty bed. Triumph claimed her, even before fear; it had been accomplished, it was morning, Sybilla by now was safe.

She did no answer Morven for moments; she lay where she had been, seeing his figure taut against the pallid light from the window; his face was lined and unshaven, his hair wild. She wanted to laugh suddenly. "She is gone," she told him calmly, blinking up at him; in spite of everything, she felt hardly awake. "She is—"

"Where? Where?" He was like a madman, shaking her; at such times, when his will was crossed, she often thought he might be mad. She heard the cold sanity of her own voice, replying. "She is married to Paul Melrose. They are many miles away by now. They were married at Gretna yesterday."

Then, in the midst of her triumph, he struck her; struck her as no man should strike any woman. His blindness made him rain blows on any part of her body he could reach; he crashed fists into her eyes, her mouth, her bosom. She struggled up, and tried to stand; but he felled her to the floor, and once there kicked her in the belly, as though she were an inert burden, something in his way. Annabel rolled aside in agony, blood streaming from her mouth and nostrils. She could no longer scream. He bent and seized her hair, dragging her by it to the door.

"Married—married—and yesterday, and no word to me!"

He kicked her downstairs. Outside the snow had begun to fall, relieving the night's bitter cold a trifle; it was still very early morning. When he had punched and kicked the woman's body out of doors, he let it lie there, in the falling snow; presently he felt the latter on his face. He was sobbing, less with anger now than self-pity. To do such a thing! And to him who was blind, blind . . .

He stumbled off. After a little Annabel raised herself in the snow. Her eyes were swollen and she could see nothing for blood and pain; he had broken some of her teeth, she thought. She could not even rise; painfully, encroaching inch upon inch along the ground, she made herself move a little; it was better to move, she had heard someone say, in the snow; otherwise one might die of cold while still feeling warm. To die quite yet would be unsuitable . . . to die, in the snow here, in only a nightshift; herself, the lady of Malvie.

After minutes she ceased to move. The snow fell for a time in small flakes, then stopped.

VIII

Livia had dismissed the Malvie carriage at the dower-house lane end. She had several reasons for doing this, although it was by then very early morning; firstly she wanted leisure to think, and the crisp bitter air drove away the weariness of the night's journey when, for lack of leisure, she had not slept. She thrust a guinea into the coachman's hand, hoping it would induce silence in him if he encountered Samson or Morven. What to say in face of any questioning of herself she had not decided.

She heard the coach-wheels trundle away, already crunching in the depth of snow which had fallen; it was unusual here, so near the sea. She huddled her furs closer to her face and walked on up towards Mains; it was, and this was her second reason, more convenient to go in this direction straight to Annabel, in the tower, and tell her what had occurred, and that the marriage had taken place as planned, without a hitch. Looking back on the conspiracy that had had to precede it, the hasty smuggling away of the little bride, this seemed incredible. Livia smiled with pleasure as she remembered the manly, protective aspect of Paul, the bridegroom. He would make Sybilla a good husband. They had been married by the smith at Gretna, in the small room where numberless other couples had stood together. Afterwards they had driven away to a nearby inn. Tomorrow they would return to Maddon. All that was accomplished, and she herself had had a glimpse of a kind of loving which, except for Abel, she had never known; a cherishing, a mutual devotion, great gentleness, one to the other. Paul would never seize Sybilla in the way Morven still, after all these years, often seized and fell on herself; his need of her was still urgent and passionate, entirely without consideration, selfish perhaps; but they had had moments together that the tame folk of this world would never know. "Whatever happens between us now, I've known that," she told herself, walking on through the snow-filled woods. The trees still held their night's burden of whiteness and had not yet shed it with its own weight; it was still too cold. The Mains slept emptily, its windows dark.

She was aware of a need to talk with Annabel about Morven, about his probable reception of the news of Sybilla's marriage. Was it beyond possibility that he would be driven insane, at least for the time, and would it be safer if they were to approach him together regarding it? The prospect had already occurred to Livia in the coach. For a man's wife and his mistress to be in league, regarding the separate salvation of his unacknowledged daughter and his unacknowledged son! It was a twisted, strange situation, but nothing here at Malvie was otherwise.

The great house reared darkly, and Annabel's tower stood with its windows unlit, though it was not likely, thought Livia, that Morven's wife had slept. Poor soul, she would be waiting in trepidation for news, anxious perhaps lest Sybilla should have been brought back again for any reason, or that there might have been an accident to the carriage meantime in the snow.

An accident in the snow. Livia came upon the prone body without, at first, knowing who it was or even that it belonged to a woman. She knelt down by it; and then, drawing a single harsh breath of horror, knew Annabel. She thought at first that Morven's wife was dead. Then she raised the head, cradling the dreadfully bruised face in her lap; and felt for the heartbeat and at last found it, though the body was almost frozen with cold, drifted over as it was with snow like a log lying in the forest. The snow by now had stopped, as though it had also done all it could to Annabel: and as Livia knelt there, the sound of the first sliding weight from the overladen branches reached her, splurging softly on the ground, as the whitened world began to wake.

She found afterwards that she had no recollection of Annabel's weight, of getting her away from the place; she must have half carried and half dragged the unconscious creature. The passage of time reduced itself so that an hour, for it must have been as long, seemed like moments, and Livia had somehow conveyed the injured woman back inside the door of Mains, her own place, instead of Malvie; she remembered telling herself Annabel must never go back to Malvie again. "He must have gone mad," her thoughts raced. "Morven must have run mad when he heard of the marriage." Had she not predicted it?

There were necessaries she herself kept ready at the dower house, dry wood and tinder, blankets and a bed; she laid Annabel on that and covered her with the blankets and then knelt down and began to kindle the fire, knowing that at all costs the sick woman must be made, and kept, warm. She fetched brandy from a place where she stored it and tried to force some of the raw spirit between Annabel's blood-blackened lips; then she fetched water and heated it on the fire, and sponged the swollen face gently. It was so badly injured that the features were almost unrecognisable; the eye-sockets had swelled and the lips and nose were battered, as was the body. As the fiery spirit went down Annabel's throat she turned her head, and moaned a little, then coughed painfully with the burning of the brandy. "It's Livia," said the other softly. It was probable, she thought, that the bruised eyes could not see. "Livia, and you are in bed at Mains. There is a fire. Presently I'll fetch someone to help us."

She had been thinking of the physician; but Annabel began to sob and cry out, and Livia knew that, for the present at any rate, this thing must not be made known. She looked about her desperately. What was she to do with the poor soul? Here, Annabel was as open to Morven's vengeance as if she had remained at Malvie. There was only one safe place; Maddon. But how to transport her there? The Malvie coach, by now would have been noted by Samson, and its return enquired about.

"Sybilla?" said Annabel, and Livia told her all was safely done, and the young pair married. The sick woman sighed, and appeared then to sink into a deep sleep, possibly by reason of the brandy. It was better not to wake her. Livia stood irresolute, wondering if she dared leave the other lying here, possibly for some hours, while she went for a farm-cart or aid of some kind; then an answer came. Beyond the window, faintly, came the clip-clop of hooves; William, returning too soon; but Livia had never been as glad of her son. She ran out; he was passing by the gate, intending no doubt to ride up through the wood, hoping to return the horse to the stables without question; Livia hailed him.

"William! Willam!"

William turned his head in the saddle, blinking slightly; he had had a willing tavern-maid, and too much wine, and his head now was thick; but there was no doubt that what he saw at this moment was his mother, clad in her furs and waving to him, and calling also, from the doorstep of Mains. Why Mains? He'd thought it was empty . . . his mother, he knew, went there by herself sometimes, but not at this time of early morning. He halted the horse, and made as if to slide out of the saddle. Livia thrust him back. "No, stay there, stay!"

She seized the reins and turned the horse's head; it was as though, William decided resentfully, she thought he had no will of his own, not even enough to control his own mount. "What is it?" he said. "I want to go to bed; I stayed away, like you said." There was, he thought, no pleasing women. The tavern-maid had mocked him by the end, and he—

"Turn round and ride as fast as you can, back to Grattan. Waken Abel and fetch back the dray. Tell him I sent you and that it's a matter of life and death. Go, now; don't stay to argue." She gave William's horse a little thrust, as if to speed it on its way; she screamed the message after her son again. "The dray! The dray! Don't waste an hour—a moment; come back as soon as may be. Tell Abel."

She watched him ride off; then went back into the house to where Annabel was, watching the sick woman's breaths rise and fall lightly, more evenly than before. If only she took no harm from the night's bitter cold there had been! At Maddon, they'd nurse her other ills, as soon as she might be conveyed there. Livia prayed William would make haste; that Abel might refuse her request never entered her reckoning. He'd always loved her, hadn't he? And all these years she hadn't ever asked him to trouble himself, except over this. If only he'd send the dray, without stopping to ask questions; if she could have gone herself without sending William, she's have done it. But how could she leave the bruised, half-dead woman, till Annabel was safe in Maddon? "Nor will I," she promised herself. Mrs. Cecily and the old magistrate could think what they liked. For now, she herself was as she'd been long years ago, the maidservant at Mains, carried up Miss Annabel's chocolate each morning. It didn't signify what had happened since, if only Abel would understand that.

He understood. The day arrived, and William and a man Abel had sent as driver carried Annabel out between them, and laid her on the straw covered with blankets. In the early morning, before even the farm-carts were about, the lady of

347

Malvie was jolted away from her inheritance; she knew nothing of that journey, or that Morven's mistress kept watch over her always, guarding her from the worst pot-holes in the road by holding her carefully in her arms. No one noted or followed them; the roads were snow-sprinkled, deeper as they journeyed inland, and it grew cold again before Maddon was reached, and placid Cecily, all of whose married life had hitherto resembled a calm pond, had now two crises to endure there, one upon another; one was Paul's marriage to Sybilla, of which he had sent word already, and that the marriage was consummated and they would soon be home. The second was the unheralded arrival of Sybilla's mother, Godfrey's widow, in no state befitting a respectable woman; it was embarrassing to know what to do with Annabel, and in the end they put her in a bed in one of the upper rooms, with the strange sullen woman who had come, wrapped in furs, and who refused meantime to leave her, as attendant. "When she's up and about, maybe," was all this socially doubtful creature would say; but by the time Annabel was up and about it was beginning to be evident the way it was with her, and that was an additional mortification to poor Cecily. At such an age, and to such a rascal as the husband had proved to be, so much so that Annabel couldn't for her own safety return to him! "And now, I daresay, she will have to remain here, with the new child when it's born," Cecily told her husband, who as he was himself growing old had little now to say regarding anything.

It was, all of it, an awkward enough welcome for a new bride; but as events proved, Sybilla fitted in so well with the way of life evinced by her husband's family that she also, truth to tell, was ashamed both of her mother, and of the situation. She settled down to become an acceptable wife to Paul, as though she had never belonged anywhere but at Maddon.

One other thing occurred. At some time during the first days, after Annabel was pronounced out of danger, Livia begged a lift in a cart which was going part way to Grattan, and later went on foot to Malvie. She walked up past the pond which Godfrey had once dug for Annabel, and which now showed only slime and duckweed; and up to the main door of Malvie, and went in. She found Morven sitting over his wine as always at that hour, and as usual said what she had to say to him in moments. She told him that she was leaving him, and would never live with him again. Then she turned and went out the way she had come, leaving him staring sightless after her. No one hindered Livia on the journey away from Malvie except the wind, which blew in her face and made the going harder. She broke the journey briefly at Grattan on her way back to the Melrose place, where no one desired her return except Annabel, who still needed her. As long as she was needed, she had promised Morven's wife, she would remain at Maddon. Afterwards, she'd return to Abel.

The village of Grattan had very little to talk about, as a rule, except its ordinary day-to-day affairs; now these were much diversified over the subsequent few years. In fact, the villagers neither knew where to begin, nor where to end. It was rumoured—this was the earliest gossip, lovingly retailed by the butcher who had followed Matt Jarvie, and was, like him, by now a kirk-elder—that Livia Judd had settled in after all again with her husband. However Abel made his next appearance on Sunday alone, and sat solitary in his pew, his best blacks by now a trifle rusty, and his big body much thinned since his fringe of hair had turned white. He was the same as ever when folk spoke to him, gentle and courteous; nobody asked him about his wife. It was thought necessary, however, for two of the elders to call, and discuss the matter, as it was one of public comment; and so they did, one day, and found Livia on her knees, scrubbing the taproom floor. She wrung out her cloth and knelt back and surveyed them, giving stare for stare.

"I expect you're after money," she said to them. The senior of the men, who was still Priddy—his wig was renewed, and his teeth wholly missing, but otherwise he was little altered from the man who had visited Godfrey Devenham at Malvie, long ago—stood his ground. That such a hussy should dare answer him, let alone look him in the eye! She should be on a repentance stool with her shamed head hanging, in view of all the congregation, and her back warmed naked with whips, and so he told Livia.

"I've had enough of you and your whips and nakedness," said Livia, "and maybe in the next world it will be less comfortable than you think for the like of yourself, Master Priddy —ay, I mind the name. Your kinsman ruined me when I was a young maid, and I hear they took money and office away from him in the end, for doing the same to others, but they took too long. I'll pay you myself for the sum you want of

Abel; he's in his bed, for he's ill, as you could have seen for yourselves." For the loss of weight Abel showed lately had shocked her; he hadn't, she thought privately, perhaps very long to live, and she knew an inward gnawing trouble often pained him; a cow had kicked him, he'd told her lately, when he was only a boy, and had climbed a wall to try and help her deliver her calf which was misplaced; a daft-like thing to do. "Here's your money," she told the elders, going to the till, "and now get out." She would replace the money later, she promised herself.

"You are residing with your husband again as a member of this parish?"

"I reside with Abel sometimes, and other times I don't; where I go then is my own business. If you want to see Abel he'll doubtless be about on Sunday." They'd never made Abel an elder, for all his good, useful life. No doubt that was her fault for leaving him in an unattended state, half single and half not. Without question many things were her fault. She'd try, now, to make it up to Abel for such time as he had left. But, at times, Miss Annabel also needed her; and then she'd take the dray and go over to Maddon. Abel understood that, and that she might be away for days, maybe, or a week. That time of the baby boy's birth—

She watched the two elders go, black broadcloth backs bristling with import; no doubt everything they'd learned, which wasn't much, would be all round Grattan as soon as someone called in for a joint of beef. Livia found it stifling, a little, after the silences of Malvie. But she'd never go back to Malvie again. Morven sat there, no doubt, now, this moment, drinking, perhaps with the man Samson by him, possibly also William Judd. William had elected to return to his real father after that time she'd left Malvie, and he'd helped them lift Miss Annabel into the cart and had then gone away. He'd say nothing about that to anyone. William said very little. He probably thought less. It was habit, not love, Livia knew, that made him stay on with Morven. He'd been used to the situation for years, and couldn't change his ways by now. Some folk were like that. She herself had been.

Livia dropped to her knees again and began to clean the floor with great circular, rhythmical sweeps of her well-formed hands and arms. It was satisfying to have a job to do; the maids cleaned in their way, but every so often, though Abel said she shouldn't, she herself would go right down on her knees, and get on with a task like this, or with cleaning the window-glass, or rubbing the brass and pewter. Things took on, she liked to think, a special shine when she did them herself; the Fleece itself looked already more cheerful, though nowadays she didn't serve ale again at the bar; not quite yet. But she used her great generous overflow of energy in every way she could to help Abel; it was like the sun coming out to see his face; and she wasn't unhappy, as she had expected. Work was an antidote to most things.

Miss Annabel had almost died giving birth to Morven's son; if she herself hadn't been there at Maddon, Liva liked to think, it would have happened. As it was, the poor creature, whom nobody wanted—her own daughter would look the other way when she came by, as if Mrs. Sybilla couldn't endure the sight of her mother's body growing big with child, when as yet she'd started none of her own to Mr. Paul, and as for Miss Clairette, she was queer these days and saw nobody. Poor Miss Annabel had crawled away, like a sick animal, at last into the little cottage they'd allowed her, on Maddon estate. It was there young Master Philip had been born. Livia herself had moved in and had stayed with the pregnant woman five weeks, during most moments of which Miss Annabel was certain the pains had come on prematurely; as it was, the child didn't come till term, and caused as little trouble then as a baby could, but that wasn't small at the best of times; and with a worn-out mother rigid with fear, it hadn't any of it, been too easy. But he was a fine little boy, and resembled nobody so much as Miss Annabel's own father, fair-haired and with fine, chiselled features, and a plump well-formed body which later would grow tall. So they'd christened him Philip; it was as if the mother didn't want to be reminded, in any way at all, of Morven. That she should have conceived at all was a miracle; the doctors had said it couldn't happen again, but doctors were often wrong. Herself, Livia thought—and Annabel in her ravings between waking and sleep had said a good deal, perhaps more than she understood herself—that possibly, for once, she had relaxed under Morven; maybe the urgency of giving time for Sybilla to escape, to get away from him and be married that night to Mr. Paul, had made Miss Annabel forget her own fears, and caused her to open and to hold the seed. It would never be known; but meantime Morven's wife begged piteously that no one at Malvie should be told; they would, she said, come at once and take Philip away from her.

"Promise you won't tell Morven?" she had cried to Livia,

seeing her stand by the small window, where the light fell on the baby's face as she held him in her arms; from the first, he'd known her as well as his own mother. "Promise," cried Annabel, and turning to look at her ravaged face—she'd never regained her looks since the beating Morven had given her, and never now would; she was become an old woman, grey-haired and thin as a bone—turning, Livia had said sadly "I can promise that, if you wish it. I don't see him. If it's left to me I shall never see him again."

"They will tell him, Uncle Hubert will be bound to tell him," said Annabel, changing position restlessly. It was as if she could take no joy in her child for fear that he should be taken from her. "They shan't have him, they shan't," she cried, and held out her arms for her baby, and Livia handed him to her at once; but he started to cry, and had to be given back again. Annabel had, again this time, no milk; but they'd found a wet-nurse for Philip Doon.

Sir Hubert Melrose however made no move to inform Malvie of the birth, which was surprising to more folk than Livia. In fact, it was kept very quiet; few people now saw Annabel, or visited the cottage at the further edge of Maddon ground. The old man himself rode over one day. He bent his head to enter at the low lintel, and Livia, who was present, curtsied; she was, as she'd been on first seeing Abel again, shocked at the changes time had wrought. This old gentleman wouldn't last out the year, or she'd be much surprised; his thin face was the colour of a plum, covered with tiny broken veins, and his eyes were suffused with blood, and his hands trembled. He came and bent over Philip who lay in his cradle, and Philip yawned in Sir Hubert's face; that made the old magistrate smile, and he said, to both the women.

"You have a handful there; when it comes to his having to have a tutor, maybe he can share one at Maddon." That was his way of saying that he hoped Paul and Sybilla would soon have children, and also that there was no need for young Philip to leave here. He looked grave when Morven was mentioned, but said little, except that he would certainly keep silence. Shortly after that he left. Hearing him ride off, Livia reflected that it was queer, come to think of it, that Sir Hubert had not made any effort already to inform Morven. This was, when all was said, the heir of Malvie, and Doon of Malvie should know of the existence of his son. She downed the feeling of pity which rose in her, despite everything, for

Morven. Morven had forfeited pity and consideration from anyone. She herself would have nothing more to do with that matter. She turned again to Morven's son; and outside, the ivy which grew on the cottage wall tapped against the tiny window. Come spring, they'd have it cut; perhaps Miss Annabel would make a garden again out of the kerchief-sized patch of rough grass there was, with a little stream winding at the end by the far wall. They'd have to keep watch, always, that Philip didn't fall into the stream, when he was older, and running about. Perhaps a set of reins, to hold on to with one hand while one got on with one's tasks with the other, would keep him out of danger.

She was constantly planning for Philip, sewing for Philip, playing with him, later teaching him rhymes and numbers. Anyone would think he was her child and Morven's.

Time had passed in such ways. Philip Doon by now was four years old.

IX

Annabel was weeding her cottage garden. Every now and again she would straighten from the task and ease her back, which grew stiff with constant bending; and also the other, more insidious pain in her left breast. The latter was like a small gnawing animal, a constant familiar; there was a hardness there which had first come eighteen months ago, and had since enlarged. She hadn't said anything about it. Pain was something to be endured, not made much of; and there were other things. There was the garden. She glanced about her now with pleasure; over the few years here, she'd made paths and a lawn, and grown marigolds and poppies, lavender, kitchen-herbs; sometimes they sent down from the great house for fennel and sage, which Cecily and Sybilla couldn't grow themselves no matter how they tried. There wasn't any accounting for such things.

She breathed the peace of the garden, silent now except for the constant purling murmur of the little stream. Philip was away today with Paul, who was himself teaching the child to ride his first pony; and yesterday Sybilla had come, full of importance, to tell her mother that at last, after five years of marriage, she and Paul could expect a child. Sybilla had sat there in some triumph, much like—Annabel could not resist the simile—a proud little well-feathered hen; she had put on flesh of late years, and dressed fashionably and knew everyone. She was, without doubt, ashamed of her eccentric mother, in her old print gown and chip-hat, and gardening-gloves, and comfortable easy shoes. Annabel didn't as a rule meet Sybilla's new friends; it was, at times, difficult to credit that she had ever given birth to this alien daughter, that she had once liked to think of as Godfrey's and her own.

Godfrey was with her now. At such times, when she was alone in the garden and at peace with herself and the world, he came to her; they could stay together in communion of spirit, saying nothing for there was no need. She knew that he approved her flowers, liked to see her interested; that was one thing which minimised the pain. Godfrey himself had known much bodily pain in his life, and she liked to think that, in a way, it brought her nearer him; the shared experience deepened their love for one another. This love, that she felt for Godfrey, differed so much from the accepted views of bodily love that she spoke of it to no one; no one, except perhaps Livia, would have understood. How strange that Morven's mistress, who had loved him with her body so well, should be almost the only person to understand the consuming love of the soul! But Annabel had said nothing even to Livia.

She bent to the weeds again now, plucking them deeply and separately, bestowing them for burning in a flat osier basket. Later, when Philip came home, they would have a bonfire. He was always active, and wild with interest about such things; often he exhausted her. It was as well that Paul was kind to the boy, would be kind no matter how many sons he had of his own, and that Livia loved him like a second mother; and Cecily, of course, was always kind. There was much kindness at Maddon. Only Sybilla, curiously her enemy now, and Clairette, a grey attenuated shadow hardly ever glimpsed in full day, marred the whole. But by the time Philip was grown he would be armoured against such things, even though she herself might not live to see him a man. Annabel was almost certain of this; it was as if she had known from the time before Philip was born that she would never see him as a man. Now she accepted it.

The gate creaked; it was a servant from Maddon, with a sealed folded note from Cecily. Annabel broke the seal and screwed up her eyes against the sunlight; her sight was not what it had been. Peering close to the letter, she read its contents. "Hubert is most unwell, and desires to see you as soon as you can come," Cecily wrote. "Will you come today, if you can?"

It was like them to make a request of it, to suit her convenience; after all, she was their guest, almost their pensioner. She said to the servant "Tell Lady Melrose I will follow you at once," and peeling off her earth-stained gloves, made her way as she was to Maddon.

Sir Hubert lay in the great bed where he had been born, and his father before him; Melroses were begotten and died here, and he would soon follow. She could tell that when she saw the light fall on his face, showing it grey, without its customary heavy colour. He smiled as he saw her, knew her, and extended a hand; she took it between her own. "Uncle Hubert, I am sorry you are not well." There was nothing else to say; a man of his age, no doubt, was dying. He knew it. "I had a thing to say to you, Annabel," he said; his voice already sounded far away. "Draw in your chair; is the room empty? This is for no one except yourself, meantime; but it was necessary by now that you should know."

He closed his eyes for instants, and she looked quickly round the great chamber; it was empty, even Cecily having left, closing the panelled door behind her without a sound; good quiet, obedient Cecily, the excellent second wife; they'd been happy, no doubt, in this room. Annabel surveyed the furnishings, many of them as old as the time of Scotland's kings; there were curious carvings on the ceiling, and the tester was faded Flemish scarlet, with the family arms as by custom, in gold and blue. It was like a king's deathbed, she thought; and shivered. Further over, a Chinese screen struck a modern note; it had been a gift from Godfrey, and the curtains also had been from him, and had come from Lyons where they had been specially woven in a design that could never be repeated, for the loom's setting had been destroyed afterwards. How strange to recall such things now, when Uncle Hubert had something important to say to her! "There is no one else here," she said gently. "What is it, Uncle Hubert?"

"It is nothing you will like to hear," he said grimly. "It concerns your son."

"Concerns Philip?" Fear clutched at Annabel. "Is he ill, is he——" She wondered, perhaps, if Philip had fallen off the pony; if he were dead, and they had chosen this way of telling her. But surely no one would be so cruel!

"And yourself, and Morven; and your father and his father, and your mother, my own dear sister Grace. It is for her sake I have kept silence all these years. Perhaps I should not have done so." He eased himself on his pillows. "Perhaps God punished me . . . when He took away my son Peter. I was bitter, I recall, about that."

"God is loving," she said to him, and knew that it was true. She straightened his pillows. "Is there anything I can fetch, Uncle Hubert? Wine, water, writing-things?" It had occurred to her that perhaps it would ease him to know that whatever it was could be written down, to save his voice which strained and was growing hoarse. But he shook his head.

"I have all my needs. Only . . . there is a box with the lawyer, which he has not opened; he will do so, on my instructions, after my death. It matters . . . now Sybilla is to bear my son a son, or daughter; before that I had yourself to consider, but now Malvie is due to Paul through his wife, and I——I must tell the truth." He moved restlessly; she watched, and through the bewilderment of her mind a word he had used struck her; Malvie. What right had Paul to hope for Malvie, except formerly through herself? And now it would be Philip who must inherit; soon, when she herself made a fresh will, she would see to that.

"Malvie will be Philip's, uncle," she said quietly. His eyes flashed and he said clearly "No. The child has no title to Malvie."

"Uncle Hubert, Philip is the son of Morven and myself; he is the heir of Malvie." As she said the words she felt a ring of pride; it had been wrong, she now knew, not to tell Morven of the birth. Why had Uncle Hubert consented to her silence? Why——

"Sybilla is the heir; it is her children who will inherit Malvie. You are Morven's wife, but Morven and yourself are both illegitimate. Your mother, my sister Grace Melrose, was married first secretly to Richard Doon, Morven's father, before he rode off to the 'Forty-five; then he strove to repudiate her, when he supposedly married the Highland woman who became Morven's mother, and he asked Grace by letter if she

356

would release him and say nothing of their former marriage ceremony. Grace was so overcome with shame and regret that she listened to me, and to our father, who hadn't wanted her tied to a Jacobite rebel in the first place; it was agreed between us to say nothing, and later we married her to Philip Doon, and you were born of that union. But in law neither you, who were born to Grace and Philip, nor Richard's son by his Highland woman, are children of wedlock. I said nothing of it all the years of your youth, although I prevented Peter from marrying you as he wished; perhaps I was wrong, as one can be. . . . Then Devenham came; and as the trustee of Malvie I sold him the place, and Sybilla is his child, and Paul's wife, and Malvie is hers by right, and her children's."

"Who knows of this?" Her lips were dry, her mind a very old woman's; all the suffering, all the bitterness and conflict, she was thinking, have been in vain; Malvie was never Morven's. His whole life has been lived for nothing. And I, and I . . . And Sybilla is not Godfrey's daughter. If I say so, what will happen?

It did not occur to her to doubt the dying man. Presently he said to her, as though he were weary of the whole matter "The evidence, your mother's certificate of marriage to Richard Doon, is with the lawyers. They had two nights together before he rode off; he visited her, as he had married her, secretly. Poor Grace, she loved him, and she had wanted to give herself to him lest they never meet again after that mad prospect of the last of the Stuarts . . . they never did. Richard died years later in France. Richard Doon was a rascal, like his son."

"No." It had suddenly become necessary to protect Morven, as she might have done when they were children; all his later injury to herself had been forgotten. "Uncle Hubert, you allowed Morven to grow up believing he was the true heir; you let him grow embittered and resentful, coveting a place he should have known could never have been his; you have let our whole lives, his and mine, be ruined and blighted by—by what? Why did you do it? Why, Uncle Hubert?" She had risen, and was staring down at the dying man.

"For my sister's sake. Was I to have her name dragged in the mud, after the disaster of Culloden, after . . . She was a Melrose." He spoke proudly, and she saw his glance waver to include the tester above the bed. "We have always been loyal to the house," he said quietly, and then closed his eyes. He did not seem any longer to be aware of her presence, and shortly, without knowing what to do, she made her way out of the room and out of Maddon, seeing no one on her journey.

After she had gone, when Sir Hubert slept, Clairette Bowes rose from where she had been sitting behind the Chinese screen, and went quietly out. She had heard everything that had been said. Her lips smiled faintly. She knew now what to do.

X

Morven Doon had lived alone since his wife and his mistress had left him, except of course for the steward Samson, and Morven's natural son William Judd. The two last sat at table with him each night over the wine; there was no longer any pretence of difference between servant and master; other staff had been dispensed with, except for the kitchens, and there were carved meats now on the sideboard to which everyone helped himself, Samson carving Morven's portion and setting it before him without a word. The meal was no longer fastidiously served, as it had been in the days of the women. The sconces in which candles burned low were of silver, it is true, but this was black from uncleaned smoke, and the gouted wax had spilled over each night on to the table in places and had not been removed. Morven drained his wine, and called for more; Samson brought it, and re-filled his master's glass and also that of William, who sat as always in silence, and of the guest who was present tonight. They did not often have guests nowadays, since the ware-houses had been sold some years before and there were, now-adays, few foreign boats in the bay.

The visitor tonight had in fact come off such a boat, landing after dark and making his way up as formerly by means of the tower entry; he was used to no other. He was Dutch Pete, Pieter van Hooghen, the old client, friend, business rival per-haps of Morven's; they had not in fact seen each other for six or seven years. Pete had a lieutenant with him. He was a big burly man, who looked like what he also was, a seafarer. He knew every run between here and Man, and all the Channel ports and the hiding-places among the low flat islands as the mouths of the great rivers Elbe and Scheldt, and the sandbanks too; he had been shipwrecked four times. His little eyes surveyed the blind man shrewdly from behind a haze of pipe-smoke; Doon had aged, the other Dutchman thought; he hadn't enough occupation, and a life without work or women was meaningless. Van Hooghen laughed shortly, and exhaled smoke. "You should come back into the business, Mynheer," he said. "What can Pitt do? There is going to be war."

"I sold out years ago. Let others have the trouble; mine is over."

"When trouble is over, life is over," said Dutch Pete. "It may be that your Pitt—" he spoke the word regretfully, as one might use a social solecism— "—has made the sale of liquor less gainful than it was. But with this Bonaparte, who dislikes the English nation—"

"We are not English, Mynheer," said Morven, smiling. "Have your years among us here in the north taught you nothing?"

"He will not know the difference, any more than that between a Corsican and a Frenchman," muttered the lieutenant into his beard. "Soon there will be war, I say; and such things as he can prevent your getting, such things as Lyons silks, spices, tapestries and Sèvres porcelain, difficult to carry and therefore very, very expensive, my friend, when they reach the market here—all this, if a man has foresight, may well, shall we say, compensate a trifle for the boredom— yes, yes, you are bored, my friend, I know well!—of having sold your warehouses to the highest bidder. There are other packhorses, and many other men, who would be willing to ride across country again, on a new venture. It is for this I have come, a long way, as you know well. Have I come for nothing?" He spread out his hands, and waited in the heavy silence for Doon to speak. Their lives had lacked savour without him, and without the landing-place below the tower.

Morven still spoke good-naturedly. "I am a law-abiding citizen now, and an old man. Try other fields; I am content with my inheritance, and a glass of taxed wine at the day's end." He fingered the wood of the oak table, he had used, Pete recalled, to boast to them that it had been brought home by his father. He said less of that nowadays. What did he do

359

with his time, the blind man? There had been a woman once, a glorious fleshly woman with black hair. Dutch Pete had coveted her for himself, but she would have none of him. Then there had been the other, the wife. A pity there was no son. "Mynheer, risk a little for us again!" said van Hooghen persuasively. "You are not so old as you think; less so than I, and I would miss the sea's swell and the knowledge, also, that I carried some matter aboard that I should not." He smiled, and the tone of his voice conveyed the warmth of the gesture to Morven. He'd had companionship, loyalty from these men. If he had the heart to begin again . . .

"I will tell you tomorrow," he said to Dutch Pete. Presently he rose and, according to his custom now it was dusk, made his rounds of the house, satisfying himself out of his own darkness that all was as it should be; Malvie, Malvie, his own, for as long as life should remain to him, so that perhaps, after all, he had not lived vainly. For a man to achieve his life's ambition was something, more than most men contrived to do. The golden lichened roof would be slate-dark now, lacking the rays of the sun. In all the rooms the things which had always known Malvie, his father's 'cello, the double portrait of Philip and Grace, Susannah's harp, the great hung beds, the carved chairs, his father's oak table, stood as always, oblivious of time, and knew that he, Doon of Malvie, passed by. Doon of Malvie! That was what he had always strained to be, what he had been born to, and had achieved.

A sound disturbed him; he turned irritably. It was William Judd.

"A woman. She came in a carriage. She says she must see you tonight." His tone was sullen. He didn't know who the woman might be; she wore a veil. Her late arrival had dragged him away from a carouse with Dutch Pete which would have lasted well into the morning; there was nothing else to do. The days passed slowly enough, here at Malvie. Why did he stay? His mother would be glad enough to have him back, and so no doubt would Abel. He hadn't asked them. He watched Morven grope for his stick and move across the room, towards the stairs. Why did a blind man have so much power over them all that it was assumed they would never leave him? "Samson won't ever leave," William told himself. "But I might, some day." The day, he knew, was increasingly distant; he could never summon the courage or energy to leave. He watched Doon descend the stairs, and saw him come face to face at last with the waiting woman.

She put back her veil then. William saw who it was. It was Miss Clairette from Maddon, dead Mr. Devenham's sister. What was she doing so late at night, driving alone in a carriage as far as Malvie? But it would be for the usual reasons, William thought; this was an old maid, soured and withered and spiteful; one had only to look at her face, with the close-set dark eyes in it like a serpent's, and the thin mouth puckered hard in a smile over loss of teeth. Doon, being blind, couldn't see her, William thought; at the least, he was spared that.

Clairette took a step forward. "It is a great many years since we last met, Morven," she said. "There are two things I must tell you. That is why I have come."

Although she knew Morven could not see her, Clairette had put back her veil as he descended the stairs; the pretentious action gave her the sensation of drama, of being the central figure in a theme of revenge for bitter wrong. Now that she saw Morven clearly, she was aware of how greatly he had aged. His hair was grey and his face lined even in candlelight. It came of living alone, she thought smugly. She announced herself, as there were no servants in evidence.

Morven smiled, bowed over her hand, and expressed no particular emotion. He would have known it was Clairette, he told himself; her odour at close quarters was unaltered. He wondered what had brought her here; was it news of Annabel? A coldness took him; since he had ejected his wife from his house, he had not uttered her name and had made no enquiry regarding her. He assumed that she would in some way have reached Maddon. His life here was entirely shut off from all influences that they might have known together; in his darkness, in his kingdom, he was of his own choice left alone.

Clairette was still silent; she had in fact found it difficult to begin, now that the moment had come for her triumph over Morven. He helped her. "You have news for me?" he said coldly. "You would not have travelled so far, assuredly, to see such as myself without some good reason. Is it—" he spoke slowly, certain that the tidings she carried must be, by contrast with his own words, bad—"is it news of my wife? How does she?"

"Your wife is well, and so is your son. He has grown; I saw them yesterday."

"My—"

It had not occurred to Clairette that the extent of his ignorance could be complete. She watched the dawning joy on his face, the progress of full understanding, of memory aiding sense; it was like seeing the sun rise over the sea, except that Clairette had never watched the sunrise. Her own face remained cold and narrow, the eyes resentful; had she given Morven Doon a moment's joy?

"Your son Philip. I wonder you never visit them."

"I—I would not be welcome. Clairette—" he came forward with hands outstretched, imploring her out of his own dark place, pleading perhaps for her liking even now, when he had his life's greatest news. "What can I do to atone, Clairette, for the gift you have just brought me? I had not known there was an heir to Malvie."

"There is not."

He stopped short; and brutally, clearly she told him the news she had overheard at Sir Hubert's deathbed. It was probable the old man would never rise therefrom again, even that he might, she thought, be dead when she returned from her journey. The possibility stayed clear in her mind as she destroyed Morven's dream, watched his hopes crumble and his face grow dark.

"Malvie was never yours," she ended triumphantly. "All your life you've nursed a fable of your own, Morven, an illusion. You have not even the name of Doon to give your son."

Suddenly he lunged forward at her, clumsily knocking himself against some object in a way which was not his wont. Clairette heard her own mocking laughter ringing through the empty place. Then fear took her and she turned and hurried out, beyond the still open door to where her carriage waited, and bundled herself inside in haste and gave orders to the coachman to drive off at once. But still she could see, perhaps would always do so, the blind man's figure in her mind and memory, and hear his voice crying after her.

"You lie! You lie! I am Doon of Malvie!"

The carriage-wheels churned off into the night.

XI

It was within the next few days that Dutch Pete received the order his heart craved, an order which would fill three ships' holds. It was a commission fraught with danger; on hearing what it was that Doon demanded, neither spices nor wine nor Lyons silks, but a commodity that would entail raiding the sources of supply engaged already by Bonaparte, with intent to blockade the English coast along lines formed from Boulogne, Dutch Pete murmured a little, and quadrupled his price. Doon paid without a murmur; he would expect delivery, he said, within ten days. Van Hooghen expostulated. Such a thing was uncertain, unpredictable! They might not easily acquire such bulk as Doon wanted. What he wanted it for did not seem prudent to Pete to ask; one never questioned Doon, or marvelled at the vagaries of his manner or his thin white devil's face, so filled with infectious gaiety as it had been two nights ago, and now dour as an old man's who has nothing left to live for. Gunpowder! If Doon wanted to blow himself and his house sky-high, it was no concern of Pete's, as long as he had the money. "It will be forthcoming," he told Doon, "in the time."

"Good." Doon said no more, and turned abruptly away from the scene of their talk; they had been alone at it, the man Samson being for once not present. Van Hooghen felt, unaccountably, safer as a rule when the mulatto was there; he was a rascal, as they all were, no doubt, but human. But this intense white devil! Dutch Pete essayed a jest, to shed the burden of strangeness from his own spirit. He repeated, for he thought it was a good one, the recent thought he had had about Doon blowing himself and Malvie sky-high.

But Doon did not laugh. "What concern is it of yours if that should happen?" he said, with his back turned so that no one now could see his face. Dutch Pete said no more.

Before that, Morven had driven over, for the first time in

years, the first since his blindness, to Maddon. He had chosen an unfortunate time; Sir Hubert was newly dead. The great house was in confusion and grief; a servant received Morven, and led him into the hall, where he was received by Paul, red-eyed for his dead father. Halfway through their greetings and condolences, and before Morven could ask about Annabel and his boy, Sybilla joined her husband; Morven could not see her, but he heard the hardness of her voice as she asked that he be shown out at once. "We do not want such persons here."

"My dear—" Morven had the impression that Paul placated his wife, spoiled her as though she were a child; she was behaving like one, he thought, a suspicious child which must at all costs have its own way. He himself could not blame her for hating him; those episodes with William, when together they had kissed her familiarly in bed, would not be forgotten by the new lady of Maddon. "My dear, Morven has come to enquire for his wife and boy. Would not your mother—?"

"Mama will not see him. Nor will she permit him to have access to Philip. Please ask that his carriage be removed from the doorway as soon as may be; others will be coming to offer their condolences about your father, and cannot pass one another in the avenue."

"You are much exercised over Paul's father," said Morven, smiling. "Have you no regard for your own?"

She bridled. "I loved Papa devotedly, and have never forgotten the way you insulted and killed him, and dragged Mama's name in the mud; please go now, or I must ask the servants to hasten your departure, and I'd be unwilling to do so in your state."

"My dearest, calm yourself," murmured Paul. Morven's smile widened.

"I will go, Sybilla, as there's no help for it; but before I do, I must inform you of a thing which perhaps you may not have known, or even suspected. Devenham was never your father; he could not have sired a child. You are my own flesh and blood, Sybilla. Take heed how you use your father, my dear; I was your mother's love long before she married Godfrey Devenham. Ask her if she remembers the pear tree."

He turned and went; and had the satisfaction of hearing a sound of horror from Sybilla, though he did not see her faint, or Paul catch her in his arms. By that time Morven was on his homeward journey, back again down the tree-lined avenue of Maddon, and already other carriages were coming up.

Sybilla miscarried of her child, and whether or not this was attributable to the thing Morven Doon had informed her of, if she believed it, or would have happened in any case as a result of grief for Sir Hubert, of whom she had been fond, the result was the same; keen disappointment was felt by both Paul and Sybilla, and also by Cecily, who had hoped as much as anyone for a continuance of her husband's family in the male line. Least affected outwardly by the occurrence, which happened soon after the funeral, was Sybilla's mother Annabel. The fact that no one had troubled to ask her whether or not she would permit Morven to meet his own son had angered her; it was, she thought, high-handed and cruel of Sybilla to act so. Also a conversation resulting from her own belated request for advice from Paul about the vexed problem of the Malvie inheritance, when she had not known to whom else to turn, had borne sour fruit. Sybilla had insisted on being present at the interview; it was as if she could bear no other woman to have many dealings with Paul, not even his own stepmother, and certainly not Annabel.

Paul had been too greatly distraught by events to give his full attention to the problem of Malvie; it was Sybilla, still commanded by her physician to lie on a day-bed, who conducted the interview. This word was coming more and more to describe Annabel's occasional dealings with her daughter and son-in-law; since Sir Hubert's death, and Cecily's retirement into widowhood in her own remote suite of apartments with her daughters, Annabel had felt like a stranger at Maddon. Even in her little cottage, in the garden she had made there with her own hands, she was beginning to feel as though each stick in the grate, each springing plant, each herb was Sybilla's, and that she herself, and little Philip, were there on sufferance only.

She tried to tell herself, as she bent and kissed Sybilla where she lay, that it was her own imagining; surely they were as welcome as they had always been! But suddenly it occurred to her that in Sybilla's beautiful, pale face, below the round brow and the curls fashionably dressed despite her late indisposition, there looked out the flat, acquisitive blue eyes of aunt Retford; why had she never noticed it before? Paul came forward, friendly, courteous, and worried as always; he had a great deal on his shoulders, poor Paul. He bowed over her hand.

"Dearest, the question of Malvie," said Sybilla fretfully. She hardly gave Annabel time to seat herself; the latter did so, and disposed her hands together in her lap to still their trembling. She saw the blue eyes light an instant on their roughened skin and earth-stained nails. No lady, undoubtedly, in Sybilla's estimation, would ever have a hole in her gardening-glove. Annabel felt laughter rise unbidden, suddenly, despite disillusion and pain. Despite everything, she had a thing Sybilla had not, and never would have; perhaps it had no name.

Paul fidgeted a little, straightening a fold of his cravat which had come awry. "Malvie is at your mother's own disposal, Sybilla," he said reproachfully. "It was clearly stated in your father's will that the inheritance was to be hers, and the disposal likewise." He looked at Sybilla and smiled, as if he could never even yet regard her without delight; the conversation, Annabel knew well, would already have taken place in some form between them.

"My father's will," murmured Sybilla, and quickly turned to an aspect she would not previously have discussed with Paul. "Mama, who was my father?"

There was silence in the room; different kinds of different silences. Paul was astonished; could his love, after her terrible ordeal, have been left with her mind disturbed, as women were said at such times to do? He made a small protective movement. Annabel, the unprotected, did not answer for some moments. She had closed her eyes, and opened them again to hear Sybilla say, maliciously,

"That man—you know who I mean—asked if you remembered the pear tree."

She sat up suddenly, and swung her legs to the ground; the gesture was surprisingly lithe and strong; she is quite better, Annabel thought. She herself was on the verge of fainting; she had the notion that her reply must be guided not only by truth—what purpose would the truth serve now?—but by considerations for Philip, for Paul, for Godfrey's shade which stood at her elbow, guiding her. She began to speak slowly, as though Godfrey spoke and not herself.

"You loved your Papa, Sybilla, did you not? I can remember when you and he were everything to each other. He left you a fortune in money—"

"What does that signify?" Sybilla sobbed; within moments, her late defences had broken down and she was almost a child again. Paul went to her.

It signifies a great deal, Annabel thought drily; but did not say it aloud. She said "If I tell you, and swear with all my heart, that Papa knew the true facts of your birth, and still made you his heiress, does that answer you, Sybilla? As you know, I loved Papa."

She had risen, and was preparing to go; the sobs from the sofa had ceased, and Sybilla, held in Paul's arms, said plaintively, as though no longer quite sure of herself.

"Then Malvie is to be mine, Mama, is it not? You will not leave it to Philip? As Papa's heiress, I have a right to it; he purchased it, and we—"

"That is my own private decision, Sybilla, as Paul has said," Annabel told her clearly. She looked round at the rich room; the gilded spindle-legged furniture Paul had lately ordered, at his wife's request, from London, and the recent portrait, by a famous painter, of Sybilla herself, in a high-waisted gown and Oriental turban, her tiny hands shown idly tying a knot in a striped silk scarf. Maddon itself was such a house as few young women in the whole world would call themselves mistress of, with a husband ready to pamper and indulge each whim, and the local society at beck and call. All that, perhaps, Sybilla lacked in material ways was a child, and children no doubt would come. Yet she wanted Malvie. She wanted it not because she had ever loved it; although it had been her home in Godfrey's lifetime, it was Godfrey himself Sybilla had adored, not the house, and it would have been the same had they chosen to move to Edinburgh or London, or to some other estate in the country. No, Annabel thought; Sybilla wanted Malvie because she could bear to part with nothing, not even the portion of her husband's heart that might have been given to herself, in the years when she was lonely. Sybilla also wanted the house, of course, in order to prevent Morven's son from obtaining it; she hated Morven. Hated him and all of his blood . . . no doubt he'd earned such hatred. But at this moment, Annabel found, she preferred her husband to Sybilla.

"I cannot discuss my will, Sybilla," she said, "but you may depend upon it that the lawyers will see that it is fair." Philip must not be left destitute; how frightening, although she knew her own state of health, it was that she must already begin to think of the possibility of the boy's life without her, and of how he would fare! She rose, and took her leave; and all the way back to the cottage reflected on her situation now, and, above all, the visit Morven had made lately when Sybilla had not permitted him to meet his son, had not even told her he had come to Maddon till afterwards. There had been Sir Hubert's death and funeral, it was true, to distract everyone; but even so . . .

Annabel asked Paul if she might have the use of the carriage on the following day. She was going, she said, into Grattan.

Annabel's reliance on Livia as a confidante, even a friend, still had power to astonish her, retaining as she did some remnant of a conventional upbringing, more so than Livia herself, whom nothing astonished. But it was true that of the few persons she still saw and talked with, Morven's former mistress, who had been a servant, was the most valued and valuable. Livia never betrayed confidences; she brought to every problem the same grave, considering quality Annabel remembered in her, enhanced by the years but prevented, by a kind of earthy humility, humour and commonsense, from becoming either omniscience or conceit.

It was to Livia she went now in her trouble; Livia, the wife of the Grattan innkeeper; social levels no longer troubled Annabel. She dressed Philip in his frieze coat and cap, and saw his shirt-frill was suitably disposed and his shoes clean. Then, herself attired in an everyday bonnet and shawl, she climbed with the little boy into Paul's comfortable, well-upholstered carriage and felt the horses spring away. Comfort to Annabel now was a remembrance of something she had once had; it never occurred to her that, by means of litigation against Morven, she could again have been a rich woman, in enjoyment of Godfrey's legacy to her and also, of Malvie. She did not grudge Morven Malvie, his heart's dream. But Philip? Sybilla's greed had wakened her mother to a realisation of Philip's coming necessity. Apart from the desire she herself now had—had had since she heard of his visit—to let Morven meet his son, it was politic, no doubt, that the father should know his heir. Morven himself was a rich man, no matter how the money had been acquired; Annabel was vague about the smuggling-years and the subsequent sale, at immense profit, of the Leith houses and the packmen's trail, and fleet of ships; the latter had in fact been mostly bought by Dutch Pete and sold again to Frenchmen, now that there might be war. Pete, and Morven also, had noses for a profitable transaction; Annabel never, except now for Philip's sake. She stared ahead of her along the familiar road, answering her son's excited questions as best she could. The child had been several times to Grattan, and loved not only Livia but Abel, who would play with him as he never had with Willliam. Poor William had been a different matter from this engaging, bright, pretty little boy, with his fair hair and Doon features and precocious intelligence. Philip himself had never even heard of his half-brother as such, although he knew Aunt Livia had a son of her own, who dealt in horses.

The inn was reached and, as soon as the ostlers had come out to the beasts' heads and arranged for their watering, Philip was out of the coach and away to Abel. The latter now took little part in the active affairs of the inn; he left it to Livia, contenting himself, as his father the smith had once done, with watching the days pass, and the sun rise and set, now that he was ill. He had grown very thin and yellow; the smile with which he greeted young Philip was as sweet as that of a pictured saint. Livia came out and gave the child a hug, and a sweetmeat, and said she'd be back; then went over to his mother.

They had greeted one another, out in the court-yard; for an instant there was only the sound of their murmured voices, and the ostlers' trampling feet in the near distance, and the familiar sight of the clear cobbles swept empty of straw. Then, in the next moment, a sound came such as neither woman, nor any other soul in Grattan or in all the countryside, had ever heard; a low growl as of thunder, but there was no storm; a quaking, so that the sturdy inn-building shook as if it were made of cards, and the houses also, and somewhere a woman screamed, but Livia and Annabel stood still, with their very gowns' stuff made to quiver by the force of the blast which came, more briefly than wind, far deeper and more intense than the wayward fanning of great fire. Never had such a sound been heard; but they knew what it was, and whence it came; from Malvie itself, over the far hill.

Malvie! Annabel gave a moan; and presently, as others came running, Livia pointed, her figure like that of a goddess predicting doom, the outstretched arm firm, splendid, decisive. The part of the sky where she pointed showed fire, already; a glow, as though the sun were setting at midday, shone

369

reflected at the horizon; such a fire must be vast, deadly, so swift as to leave no living thing.

"Come," said Livia, and without another word she helped the other woman into the carriage, and got in herself. The coachman leapt to his place again; within moments they were off, not even taking time to tell Abel to look after Philip till they returned. They knew he would do so without asking.

XII

The colours made fountains and exploded before Morven's eyes; they were green and gold, purple and a geranium red which was not the colour of blood, such as he remembered from years ago when he first went blind. They gyrated and behaved in a manner indescribable to himself, as though his eyes and ears were correlated. Later it came to him that they were associated with a noise, and roaring; still later on he remembered why. He recalled the packages stowed in every imaginable corner of Malvie, from the carved tunnel of the cavern entrance to the Flodden tower, the east wing built in his grandfather's time, the cupboards, the back stairs, every cranny where, even in the time when servants abounded here, nobody would have discovered an untoward thing. He had bestowed them himself, knowing, in his blindness, every hidden place. There was not a corner of Malvie which could escape once he had lit the fuse which led to the store below the tower, and he himself would mount then to the room above, where he had been born, and listen for the last time to the sea sounding, before all other sounds ceased for him. He would die with Malvie.

Before then, he had sent away the remaining servants. He had given them all silver, a sum of forty days' service as the law expected of him; he laughed; at times he adhered to the dictates of the law. He had also sent away William and Samson. "Go and take a few days' holiday," he had said to both men. He had also given them money to spend. Afterwards he wondered if he had persuaded Samson sufficiently of the need to go; the man had sounded puzzled, perhaps suspicious. Samson, the son of a prostitute and a prizefighter, had enough of this world's sharp sense to do well in it, whatever became of Malvie and himself. He had no fear for Samson. William was a different matter; he, Morven, had never felt the affection for the young man that he should have done for his own son, that he would have done for Annabel's son Philip, if only, if only . . .

Annabel.

Morven gave much thought to her in those last days, especially as regarded the matter of her worldly provision and income, also Philip's. He had left them each a separate legacy, and after his own death, with that and the reversion of Godfrey's jointure, Annabel would be a very rich woman. She might, he thought wryly, marry a third time. There would be nothing to prevent her; and with money, and beauty, she would be much sought after. He still saw Annabel in his mind's eye as the exquisite young girl in a buttercup-yellow gown, with curled bright hair, that time at Cecily's wedding to old Sir Hubert Melrose.

And Livia?

Strangely, he had thought less of Livia than of Annabel. He had left her some money, less than the sum allotted to his wife. Livia was his bone and his flesh; no explanations were necessary between them; wherever his ghost was compelled to wander, if it might no longer be at Malvie, it should be near Livia somewhere. She would know this, with the extra sense she had, handed down from her remote, unpredictable ancestors. There was no need for him even to see—how he still used the verb pertaining to sight!—to see Livia again. They had loved as few lovers in the world had ever done; Abélard and Héloïse, or the doomed boy and girl of Verona. He and she had lived, in those times together, as intensely as if a thousand years had been theirs, and he could not complain of too short a life.

That should end now. After Samson and the rest had ridden off, Morven had taken his staff and walked once, for the last time, about the precincts of Malvie. The great empty house echoed to the sound of his footsteps; as long before, when he was a young man, he had fingered his father's violoncello, strayed through the attics, felt the carvings of great escutcheons above the stone hearths of hall and withdrawing-room. He had pictured the scenes which must have taken place in Malvie, some of which he had himself witnessed; the gatherings of mediaeval days, when Doons had ridden out on crusade—poor Kitty's unvarying cry, he remembered now—and later in the time of the Union, and the days of Montrose. He mounted the twining steps of his tower and thought how it had been built in the year of Scotland's bane, so that the young bride of the Doon laird who had gone with his men to the Border, to aid the King, could mount it and watch, like the Queen of Scots at Linlithgow, for a husband who never again rode home from Flodden Field. He descended a floor and went again to the room which had seen his own birth, where Annabel had lived alone for many years long after; but it was not his wife he thought of now, but his mother; unknown, incalculable Helen Doon, hailing from the country of blue hills and fey folk, of loyalty and undying feuds and proud, ancient blood. He himself was half Highland; was that why he had differed so much from the tame people here? They had disowned him, Morven, almost from the onset, not only because his father had ridden off to the Prince's side.

He was out of place and time; he was better gone, and everyone, of those who were left, Annabel, young Philip, Livia, Abel, the Maddon folk, would be relieved enough to hear of his death, though some would no doubt feel grief. He had gone down then and, taking a tinder, had set a light to the slow fuse that would crawl towards the first of the packages of gunpowder Dutch Pete had brought by order of his own from France. Bonaparte's gunpowder, destined to blow up at least a part of the land that general most hated . . . it should do its duty, Morven thought. Malvie, by rights never his, was not for him to contemplate longer, nor could he bear to watch the calm possession of the place he had loved by Madam Sybilla and her tame Melrose spouse. That marriage had been one of bantams, of mealworms; he'd had no part in it, though he regretted, now, his white-hot anger against Annabel that had caused him to use her at the last so shamefully. The money, he thought, would signify his own belated apology, when the time came.

Then he had returned to his birth-room, and had lit a pipe, and had sat listening to the sea below Malvie. When the explosion came, it would set off a train starting below the place where he sat; there was no possibility that he would escape death. He thought of death as a friend, already welcoming.

Then a noise came; but it was not the rumble and tremor

of the fuse lit below the tower. It was the sound of footsteps, hesitant, a little; as if uncertain of their owner's welcome. Morven felt his heart pound with anger; who had disobeyed him at such a moment and come back?

"Doon?"

It was Samson; the mulatto boy he'd rescued from a corn-crock, saved from hanging *in terrorem* by George III's colonial redcoats. Morven turned, a sardonic grin on his face. "You should not have come back," he said; "why did you do so? Get away out."

Samson tried to explain himself; he was not in fact certain why he had felt a need to return, and bring William also. He had felt, and had persuaded the younger man to feel, that all was not well; the servants had been dismissed, they themselves had been sent off without reason on a sudden holiday; what was Doon doing, or meaning to do, in the great house alone?

"Let us return," he had said to William Judd, and the latter, who seldom thought or argued for himself, had merely turned his horse's head, and had followed Samson's own lead back to Malvie. He was stabling the horses now in the groom's absence. Not another soul was in the place.

"You have come back only to die with me," said Morven. "Leave while there is still time, if you can."

Even as he spoke there came a violent explosion, from beneath their feet; it was as if the stones of the floor were pulled apart, and the tower itself collapsed like a broken toy. Morven could see nothing; he could not see Samson's agonised face, the whites of the eyes protruding in terror, and the man's body propelled forwards. He could only feel the arms, the strong brown arms with the muscles of a prize-fighter, seizing him and throwing him, throwing him into space that seemed as limitless as hell's pit, and he hurtled down, down, his body a thing without will, without weight, nothing.

All around Morven's falling body the explosions ignited and roared and trembled; he felt already the intense resulting heat of fire. Then there was nothing any more but darkness about him; darkness, and quiet, and peace.

The scene which greeted the two women as they arrived over the hill in the carriage was as bleak, unfamiliar and desolate as a landscape off the moon. Where there had once been roofs and gables, the tower, even certain remembered

373

rocks, threw as nothing; nothing now but a jumble of desolation, a madman's giant game of bricks and rubble. Here and there, the remains of a vaulted arch, or a chimney-flue, stood up, black and clear against the remaining flames which reared behind like a backdrop; soon, for they had been engendered only by the force of the blast, as there was little wind, they subsided. Smoke rose where they had been, achieving grey vertical spirals, as though volcanoes lived beneath and had breathed vapour gently. Such a place might have been the aftermath of battle, littered with the bodies of the dead. But at first when they stepped out of the carriage and walked over to where the house had once stood, there was no one to be seen; nothing.

It was the coachman who found the thing, not Livia or Annabel. He gave a cry, and then came running over, stumbling on the uncertain looseness of the stones. The man's face was white as curd; he could only stammer, and point at a place on the ground where some object lay. It was a man's severed arm, still in the grey cloth sleeve; still with frilled laundered linen at the wrist, and a ring on the finger. The palm was turned upwards, the fingers curled a little and relaxed as if in a form of death which had come expectedly, decently. The skin of the palms and of the nails was pink. The back of the hand was dusky, and the wrist and, when they exposed it, the arm. Search as they might, search as others later did, it was all anyone ever found of Samson.

Presently Annabel turned to the coachman; he was trembling, with beads of sweat on his brow. "Go back to the carriage," she said to him, "and wait for us. We will come in a little while." Strange, she told herself, that in a crisis, even less indescribable than this, it was the women who were supposed to faint and grow pale, to scream, to render themselves useless in emergency. But both she and Livia were ice-cold in resolution to go on looking, if need be, till nightfall for Morven. After that they must go back for lights and other aid . . . At the moment, it hardly seemed that other eyes could see more, or men find more even armed with spades and pickaxes; Malvie, or the place where it had been, was as obliterated, its foundations laid as flat, as by a blast from the anger of God. "There is nowhere else to look," she told herself, with a curious fatality. "He is dead, he must have wished to die so."

A cry came. She had forgotten Livia, picking her own way about among the disordered rubble. Annabel had herself lost the sense of direction which would have told her where there had once been steps, cut deep in the rock, going down to the little beach and the sea. But Livia had found the place, and was calling her; she picked up her skirts and ran, holding her free hand against her afflicted breast to suppress the constant pain. Livia had already found . . . what?

She said nothing as she ran. She did not, as a thousand women would have done, call out "Is he there? Is he dead? Is he whole?" after the shocking bodiless limb they had just seen, its wrenched vessel-ends hardly soaked with living blood before sealing. She kept silence; and heard her breath rasping in her throat, and felt great fear.

But Livia knelt there by Morven, with his head in her lap. She had found him lying thrown clear of all harm, lying with his head down below body-level on the steps so that she had feared his neck might be broken in the fall; she had gathered him, as one would gather a dead child, into her arms, and nursed him, and felt certain she had heard no crunch of severed bones, seen no wry lolling, and that if he were indeed dead, he had died with his body unbroken; there was no visible mark on him.

She was crying, now that the search was ended and Morven was found; she laid her cheek, warm and wet with tears, against his face, and found when she lifted it away that she had herself smeared him with dirt and soot; she must have searched so close to the dying flames that she had been grimed by them, whereas he was clean. He couldn't have been in the explosion; something or someone had already thrown him clear. Was it—

"Where is William?" she said aloud. It occurred to her that her own earlier anxiety should have been for their son also. Later they would search for William. She saw Morven move then, heard him sigh. By that time Annabel had reached them; and like Morven's mistress knelt down, and chafed his hands in her own, so that, when his eyes opened, hers, not Livia's, was the face he first saw.

And he saw her. Both women knew that he did so; the eyes which had for so long been bright, impersonal, void, focussed suddenly. Morven smiled.

"Annabel," he said wonderingly; and again, as if it were a dream and not reality, "Annabel!"

It was not that the village of Grattan had often lacked a *cause célèbre,* since the coming of Livia in the first place to the Fleece. But the latest escapade almost defied repetition; it was as though denizens had arrived from the moon, or from Africa, although it was early known that Samson, who according to the village—which lacked comparison—had been as black as the ebony chiefs of Ashanti, would never be seen among them again. A shudder passed briefly among the serving-maids, the tradesmen who had dealt with him, the seafaring men he had known, for the manner of his death had been horrible, though swift. Then he was forgotten, except when some old man told his grandchildren that once upon a time, near the village, there had stood a great house named Malvie, and in the house had lived a man as black as coal who they said was a servant of the devil.

The devil himself was laid tenderly meantime in bed at the Fleece, with the attendance of Mistress Judd (and everybody knew what had passed between those two, not a doubt of it, all those years) and her husband, who though ill himself sat many an hour by the sleeping Morven Doon, remembering the days of Bart and Aaron, as well as other things. That was strange enough; but in addition, betraying her class in a way great folk seldom did, the wife of Doon, who had left him years ago, was staying at the inn also, helping with the rest to nurse him back to health; and with her a little boy, who it was said was Doon's own son, and the older villagers could swear to it that at the least, he resembled the old laird Philip very greatly. But the cataclysm that had demolished Malvie had broken down, also, seemingly, the walls between master and servant, mistress and maid, husband and lover; nobody in Grattan knew exactly where they were, or where anyone was, and even the elders of the kirk, after one sharp retort from Livia Judd's ready tongue, kept their distance, and did not trouble the sick man who had once been blind.

For this was the greatest astonishment of all; the restoring of sight to Morven Doon.

Such things didn't happen, said the gossips; he must have feigned blindness all these years. How, in any case, could a blind man have achieved the things Morven was said to have done? What these were, they found when they tried to specify, were and had always been shrouded in mystery; there were rumours of a line of packmen passing, in silent files in the dark of the moon; ghost-ships, moving in on no tide, and out beyond the horizon where they had come from, no man knew whither. It was better not to ask of such things, and a generation reared to say nothing of the smuggling-trade, knowing the fate that befell informers, kept their silence. But the other legends concerning Morven Doon were common property; how his wife had been carried off, a bruised half-dead thing in a common dray, and no one knew when she had given birth to her son, after living—they said—as a hermit, a nun, in the tower alone all those years. Then there was the memory, clear yet, of how *he*—they often did not mention Morven's name, as if to do so would raise powers which might not subside again easily—of how *he* had come by one night, when the wind had risen, and had shown his blind face an instant at the taproom of the Fleece, and had bewitched Abel's wife, and had borne her away. The fact that spoiled the ending to such a tale was that Livia, nowadays, had returned to Abel and was, as far as anyone could see, his loved and loving wife again; there had been no flogging at the cart's tail in the public streets, no sinking of a demon-ship when a lover, who was really the devil, set his giant hoof on the deck to submerge it, and the faithless wife and mother with it, as had happened in the old, approved song. No, nothing had fallen out as it should; there was no improving moral to regale the children with, telling them to mind their ways if they would not end like Livia Judd, or Morven Doon. Livia was prosperous as ever, hard-working, stouter a little, but less flabby than she'd been; a streak of white at the side of her black hair added to her attractions, and her bosom was as queenly as ever, her ankle as neatly turned. As for the blindness—well, the minister had a thing to say about that. "It is a notable matter that the mind, and its state, can affect the body in ways we do not yet understand, nor does any physician," he had told an enquirer. And he quoted the blind man who was healed in the Bible; but the listener went away nevertheless unconvinced that the explosion of Malvie could have any connection with Holy Writ. Its cause, like the memory of packmen by night, had been little spoken of in Grattan.

Miss Sybilla—like her mother, known always by her maiden title with which they had watched her grow up— Miss Sybilla had driven over, looking petulant, and wearing a new half-mourning bonnet, with Mr. Paul in silence by her side. They had disappeared into the Fleece before driving on, it was supposed, to view for themselves the ruins of Malvie; then they had returned at great speed through the village without stopping a second time. One woman recalled seeing Miss

Sybilla's face then, and it was bright-cheeked with anger. "She'll have lost a fine inheritance," said the woman.

"No, no, it would go to young Master Philip."

They argued, the neighbours, back and forth over the matter; but as there was nothing left of the house at all, even the Mains having been so shaken by the blast of the explosion that a wall had subsided and showed a great crack, so that the house would be unsafe to live in—as there was nothing left, and as they knew even less of the contents of Godfrey Devenham's will, their curiosity had to remain unsatisfied. It leaked out, however, through a maidservant at the Fleece, that Miss Sybilla had had a fair set-to with her mother.

"She says, Miss Annabel says, that she won't leave him till he's well, no matter what he did to her," reported the girl, wide-eyed. "And Miss Sybilla says 'Mama', she says, 'where's your proper shame? He keeps his mistress here, and you also, and after the way he used us both at Malvie'—"

But one of the neighbours hushed the girl, and said no unmarried maid should speak so. Certainly Mistress Judd aided Miss Annabel in nursing the poor blind gentleman, who had nowhere else to lay his head; that was as it should be.

"But he is not blind now, that is the thing," announced the young maid, who accordingly had the last word. "He is no more blind than you or me. From the time they found him in the ruins of Malvie, he could see; do you suppose as they're saying, it is a miracle?"

And no one could answer her.

Annabel and Livia, and Morven, who was now allowed by the physician to be out of bed, and Abel, who would shortly take to it never to leave it again, sat together round the Fleece kitchen fire, drinking toddy. Every so often Livia would rise from her place and, leaning over the steaming bowl, stir and serve the mixture with a silver ladle, borne on a long twisted handle of age-darkened wood. She wore her snowy goffered cap and apron; being Livia, they were as clean at the day's end as they had looked at the beginning. The servants had all gone to bed, young Philip long ago, and any customers also; the hour was late. It was the only time the four friends had to talk among themselves.

That they should be friends, after all that had passed, was astonishing if one misunderstood human nature, less so perhaps if one did not. To Morven, so long accustomed to live in darkness, it had taken a little time to realise that the thin, ill woman, lacking any colour in her face, with grey hair, only the eyes remaining unchanged, was Annabel after twenty years. He had known her at once; the change had not till later been brought close to him. He had known Livia also, and Abel; the latter white-haired, yellow, and scraggy now with a stoop when he walked; the physician made no bones about it; Abel had not many months to live. When he died, Livia no doubt would keep on the Fleece, or sell it at a profit.

Watching Livia, so changed and yet the same, diverted Morven; he had not known her inner resources, the way in which she had been able to turn disaster to her aid, at the time he himself had been imprisoned and blinded; the way in which she had carved out a life for herself since, despite his return when he had again torn her out of it. She could become, if she so wished, a respected figure for the rest of her days, or, or . . .

William. Morven stared at the fire for instants, regretting that he had never in his life seen that first-born son's face, or could feel deep emotion now he was dead. It was curious that the fruit of his and Livia's early passion, the love-child who should have occupied their hearts to exclusion of all others, had hardly touched either of them; he himself, he saw now, had driven William away long ago. He had, in his own way, killed William; sapped him of initiative, sent him off that last time without explanation, almost made him return at Samson's bidding; but he would not have asked William or Samson either, to die in the holocaust for his sake. That Samson should have died still tormented Morven in the night hours. "He should have lived to be old," he thought.

"What are you thinking of, Morven?" said Abel Judd.

He drew on his pipe; the men found comfort in smoking long pipes of contraband tobacco, sometimes cooled by passing first through water and sometimes not. Morven surveyed Abel now, aware that he was looking at a living saint; who else would have endured him again under their roof, let alone ministered to him, after what had passed? He had denied Abel his inheritance from his father, taken away his wife; and yet now, again, they were friends. Morven sipped his toddy. "I was thinking of many things," he replied, "and of the fact that I must soon leave here. I have trespassed on your kindness too long."

No one glanced at Annabel; would she go with Morven,

and if so, where would they go to? "You have the smithy cottage," said Abel uncertainly. It had been, over the years of Morven's occupation at Malvie, repaired a little, and a herd and his wife had lived in it for a year or two; it was better than nothing, the Mains being gone, and Annabel herself had inhabited a worse cottage at Maddon. But Morven shook his head, smiling a little.

"Later, when I return, I may grow old there, it is my own at least, not like—" But he veered away from the forbidden subject. "I am going on a journey," he said. No one spoke, and his smile widened. "You do not ask me where," he told them. He turned to survey Annabel, who sat nursing her own toddy-cup, not drinking much of it; the great gold-flecked eyes in her thin face had never left him. "Not a wife in a thousand but would scold her man and say "Where are you going—when will you be back?' But never you, my dear. You leave me free, as I need to be always." He took her hand, and kissed it. "We four may say all things in presence of one another," he told the company. "I can say to all of you—" he spoke with difficulty—"that since I regained my sight, by whatever means, I have to realise that what I lived for was one dream out of many, and an idle dream at that. What does a house of stone and mortar signify, when the grass grows and the sky is bright by day and has stars by night? After so long in darkness, it gives me great joy, I find, to regard the sky. I sit here—as you know, Abel—idly in the yard, staring up at the clouds that pass by with the wind, taking pleasure in them. I can hold an insect in the palm of my hand, and remark its colours, and see how the undersides of leaves are different from the upper; a hundred thousand things I never took time for in my youth. But then I thought of nothing at all save only Malvie, and how to regain it."

"It's strange to think, Morven, that you were seven years in Australia, and never saw it yet," said Livia, filling up his toddy. "Would you want to voyage that way again?" She cast a direct glance at him, as if it were nothing to her where he went; but he gripped her wrist for a moment with his fingers.

"Not so far, lass, not so far," he said. "I may go to see the blue hills of my mother's country of Morven for the first time, and follow the course of the lochs inland, and look for the deer. Later I'll return, and maybe—"

Livia withdrew her hand. "I'll not leave Abel again, for

you or any man," she said. "You know that."

"I doubt I'll not be here, love," said her husband. He spoke with such calm that all three turned their heads and gazed at him, astonished at his tranquillity regarding his coming death. "When I'm gone—and Annabel here—"

Annabel shook her head quickly. It must not, she told him without words, be made impossible for Morven to go on his journey by telling him, as she had not herself done yet, that her own life might be little more prolonged than Abel's. Another year, the physician had said; and there would be increasing pain. They would have to give her laudanum, such things, towards the end; what use to keep Morven beating his wings against such a cage? "Let Morven go, and see what he chooses to, and return when he will," she said, smiling. "Who can tell what will happen to anyone? Not one of us here but has had a fortune which differs from our neighbours', which could not have been predicted at any of our births." She looked round, and thought of all their separate arrivals in the world; Livia's in a cowshed, her own at Malvie, Morven's in the Flodden tower above the sea, where not far off Abel had already been born to the blacksmith's wife in their cottage. Morven now, and Livia in the end, she dared say, would live in the cottage together, when she and Abel were gone. It wouldn't do—she bit her lip on threatened laughter—to keep Morven on here as the landlord of the Fleece. He wouldn't fit into the necessity of keeping to all hours. He—

Pain came, and Annabel closed her eyes for an instant. "I'm tipsy, Livia, with your good brew," she said, "and I think I'll go to bed." She slept with little Philip in a small room at the back of the inn, one which was never as a rule used for customers. The boy himself would be asleep long ago; Morven had been in to him as usual to say goodnight. It would be safe, a blessed thing, to be able to leave Philip in charge of Livia and Morven together, after she was gone. The child loved them both and they him.

She stood with Livia and Abel next day to watch Morven depart. They had all of them begged him to stay longer; he was not strong enough to travel yet, they said; but he laughed. "I survived the hell-voyage between decks, blind as a mole, with only poor Tom Neilson to lift me out of my own filth for seven months," he said. "Now I'm my own man again," and they could see that he was eager to be gone, and not one

381

among them tried to restrain him. It had never, in any case, been possible to order Morven Doon.

There were tears in the two women's eyes as they watched the thin cloaked figure go, the staff borne now in one hand like a standard in battle, no longer an invalid's prop; at the turn of the road he looked back, and raised a hand to them before going on. Philip tugged at Livia's hand. "I want to go with Papa," he said. He had said it already, before Morven left; and had been told that perhaps later, when he was taller and older, he should go by his father's side wherever he went. "Now you must stay to look after Mama," Morven had told him, and the little boy alternated between pleasure at his own new importance and sorrow that, for a time at any rate, he must part from the fascinating personage with whom he had lately become acquainted, who was his father, Mama and Aunt Livia told him; and who had wonderful stories of places where yams grew, and men lived who knocked out a front tooth to placate a special god, and other such things. There would be more stories, no doubt, when Papa returned. "When will that be?" Philip asked, looking up at the adults who stood round him and who all, even Uncle Abel, had tears in their eyes, though Philip had been told it was only children who cried. "When?" For he had been, as an only child, so much accustomed to his own sole company that he could not yet understand that nobody but himself could follow the the progress of unspoken thoughts. But Abel Judd did his best.

"Soon, maybe," he said to the boy, and took his hand from Livia. "Come with me now, and we'll clean the ale-taps; would you like that?" And Philip, looking forward to being put in a leather apron, like a real tavern-server, and helping Abel make the taproom ready for the customers when they came, went off readily, not even looking back, as Morven had lately done, at the women who were left alone.

And now there remained only the pair of them, side by side in the cobbled yard, with the road empty. Annabel looked at Livia, and both of them sighed. Then they laughed; it had long ago become a matter for lightness of heart, this strange love they both felt for the man who had lately gone. "He'll be back, maybe," Livia said. Then her eyes lost their laughter. "You, love," she said, "You yourself—you're not well, are you, Annabel? I noticed it, but didn't speak."

Annabel looked at her; the beautiful, variegated eyes were again as they had been when she was a young girl, vulnerable to understanding and pain. Otherwise how she had changed!

Livia thought. She was scarcely able to keep back her tears, no longer for Morven but for his wife.

"It's the same as Abel has wrong with him, isn't it?" she said gently, and the other nodded.

"We'll both have gone, Abel and I, perhaps, when—when Morven comes home again. Then you and he—"

"Ah, never speak so! You know well I'd live in a ditch in midwinter with Morven, having left a good bright fire in a hearth for his sake; it's what I did, to all intents, once in my fool's life at any rate. But rather than take away what's yours by rights, and Abel's too, again, I'd—"

"What would you do?" said Annabel, smiling. She seemed, despite the ravaged face and body and the once-bright hair, suddenly gay, as if all care had been lifted away from her. "Many waters, they say, can't quench love . . . even in a ditch."

"You're different." The other woman spoke almost fiercely.

"Which of us is not nowadays? But I have always felt that since Malvie went, the world was a lighter place; as if with its going the evil went out of Morven. It's a bad thing to want a place, or person, too much. But I myself have the consolation that whenever I go—and it will not be long, Livia —Godfrey will be waiting for me. You didn't know how I loved Godfrey, in the end; it wasn't a love of the body, such as you feel for Morven."

"I feel more," said Livia.

"But you love Abel as well. You can't fail to; he is so good a man, and has remained so whatever befell. I've grown fond of Abel myself since coming here; how much we all love one another! There is no sadness left, no regret—except for those who died. That's over, as many things are." Annabel shut her eyes briefly in a gesture Livia had come to recognize; it meant her cancer gnawed at her.

"The pain's not over yet," said Livia roundly. "I'll ease that, as I can. I've nursed Abel these many months with it, and I know what to do, as far as it can be done. You know you can stay on here, you and Philip." She had given up calling him Master Philip long ago; it was one indication of the change in their respective relationships. "Afterwards," said Livia, "—well, what I'd once set aside for William will be Philip's. They're both Morven's flesh, which is what matters. Perhaps he'll make a preacher."

"Perhaps not," said Annabel, who knew her son.

Livia laughed, "He'll be what he likes," she said, "like his father. I'll see he doesn't have the troubles to contend with that Morven had, when he was a boy; no home of his own, no one to care what became of him in the end or at the beginning. I'll give Philip all that, and more, as if I were his own mother, and I'll see that he remembers you, and—"

"Dear Livia," said Annabel, "I know you will." She leaned on the other's arm, and together they went back again into the inn.